Nancy Drew®

The Palace of Wisdom

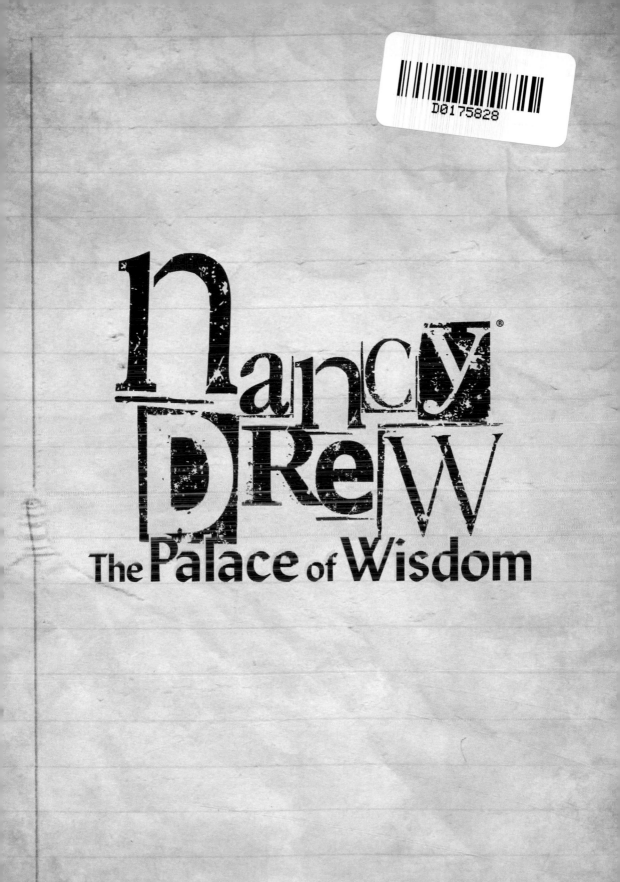

Nancy Drew
The Palace of Wisdom

WRITER
Kelly Thompson

ARTIST
Jenn St-Onge

COLORIST
Triona Farrell

LETTERER
Ariana Maher

COLLECTION COVER BY
Jenn St-Onge

COLLECTION DESIGN BY
Cathleen Heard

EDITED AND PACKAGED BY
Nate Cosby

DEAREST NANCY,

I Know what YOU DID.

I KNOW YOU'VE

TRIED to FORGET.

BUT MEMORY IS long.

AND SO IS LIFE, or at

LEAST it SHOULD be.

WHAT WOULD YOUR

Mother SAY IF SHE

WAS ALIVE TO SAY IT,

NANCY DREW?

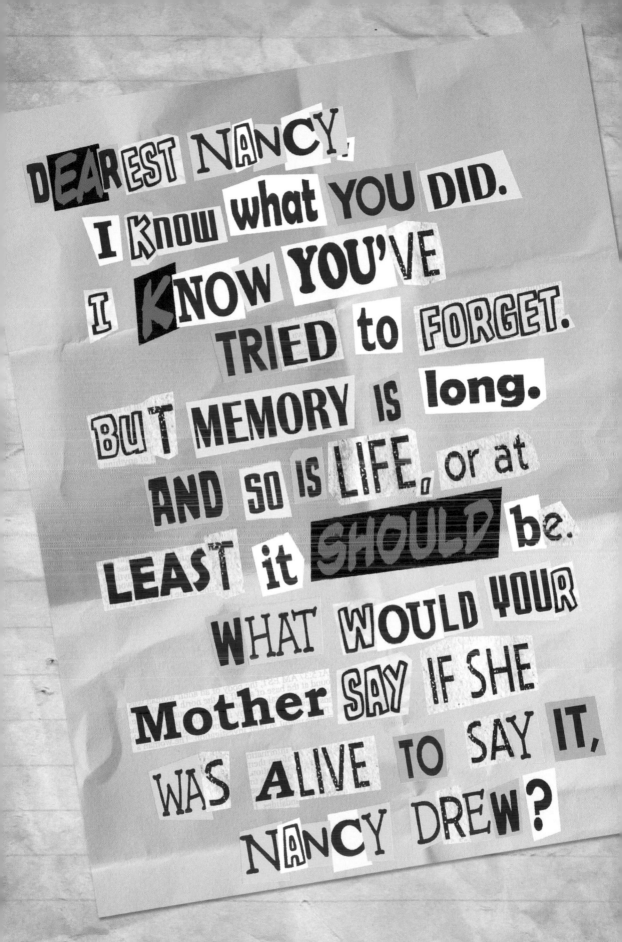

DYNAMITE®

Online at www.DYNAMITE.com
On Facebook /Dynamitecomics
On Instagram /Dynamitecomics
On Tumblr dynamitecomics.tumblr.com
On Twitter @dynamitecomics
On YouTube /Dynamitecomics

Nick Barrucci, CEO / Publisher
Juan Collado, President / COO
Brandon Dante Primavera, V.P. of IT and Operations

Joe Rybandt, Executive Editor
Matt Idelson, Senior Editor
Kevin Ketner, Editor

Cathleen Heard, Art Director
Rachel Kilbury, Digital Multimedia Associate
Alexis Persson, Graphic Designer
Katie Hidalgo, Graphic Designer

Alan Payne, V.P. of Sales and Marketing
Rex Wang, Director of Consumer Sales
Pat O'Connell, Sales Manager
Vincent Faust, Marketing Coordinator

Jay Spence, Director of Product Development
Mariano Nicieza, Director of Research & Development

Amy Jackson, Administrative Coordinator

Trade Paperback ISBN13: 978-1-5241-0849-6
Hardcover ISBN13: 978-1-5241-1463-3
Second Printing   10 9 8 7 6 5 4 3 2 1

chapTeR onE

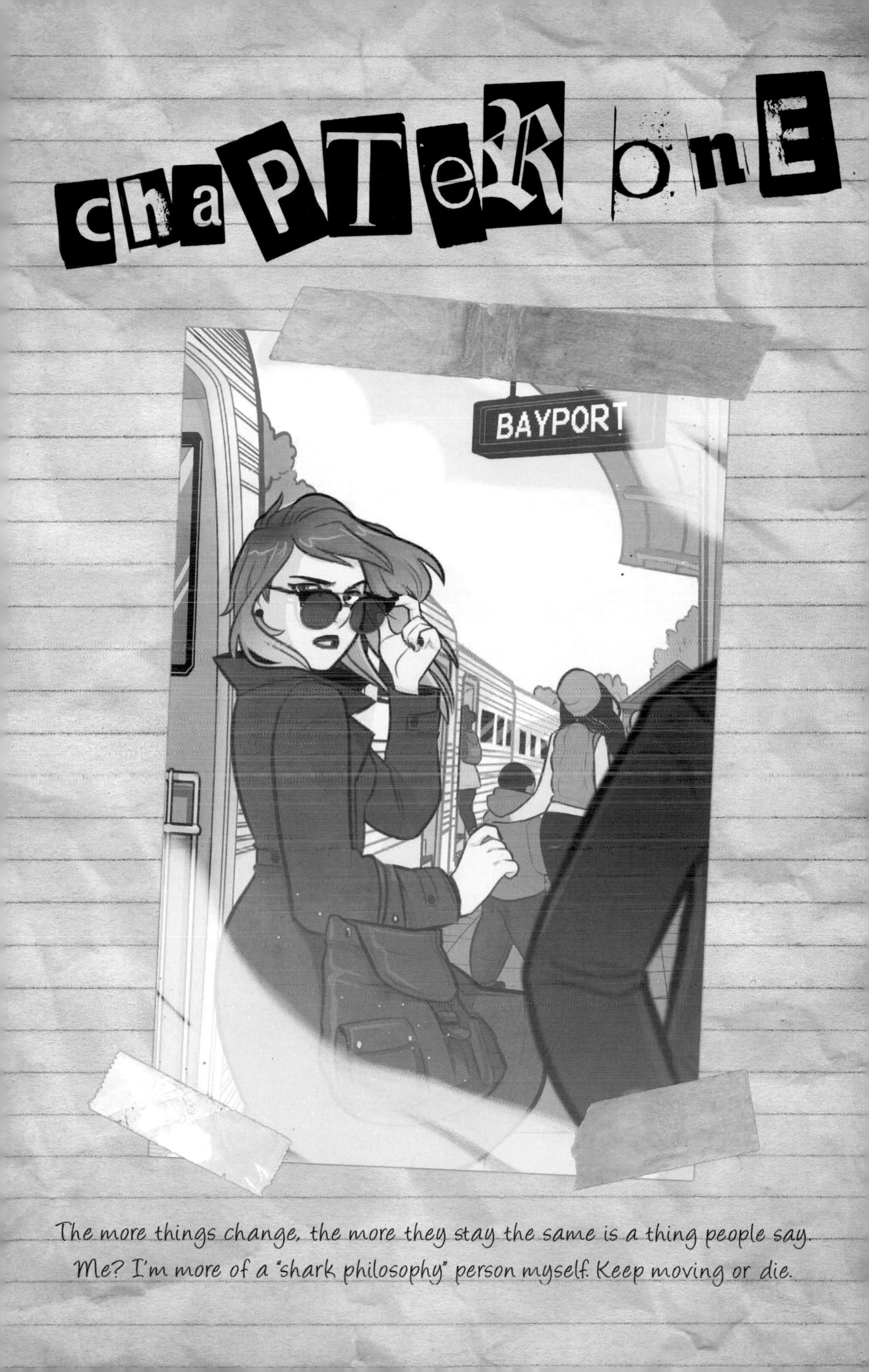
BAYPORT

The more things change, the more they stay the same is a thing people say. Me? I'm more of a "shark philosophy" person myself. Keep moving or die.

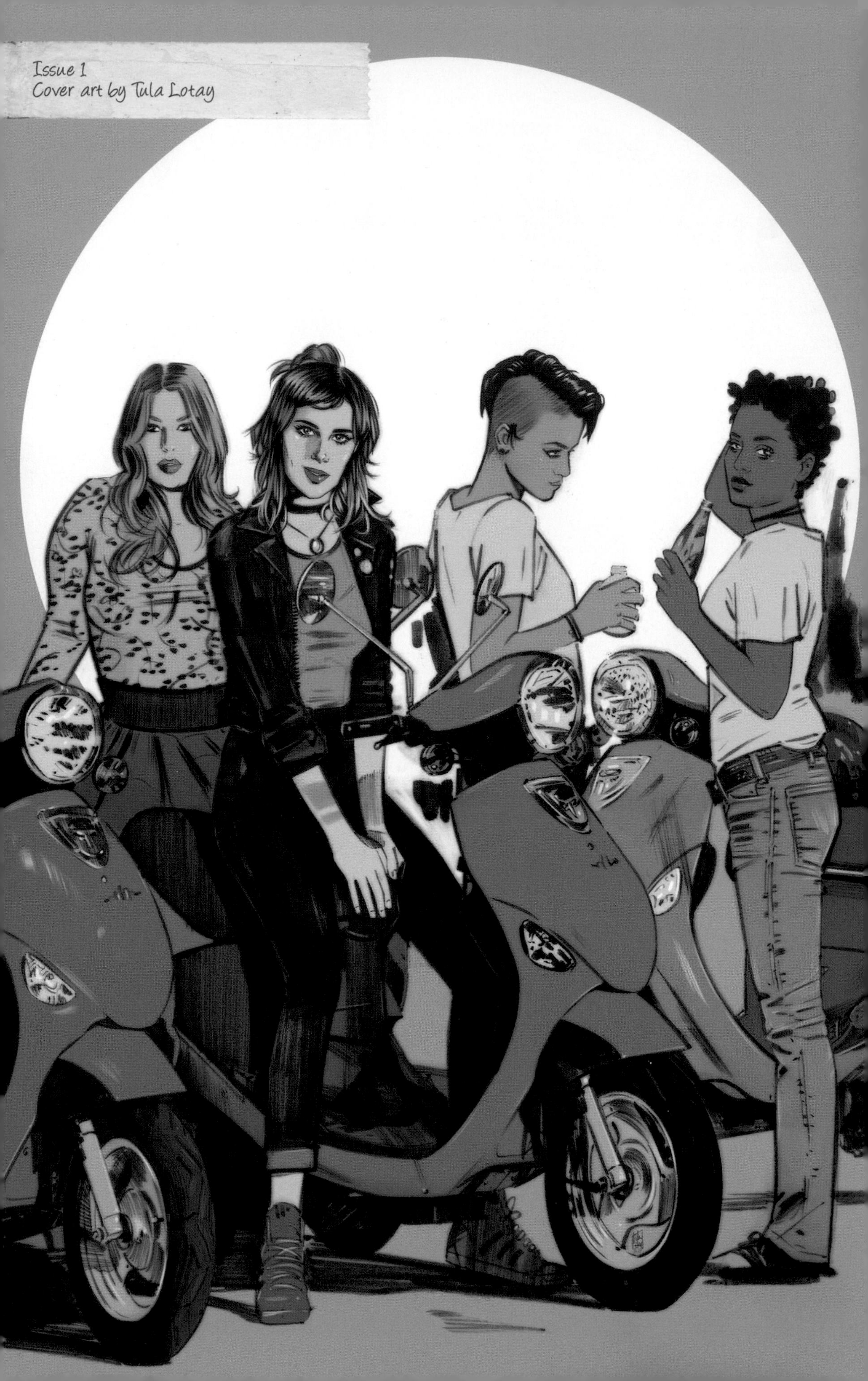

Issue 1
Cover art by Tula Lotay

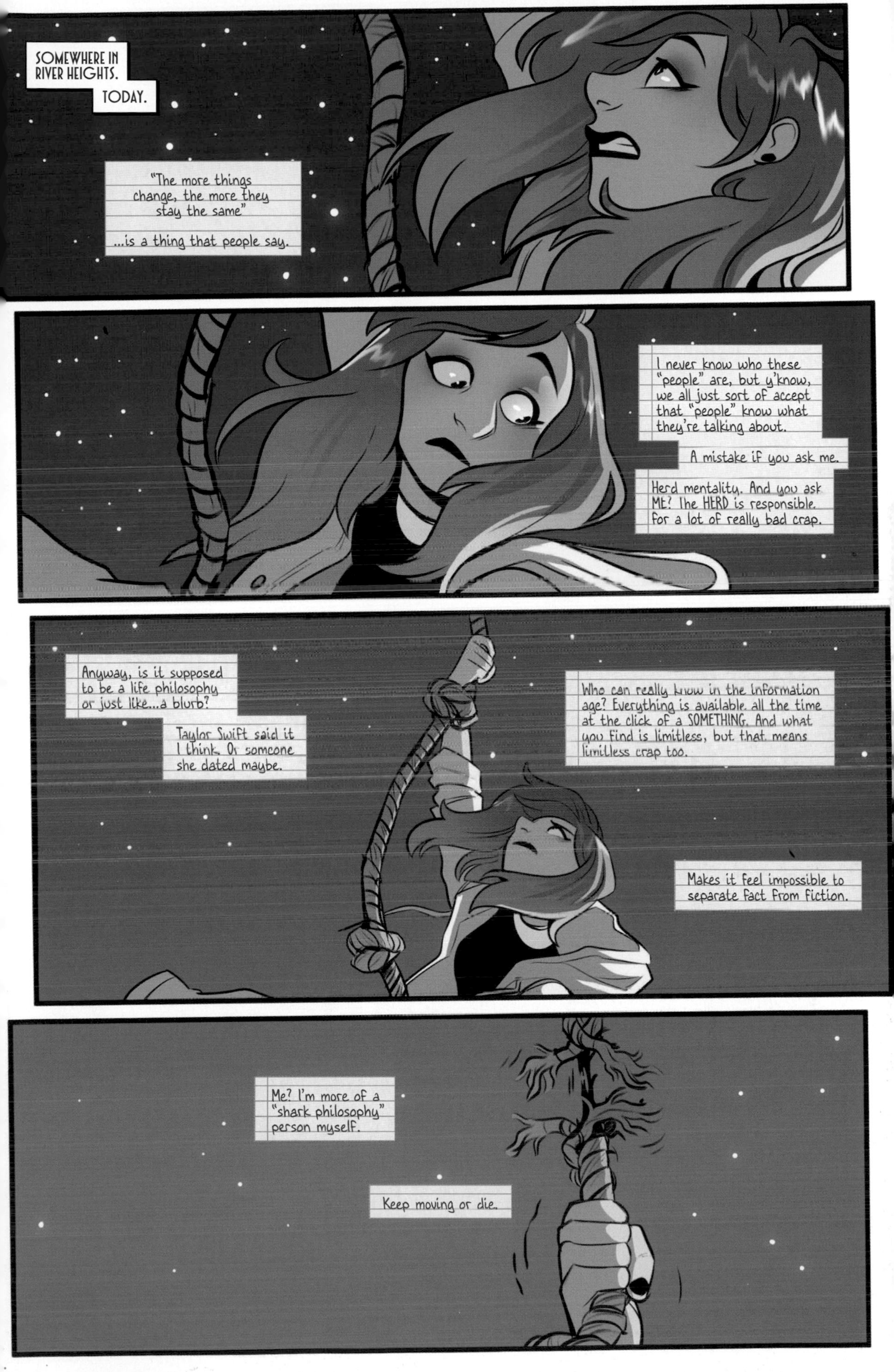

SOMEWHERE IN RIVER HEIGHTS.
TODAY.
"The more things change, the more they stay the same"
...is a thing that people say.
I never know who these "people" are, but y'know, we all just sort of accept that "people" know what they're talking about.
A mistake if you ask me.
Herd mentality. And you ask ME? The HERD is responsible for a lot of really bad crap.
Anyway, is it supposed to be a life philosophy or just like...a blurb?
Taylor Swift said it I think. Or someone she dated maybe.
Who can really know in the information age? Everything is available all the time at the click of a SOMETHING. And what you find is limitless, but that means limitless crap too.
Makes it feel impossible to separate fact from fiction.
Me? I'm more of a "shark philosophy" person myself.
Keep moving or die.

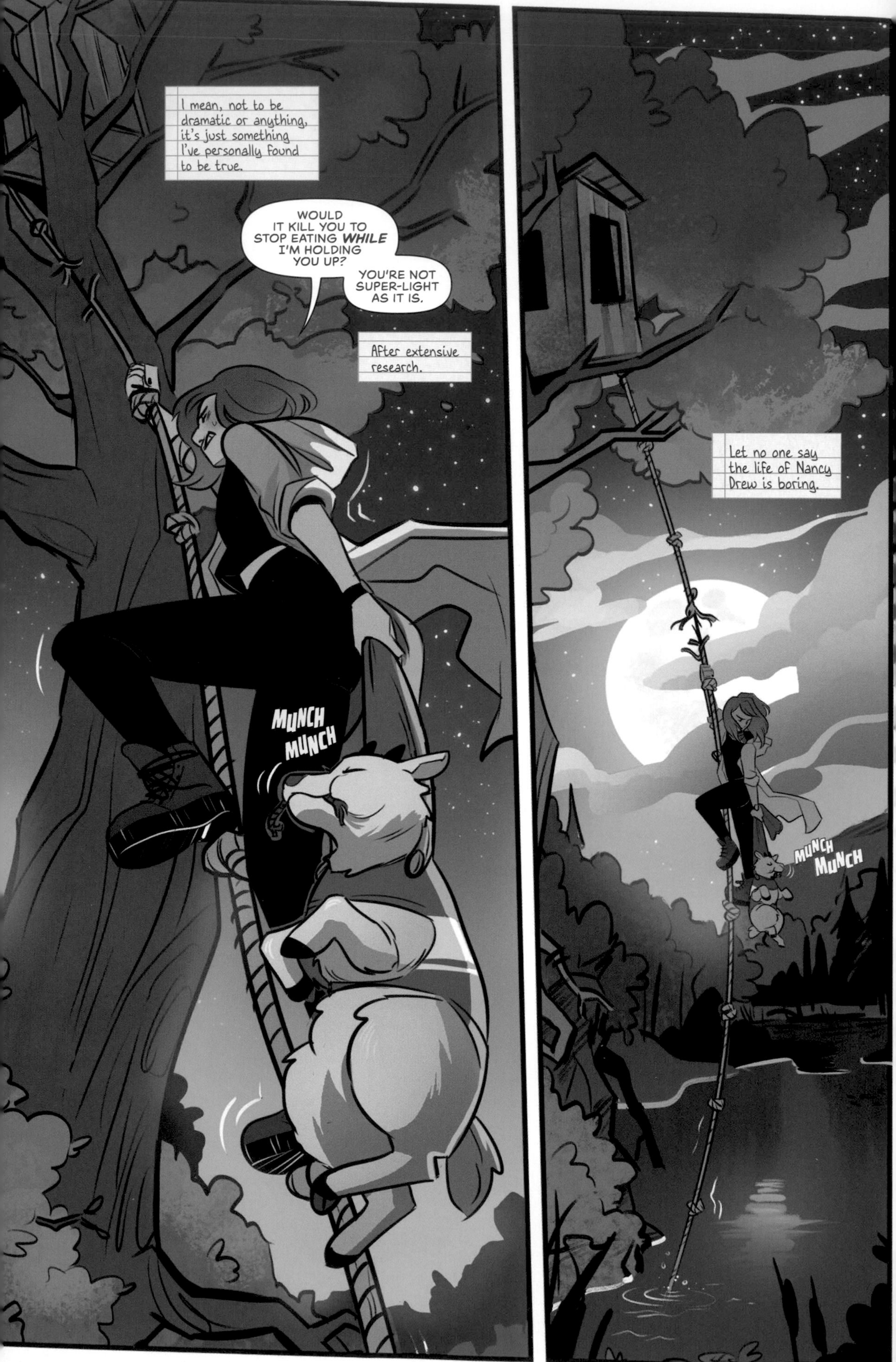

I mean, not to be dramatic or anything, it's just something I've personally found to be true.
WOULD IT KILL YOU TO STOP EATING WHILE I'M HOLDING YOU UP?
YOU'RE NOT SUPER-LIGHT AS IT IS.
After extensive research.
MUNCH MUNCH
Let no one say the life of Nancy Drew is boring.
MUNCH MUNCH

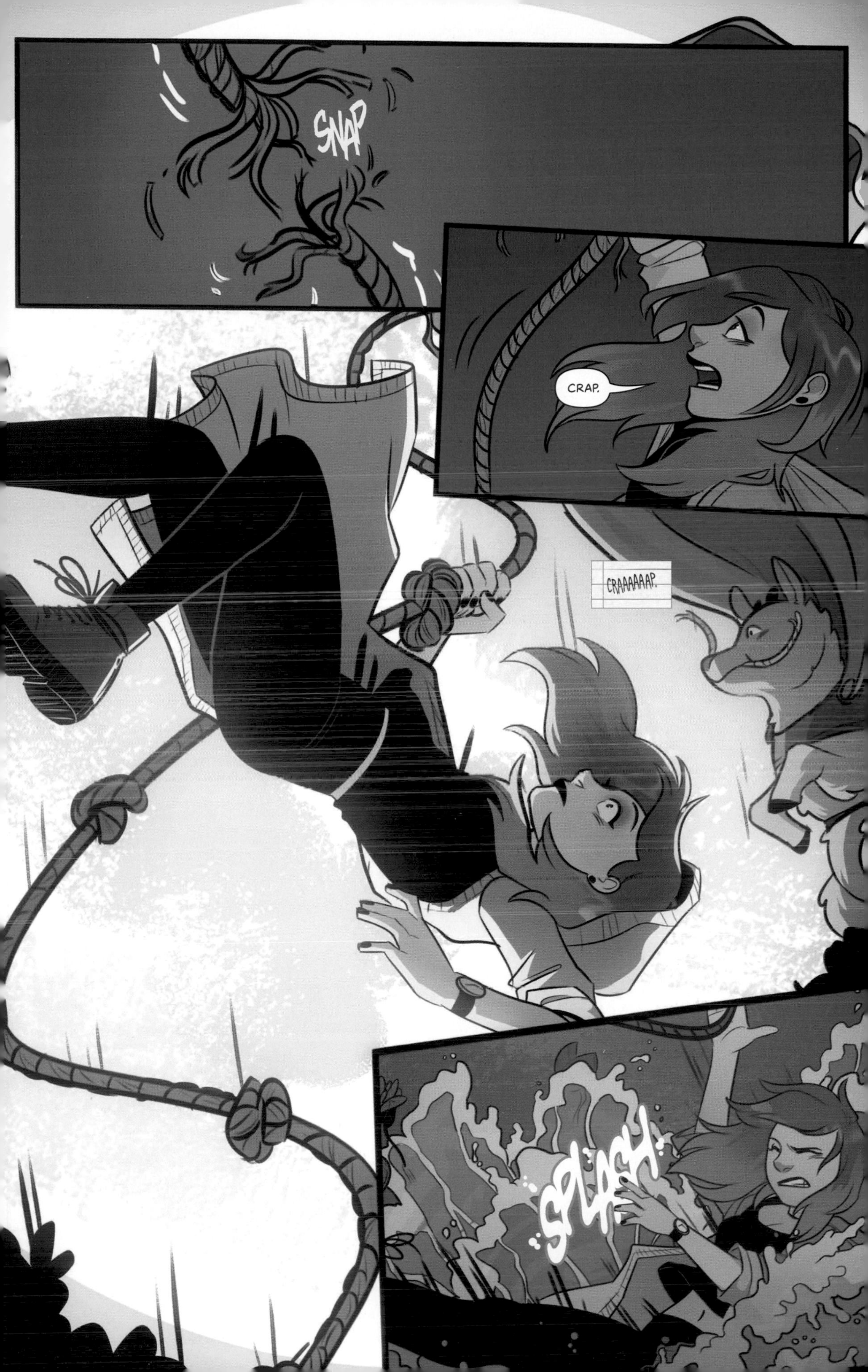
SNAP
CRAP.
CRAAAAAAP.
SPLASH

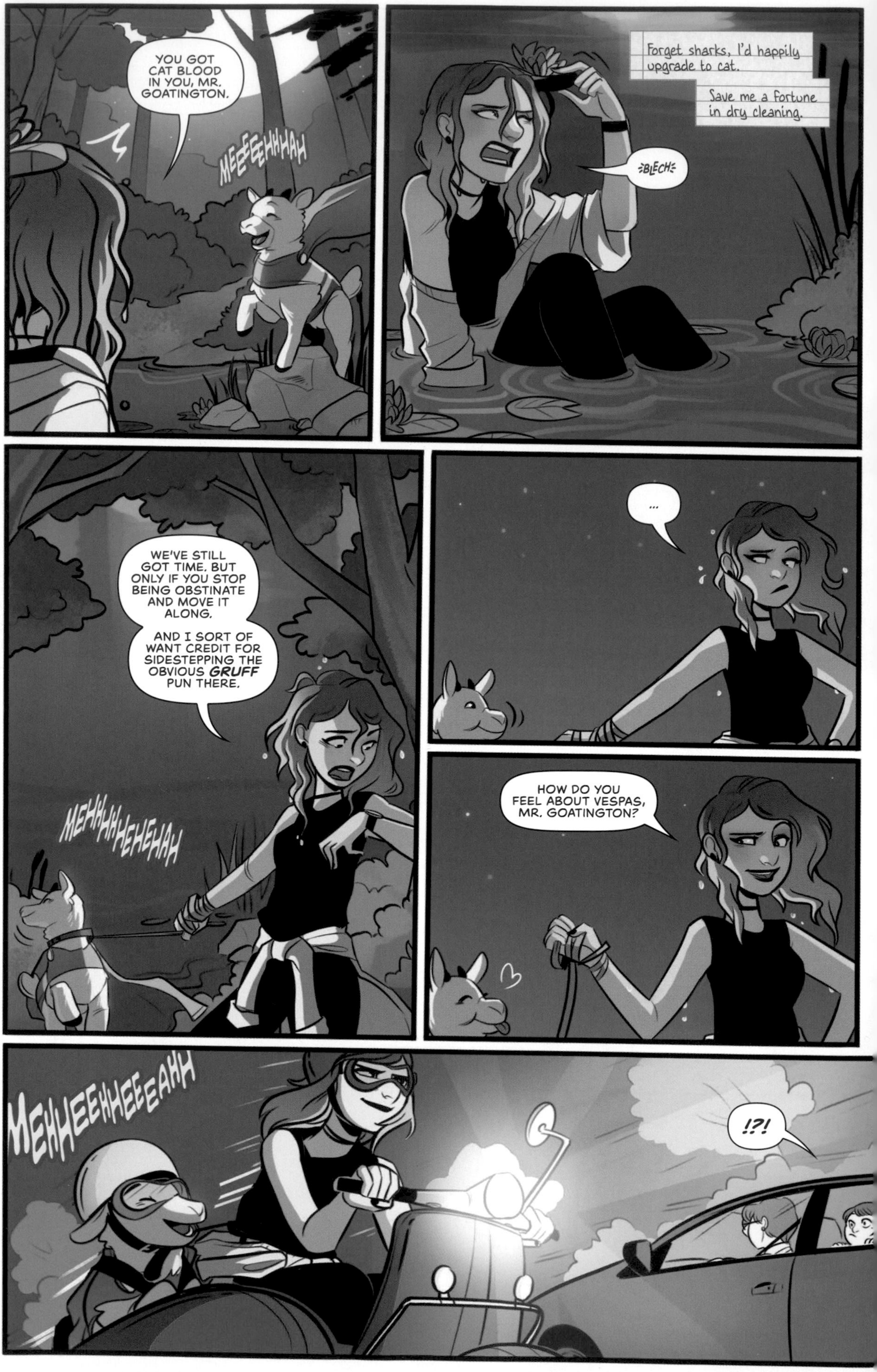
YOU GOT CAT BLOOD IN YOU, MR. GOATINGTON.
MEEEEHHHAH
Forget sharks, I'd happily upgrade to cat.
Save me a fortune in dry cleaning.
BLECH
WE'VE STILL GOT TIME, BUT ONLY IF YOU STOP BEING OBSTINATE AND MOVE IT ALONG.
AND I SORT OF WANT CREDIT FOR SIDESTEPPING THE OBVIOUS GRUFF PUN THERE.
MEHHHHEHEHAH
...
HOW DO YOU FEEL ABOUT VESPAS, MR. GOATINGTON?
MEHHEEHHEEEAHH
!?!

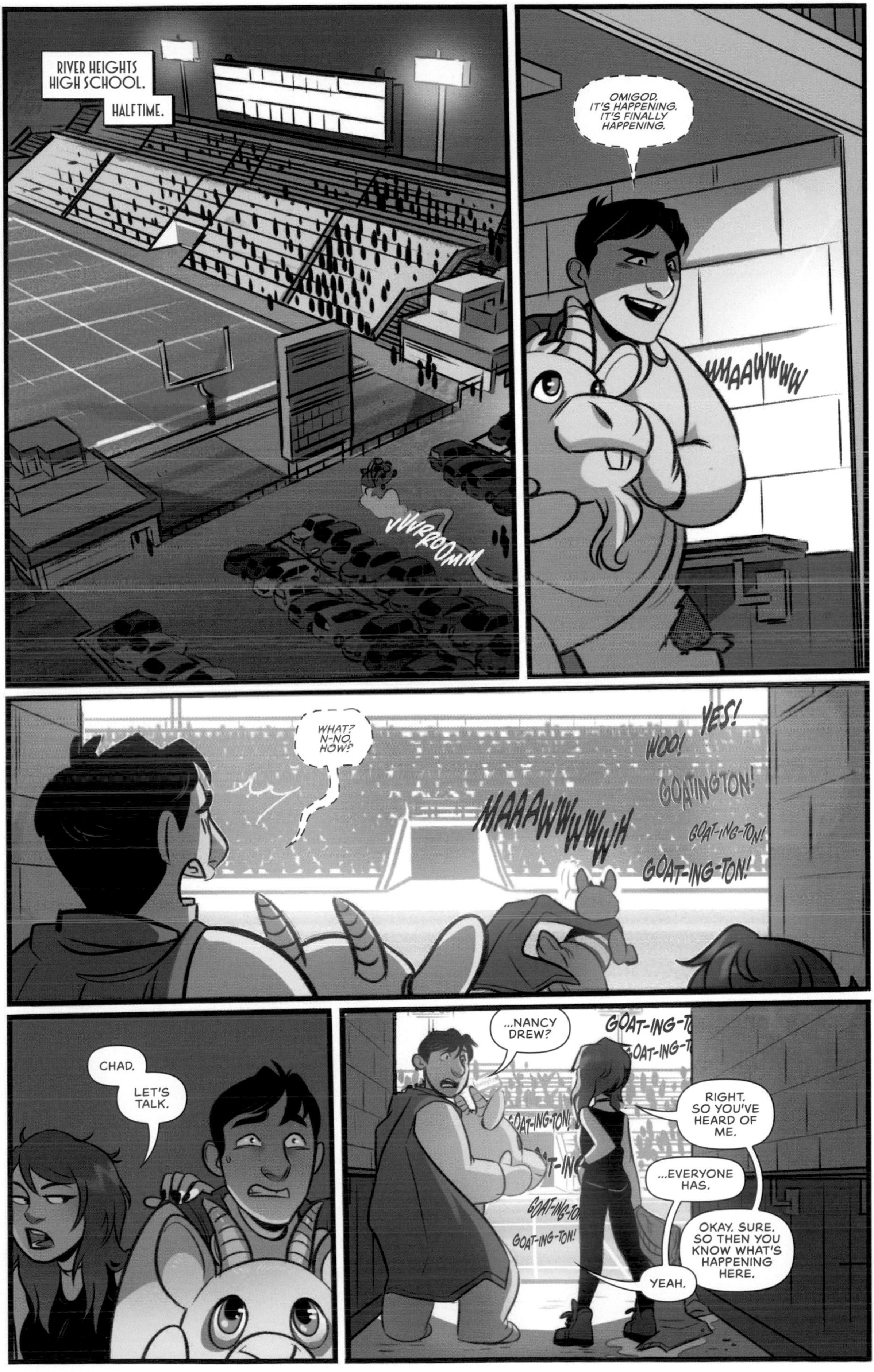

RIVER HEIGHTS HIGH SCHOOL.
HALFTIME.
VVVRROOMM
OMIGOD, IT'S HAPPENING. IT'S FINALLY HAPPENING.
MMAAWWWW
WHAT? N-NO, HOW?
MAAAWWWWWH
YES!
WOO!
GOATINGTON!
GOAT-ING-TON!
GOAT-ING-TON!
CHAD.
LET'S TALK.
...NANCY DREW?
RIGHT. SO YOU'VE HEARD OF ME.
...EVERYONE HAS.
OKAY, SURE. SO THEN YOU KNOW WHAT'S HAPPENING HERE.
YEAH.
GOAT-ING-TON!

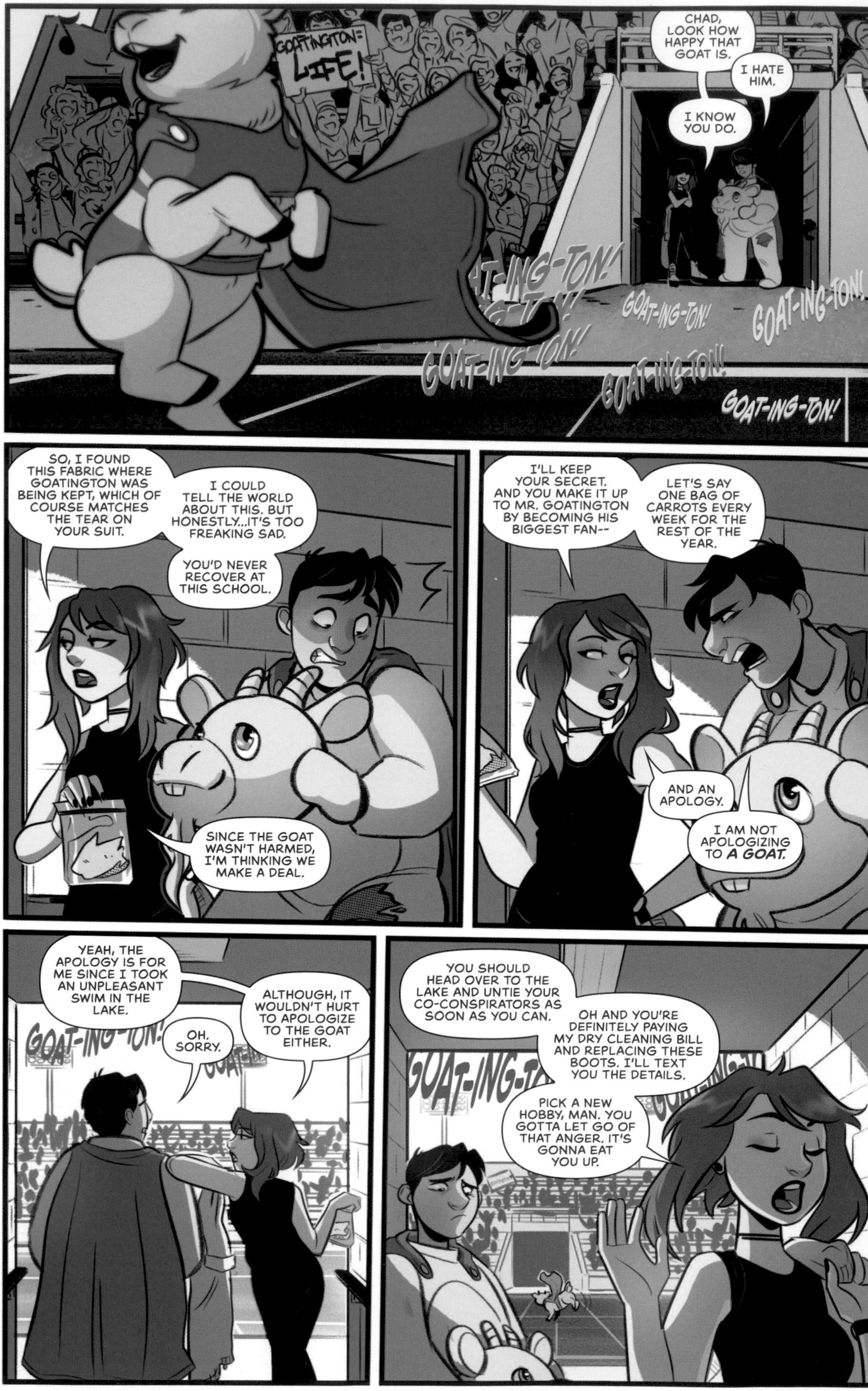
GOATINGTON = LIFE!
CHAD, LOOK HOW HAPPY THAT GOAT IS.
I HATE HIM.
I KNOW YOU DO.
GOAT-ING-TON!
GOAT-ING-TON!
GOAT-ING-TON!
GOAT-ING-TON!
GOAT-ING-TON!
SO, I FOUND THIS FABRIC WHERE GOATINGTON WAS BEING KEPT, WHICH OF COURSE MATCHES THE TEAR ON YOUR SUIT.
I COULD TELL THE WORLD ABOUT THIS. BUT HONESTLY...IT'S TOO FREAKING SAD.
YOU'D NEVER RECOVER AT THIS SCHOOL.
SINCE THE GOAT WASN'T HARMED, I'M THINKING WE MAKE A DEAL.
I'LL KEEP YOUR SECRET. AND YOU MAKE IT UP TO MR. GOATINGTON BY BECOMING HIS BIGGEST FAN--
LET'S SAY ONE BAG OF CARROTS EVERY WEEK FOR THE REST OF THE YEAR.
AND AN APOLOGY.
I AM NOT APOLOGIZING TO A GOAT.
YEAH, THE APOLOGY IS FOR ME SINCE I TOOK AN UNPLEASANT SWIM IN THE LAKE.
OH. SORRY.
ALTHOUGH, IT WOULDN'T HURT TO APOLOGIZE TO THE GOAT EITHER.
GOAT-ING-TON!
YOU SHOULD HEAD OVER TO THE LAKE AND UNTIE YOUR CO-CONSPIRATORS AS SOON AS YOU CAN.
OH AND YOU'RE DEFINITELY PAYING MY DRY CLEANING BILL AND REPLACING THESE BOOTS. I'LL TEXT YOU THE DETAILS.
PICK A NEW HOBBY, MAN. YOU GOTTA LET GO OF THAT ANGER. IT'S GONNA EAT YOU UP.

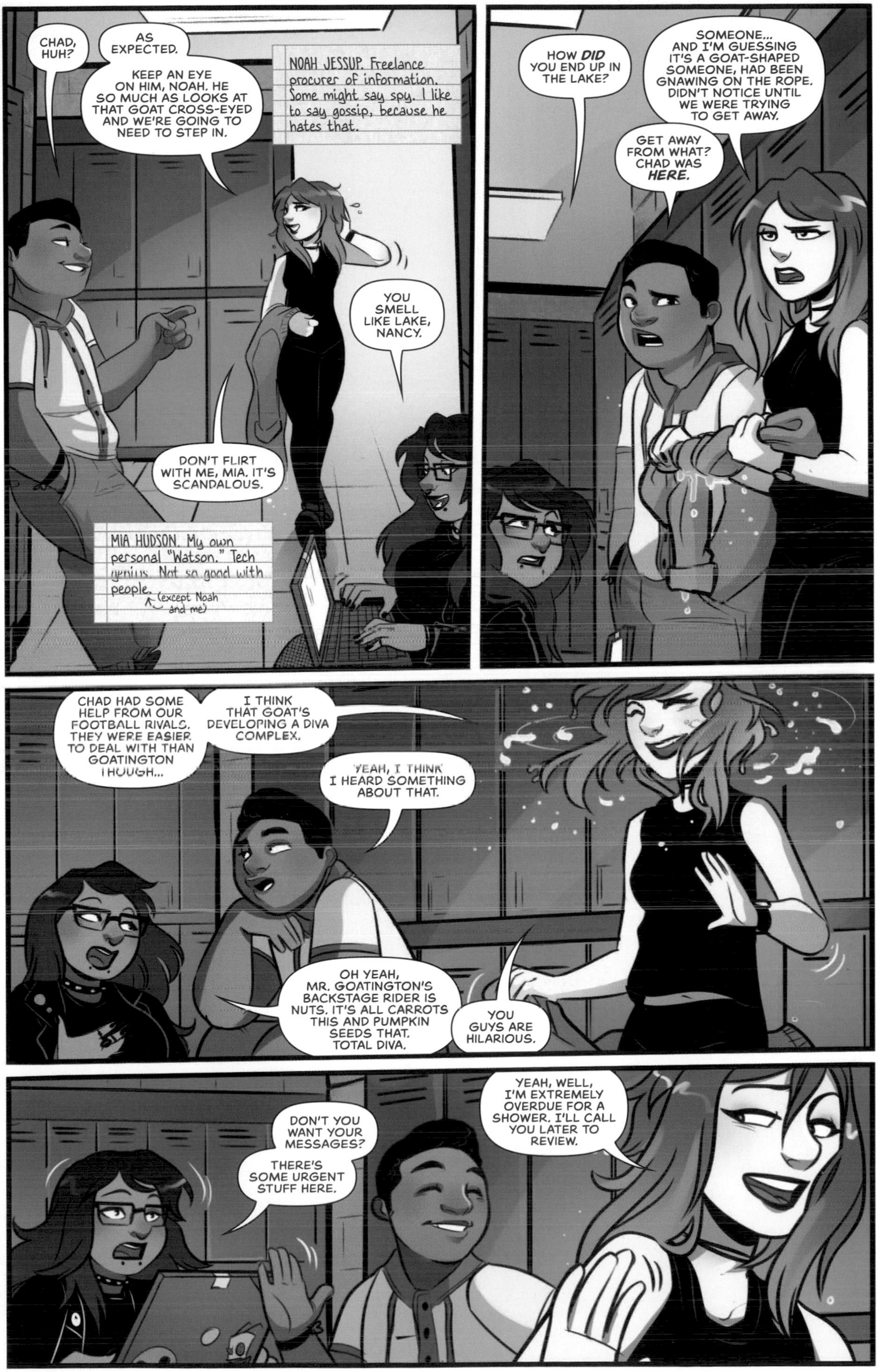
CHAD, HUH?
AS EXPECTED.
KEEP AN EYE ON HIM, NOAH. HE SO MUCH AS LOOKS AT THAT GOAT CROSS-EYED AND WE'RE GOING TO NEED TO STEP IN.
NOAH JESSUP. Freelance procurer of information. Some might say spy. I like to say gossip, because he hates that.
YOU SMELL LIKE LAKE, NANCY.
DON'T FLIRT WITH ME, MIA. IT'S SCANDALOUS.
MIA HUDSON. My own personal "Watson." Tech genius. Not so good with people. (except Noah and me)
HOW DID YOU END UP IN THE LAKE?
SOMEONE... AND I'M GUESSING IT'S A GOAT-SHAPED SOMEONE, HAD BEEN GNAWING ON THE ROPE. DIDN'T NOTICE UNTIL WE WERE TRYING TO GET AWAY.
GET AWAY FROM WHAT? CHAD WAS HERE.
CHAD HAD SOME HELP FROM OUR FOOTBALL RIVALS. THEY WERE EASIER TO DEAL WITH THAN GOATINGTON THOUGH...
I THINK THAT GOAT'S DEVELOPING A DIVA COMPLEX.
YEAH, I THINK I HEARD SOMETHING ABOUT THAT.
OH YEAH, MR. GOATINGTON'S BACKSTAGE RIDER IS NUTS. IT'S ALL CARROTS THIS AND PUMPKIN SEEDS THAT. TOTAL DIVA.
YOU GUYS ARE HILARIOUS.
DON'T YOU WANT YOUR MESSAGES?
THERE'S SOME URGENT STUFF HERE.
YEAH, WELL, I'M EXTREMELY OVERDUE FOR A SHOWER. I'LL CALL YOU LATER TO REVIEW.

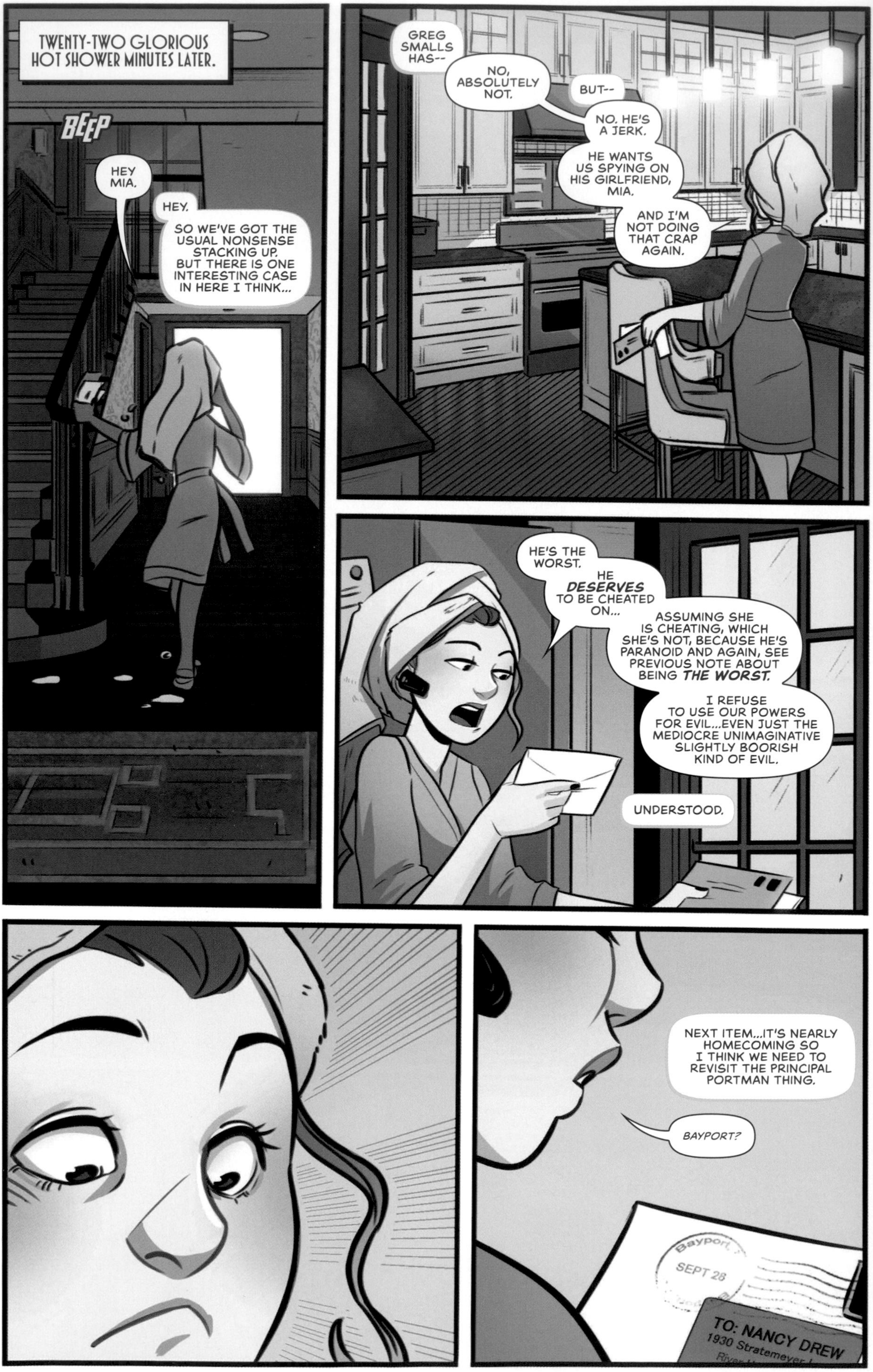
TWENTY-TWO GLORIOUS HOT SHOWER MINUTES LATER.
BEEP
HEY MIA.
HEY.
SO WE'VE GOT THE USUAL NONSENSE STACKING UP. BUT THERE IS ONE INTERESTING CASE IN HERE I THINK...
GREG SMALLS HAS--
NO, ABSOLUTELY NOT.
BUT--
NO. HE'S A JERK.
HE WANTS US SPYING ON HIS GIRLFRIEND, MIA.
AND I'M NOT DOING THAT CRAP AGAIN.
HE'S THE WORST.
HE DESERVES TO BE CHEATED ON...
ASSUMING SHE IS CHEATING, WHICH SHE'S NOT, BECAUSE HE'S PARANOID AND AGAIN, SEE PREVIOUS NOTE ABOUT BEING THE WORST.
I REFUSE TO USE OUR POWERS FOR EVIL...EVEN JUST THE MEDIOCRE UNIMAGINATIVE SLIGHTLY BOORISH KIND OF EVIL.
UNDERSTOOD.
NEXT ITEM...IT'S NEARLY HOMECOMING SO I THINK WE NEED TO REVISIT THE PRINCIPAL PORTMAN THING.
BAYPORT?
Bayport
SEPT 28
TO: NANCY DREW
1930 Stratemeyer

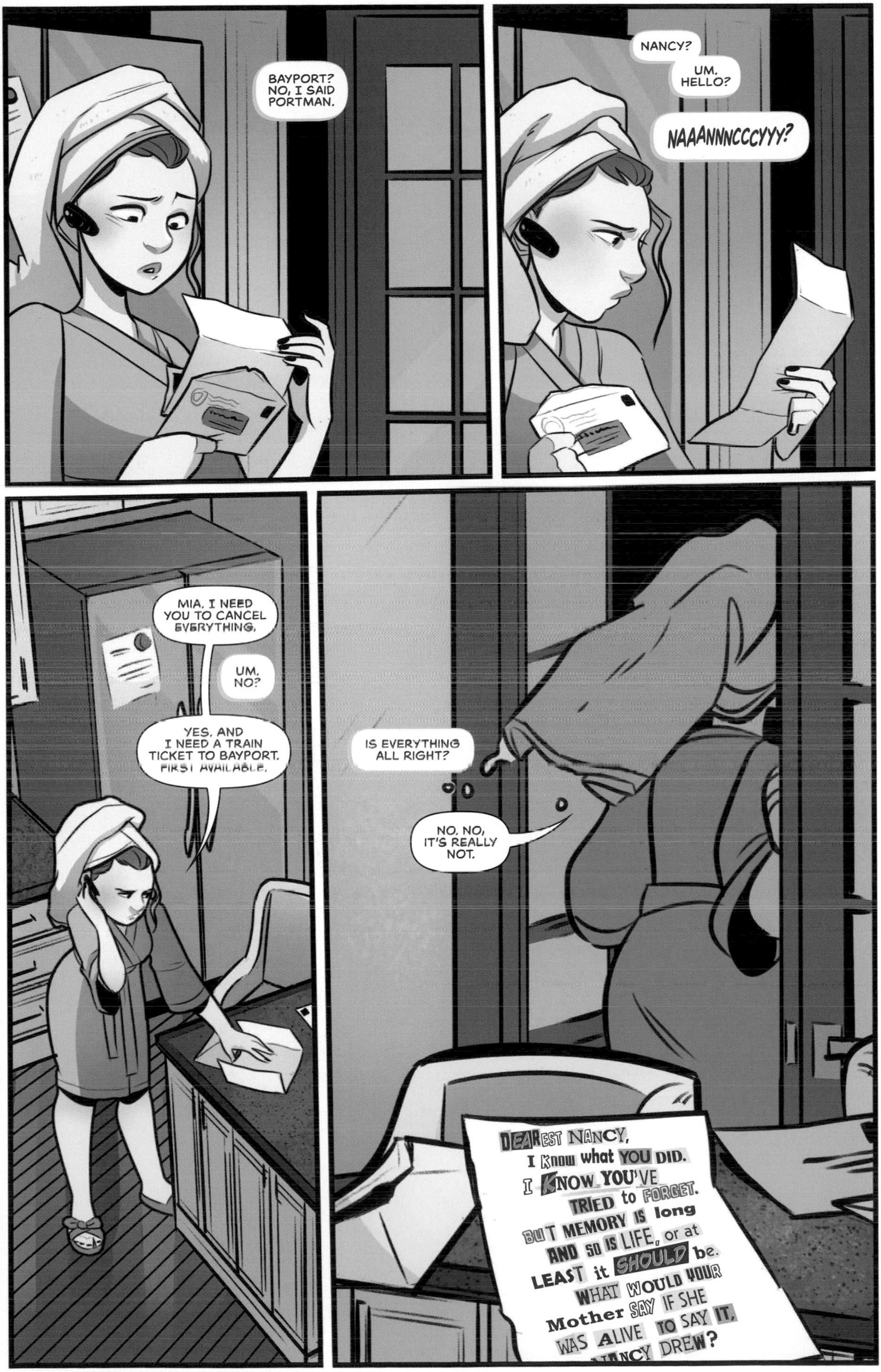
BAYPORT? NO, I SAID PORTMAN.
NANCY?
UM. HELLO?
NAAANNNCCCYYY?
MIA, I NEED YOU TO CANCEL EVERYTHING.
UM, NO?
YES, AND I NEED A TRAIN TICKET TO BAYPORT. FIRST AVAILABLE.
IS EVERYTHING ALL RIGHT?
NO, NO, IT'S REALLY NOT.
DEAREST NANCY,
I Know what YOU DID.
I KNOW YOU'VE TRIED to FORGET.
BUT MEMORY IS long AND SO IS LIFE, or at LEAST it SHOULD be.
WHAT WOULD YOUR Mother SAY IF SHE WAS ALIVE TO SAY IT,
NANCY DREW?

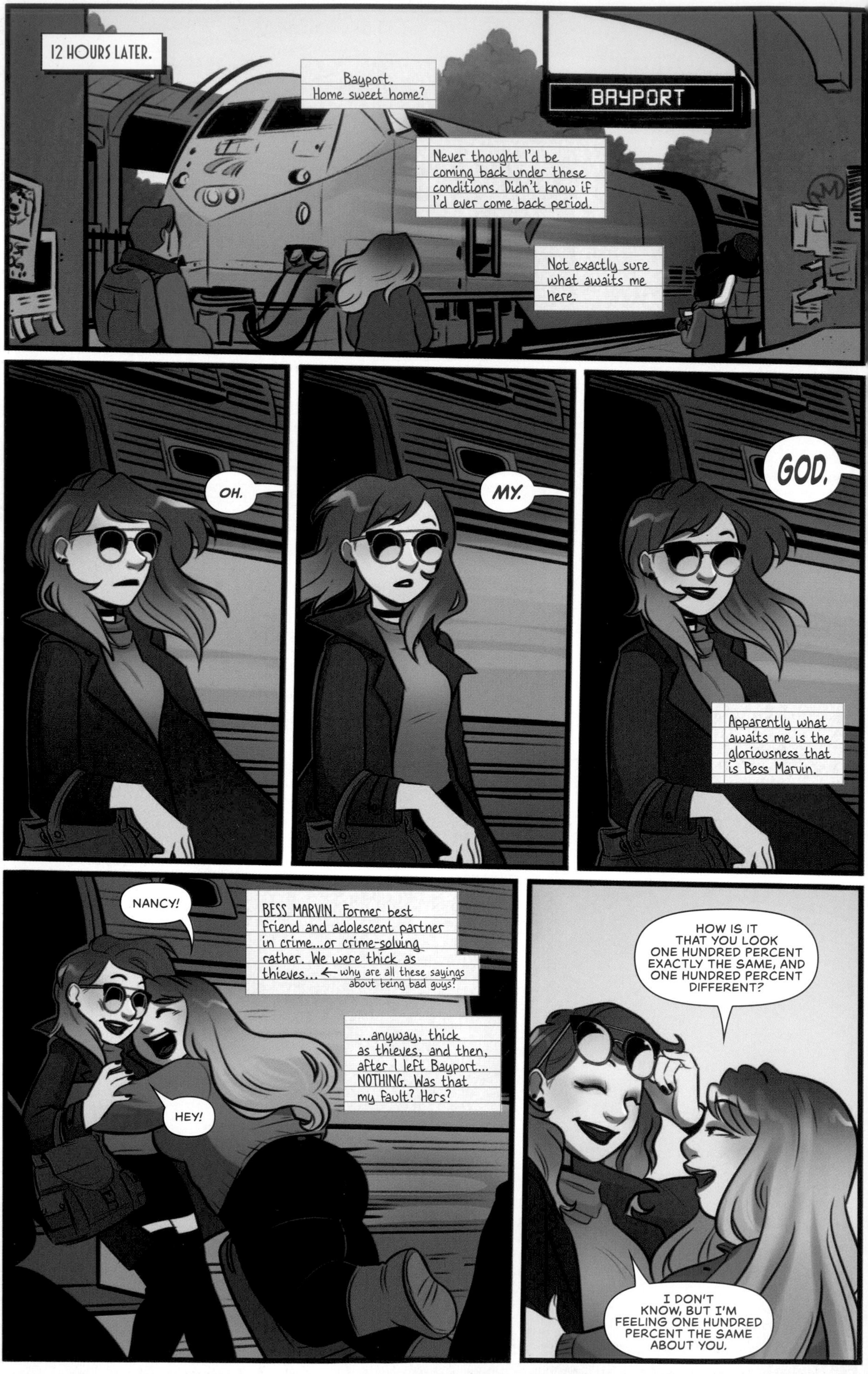
12 HOURS LATER.
Bayport. Home sweet home?
BAYPORT
Never thought I'd be coming back under these conditions. Didn't know if I'd ever come back period.
Not exactly sure what awaits me here.
OH.
MY.
GOD.
Apparently what awaits me is the gloriousness that is Bess Marvin.
NANCY!
BESS MARVIN. Former best friend and adolescent partner in crime...or crime-solving rather. We were thick as thieves... ← why are all these sayings about being bad guys?
...anyway, thick as thieves, and then, after I left Bayport... NOTHING. Was that my fault? Hers?
HEY!
HOW IS IT THAT YOU LOOK ONE HUNDRED PERCENT EXACTLY THE SAME, AND ONE HUNDRED PERCENT DIFFERENT?
I DON'T KNOW, BUT I'M FEELING ONE HUNDRED PERCENT THE SAME ABOUT YOU.

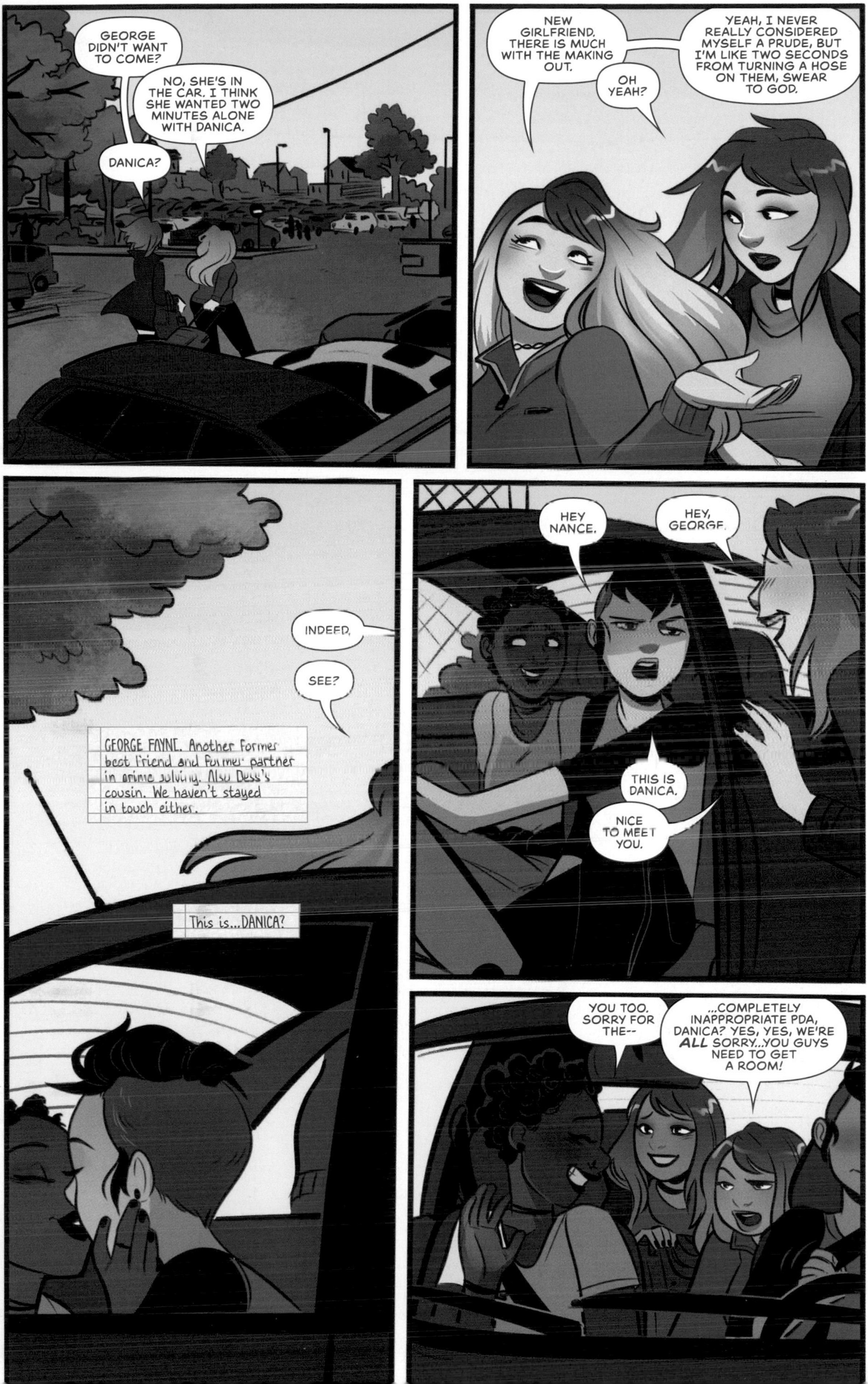
GEORGE DIDN'T WANT TO COME?
NO, SHE'S IN THE CAR. I THINK SHE WANTED TWO MINUTES ALONE WITH DANICA.
DANICA?
NEW GIRLFRIEND. THERE IS MUCH WITH THE MAKING OUT.
OH YEAH?
YEAH, I NEVER REALLY CONSIDERED MYSELF A PRUDE, BUT I'M LIKE TWO SECONDS FROM TURNING A HOSE ON THEM, SWEAR TO GOD.
INDEED.
SEE?
GEORGE FAYNE. Another former best friend and former partner in crime solving. Also Bess's cousin. We haven't stayed in touch either.
This is...DANICA?
HEY NANCE.
HEY, GEORGE.
THIS IS DANICA.
NICE TO MEET YOU.
YOU TOO. SORRY FOR THE--
...COMPLETELY INAPPROPRIATE PDA, DANICA? YES, YES, WE'RE ALL SORRY...YOU GUYS NEED TO GET A ROOM!

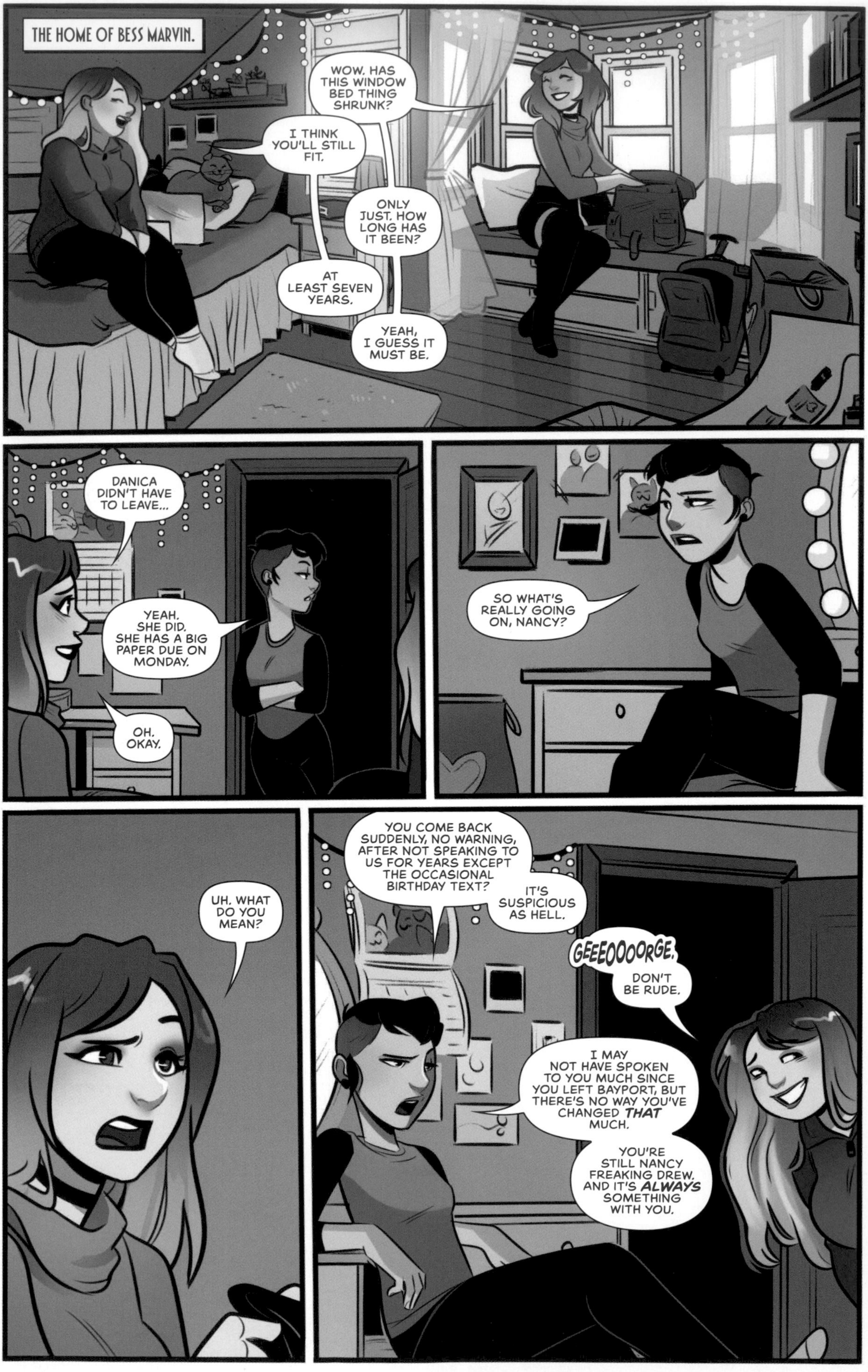
THE HOME OF BESS MARVIN.
WOW. HAS THIS WINDOW BED THING SHRUNK?
I THINK YOU'LL STILL FIT.
ONLY JUST. HOW LONG HAS IT BEEN?
AT LEAST SEVEN YEARS.
YEAH, I GUESS IT MUST BE.
DANICA DIDN'T HAVE TO LEAVE...
YEAH. SHE DID. SHE HAS A BIG PAPER DUE ON MONDAY.
OH. OKAY.
SO WHAT'S REALLY GOING ON, NANCY?
UH. WHAT DO YOU MEAN?
YOU COME BACK SUDDENLY, NO WARNING, AFTER NOT SPEAKING TO US FOR YEARS EXCEPT THE OCCASIONAL BIRTHDAY TEXT?
IT'S SUSPICIOUS AS HELL.
GEEEOOOORGE. DON'T BE RUDE.
I MAY NOT HAVE SPOKEN TO YOU MUCH SINCE YOU LEFT BAYPORT, BUT THERE'S NO WAY YOU'VE CHANGED *THAT* MUCH.
YOU'RE STILL NANCY FREAKING DREW. AND IT'S *ALWAYS* SOMETHING WITH YOU.

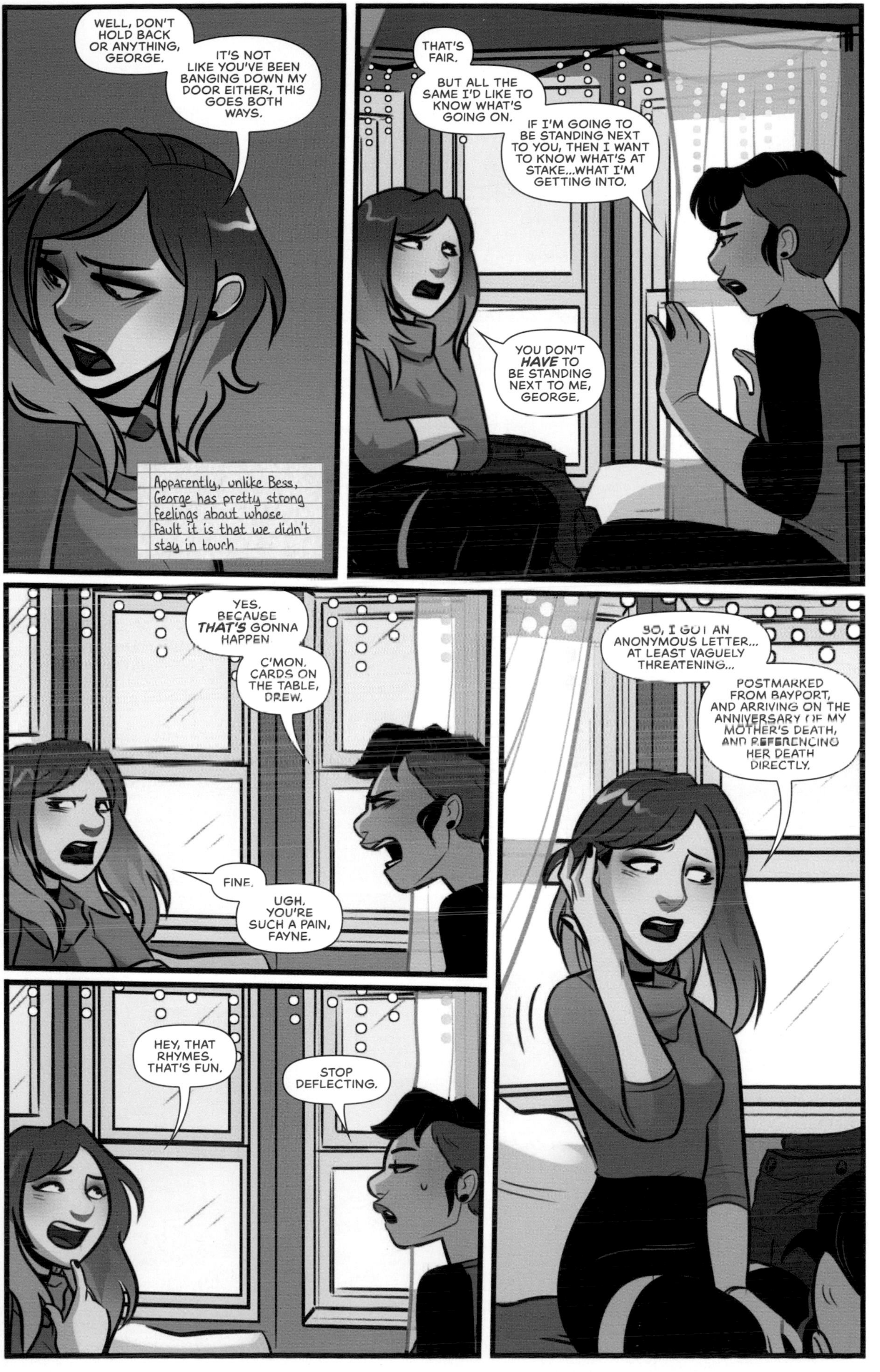

WELL, DON'T HOLD BACK OR ANYTHING, GEORGE.
IT'S NOT LIKE YOU'VE BEEN BANGING DOWN MY DOOR EITHER, THIS GOES BOTH WAYS.
Apparently, unlike Bess, George has pretty strong feelings about whose fault it is that we didn't stay in touch.
THAT'S FAIR.
BUT ALL THE SAME I'D LIKE TO KNOW WHAT'S GOING ON.
IF I'M GOING TO BE STANDING NEXT TO YOU, THEN I WANT TO KNOW WHAT'S AT STAKE...WHAT I'M GETTING INTO.
YOU DON'T *HAVE* TO BE STANDING NEXT TO ME, GEORGE.
YES. BECAUSE *THAT'S* GONNA HAPPEN.
C'MON. CARDS ON THE TABLE, DREW.
FINE.
UGH. YOU'RE SUCH A PAIN, FAYNE.
HEY, THAT RHYMES. THAT'S FUN.
STOP DEFLECTING.
SO, I GOT AN ANONYMOUS LETTER... AT LEAST VAGUELY THREATENING...
POSTMARKED FROM BAYPORT, AND ARRIVING ON THE ANNIVERSARY OF MY MOTHER'S DEATH, AND REFERENCING HER DEATH DIRECTLY.

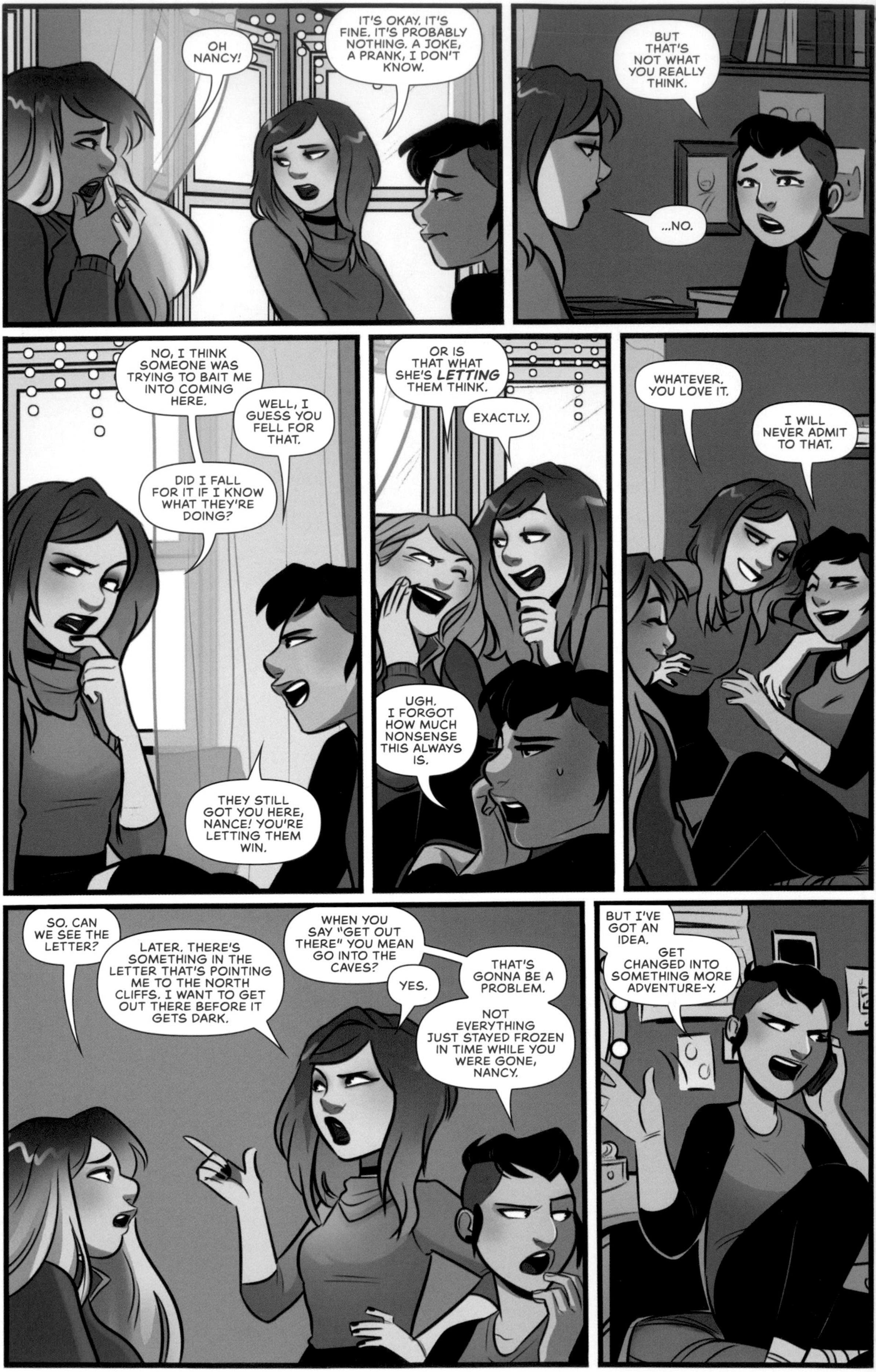
OH NANCY!
IT'S OKAY. IT'S FINE. IT'S PROBABLY NOTHING. A JOKE, A PRANK, I DON'T KNOW.
BUT THAT'S NOT WHAT YOU REALLY THINK.
...NO.
NO, I THINK SOMEONE WAS TRYING TO BAIT ME INTO COMING HERE.
WELL, I GUESS YOU FELL FOR THAT.
DID I FALL FOR IT IF I KNOW WHAT THEY'RE DOING?
THEY STILL GOT YOU HERE, NANCE! YOU'RE LETTING THEM WIN.
OR IS THAT WHAT SHE'S LETTING THEM THINK.
EXACTLY.
UGH. I FORGOT HOW MUCH NONSENSE THIS ALWAYS IS.
WHATEVER. YOU LOVE IT.
I WILL NEVER ADMIT TO THAT.
SO, CAN WE SEE THE LETTER?
LATER. THERE'S SOMETHING IN THE LETTER THAT'S POINTING ME TO THE NORTH CLIFFS. I WANT TO GET OUT THERE BEFORE IT GETS DARK.
WHEN YOU SAY "GET OUT THERE" YOU MEAN GO INTO THE CAVES?
YES.
THAT'S GONNA BE A PROBLEM.
NOT EVERYTHING JUST STAYED FROZEN IN TIME WHILE YOU WERE GONE, NANCY.
BUT I'VE GOT AN IDEA.
GET CHANGED INTO SOMETHING MORE ADVENTURE-Y.

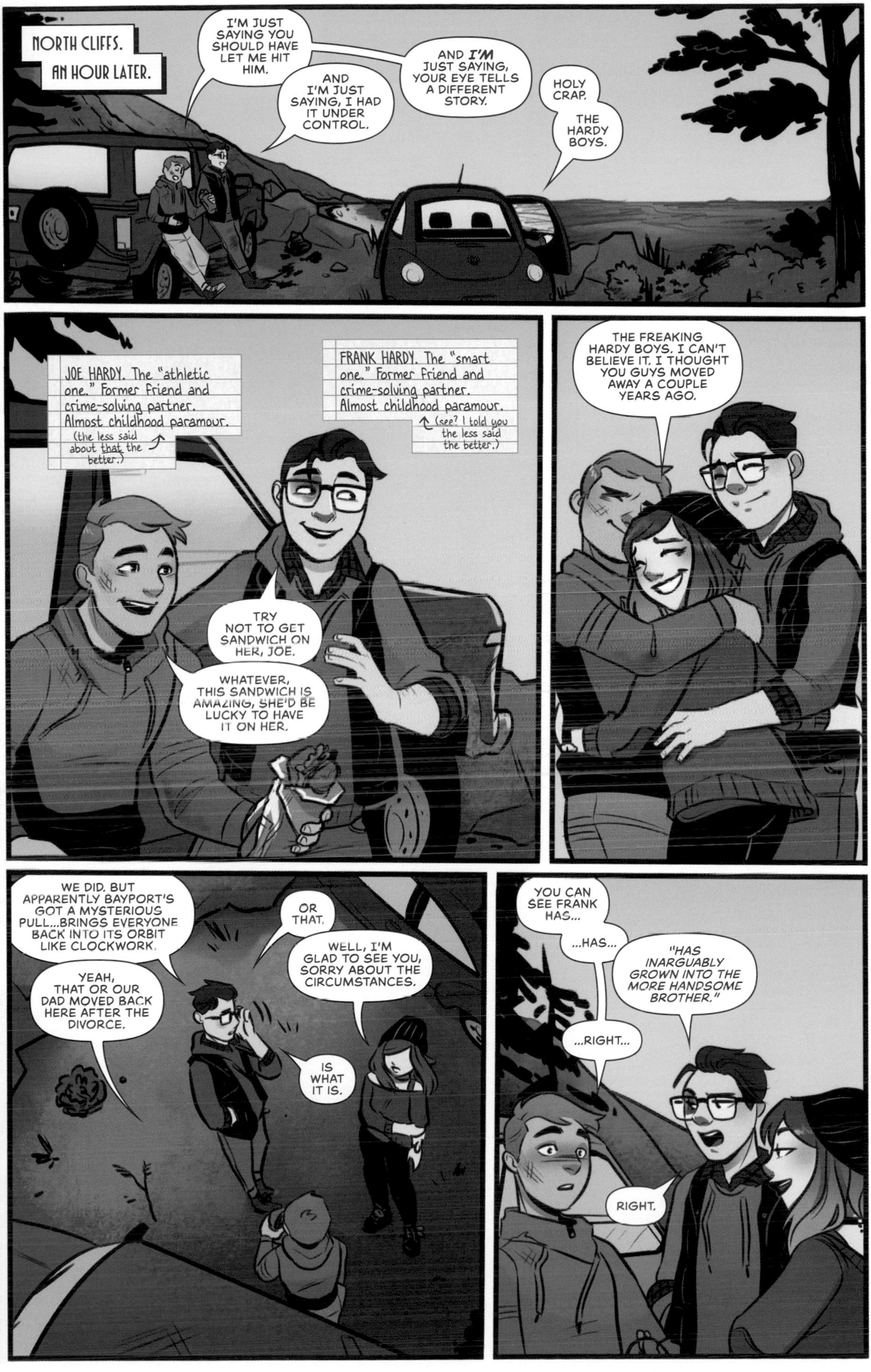
NORTH CLIFFS.
AN HOUR LATER.
I'M JUST SAYING YOU SHOULD HAVE LET ME HIT HIM.
AND I'M JUST SAYING, I HAD IT UNDER CONTROL.
AND I'M JUST SAYING, YOUR EYE TELLS A DIFFERENT STORY.
HOLY CRAP.
THE HARDY BOYS.
JOE HARDY. The "athletic one." Former friend and crime-solving partner. Almost childhood paramour.
(the less said about that the better.)
FRANK HARDY. The "smart one." Former friend and crime-solving partner. Almost childhood paramour.
(see? I told you the less said the better.)
TRY NOT TO GET SANDWICH ON HER, JOE.
WHATEVER, THIS SANDWICH IS AMAZING, SHE'D BE LUCKY TO HAVE IT ON HER.
THE FREAKING HARDY BOYS. I CAN'T BELIEVE IT. I THOUGHT YOU GUYS MOVED AWAY A COUPLE YEARS AGO.
WE DID, BUT APPARENTLY BAYPORT'S GOT A MYSTERIOUS PULL...BRINGS EVERYONE BACK INTO ITS ORBIT LIKE CLOCKWORK.
YEAH, THAT OR OUR DAD MOVED BACK HERE AFTER THE DIVORCE.
OR THAT.
WELL, I'M GLAD TO SEE YOU, SORRY ABOUT THE CIRCUMSTANCES.
IS WHAT IT IS.
YOU CAN SEE FRANK HAS...
...HAS...
"HAS INARGUABLY GROWN INTO THE MORE HANDSOME BROTHER."
...RIGHT...
RIGHT.

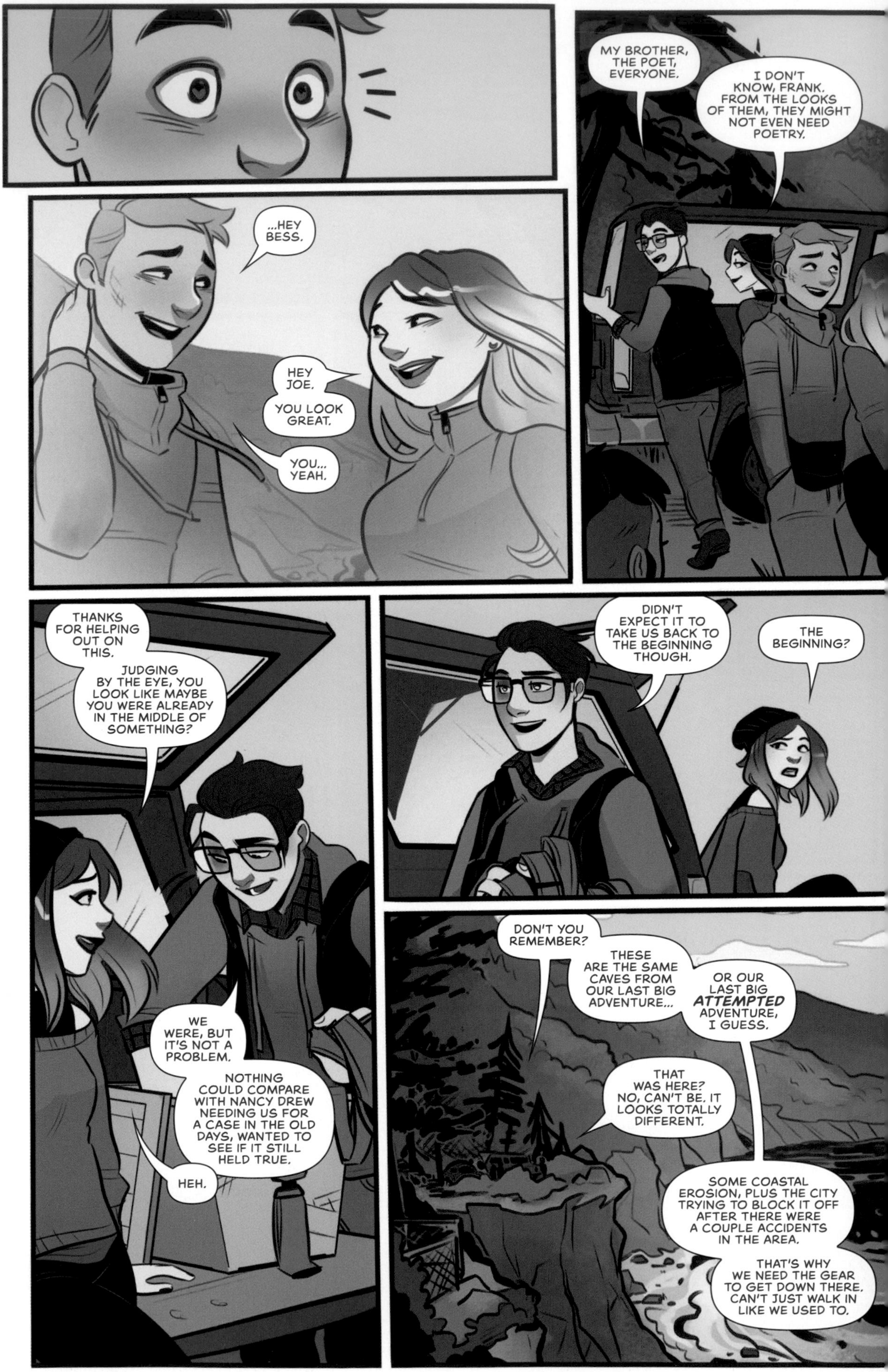
MY BROTHER, THE POET, EVERYONE.
I DON'T KNOW, FRANK. FROM THE LOOKS OF THEM, THEY MIGHT NOT EVEN NEED POETRY.
...HEY BESS.
HEY JOE.
YOU LOOK GREAT.
YOU... YEAH.
THANKS FOR HELPING OUT ON THIS.
JUDGING BY THE EYE, YOU LOOK LIKE MAYBE YOU WERE ALREADY IN THE MIDDLE OF SOMETHING?
WE WERE, BUT IT'S NOT A PROBLEM.
NOTHING COULD COMPARE WITH NANCY DREW NEEDING US FOR A CASE IN THE OLD DAYS, WANTED TO SEE IF IT STILL HELD TRUE.
HEH.
DIDN'T EXPECT IT TO TAKE US BACK TO THE BEGINNING THOUGH.
THE BEGINNING?
DON'T YOU REMEMBER?
THESE ARE THE SAME CAVES FROM OUR LAST BIG ADVENTURE...
OR OUR LAST BIG ***ATTEMPTED*** ADVENTURE, I GUESS.
THAT WAS HERE? NO, CAN'T BE. IT LOOKS TOTALLY DIFFERENT.
SOME COASTAL EROSION, PLUS THE CITY TRYING TO BLOCK IT OFF AFTER THERE WERE A COUPLE ACCIDENTS IN THE AREA.
THAT'S WHY WE NEED THE GEAR TO GET DOWN THERE. CAN'T JUST WALK IN LIKE WE USED TO.

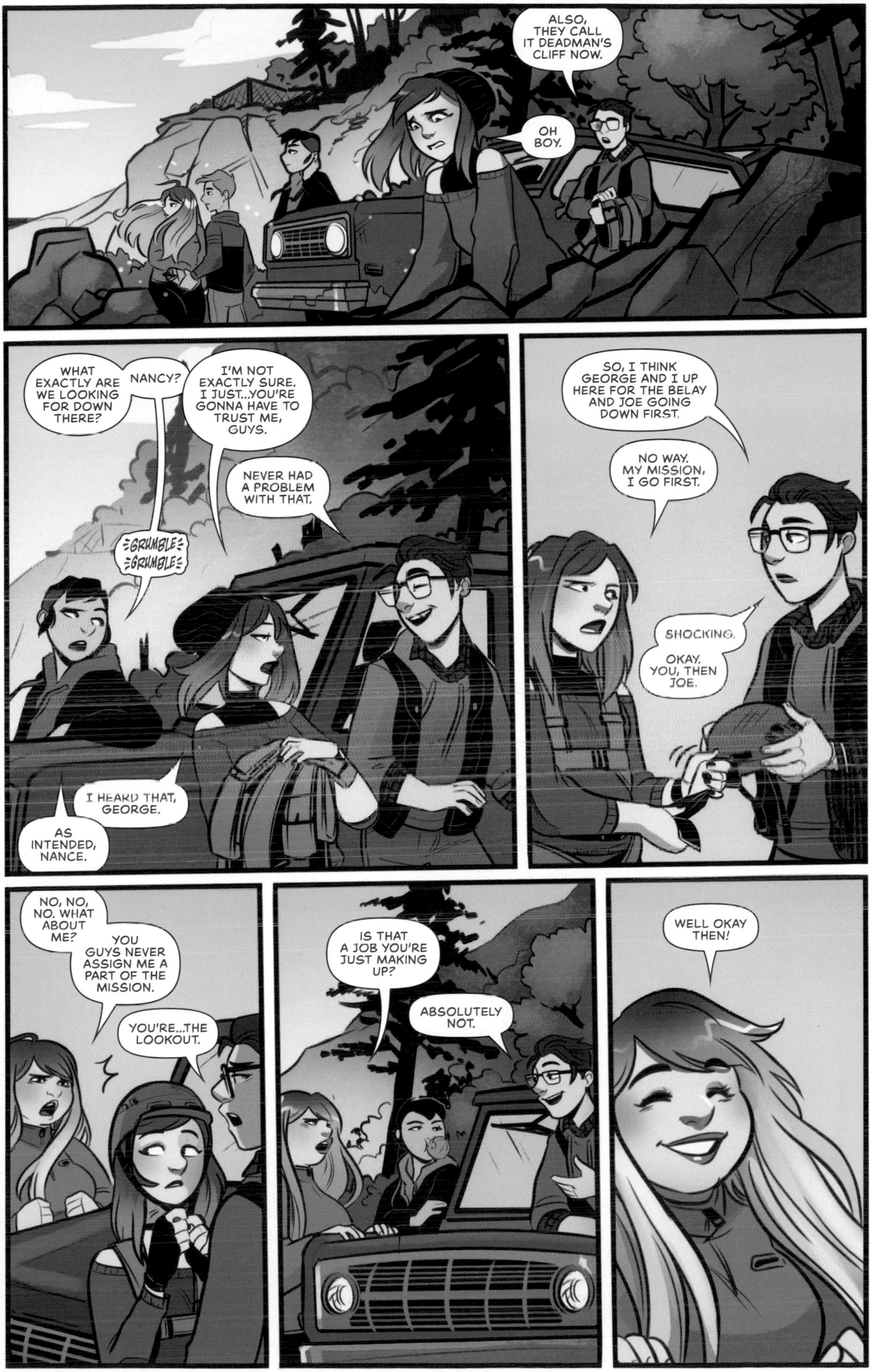
ALSO, THEY CALL IT DEADMAN'S CLIFF NOW.
OH BOY.
WHAT EXACTLY ARE WE LOOKING FOR DOWN THERE?
NANCY?
I'M NOT EXACTLY SURE. I JUST...YOU'RE GONNA HAVE TO TRUST ME, GUYS.
NEVER HAD A PROBLEM WITH THAT.
GRUMBLE GRUMBLE
I HEARD THAT, GEORGE.
AS INTENDED, NANCE.
SO, I THINK GEORGE AND I UP HERE FOR THE BELAY AND JOE GOING DOWN FIRST.
NO WAY. MY MISSION, I GO FIRST.
SHOCKING.
OKAY. YOU, THEN JOE.
NO, NO, NO. WHAT ABOUT ME?
YOU GUYS NEVER ASSIGN ME A PART OF THE MISSION.
YOU'RE...THE LOOKOUT.
IS THAT A JOB YOU'RE JUST MAKING UP?
ABSOLUTELY NOT.
WELL OKAY THEN!

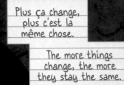

Change your friends, change your city, change your mission. You're still hanging by a thread...

Plus ça change, plus c'est la même chose.

The more things change, the more they stay the same.

Yeah. We brought that back.

It's French by the way. Jean-Baptiste Alphonse Karr, 1849, not Taylor Swift.

SLACK!

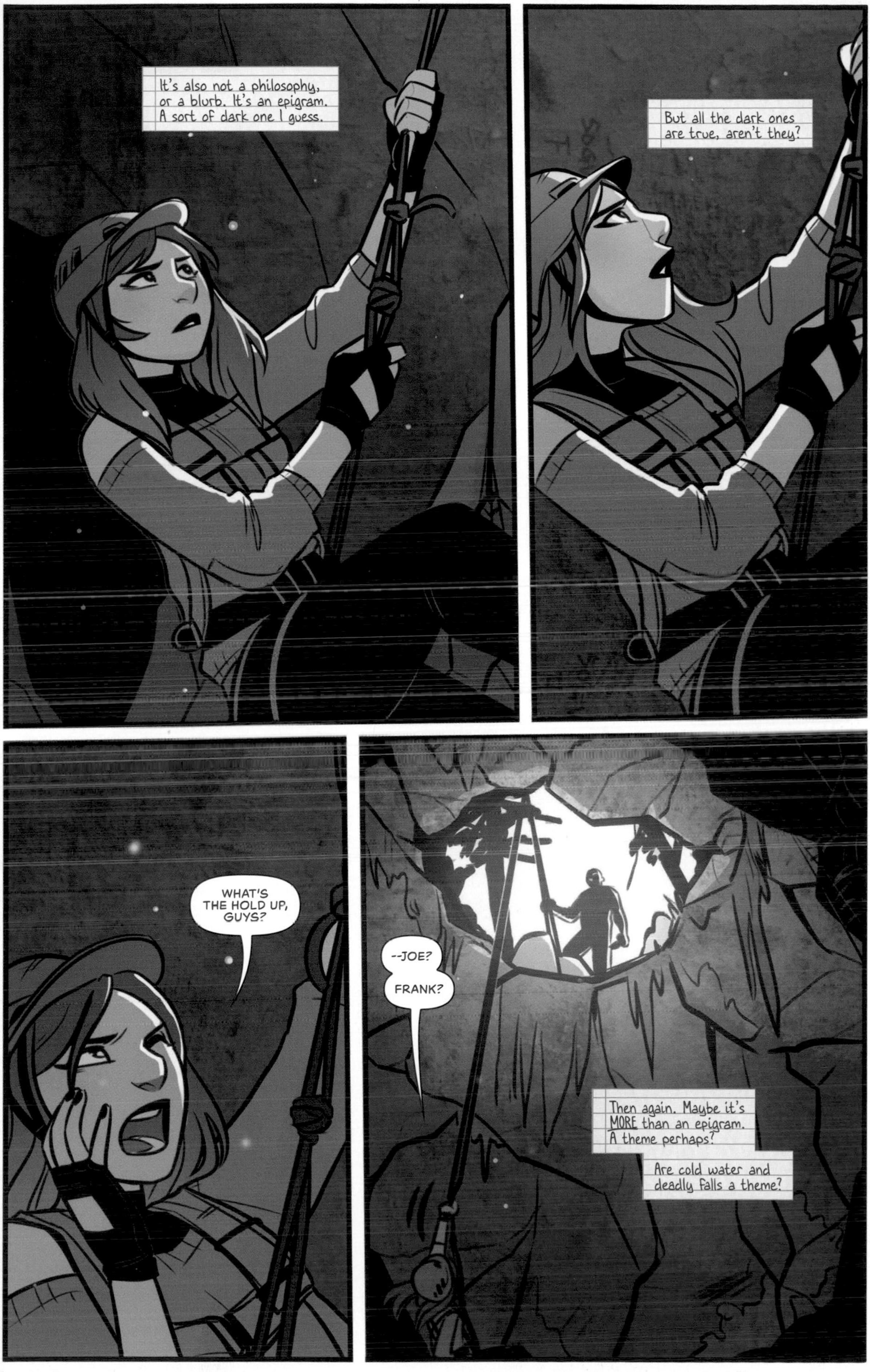
It's also not a philosophy, or a blurb. It's an epigram. A sort of dark one I guess.
But all the dark ones are true, aren't they?
WHAT'S THE HOLD UP, GUYS?
--JOE?
FRANK?
Then again. Maybe it's MORE than an epigram. A theme perhaps?
Are cold water and deadly falls a theme?

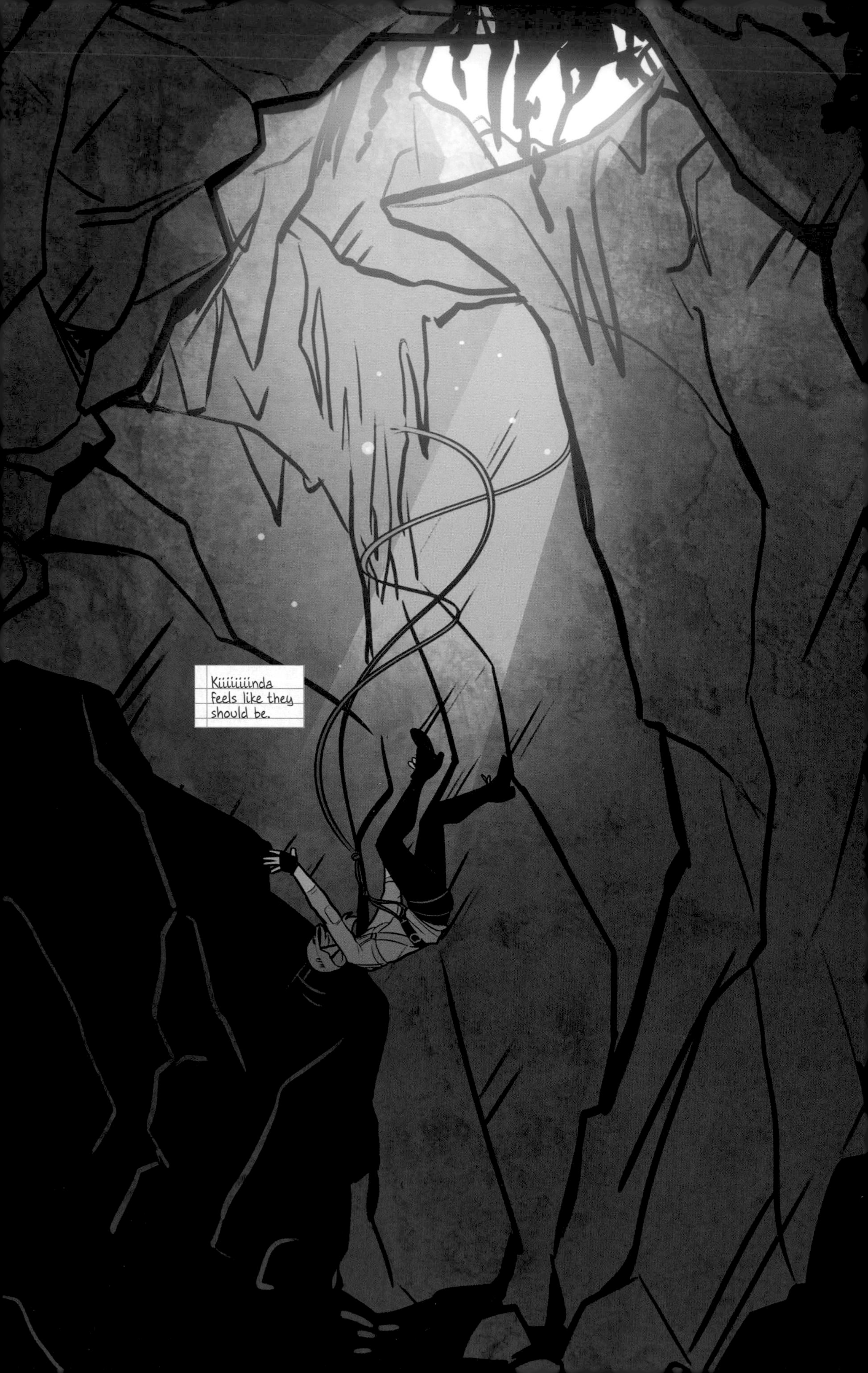
Kiiiiiiiinda feels like they should be.

And things just got way more complicated.

CHAPTER TWO

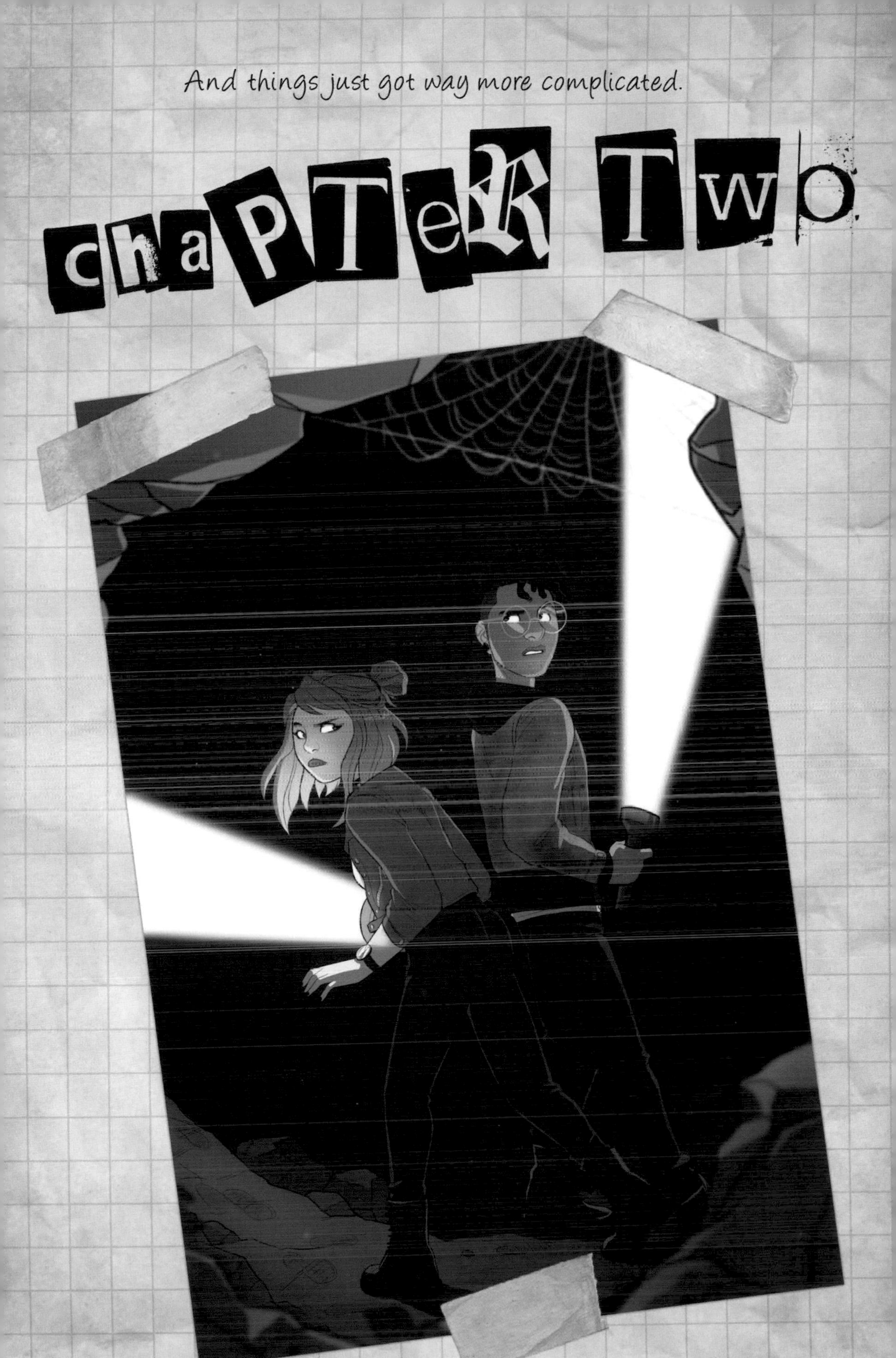

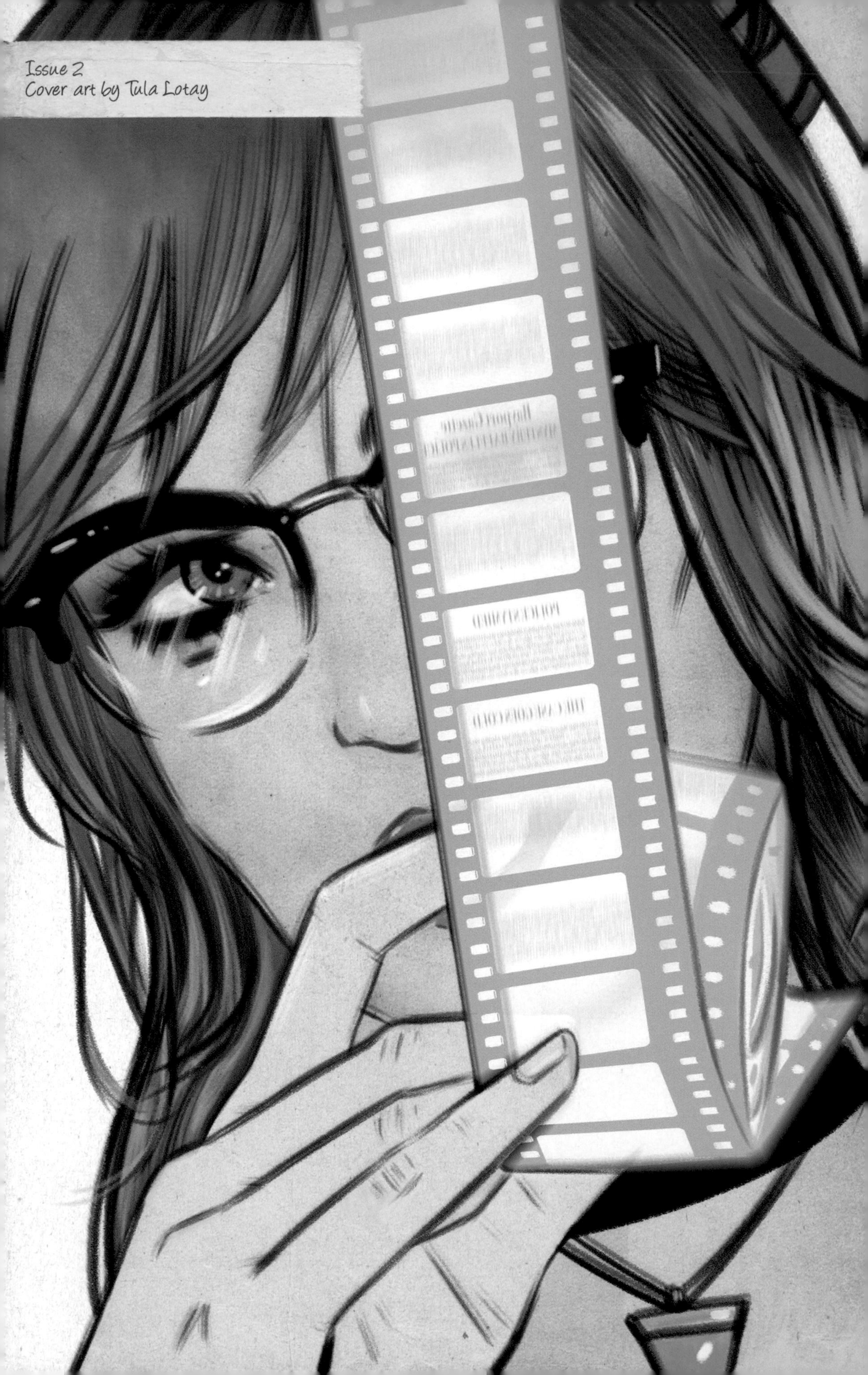

Issue 2
Cover art by Tula Lotay

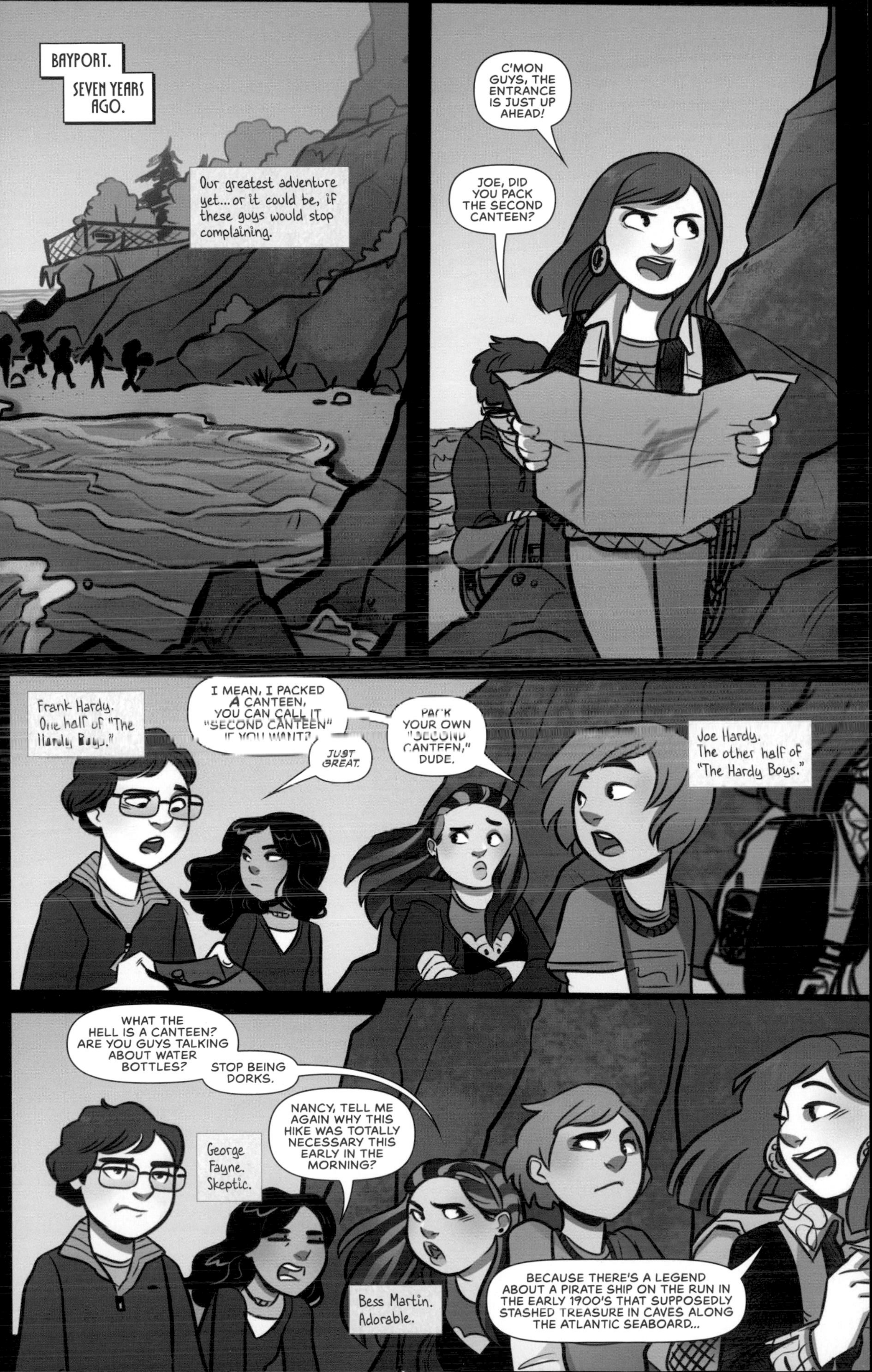
BAYPORT.
SEVEN YEARS AGO.
Our greatest adventure yet... or it could be, if these guys would stop complaining.
C'MON GUYS, THE ENTRANCE IS JUST UP AHEAD!
JOE, DID YOU PACK THE SECOND CANTEEN?
Frank Hardy. One half of "The Hardy Boys."
I MEAN, I PACKED A CANTEEN, YOU CAN CALL IT "SECOND CANTEEN" IF YOU WANT?
JUST GREAT.
PACK YOUR OWN "SECOND CANTEEN," DUDE.
Joe Hardy. The other half of "The Hardy Boys."
WHAT THE HELL IS A CANTEEN? ARE YOU GUYS TALKING ABOUT WATER BOTTLES?
STOP BEING DORKS.
George Fayne. Skeptic.
NANCY, TELL ME AGAIN WHY THIS HIKE WAS TOTALLY NECESSARY THIS EARLY IN THE MORNING?
Bess Martin. Adorable.
BECAUSE THERE'S A LEGEND ABOUT A PIRATE SHIP ON THE RUN IN THE EARLY 1900'S THAT SUPPOSEDLY STASHED TREASURE IN CAVES ALONG THE ATLANTIC SEABOARD...

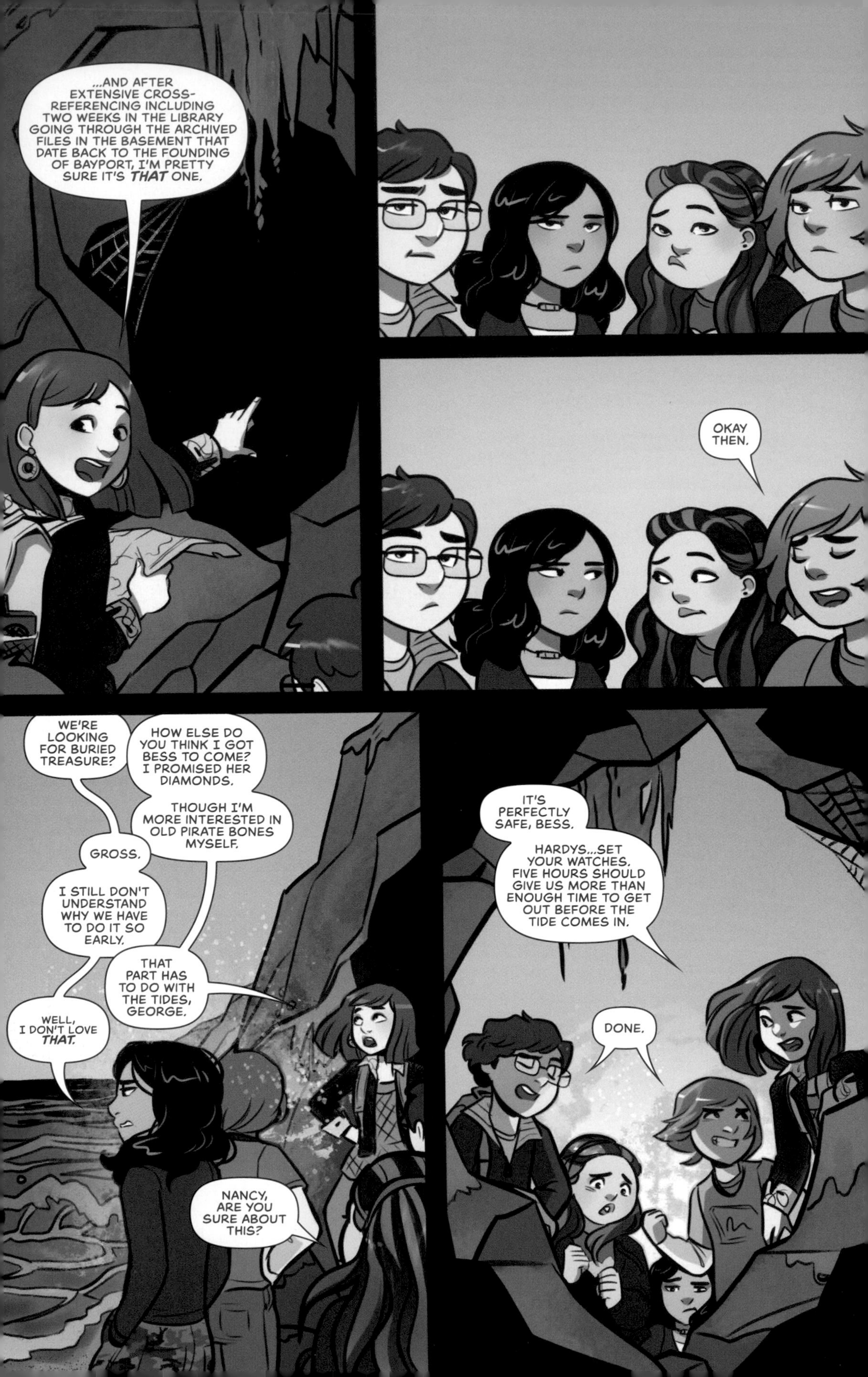
...AND AFTER EXTENSIVE CROSS-REFERENCING INCLUDING TWO WEEKS IN THE LIBRARY GOING THROUGH THE ARCHIVED FILES IN THE BASEMENT THAT DATE BACK TO THE FOUNDING OF BAYPORT, I'M PRETTY SURE IT'S ***THAT*** ONE.
OKAY THEN.
WE'RE LOOKING FOR BURIED TREASURE?
HOW ELSE DO YOU THINK I GOT BESS TO COME? I PROMISED HER DIAMONDS.
THOUGH I'M MORE INTERESTED IN OLD PIRATE BONES MYSELF.
GROSS.
I STILL DON'T UNDERSTAND WHY WE HAVE TO DO IT SO EARLY.
THAT PART HAS TO DO WITH THE TIDES, GEORGE.
WELL, I DON'T LOVE ***THAT.***
NANCY, ARE YOU SURE ABOUT THIS?
IT'S PERFECTLY SAFE, BESS.
HARDYS...SET YOUR WATCHES. FIVE HOURS SHOULD GIVE US MORE THAN ENOUGH TIME TO GET OUT BEFORE THE TIDE COMES IN.
DONE.

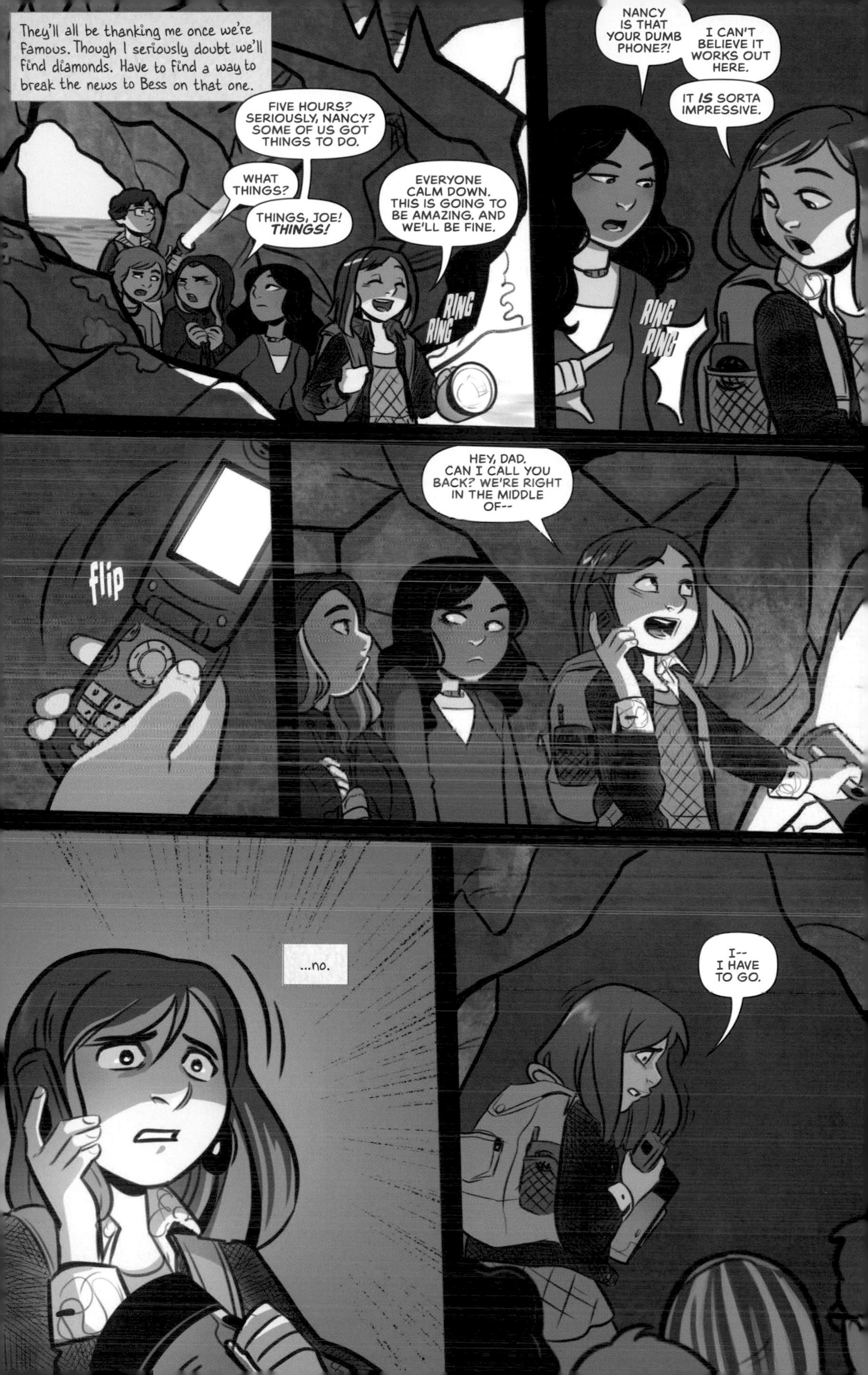
They'll all be thanking me once we're famous. Though I seriously doubt we'll find diamonds. Have to find a way to break the news to Bess on that one.
FIVE HOURS? SERIOUSLY, NANCY? SOME OF US GOT THINGS TO DO.
WHAT THINGS?
THINGS, JOE! THINGS!
EVERYONE CALM DOWN. THIS IS GOING TO BE AMAZING. AND WE'LL BE FINE.
RING RING
NANCY IS THAT YOUR DUMB PHONE?!
I CAN'T BELIEVE IT WORKS OUT HERE.
IT IS SORTA IMPRESSIVE.
RING RING
flip
HEY, DAD. CAN I CALL YOU BACK? WE'RE RIGHT IN THE MIDDLE OF--
...no.
I-- I HAVE TO GO.

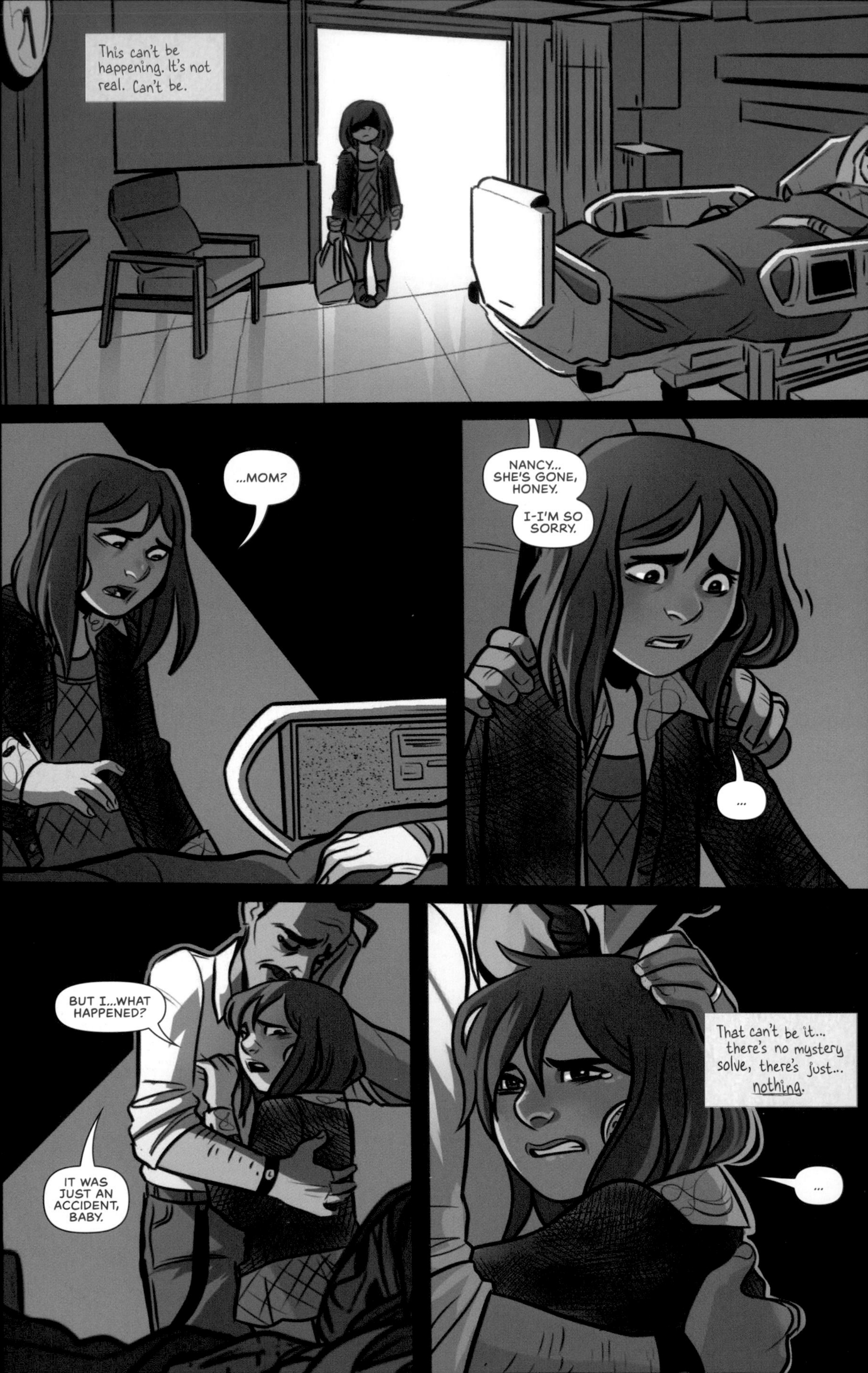
This can't be happening. It's not real. Can't be.
...MOM?
NANCY... SHE'S GONE, HONEY.
I-I'M SO SORRY.
...
BUT I...WHAT HAPPENED?
IT WAS JUST AN ACCIDENT, BABY.
That can't be it... there's no mystery solve, there's just... nothing.
...

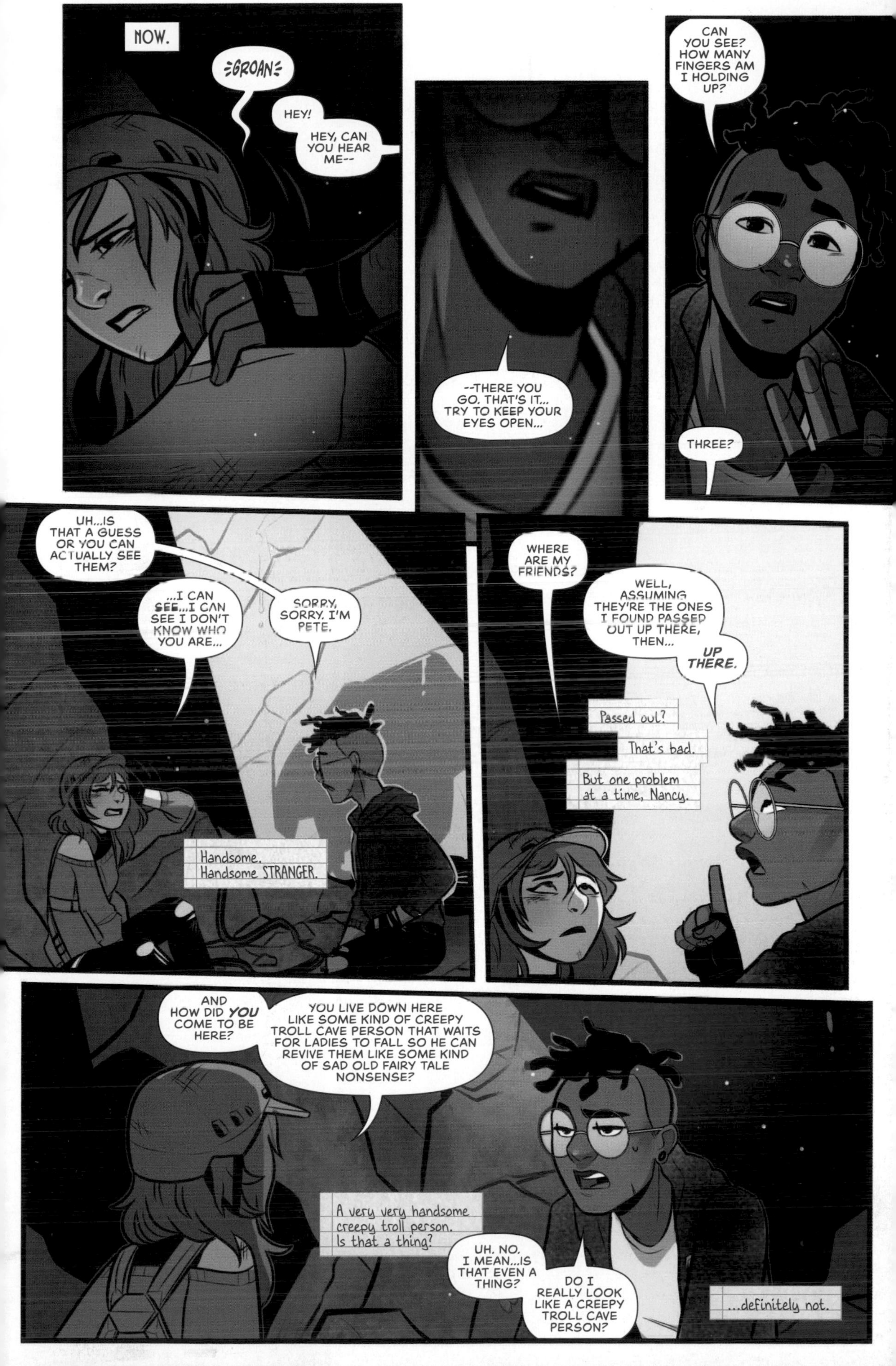
NOW.
GROAN
HEY!
HEY, CAN YOU HEAR ME--
--THERE YOU GO. THAT'S IT... TRY TO KEEP YOUR EYES OPEN...
CAN YOU SEE? HOW MANY FINGERS AM I HOLDING UP?
THREE?
UH...IS THAT A GUESS OR YOU CAN ACTUALLY SEE THEM?
...I CAN SEE...I CAN SEE I DON'T KNOW WHO YOU ARE...
SORRY, SORRY. I'M PETE.
Handsome.
Handsome STRANGER.
WHERE ARE MY FRIENDS?
WELL, ASSUMING THEY'RE THE ONES I FOUND PASSED OUT UP THERE, THEN...
UP THERE.
Passed out?
That's bad.
But one problem at a time, Nancy.
AND HOW DID YOU COME TO BE HERE?
YOU LIVE DOWN HERE LIKE SOME KIND OF CREEPY TROLL CAVE PERSON THAT WAITS FOR LADIES TO FALL SO HE CAN REVIVE THEM LIKE SOME KIND OF SAD OLD FAIRY TALE NONSENSE?
A very very handsome creepy troll person. Is that a thing?
UH. NO. I MEAN...IS THAT EVEN A THING?
DO I REALLY LOOK LIKE A CREEPY TROLL CAVE PERSON?
...definitely not.

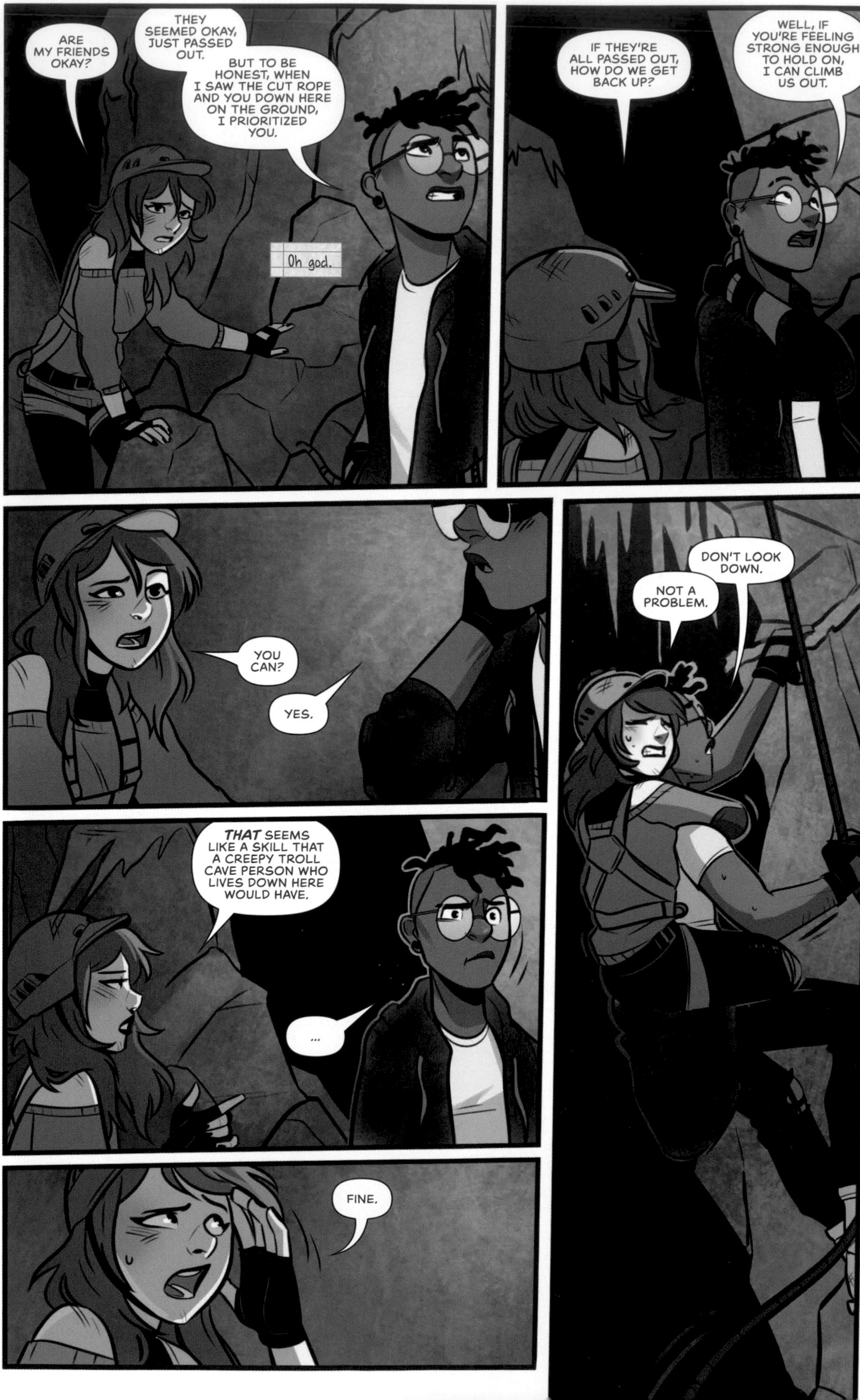
ARE MY FRIENDS OKAY?
THEY SEEMED OKAY, JUST PASSED OUT.
BUT TO BE HONEST, WHEN I SAW THE CUT ROPE AND YOU DOWN HERE ON THE GROUND, I PRIORITIZED YOU.
Oh god.
IF THEY'RE ALL PASSED OUT, HOW DO WE GET BACK UP?
WELL, IF YOU'RE FEELING STRONG ENOUGH TO HOLD ON, I CAN CLIMB US OUT.
YOU CAN?
YES.
THAT SEEMS LIKE A SKILL THAT A CREEPY TROLL CAVE PERSON WHO LIVES DOWN HERE WOULD HAVE.
...
FINE.
DON'T LOOK DOWN.
NOT A PROBLEM.

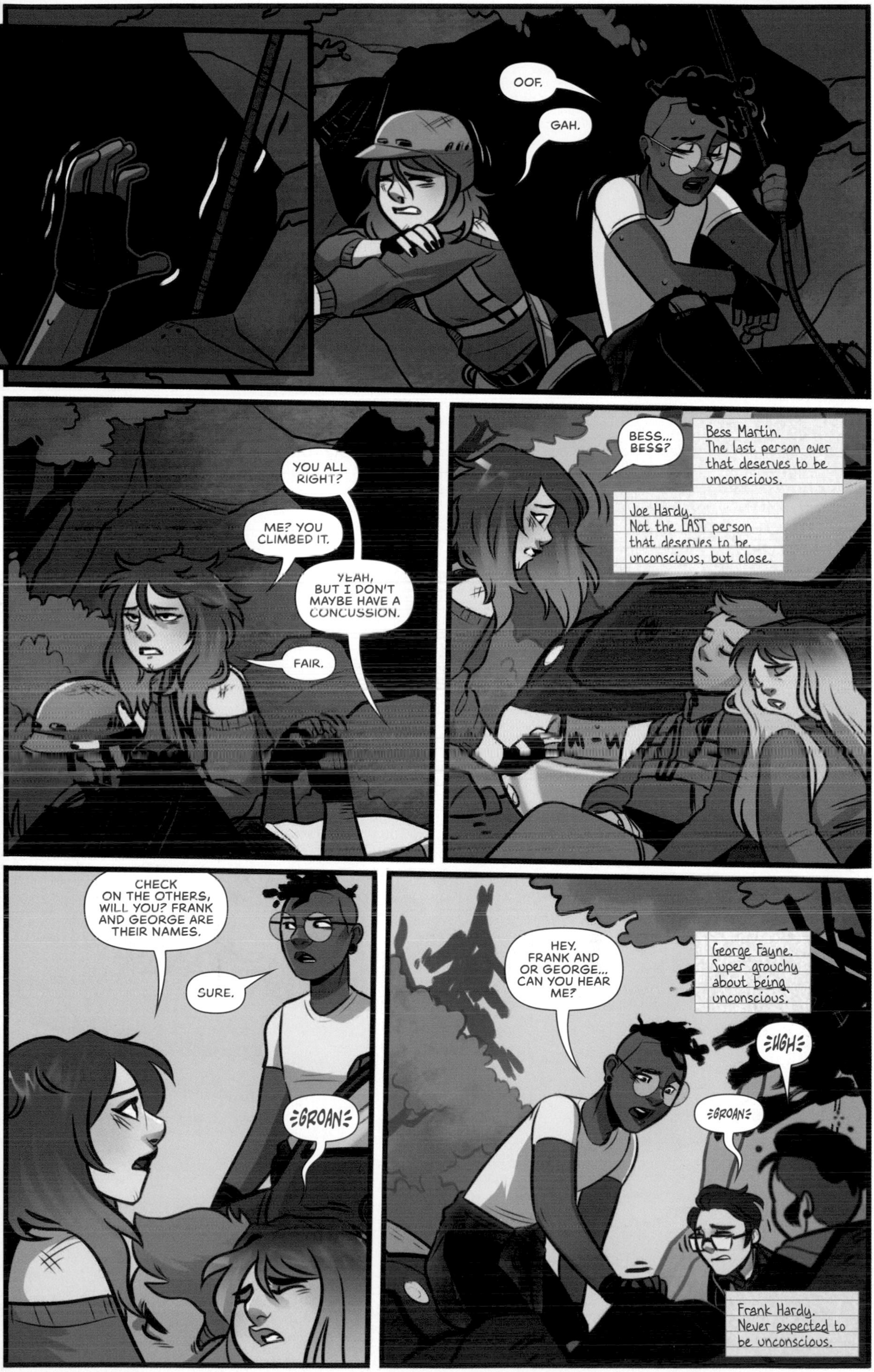
OOF.
GAH.
YOU ALL RIGHT?
ME? YOU CLIMBED IT.
YEAH, BUT I DON'T MAYBE HAVE A CONCUSSION.
FAIR.
BESS... BESS?
Bess Martin. The last person ever that deserves to be unconscious.
Joe Hardy. Not the LAST person that deserves to be unconscious, but close.
CHECK ON THE OTHERS, WILL YOU? FRANK AND GEORGE ARE THEIR NAMES.
SURE.
GROAN
HEY. FRANK AND OR GEORGE... CAN YOU HEAR ME?
George Fayne. Super grouchy about being unconscious.
UGH
GROAN
Frank Hardy. Never expected to be unconscious.

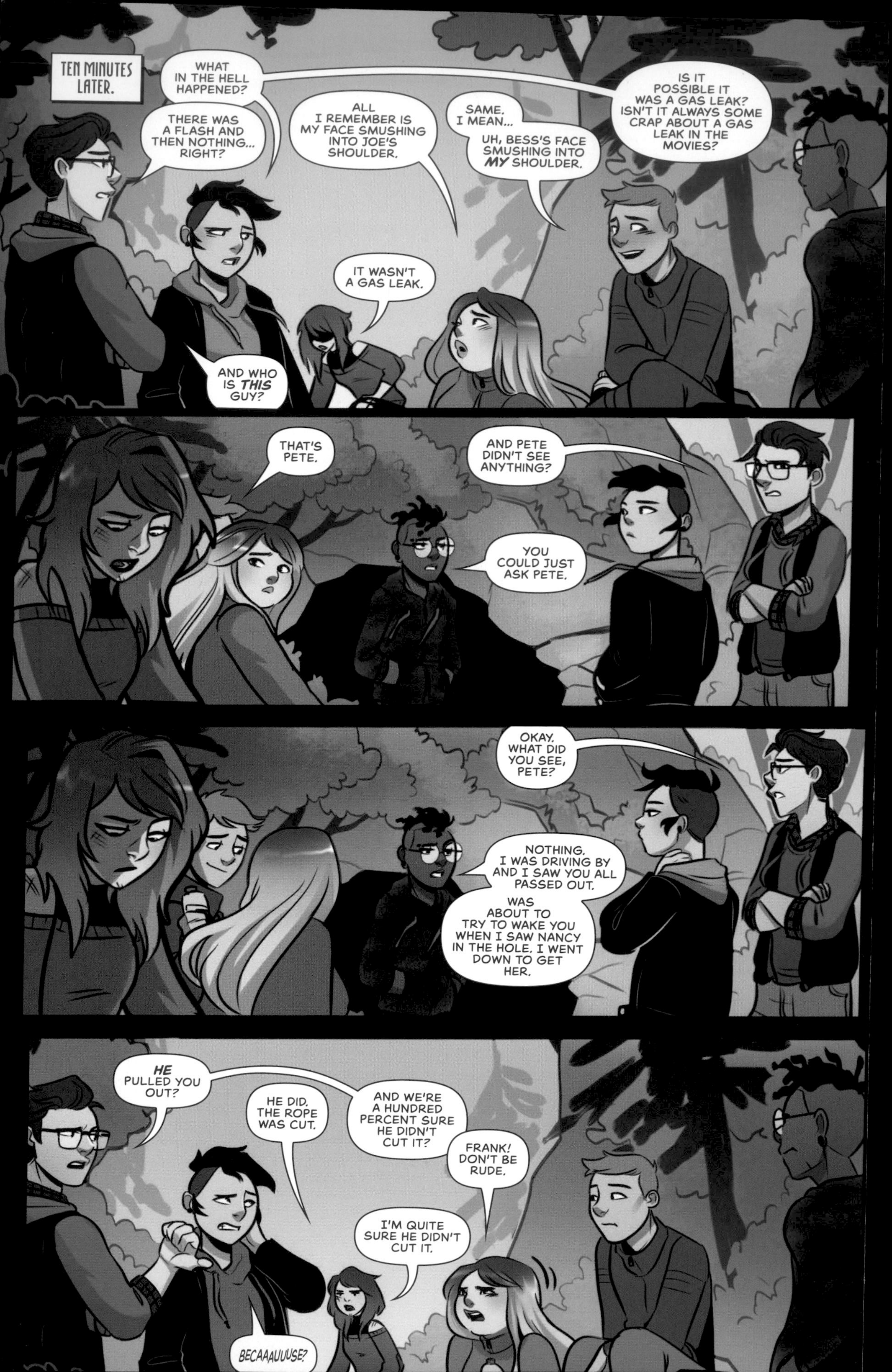

TEN MINUTES LATER.
WHAT IN THE HELL HAPPENED?
IS IT POSSIBLE IT WAS A GAS LEAK? ISN'T IT ALWAYS SOME CRAP ABOUT A GAS LEAK IN THE MOVIES?
THERE WAS A FLASH AND THEN NOTHING... RIGHT?
ALL I REMEMBER IS MY FACE SMUSHING INTO JOE'S SHOULDER.
SAME. I MEAN...
UH, BESS'S FACE SMUSHING INTO MY SHOULDER.
IT WASN'T A GAS LEAK.
AND WHO IS THIS GUY?
THAT'S PETE.
AND PETE DIDN'T SEE ANYTHING?
YOU COULD JUST ASK PETE.
OKAY. WHAT DID YOU SEE, PETE?
NOTHING. I WAS DRIVING BY AND I SAW YOU ALL PASSED OUT.
WAS ABOUT TO TRY TO WAKE YOU WHEN I SAW NANCY IN THE HOLE. I WENT DOWN TO GET HER.
HE PULLED YOU OUT?
HE DID. THE ROPE WAS CUT.
AND WE'RE A HUNDRED PERCENT SURE HE DIDN'T CUT IT?
FRANK! DON'T BE RUDE.
I'M QUITE SURE HE DIDN'T CUT IT.
BECAAAUUUSE?

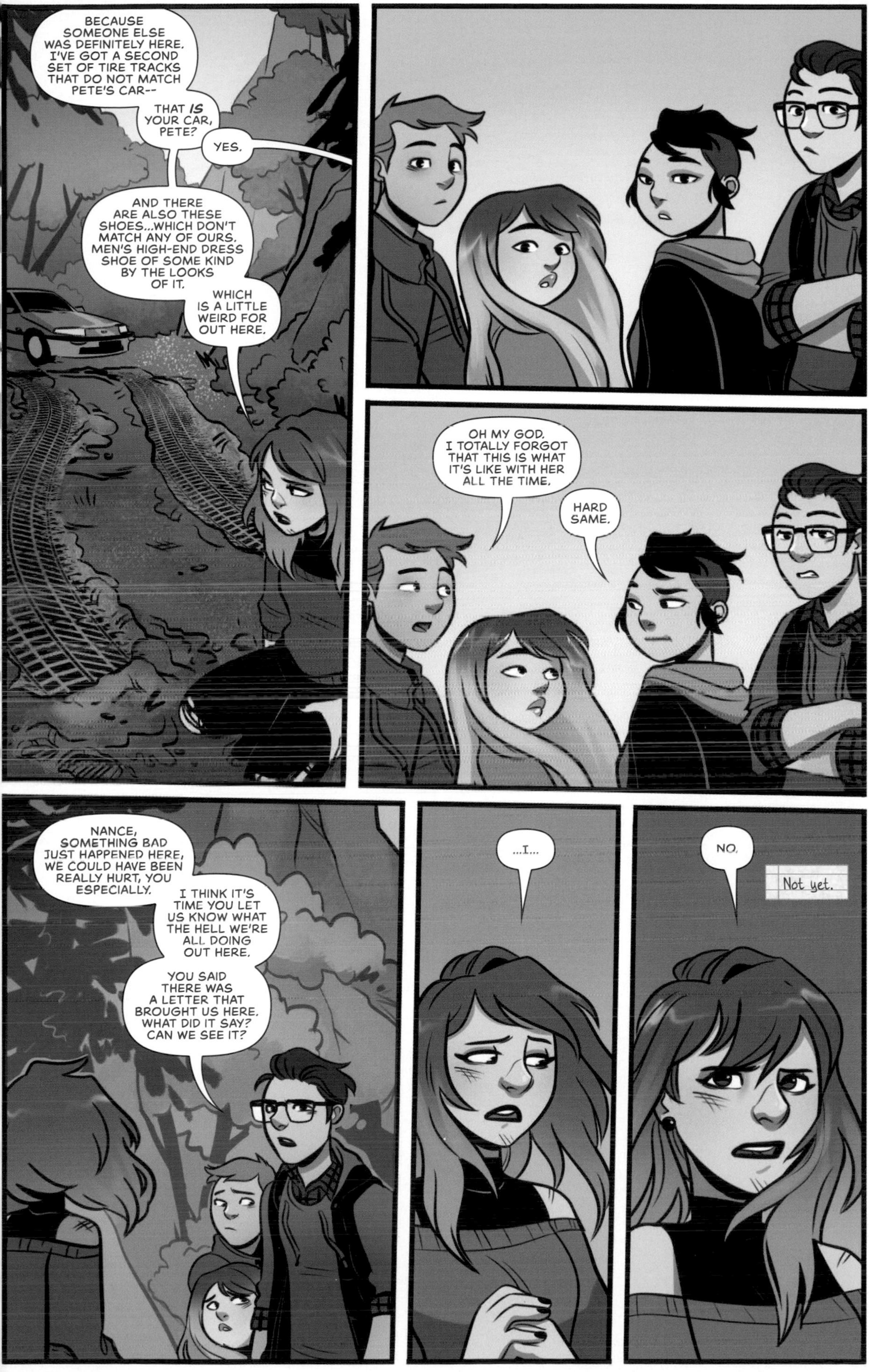
BECAUSE SOMEONE ELSE WAS DEFINITELY HERE. I'VE GOT A SECOND SET OF TIRE TRACKS THAT DO NOT MATCH PETE'S CAR--
THAT *IS* YOUR CAR, PETE?
YES.
AND THERE ARE ALSO THESE SHOES...WHICH DON'T MATCH ANY OF OURS. MEN'S HIGH-END DRESS SHOE OF SOME KIND BY THE LOOKS OF IT.
WHICH IS A LITTLE WEIRD FOR OUT HERE.
OH MY GOD, I TOTALLY FORGOT THAT THIS IS WHAT IT'S LIKE WITH HER ALL THE TIME.
HARD SAME.
NANCE, SOMETHING BAD JUST HAPPENED HERE, WE COULD HAVE BEEN REALLY HURT, YOU ESPECIALLY.
I THINK IT'S TIME YOU LET US KNOW WHAT THE HELL WE'RE ALL DOING OUT HERE.
YOU SAID THERE WAS A LETTER THAT BROUGHT US HERE. WHAT DID IT SAY? CAN WE SEE IT?
...I...
NO.
Not yet.

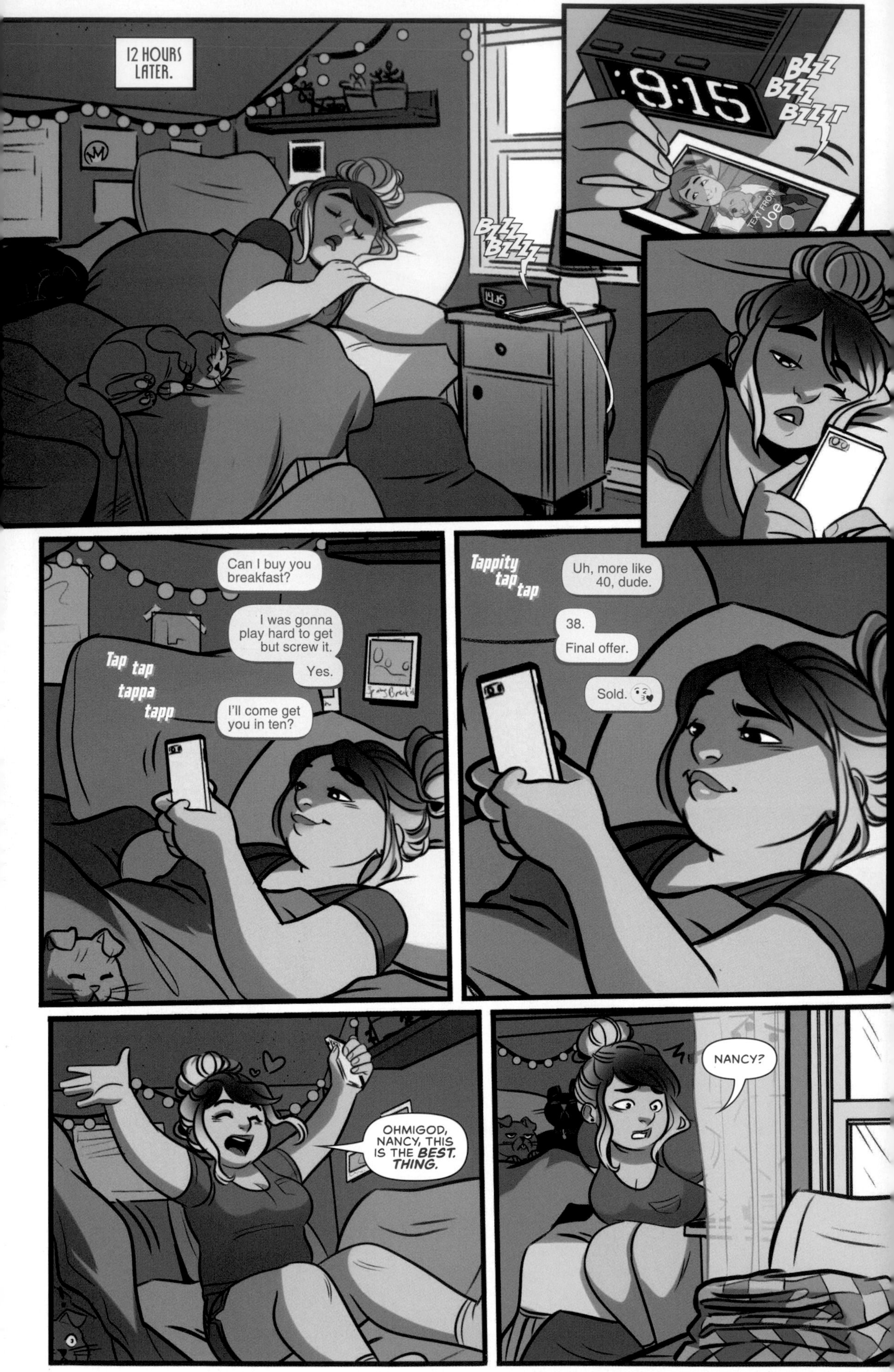
12 HOURS LATER.
BZZZ BZZZ
9:15
BZZZ BZZZ BZZZT
TEXT FROM Joe
Can I buy you breakfast?
I was gonna play hard to get but screw it.
Yes.
Tap tap tappa tapp
I'll come get you in ten?
Tappity tap tap
Uh, more like 40, dude.
38.
Final offer.
Sold.
OHMIGOD, NANCY, THIS IS THE BEST. THING.
NANCY?

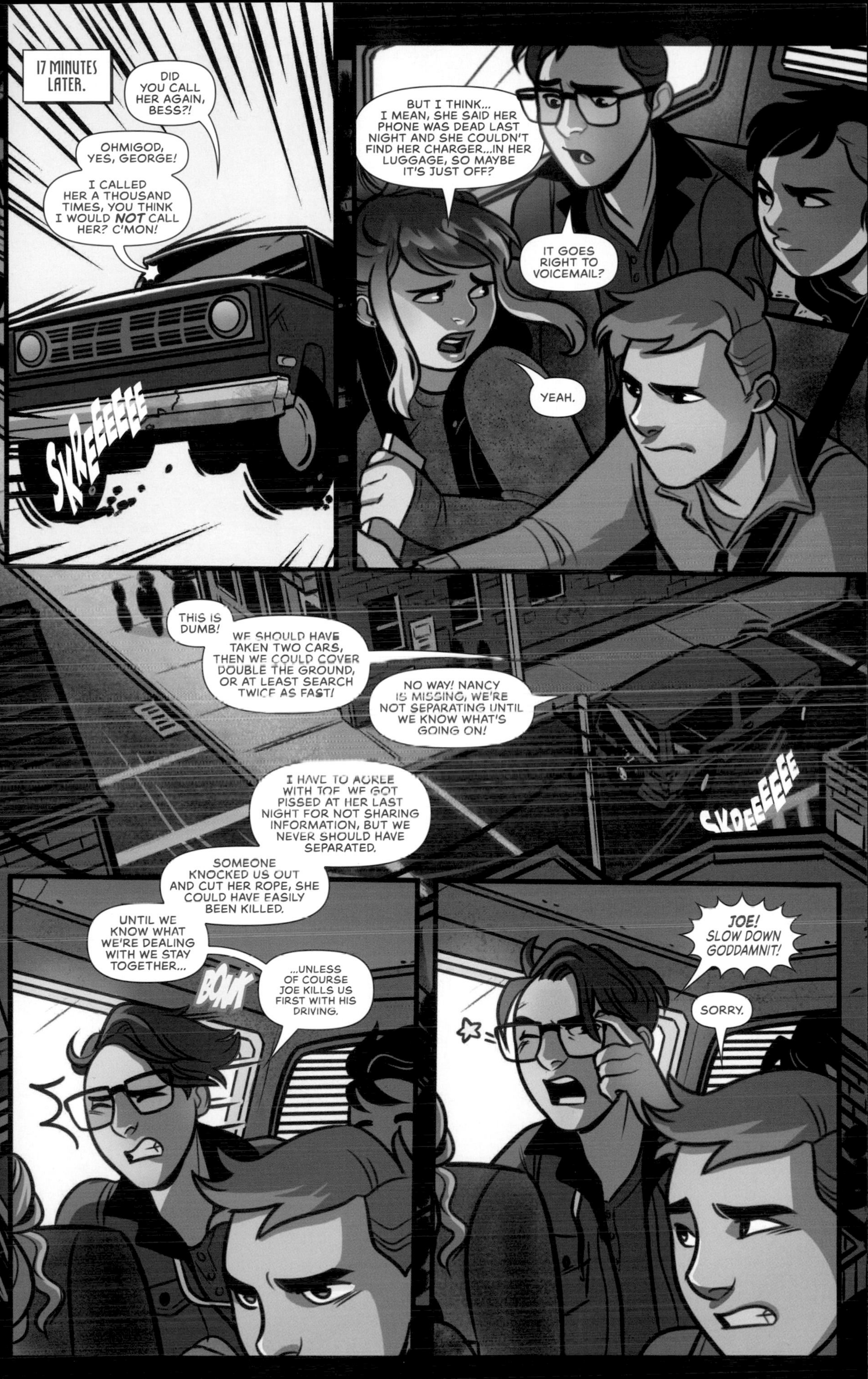
17 MINUTES LATER.
DID YOU CALL HER AGAIN, BESS?!
OHMIGOD, YES, GEORGE!
I CALLED HER A THOUSAND TIMES, YOU THINK I WOULD NOT CALL HER? C'MON!
SKREEEEEE
BUT I THINK... I MEAN, SHE SAID HER PHONE WAS DEAD LAST NIGHT AND SHE COULDN'T FIND HER CHARGER...IN HER LUGGAGE, SO MAYBE IT'S JUST OFF?
IT GOES RIGHT TO VOICEMAIL?
YEAH.
THIS IS DUMB!
WE SHOULD HAVE TAKEN TWO CARS, THEN WE COULD COVER DOUBLE THE GROUND, OR AT LEAST SEARCH TWICE AS FAST!
NO WAY! NANCY IS MISSING, WE'RE NOT SEPARATING UNTIL WE KNOW WHAT'S GOING ON!
SKREEEEE
I HAVE TO AGREE WITH JOE. WE GOT PISSED AT HER LAST NIGHT FOR NOT SHARING INFORMATION, BUT WE NEVER SHOULD HAVE SEPARATED.
SOMEONE KNOCKED US OUT AND CUT HER ROPE, SHE COULD HAVE EASILY BEEN KILLED.
UNTIL WE KNOW WHAT WE'RE DEALING WITH WE STAY TOGETHER...
BONK
...UNLESS OF COURSE JOE KILLS US FIRST WITH HIS DRIVING.
JOE! SLOW DOWN GODDAMNIT!
SORRY.

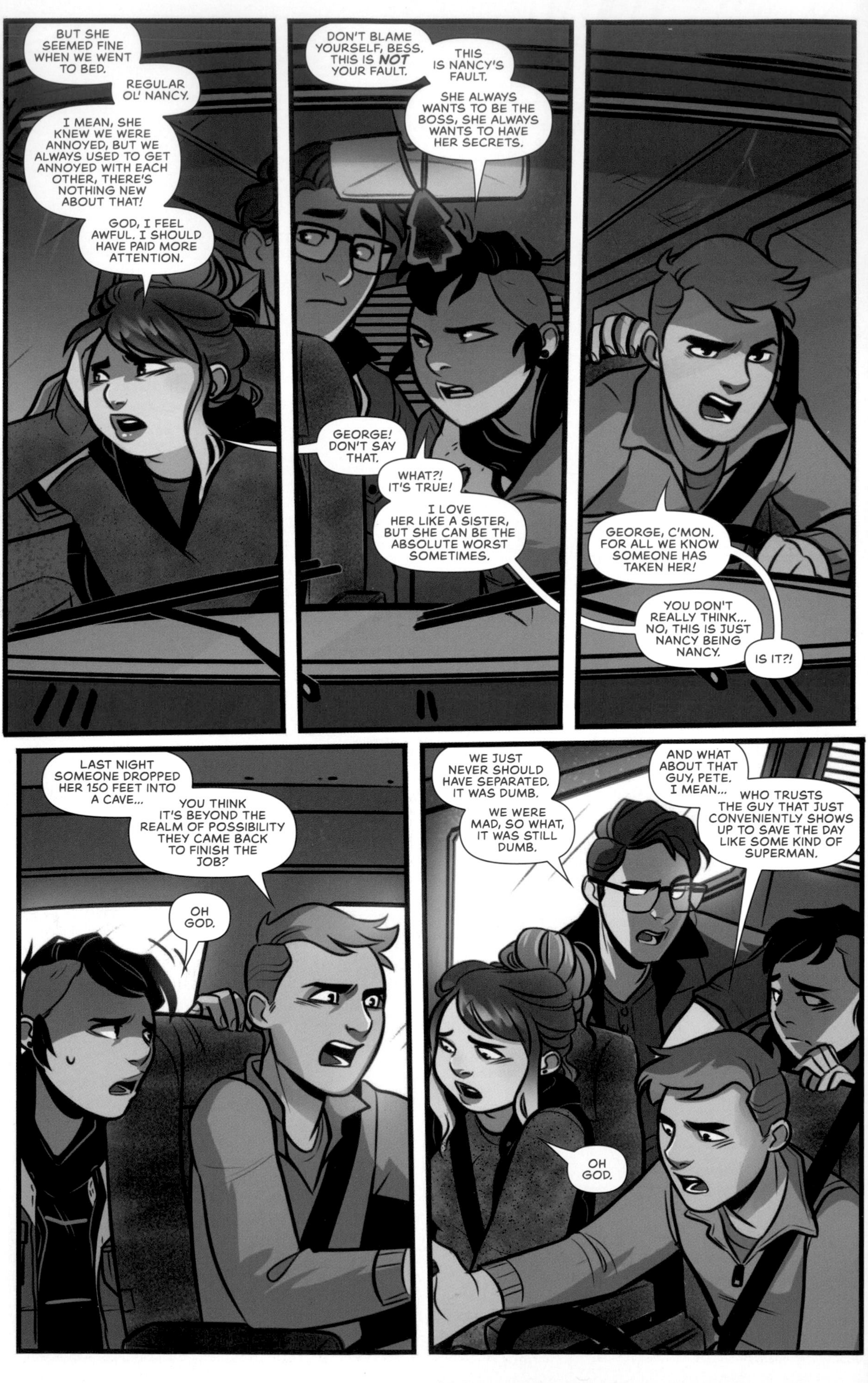
BUT SHE SEEMED FINE WHEN WE WENT TO BED.
REGULAR OL' NANCY.
I MEAN, SHE KNEW WE WERE ANNOYED, BUT WE ALWAYS USED TO GET ANNOYED WITH EACH OTHER, THERE'S NOTHING NEW ABOUT THAT!
GOD, I FEEL AWFUL. I SHOULD HAVE PAID MORE ATTENTION.
DON'T BLAME YOURSELF, BESS. THIS IS NOT YOUR FAULT.
THIS IS NANCY'S FAULT.
SHE ALWAYS WANTS TO BE THE BOSS, SHE ALWAYS WANTS TO HAVE HER SECRETS.
GEORGE! DON'T SAY THAT.
WHAT?! IT'S TRUE!
I LOVE HER LIKE A SISTER, BUT SHE CAN BE THE ABSOLUTE WORST SOMETIMES.
GEORGE, C'MON. FOR ALL WE KNOW SOMEONE HAS TAKEN HER!
YOU DON'T REALLY THINK... NO, THIS IS JUST NANCY BEING NANCY.
IS IT?!
LAST NIGHT SOMEONE DROPPED HER 150 FEET INTO A CAVE...
YOU THINK IT'S BEYOND THE REALM OF POSSIBILITY THEY CAME BACK TO FINISH THE JOB?
OH GOD.
WE JUST NEVER SHOULD HAVE SEPARATED. IT WAS DUMB.
WE WERE MAD, SO WHAT, IT WAS STILL DUMB.
AND WHAT ABOUT THAT GUY, PETE. I MEAN...
WHO TRUSTS THE GUY THAT JUST CONVENIENTLY SHOWS UP TO SAVE THE DAY LIKE SOME KIND OF SUPERMAN.
OH GOD.

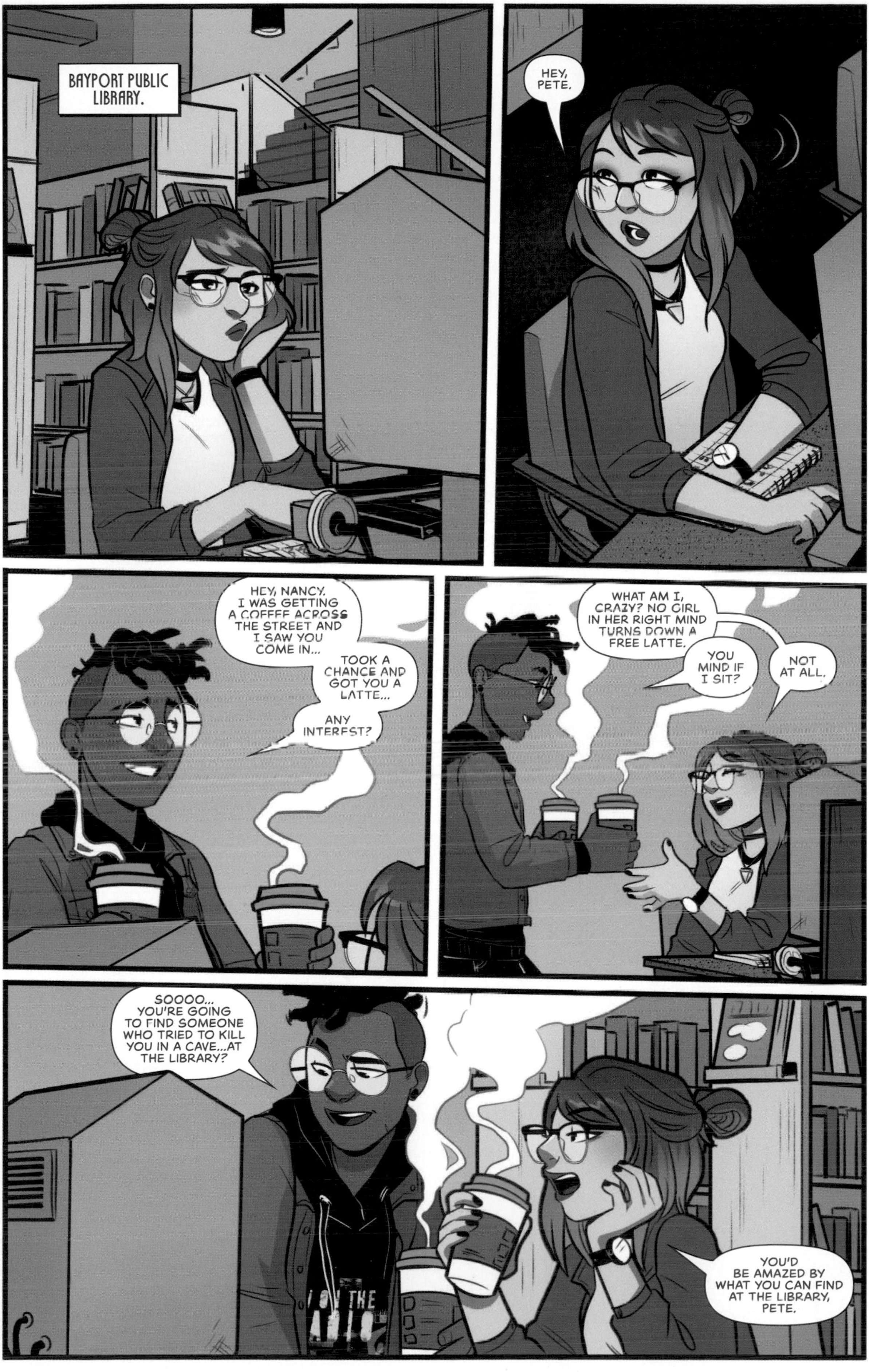
BAYPORT PUBLIC LIBRARY.
HEY, PETE.
HEY, NANCY. I WAS GETTING A COFFEE ACROSS THE STREET AND I SAW YOU COME IN...
TOOK A CHANCE AND GOT YOU A LATTE...
ANY INTEREST?
WHAT AM I, CRAZY? NO GIRL IN HER RIGHT MIND TURNS DOWN A FREE LATTE.
YOU MIND IF I SIT?
NOT AT ALL.
SOOOO... YOU'RE GOING TO FIND SOMEONE WHO TRIED TO KILL YOU IN A CAVE...AT THE LIBRARY?
YOU'D BE AMAZED BY WHAT YOU CAN FIND AT THE LIBRARY, PETE.

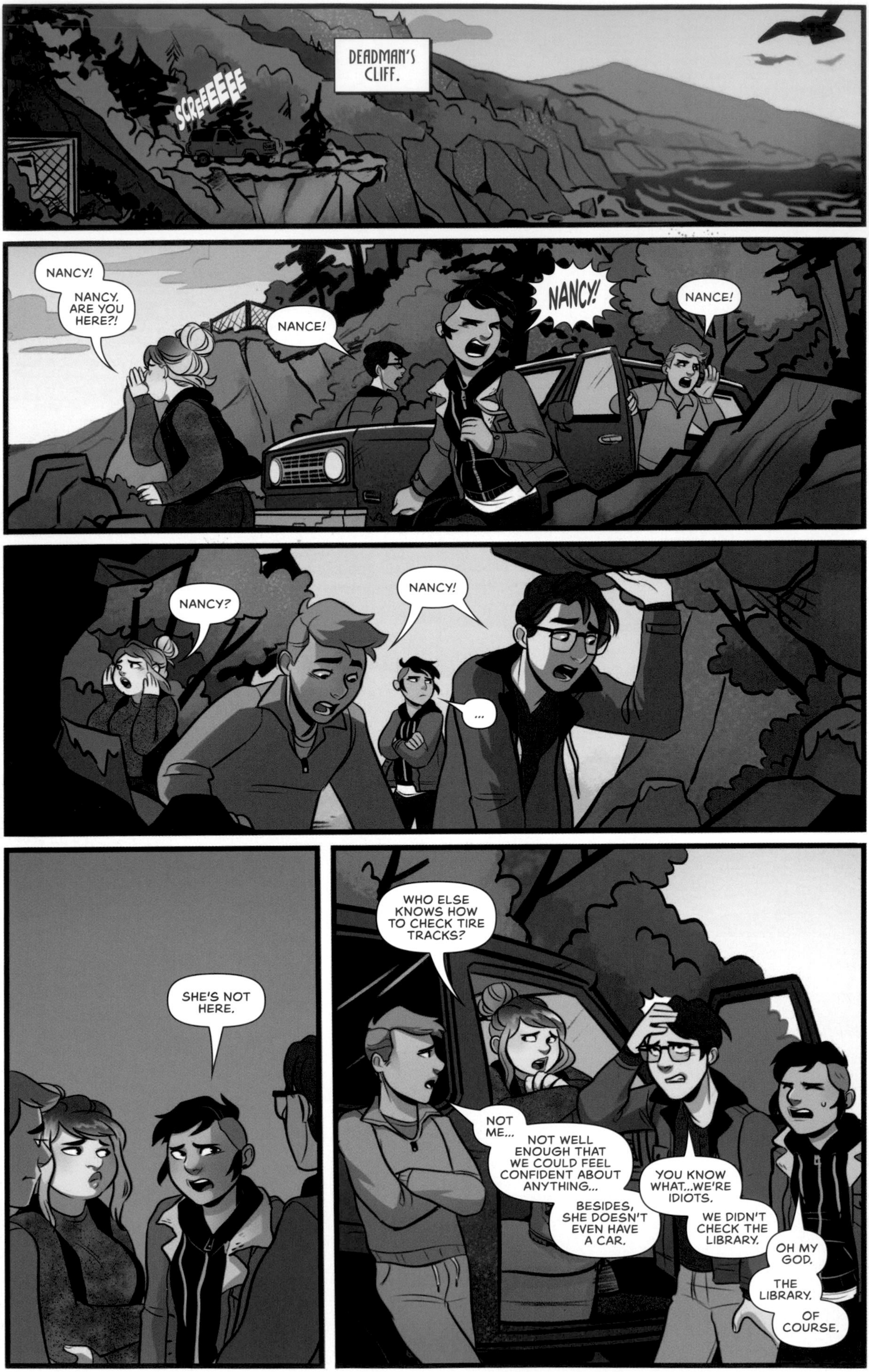
DEADMAN'S CLIFF.
SCREEEEEE
NANCY!
NANCY, ARE YOU HERE?!
NANCE!
NANCY!
NANCE!
NANCY?
NANCY!
...
SHE'S NOT HERE.
WHO ELSE KNOWS HOW TO CHECK TIRE TRACKS?
NOT ME...
NOT WELL ENOUGH THAT WE COULD FEEL CONFIDENT ABOUT ANYTHING...
BESIDES, SHE DOESN'T EVEN HAVE A CAR.
YOU KNOW WHAT...WE'RE IDIOTS.
WE DIDN'T CHECK THE LIBRARY.
OH MY GOD.
THE LIBRARY.
OF COURSE.

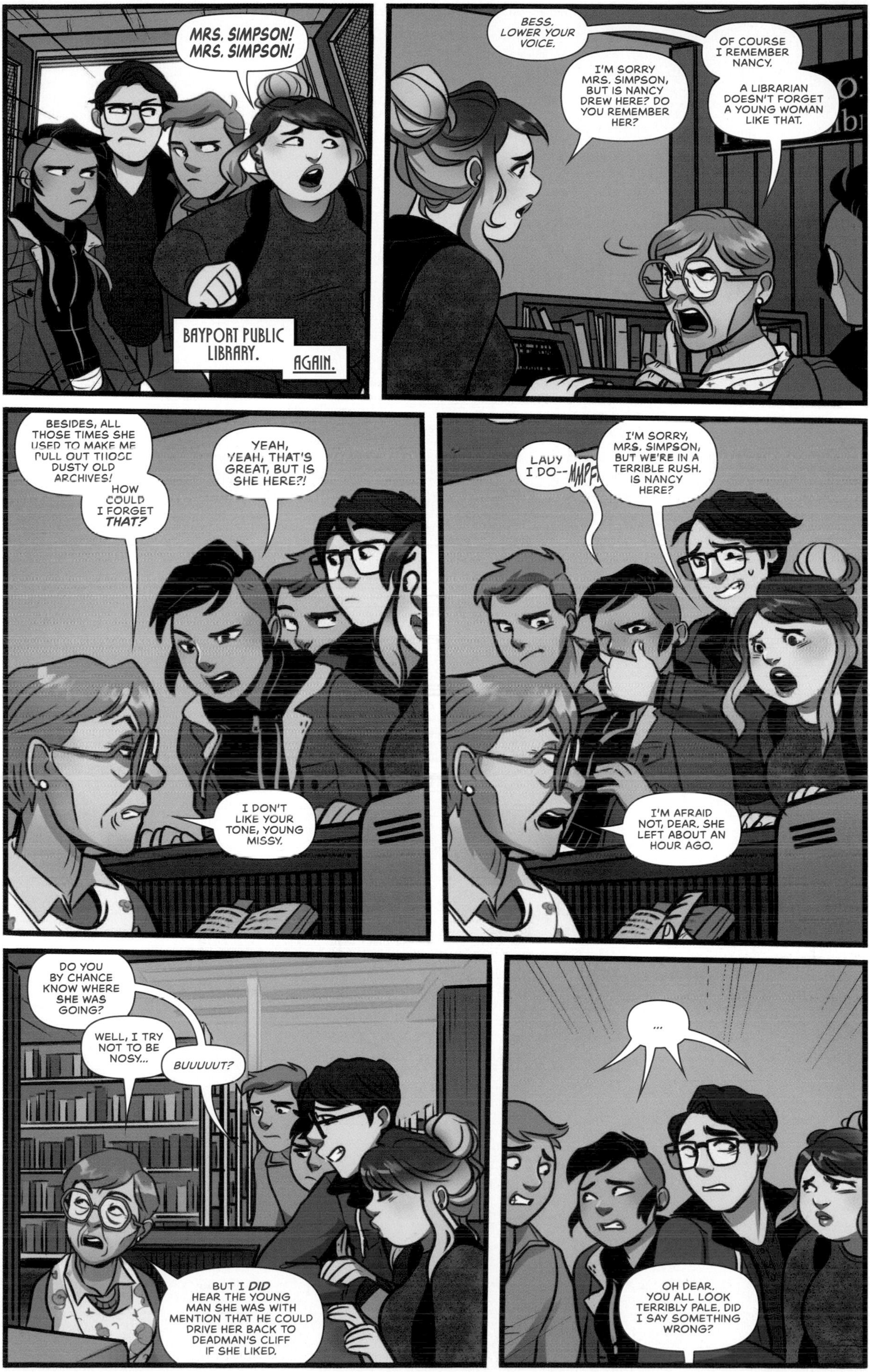
MRS. SIMPSON! MRS. SIMPSON!
BAYPORT PUBLIC LIBRARY.
AGAIN.
BESS. LOWER YOUR VOICE.
I'M SORRY MRS. SIMPSON, BUT IS NANCY DREW HERE? DO YOU REMEMBER HER?
OF COURSE I REMEMBER NANCY.
A LIBRARIAN DOESN'T FORGET A YOUNG WOMAN LIKE THAT.
BESIDES, ALL THOSE TIMES SHE USED TO MAKE ME PULL OUT THOSE DUSTY OLD ARCHIVES!
HOW COULD I FORGET *THAT?*
YEAH, YEAH, THAT'S GREAT, BUT IS SHE HERE?!
I DON'T LIKE YOUR TONE, YOUNG MISSY.
LADY I DO--
MMPF!
I'M SORRY, MRS. SIMPSON, BUT WE'RE IN A TERRIBLE RUSH. IS NANCY HERE?
I'M AFRAID NOT, DEAR. SHE LEFT ABOUT AN HOUR AGO.
DO YOU BY CHANCE KNOW WHERE SHE WAS GOING?
WELL, I TRY NOT TO BE NOSY...
BUUUUUT?
BUT I *DID* HEAR THE YOUNG MAN SHE WAS WITH MENTION THAT HE COULD DRIVE HER BACK TO DEADMAN'S CLIFF IF SHE LIKED.
...
OH DEAR. YOU ALL LOOK TERRIBLY PALE. DID I SAY SOMETHING WRONG?

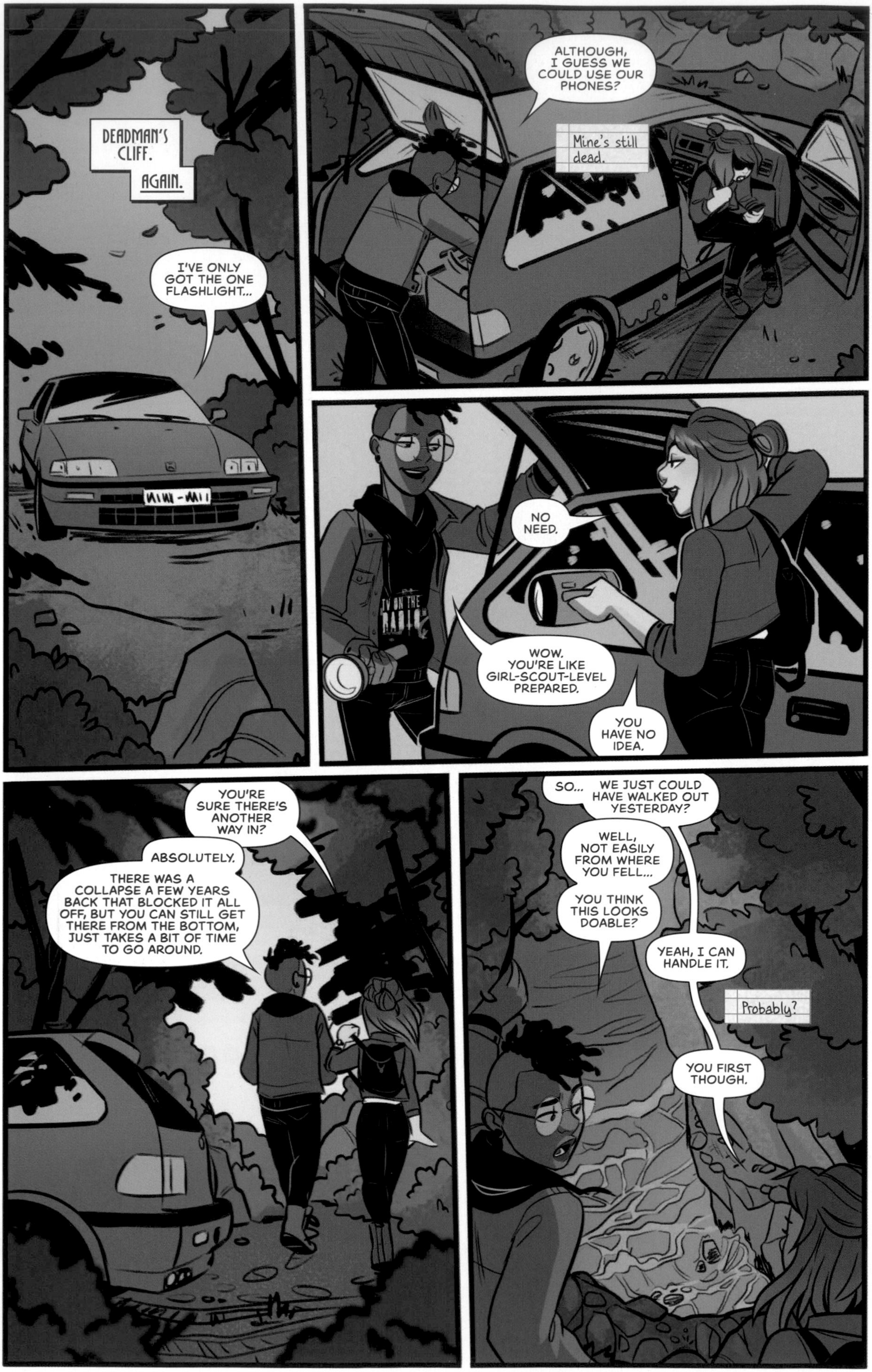
DEADMAN'S CLIFF.
AGAIN.
I'VE ONLY GOT THE ONE FLASHLIGHT...
ALTHOUGH, I GUESS WE COULD USE OUR PHONES?
Mine's still dead.
NO NEED.
WOW. YOU'RE LIKE GIRL-SCOUT-LEVEL PREPARED.
YOU HAVE NO IDEA.
YOU'RE SURE THERE'S ANOTHER WAY IN?
ABSOLUTELY.
THERE WAS A COLLAPSE A FEW YEARS BACK THAT BLOCKED IT ALL OFF, BUT YOU CAN STILL GET THERE FROM THE BOTTOM, JUST TAKES A BIT OF TIME TO GO AROUND.
SO... WE JUST COULD HAVE WALKED OUT YESTERDAY?
WELL, NOT EASILY FROM WHERE YOU FELL...
YOU THINK THIS LOOKS DOABLE?
YEAH, I CAN HANDLE IT.
Probably?
YOU FIRST THOUGH.

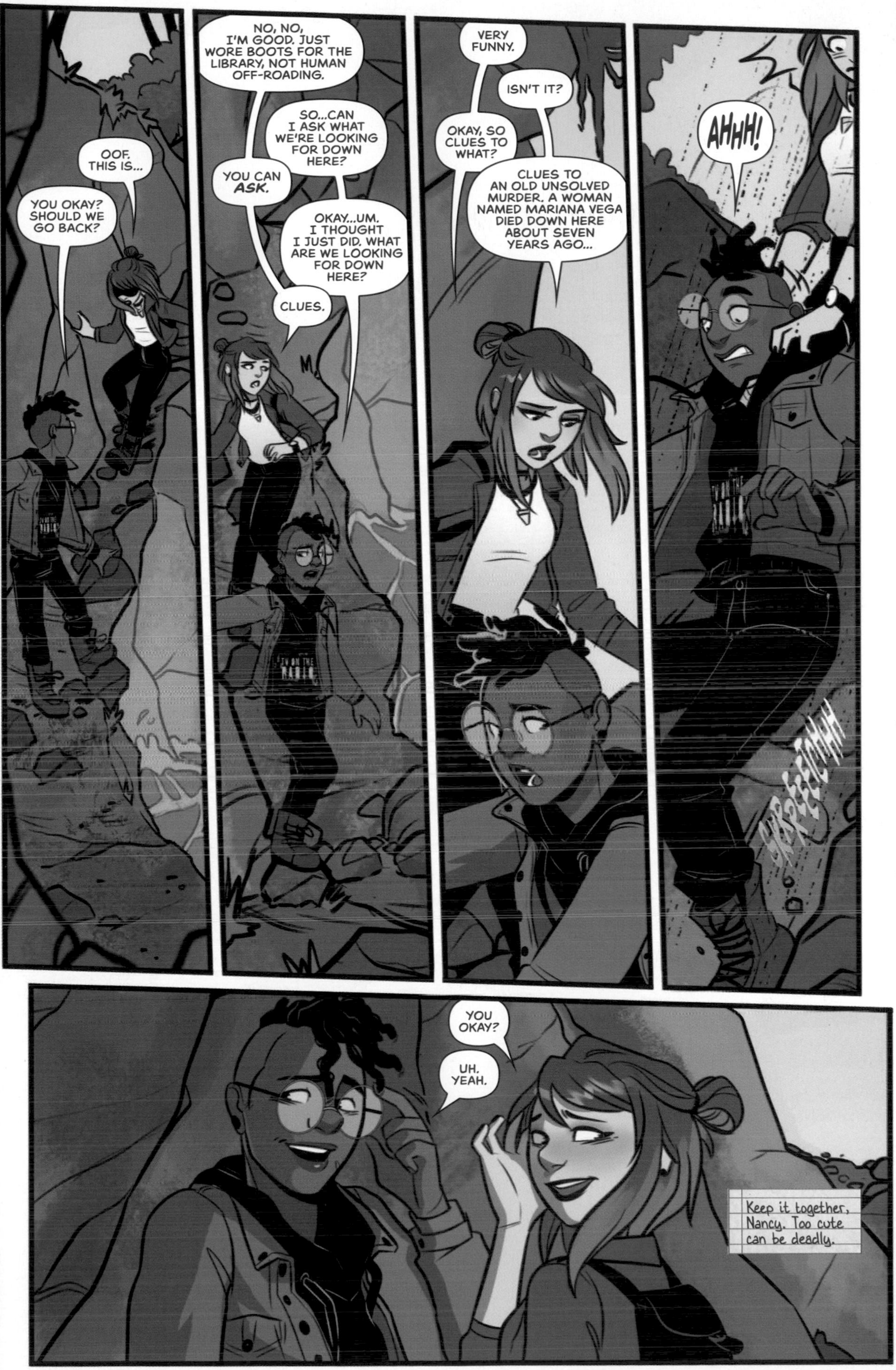
OOF. THIS IS...
YOU OKAY? SHOULD WE GO BACK?
NO, NO, I'M GOOD. JUST WORE BOOTS FOR THE LIBRARY, NOT HUMAN OFF-ROADING.
SO...CAN I ASK WHAT WE'RE LOOKING FOR DOWN HERE?
YOU CAN ASK.
OKAY...UM. I THOUGHT I JUST DID. WHAT ARE WE LOOKING FOR DOWN HERE?
CLUES.
VERY FUNNY.
ISN'T IT?
OKAY, SO CLUES TO WHAT?
CLUES TO AN OLD UNSOLVED MURDER. A WOMAN NAMED MARIANA VEGA DIED DOWN HERE ABOUT SEVEN YEARS AGO...
AHHH!
SKRREE
YOU OKAY?
UH. YEAH.
Keep it together, Nancy. Too cute can be deadly.

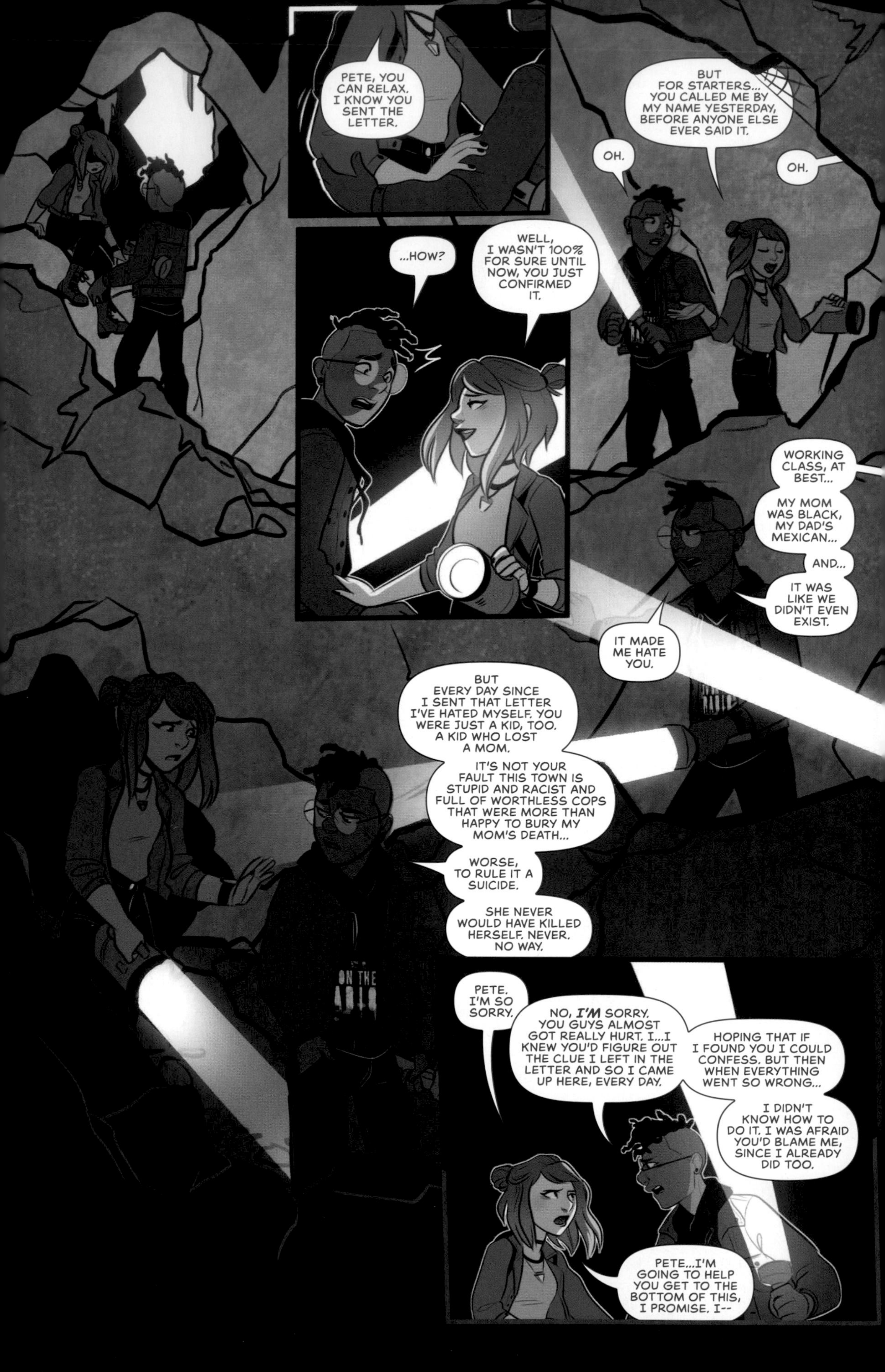

PETE, YOU CAN RELAX. I KNOW YOU SENT THE LETTER.
...HOW?
WELL, I WASN'T 100% FOR SURE UNTIL NOW, YOU JUST CONFIRMED IT.
BUT FOR STARTERS... YOU CALLED ME BY MY NAME YESTERDAY, BEFORE ANYONE ELSE EVER SAID IT.
OH.
OH.
WORKING CLASS, AT BEST...
MY MOM WAS BLACK, MY DAD'S MEXICAN...
AND...
IT WAS LIKE WE DIDN'T EVEN EXIST.
IT MADE ME HATE YOU.
BUT EVERY DAY SINCE I SENT THAT LETTER I'VE HATED MYSELF. YOU WERE JUST A KID, TOO. A KID WHO LOST A MOM.
IT'S NOT YOUR FAULT THIS TOWN IS STUPID AND RACIST AND FULL OF WORTHLESS COPS THAT WERE MORE THAN HAPPY TO BURY MY MOM'S DEATH...
WORSE, TO RULE IT A SUICIDE.
SHE NEVER WOULD HAVE KILLED HERSELF. NEVER. NO WAY.
ON THE RADIO
PETE. I'M SO SORRY.
NO, ***I'M*** SORRY. YOU GUYS ALMOST GOT REALLY HURT. I...I KNEW YOU'D FIGURE OUT THE CLUE I LEFT IN THE LETTER AND SO I CAME UP HERE, EVERY DAY.
HOPING THAT IF I FOUND YOU I COULD CONFESS. BUT THEN WHEN EVERYTHING WENT SO WRONG...
I DIDN'T KNOW HOW TO DO IT. I WAS AFRAID YOU'D BLAME ME, SINCE I ALREADY DID TOO.
PETE...I'M GOING TO HELP YOU GET TO THE BOTTOM OF THIS, I PROMISE. I--

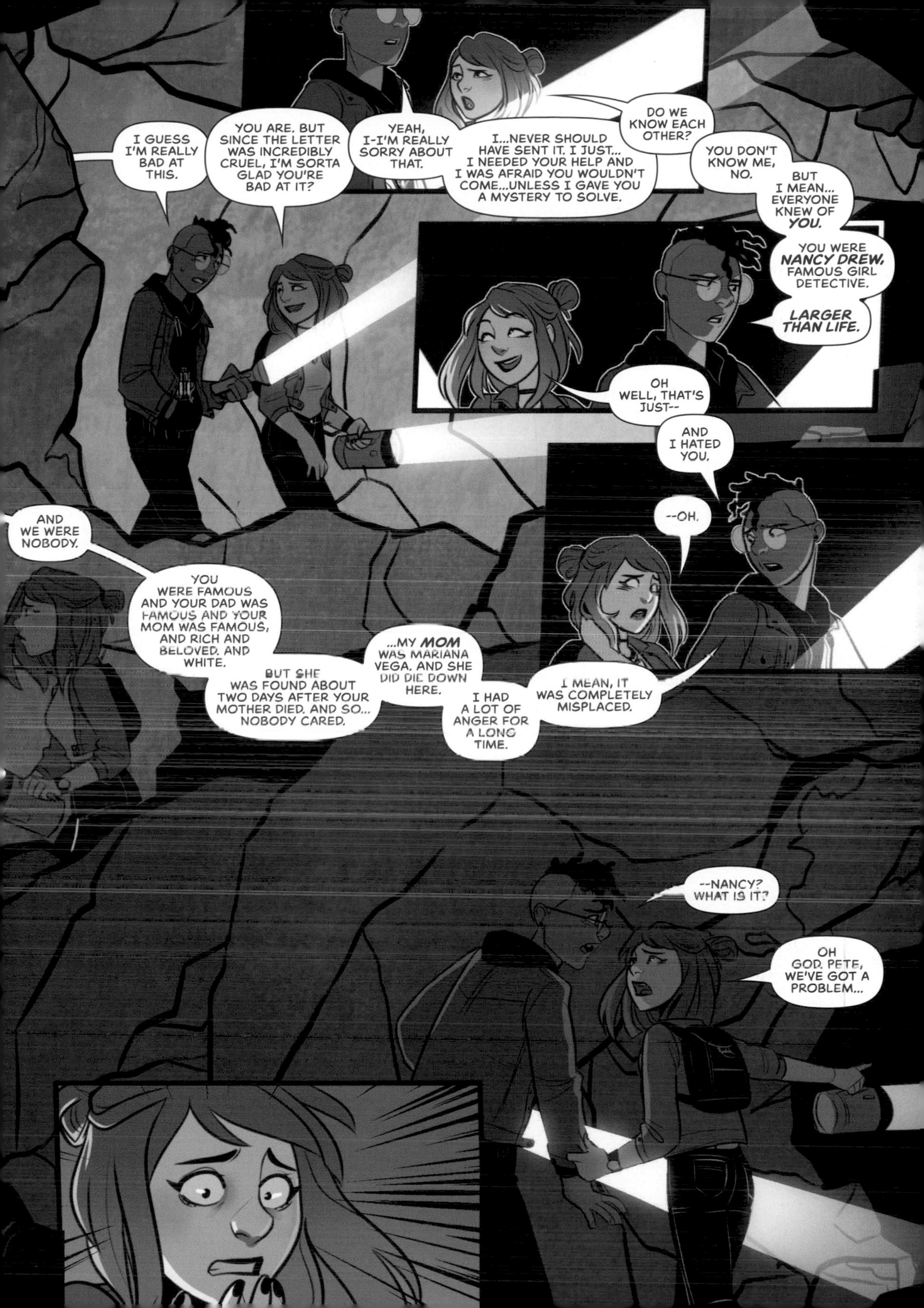
I GUESS I'M REALLY BAD AT THIS.
YOU ARE. BUT SINCE THE LETTER WAS INCREDIBLY CRUEL, I'M SORTA GLAD YOU'RE BAD AT IT?
YEAH, I-I'M REALLY SORRY ABOUT THAT.
I...NEVER SHOULD HAVE SENT IT. I JUST... I NEEDED YOUR HELP AND I WAS AFRAID YOU WOULDN'T COME...UNLESS I GAVE YOU A MYSTERY TO SOLVE.
DO WE KNOW EACH OTHER?
YOU DON'T KNOW ME, NO.
BUT I MEAN... EVERYONE KNEW OF *YOU.*
YOU WERE *NANCY DREW,* FAMOUS GIRL DETECTIVE.
LARGER THAN LIFE.
OH WELL, THAT'S JUST--
AND I HATED YOU.
--OH.
AND WE WERE NOBODY.
YOU WERE FAMOUS AND YOUR DAD WAS FAMOUS AND YOUR MOM WAS FAMOUS, AND RICH AND BELOVED. AND WHITE.
BUT SHE WAS FOUND ABOUT TWO DAYS AFTER YOUR MOTHER DIED. AND SO... NOBODY CARED.
...MY *MOM* WAS MARIANA VEGA. AND SHE DID DIE DOWN HERE.
I HAD A LOT OF ANGER FOR A LONG TIME.
I MEAN, IT WAS COMPLETELY MISPLACED.
--NANCY? WHAT IS IT?
OH GOD. PETE, WE'VE GOT A PROBLEM...

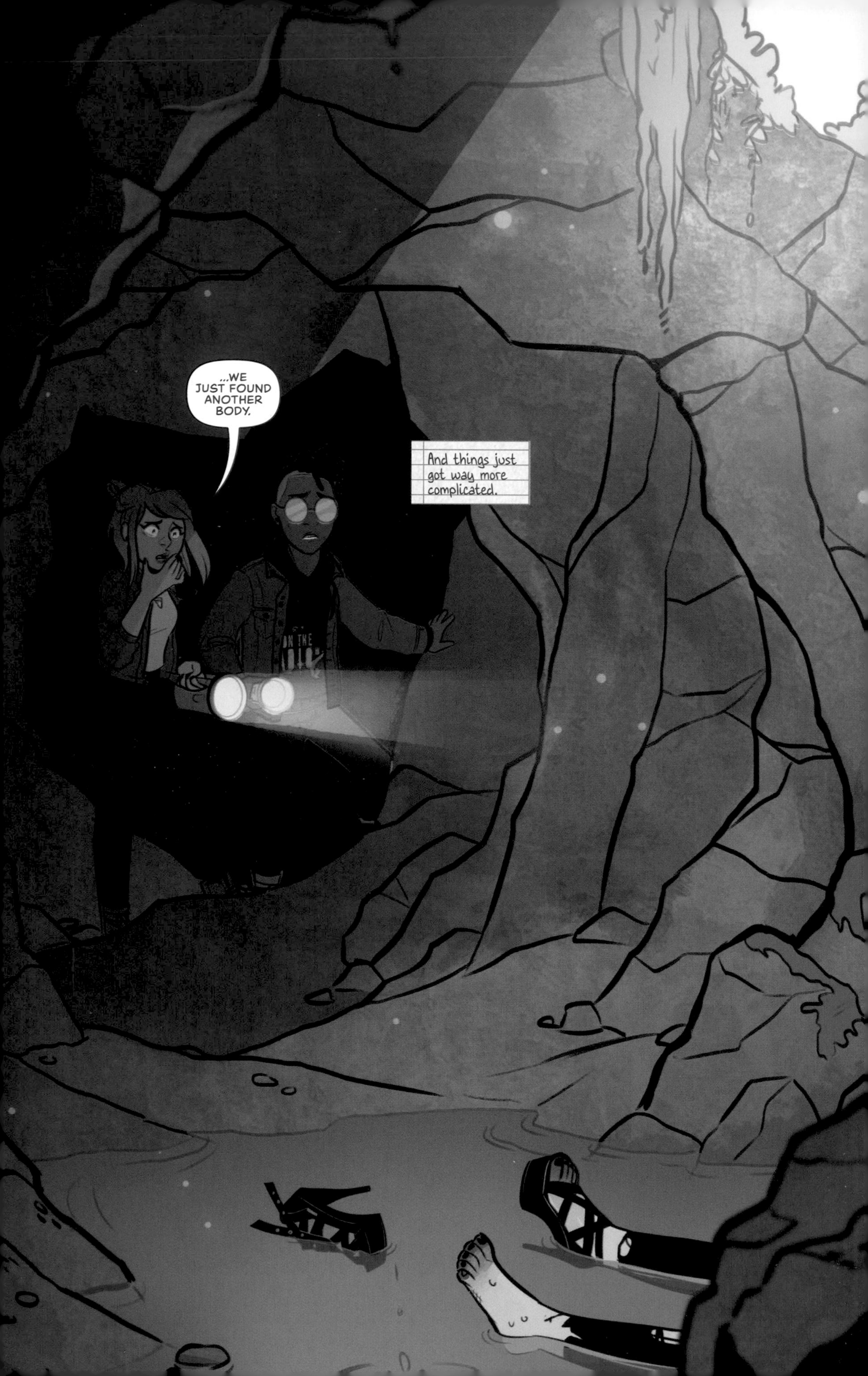
...WE JUST FOUND ANOTHER BODY.
And things just got way more complicated.

chapTeR ThREE

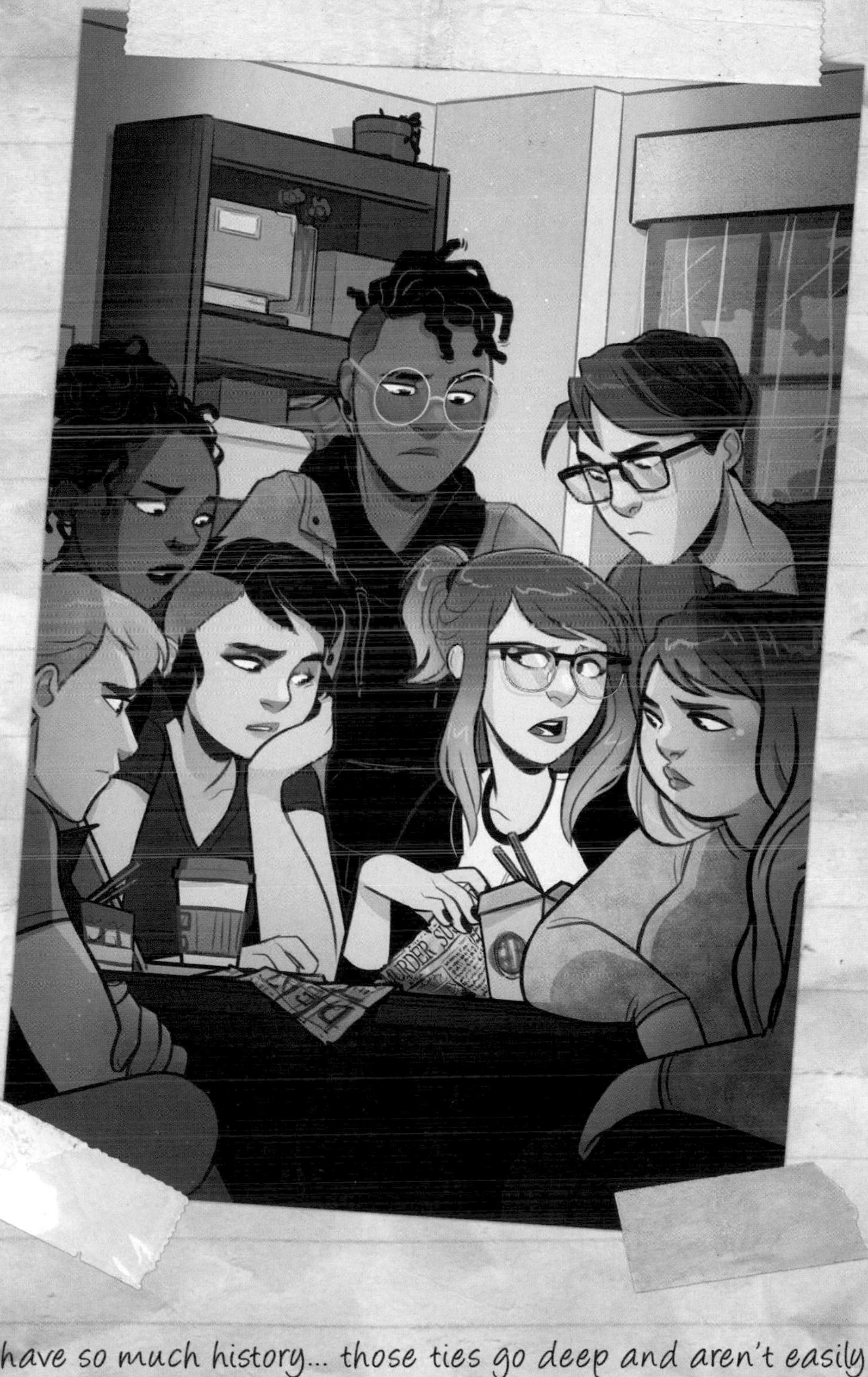

We have so much history... those ties go deep and aren't easily cut.

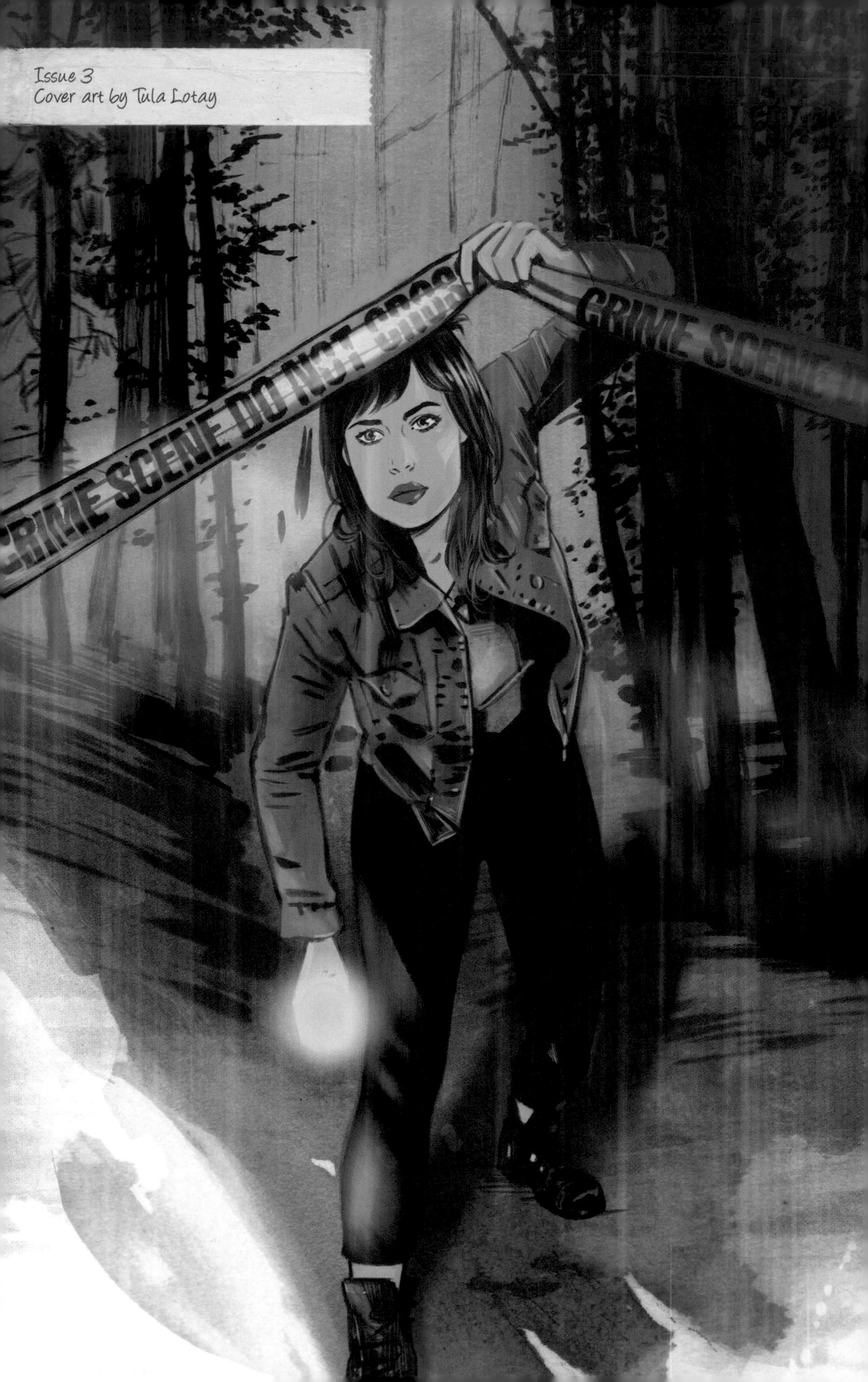

Issue 3
Cover art by Tula Lotay

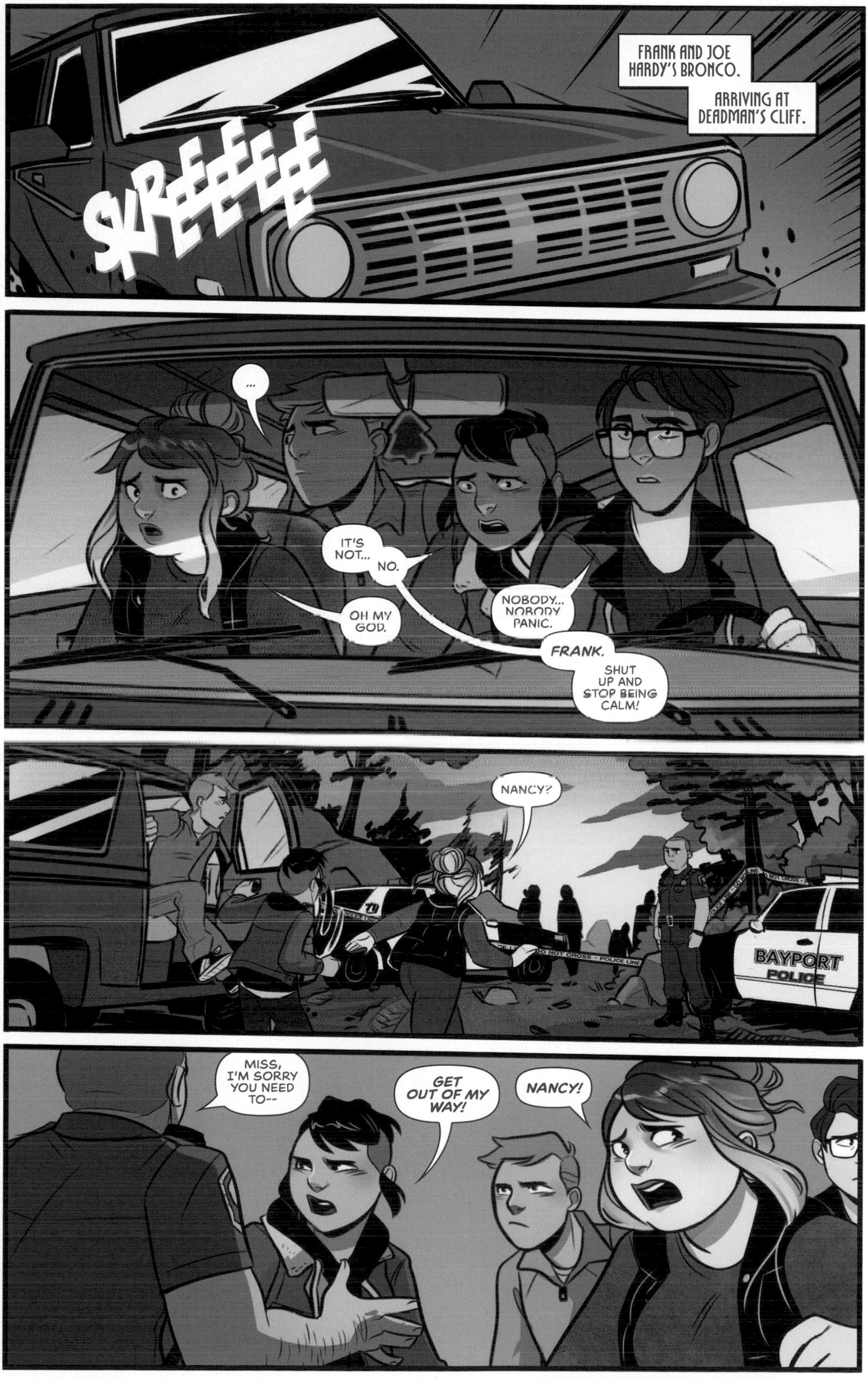
FRANK AND JOE HARDY'S BRONCO.
ARRIVING AT DEADMAN'S CLIFF.
SKREEEEEEE
...
IT'S NOT... NO.
OH MY GOD.
NOBODY... NOBODY PANIC.
FRANK.
SHUT UP AND STOP BEING CALM!
NANCY?
BAYPORT POLICE
DO NOT CROSS – POLICE LINE
MISS, I'M SORRY YOU NEED TO--
GET OUT OF MY WAY!
NANCY!

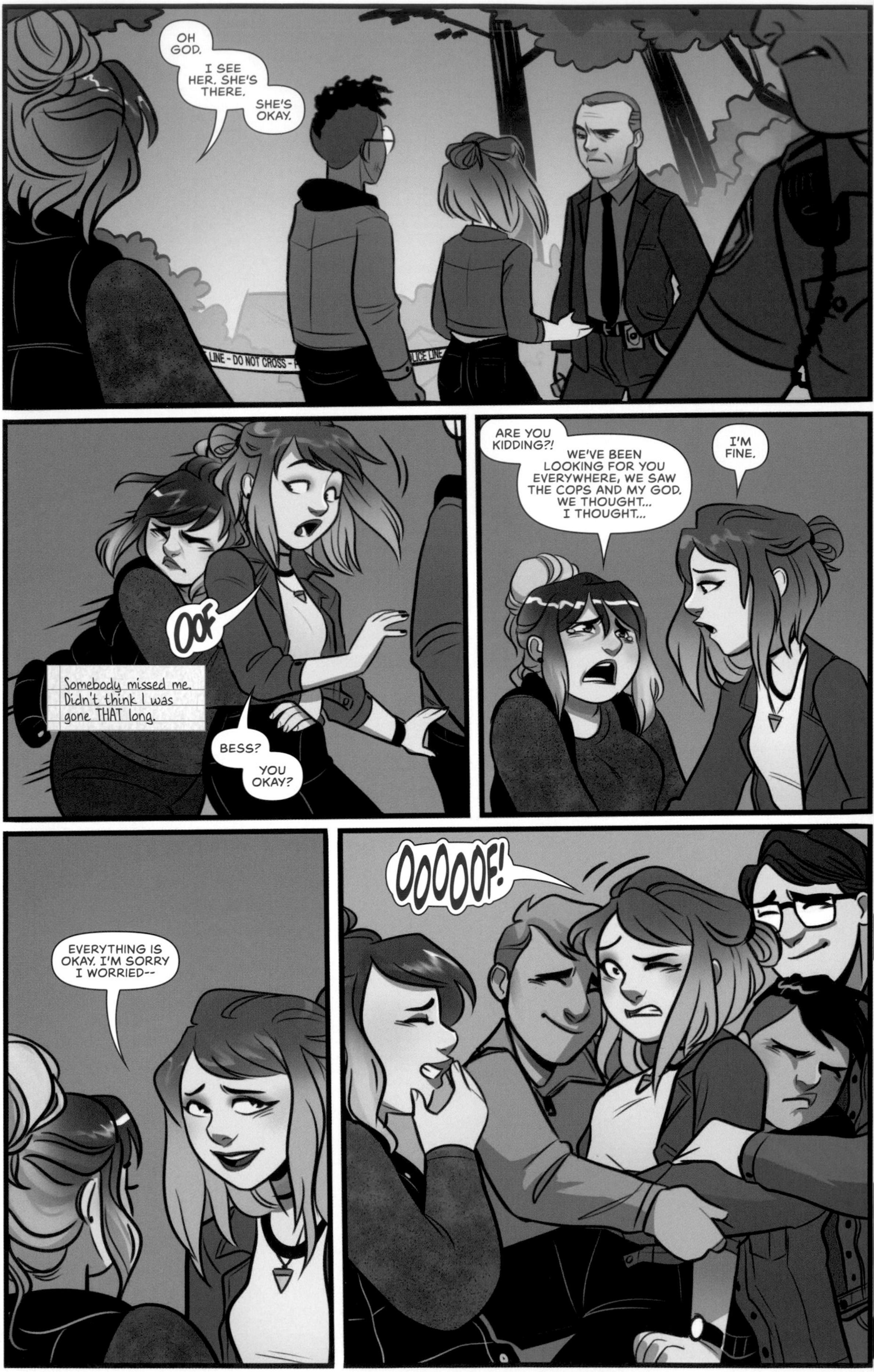
OH GOD.
I SEE HER. SHE'S THERE.
SHE'S OKAY.
LINE - DO NOT CROSS -
POLICE LINE
OOF
Somebody missed me. Didn't think I was gone THAT long.
BESS?
YOU OKAY?
ARE YOU KIDDING?!
WE'VE BEEN LOOKING FOR YOU EVERYWHERE, WE SAW THE COPS AND MY GOD. WE THOUGHT... I THOUGHT...
I'M FINE.
EVERYTHING IS OKAY. I'M SORRY I WORRIED--
OOOOOF!

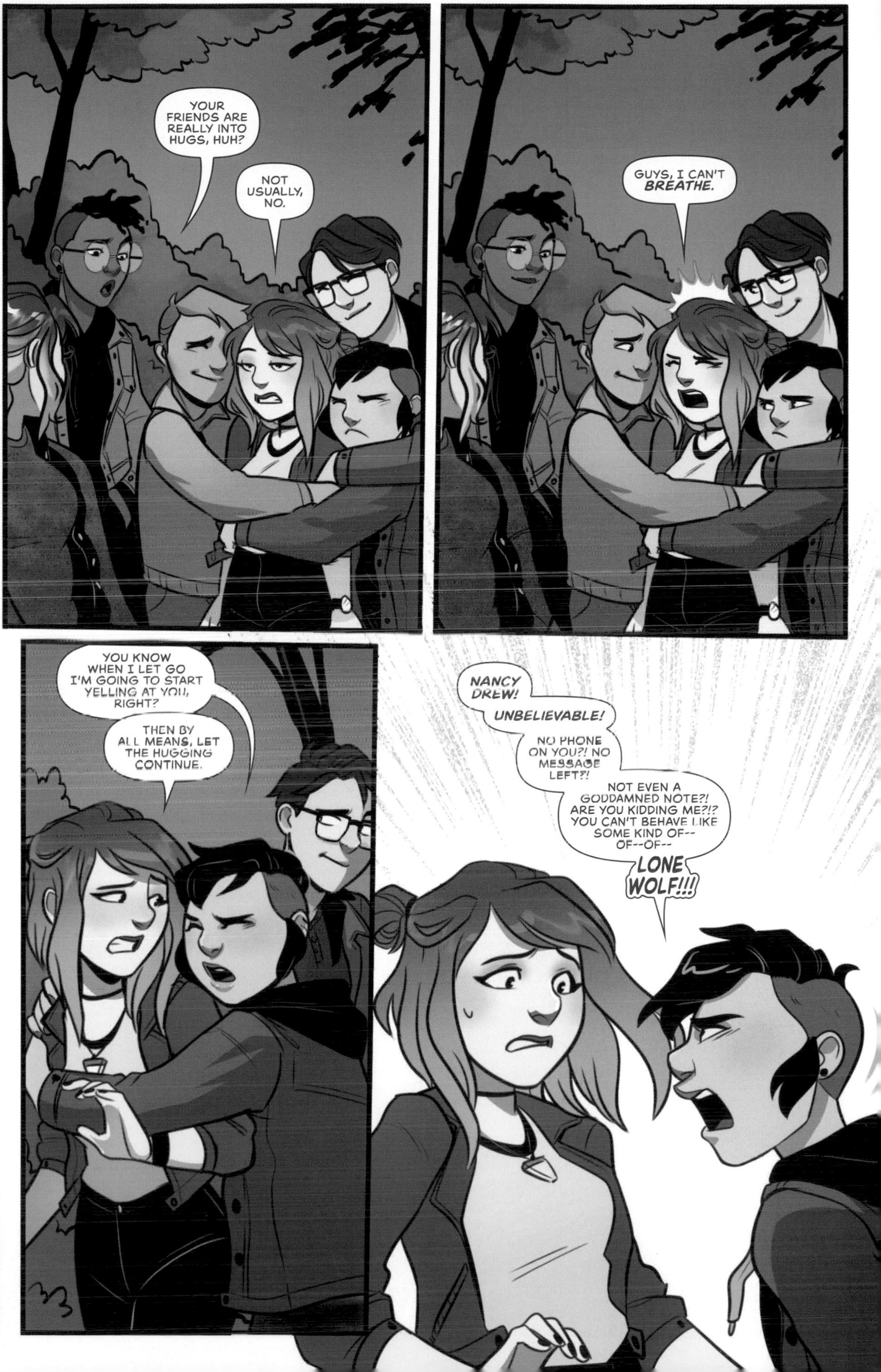
YOUR FRIENDS ARE REALLY INTO HUGS, HUH?
NOT USUALLY, NO.
GUYS, I CAN'T *BREATHE.*
YOU KNOW WHEN I LET GO I'M GOING TO START YELLING AT YOU, RIGHT?
THEN BY ALL MEANS, LET THE HUGGING CONTINUE.
NANCY DREW!
UNBELIEVABLE!
NO PHONE ON YOU?! NO MESSAGE LEFT?!
NOT EVEN A GODDAMNED NOTE?! ARE YOU KIDDING ME?!? YOU CAN'T BEHAVE LIKE SOME KIND OF-- OF--OF--
LONE WOLF!!!

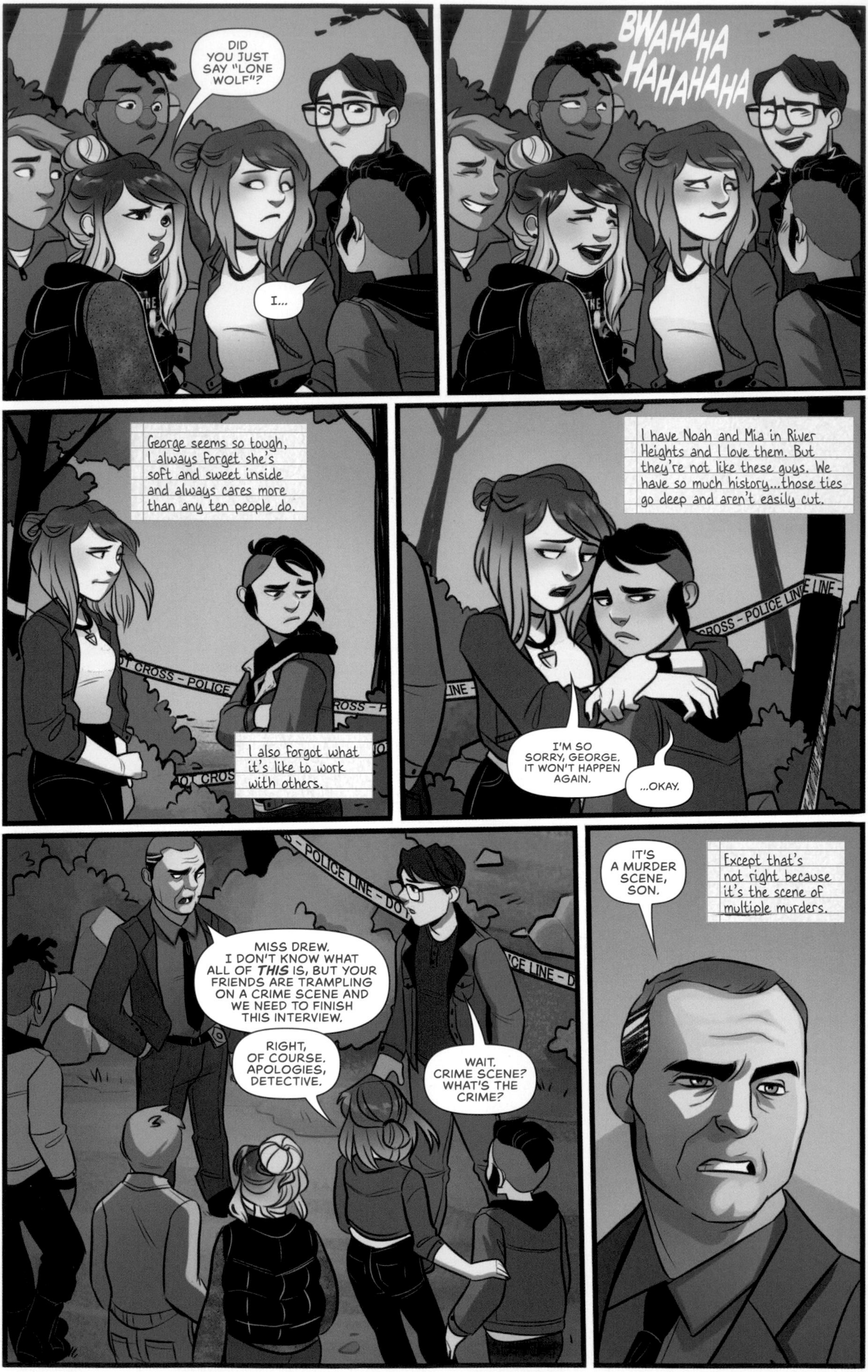
DID YOU JUST SAY "LONE WOLF"?
I...
BWAHAHA HAHAHAHA
George seems so tough, I always forget she's soft and sweet inside and always cares more than any ten people do.
I also forgot what it's like to work with others.
I have Noah and Mia in River Heights and I love them. But they're not like these guys. We have so much history...those ties go deep and aren't easily cut.
I'M SO SORRY, GEORGE. IT WON'T HAPPEN AGAIN.
...OKAY.
MISS DREW. I DON'T KNOW WHAT ALL OF THIS IS, BUT YOUR FRIENDS ARE TRAMPLING ON A CRIME SCENE AND WE NEED TO FINISH THIS INTERVIEW.
RIGHT, OF COURSE. APOLOGIES, DETECTIVE.
WAIT. CRIME SCENE? WHAT'S THE CRIME?
IT'S A MURDER SCENE, SON.
Except that's not right because it's the scene of multiple murders.

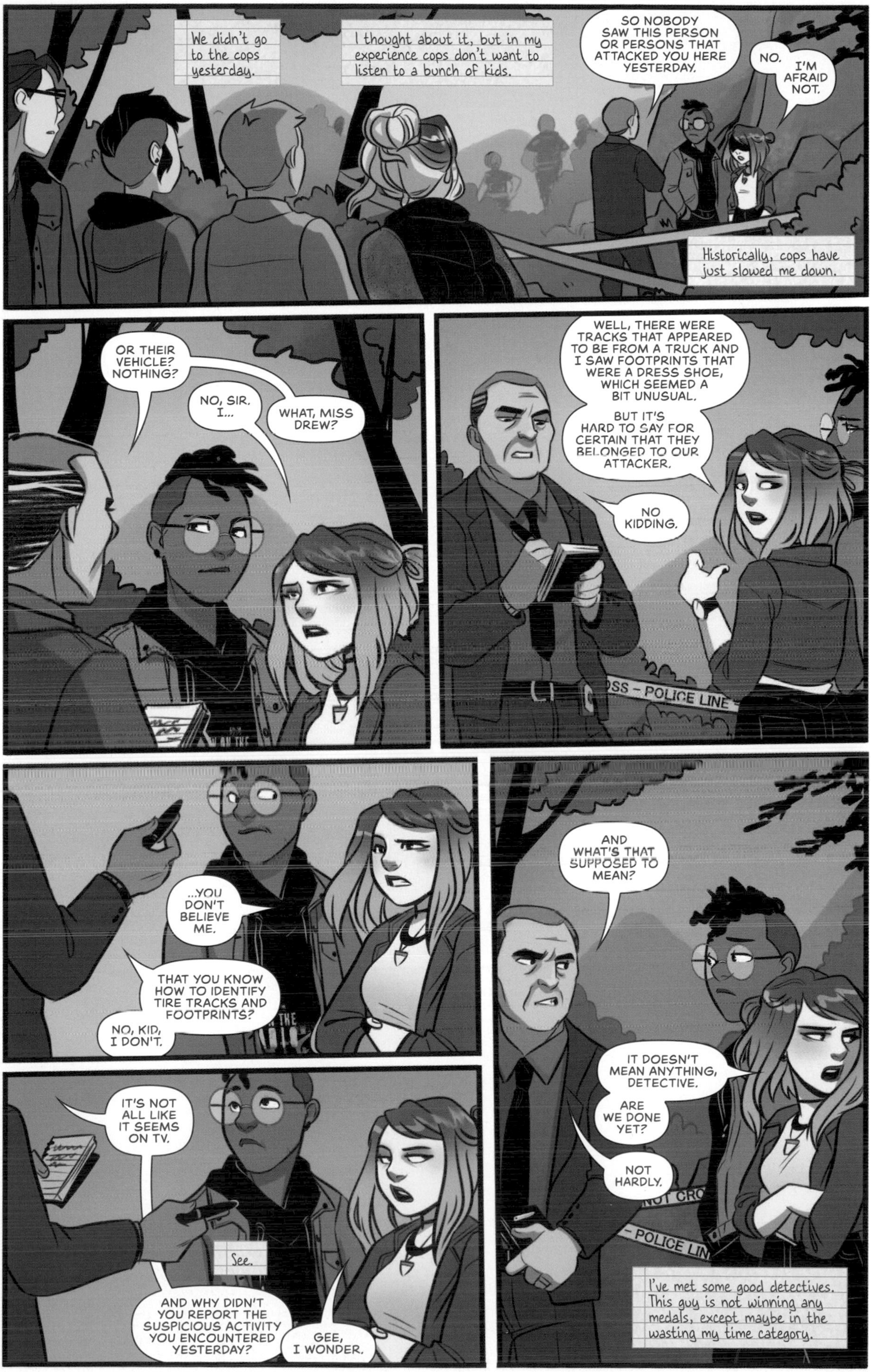
We didn't go to the cops yesterday.
I thought about it, but in my experience cops don't want to listen to a bunch of kids.
SO NOBODY SAW THIS PERSON OR PERSONS THAT ATTACKED YOU HERE YESTERDAY.
NO.
I'M AFRAID NOT.
Historically, cops have just slowed me down.
OR THEIR VEHICLE? NOTHING?
NO, SIR. I...
WHAT, MISS DREW?
WELL, THERE WERE TRACKS THAT APPEARED TO BE FROM A TRUCK AND I SAW FOOTPRINTS THAT WERE A DRESS SHOE, WHICH SEEMED A BIT UNUSUAL.
BUT IT'S HARD TO SAY FOR CERTAIN THAT THEY BELONGED TO OUR ATTACKER.
NO KIDDING.
...YOU DON'T BELIEVE ME.
THAT YOU KNOW HOW TO IDENTIFY TIRE TRACKS AND FOOTPRINTS?
NO, KID, I DON'T.
IT'S NOT ALL LIKE IT SEEMS ON TV.
See.
AND WHY DIDN'T YOU REPORT THE SUSPICIOUS ACTIVITY YOU ENCOUNTERED YESTERDAY?
GEE, I WONDER.
AND WHAT'S THAT SUPPOSED TO MEAN?
IT DOESN'T MEAN ANYTHING, DETECTIVE.
ARE WE DONE YET?
NOT HARDLY.
I've met some good detectives. This guy is not winning any medals, except maybe in the wasting my time category.

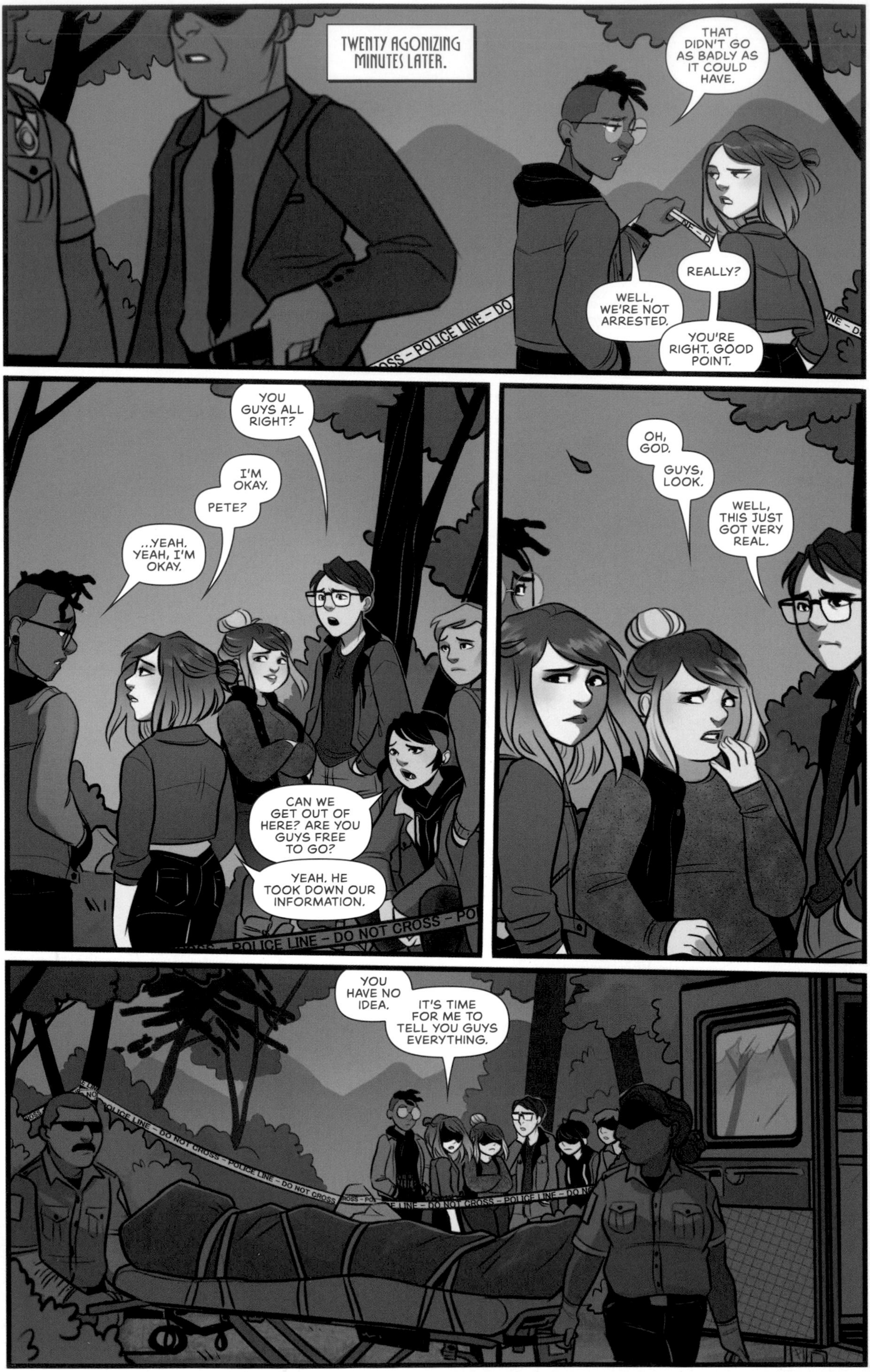
TWENTY AGONIZING MINUTES LATER.
THAT DIDN'T GO AS BADLY AS IT COULD HAVE.
REALLY?
WELL, WE'RE NOT ARRESTED.
YOU'RE RIGHT. GOOD POINT.
POLICE LINE - DO
YOU GUYS ALL RIGHT?
I'M OKAY.
PETE?
...YEAH. YEAH, I'M OKAY.
CAN WE GET OUT OF HERE? ARE YOU GUYS FREE TO GO?
YEAH. HE TOOK DOWN OUR INFORMATION.
POLICE LINE - DO NOT CROSS
OH, GOD.
GUYS, LOOK.
WELL, THIS JUST GOT VERY REAL.
YOU HAVE NO IDEA.
IT'S TIME FOR ME TO TELL YOU GUYS EVERYTHING.
POLICE LINE - DO NOT CROSS - POLICE LINE - DO NOT CROSS

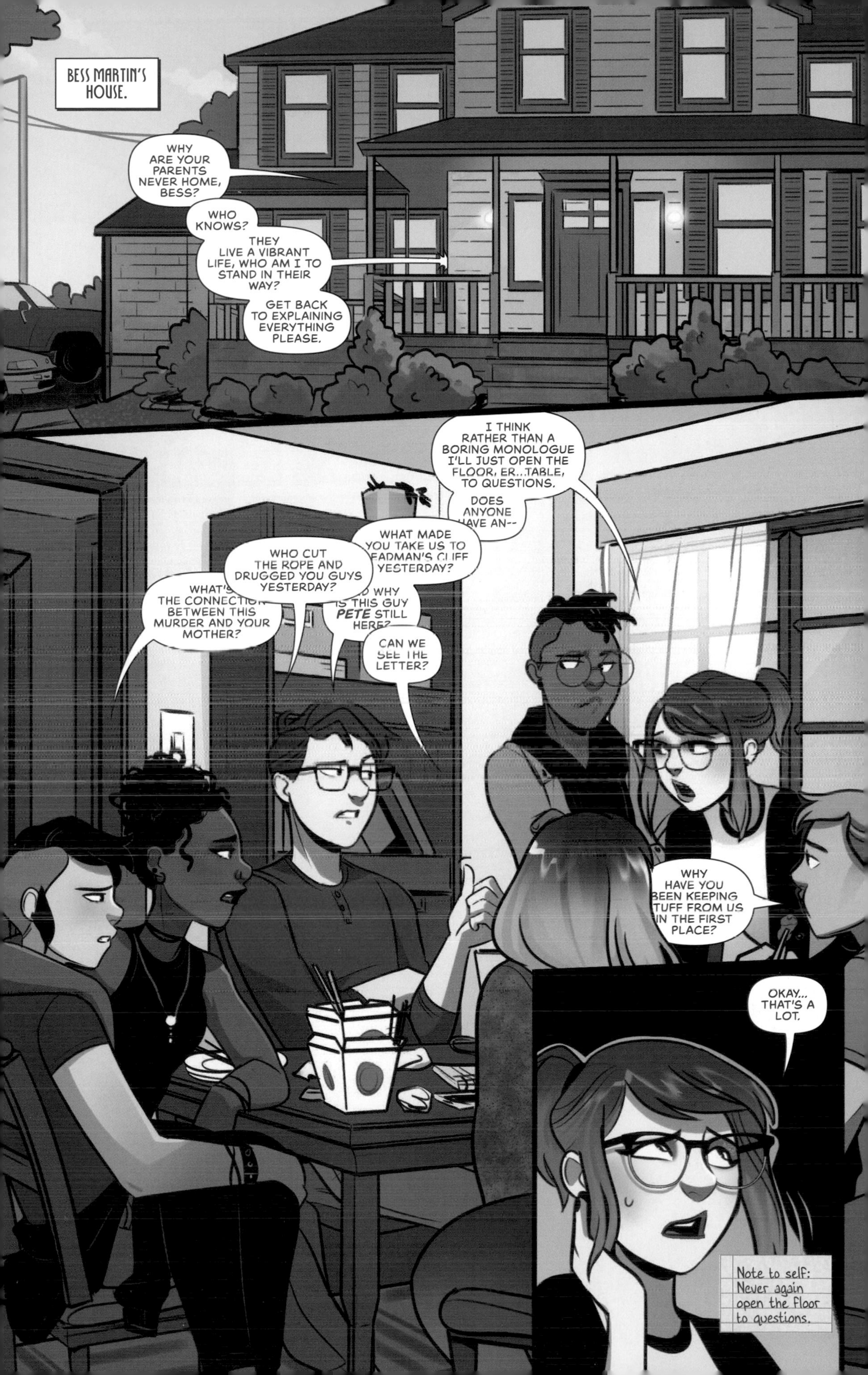
BESS MARTIN'S HOUSE.
WHY ARE YOUR PARENTS NEVER HOME, BESS?
WHO KNOWS?
THEY LIVE A VIBRANT LIFE, WHO AM I TO STAND IN THEIR WAY?
GET BACK TO EXPLAINING EVERYTHING PLEASE.
I THINK RATHER THAN A BORING MONOLOGUE I'LL JUST OPEN THE FLOOR, ER...TABLE, TO QUESTIONS.
DOES ANYONE HAVE AN--
WHAT MADE YOU TAKE US TO EADMAN'S CLIFF YESTERDAY?
WHO CUT THE ROPE AND DRUGGED YOU GUYS YESTERDAY?
WHAT'S THE CONNECTIO BETWEEN THIS MURDER AND YOUR MOTHER?
D WHY IS THIS GUY PETE STILL HERE?
CAN WE SEE THE LETTER?
WHY HAVE YOU BEEN KEEPING TUFF FROM US IN THE FIRST PLACE?
OKAY... THAT'S A LOT.
Note to self: Never again open the floor to questions.

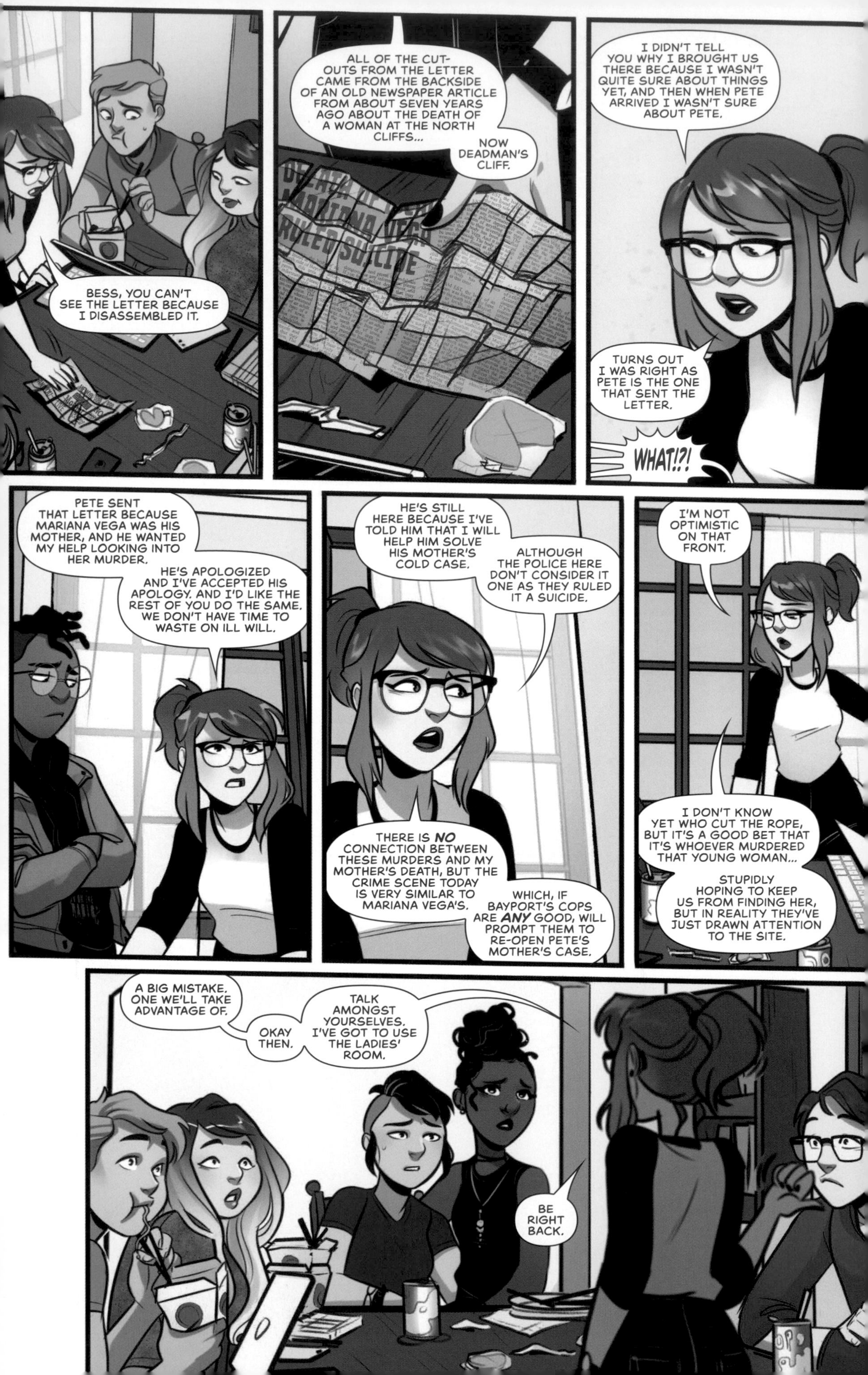
BESS, YOU CAN'T SEE THE LETTER BECAUSE I DISASSEMBLED IT.
ALL OF THE CUT-OUTS FROM THE LETTER CAME FROM THE BACKSIDE OF AN OLD NEWSPAPER ARTICLE FROM ABOUT SEVEN YEARS AGO ABOUT THE DEATH OF A WOMAN AT THE NORTH CLIFFS...
NOW DEADMAN'S CLIFF.
I DIDN'T TELL YOU WHY I BROUGHT US THERE BECAUSE I WASN'T QUITE SURE ABOUT THINGS YET, AND THEN WHEN PETE ARRIVED I WASN'T SURE ABOUT PETE.
TURNS OUT I WAS RIGHT AS PETE IS THE ONE THAT SENT THE LETTER.
WHAT!?!
PETE SENT THAT LETTER BECAUSE MARIANA VEGA WAS HIS MOTHER, AND HE WANTED MY HELP LOOKING INTO HER MURDER.
HE'S APOLOGIZED AND I'VE ACCEPTED HIS APOLOGY, AND I'D LIKE THE REST OF YOU DO THE SAME. WE DON'T HAVE TIME TO WASTE ON ILL WILL.
HE'S STILL HERE BECAUSE I'VE TOLD HIM THAT I WILL HELP HIM SOLVE HIS MOTHER'S COLD CASE.
ALTHOUGH THE POLICE HERE DON'T CONSIDER IT ONE AS THEY RULED IT A SUICIDE.
THERE IS **NO** CONNECTION BETWEEN THESE MURDERS AND MY MOTHER'S DEATH, BUT THE CRIME SCENE TODAY IS VERY SIMILAR TO MARIANA VEGA'S.
WHICH, IF BAYPORT'S COPS ARE **ANY** GOOD, WILL PROMPT THEM TO RE-OPEN PETE'S MOTHER'S CASE.
I'M NOT OPTIMISTIC ON THAT FRONT.
I DON'T KNOW YET WHO CUT THE ROPE, BUT IT'S A GOOD BET THAT IT'S WHOEVER MURDERED THAT YOUNG WOMAN...
STUPIDLY HOPING TO KEEP US FROM FINDING HER, BUT IN REALITY THEY'VE JUST DRAWN ATTENTION TO THE SITE.
A BIG MISTAKE, ONE WE'LL TAKE ADVANTAGE OF.
OKAY THEN.
TALK AMONGST YOURSELVES. I'VE GOT TO USE THE LADIES' ROOM.
BE RIGHT BACK.

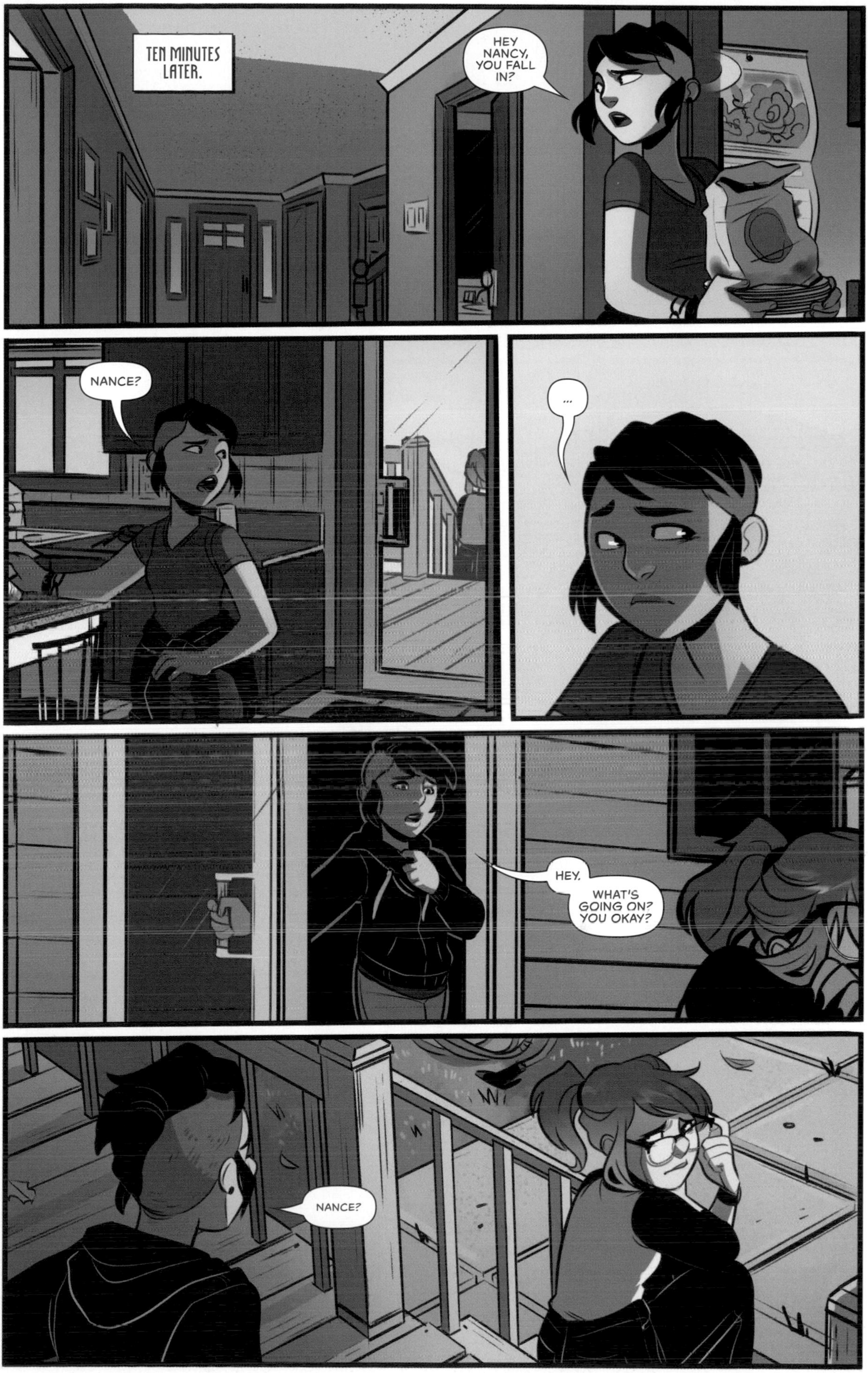
TEN MINUTES LATER.
HEY NANCY, YOU FALL IN?
NANCE?
...
HEY,
WHAT'S GOING ON? YOU OKAY?
NANCE?

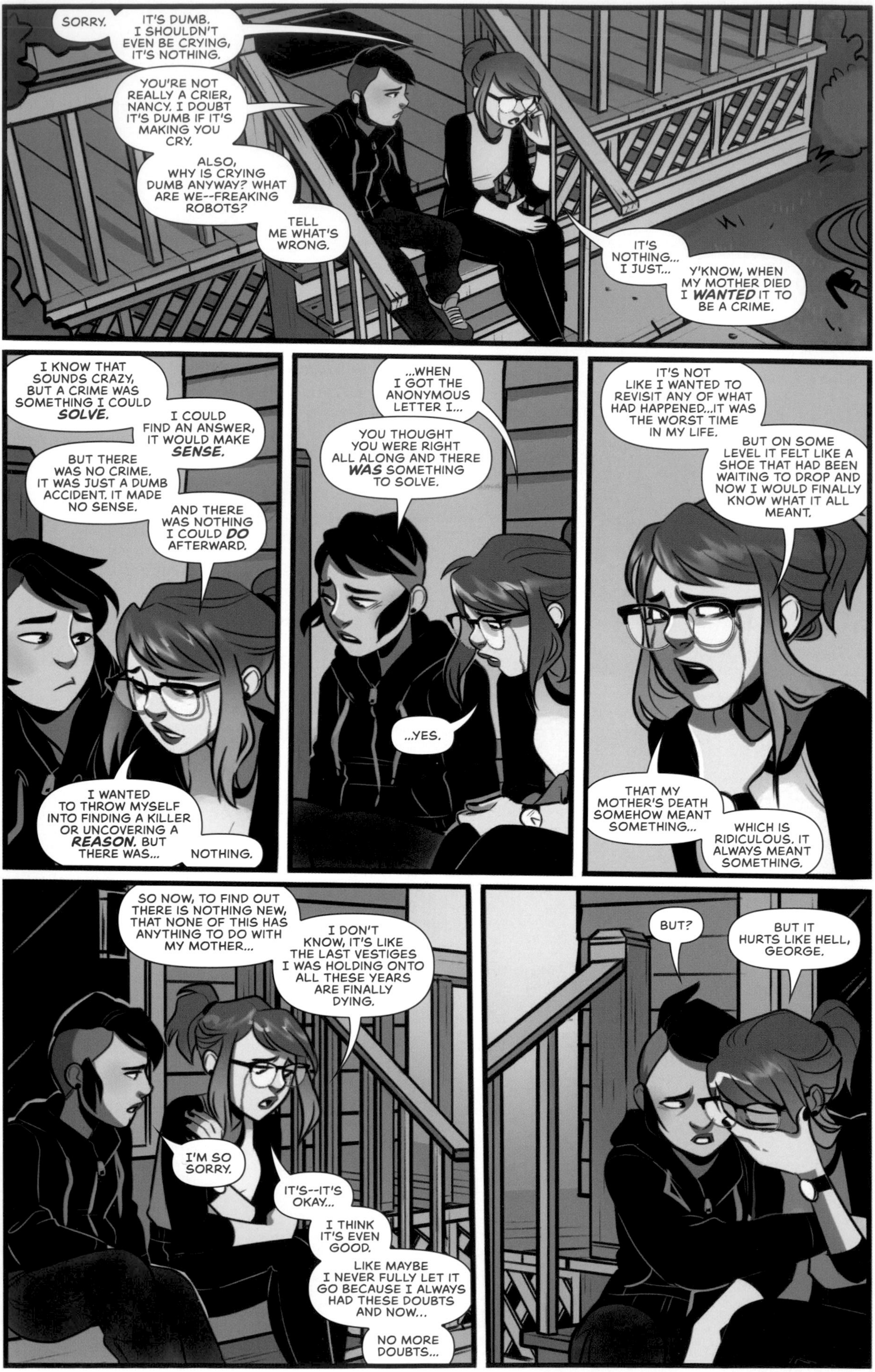
SORRY.
IT'S DUMB. I SHOULDN'T EVEN BE CRYING. IT'S NOTHING.
YOU'RE NOT REALLY A CRIER, NANCY. I DOUBT IT'S DUMB IF IT'S MAKING YOU CRY.
ALSO, WHY IS CRYING DUMB ANYWAY? WHAT ARE WE--FREAKING ROBOTS?
TELL ME WHAT'S WRONG.
IT'S NOTHING... I JUST...
Y'KNOW, WHEN MY MOTHER DIED I ***WANTED*** IT TO BE A CRIME.
I KNOW THAT SOUNDS CRAZY, BUT A CRIME WAS SOMETHING I COULD ***SOLVE.***
I COULD FIND AN ANSWER, IT WOULD MAKE ***SENSE.***
BUT THERE WAS NO CRIME. IT WAS JUST A DUMB ACCIDENT. IT MADE NO SENSE.
AND THERE WAS NOTHING I COULD ***DO*** AFTERWARD.
I WANTED TO THROW MYSELF INTO FINDING A KILLER OR UNCOVERING A ***REASON.*** BUT THERE WAS...
NOTHING.
...WHEN I GOT THE ANONYMOUS LETTER I...
YOU THOUGHT YOU WERE RIGHT ALL ALONG AND THERE ***WAS*** SOMETHING TO SOLVE.
...YES.
IT'S NOT LIKE I WANTED TO REVISIT ANY OF WHAT HAD HAPPENED...IT WAS THE WORST TIME IN MY LIFE.
BUT ON SOME LEVEL IT FELT LIKE A SHOE THAT HAD BEEN WAITING TO DROP AND NOW I WOULD FINALLY KNOW WHAT IT ALL MEANT.
THAT MY MOTHER'S DEATH SOMEHOW MEANT SOMETHING...
WHICH IS RIDICULOUS. IT ALWAYS MEANT SOMETHING.
SO NOW, TO FIND OUT THERE IS NOTHING NEW, THAT NONE OF THIS HAS ANYTHING TO DO WITH MY MOTHER...
I DON'T KNOW, IT'S LIKE THE LAST VESTIGES I WAS HOLDING ONTO ALL THESE YEARS ARE FINALLY DYING.
I'M SO SORRY.
IT'S--IT'S OKAY...
I THINK IT'S EVEN GOOD.
LIKE MAYBE I NEVER FULLY LET IT GO BECAUSE I ALWAYS HAD THESE DOUBTS AND NOW...
NO MORE DOUBTS...
BUT?
BUT IT HURTS LIKE HELL, GEORGE.

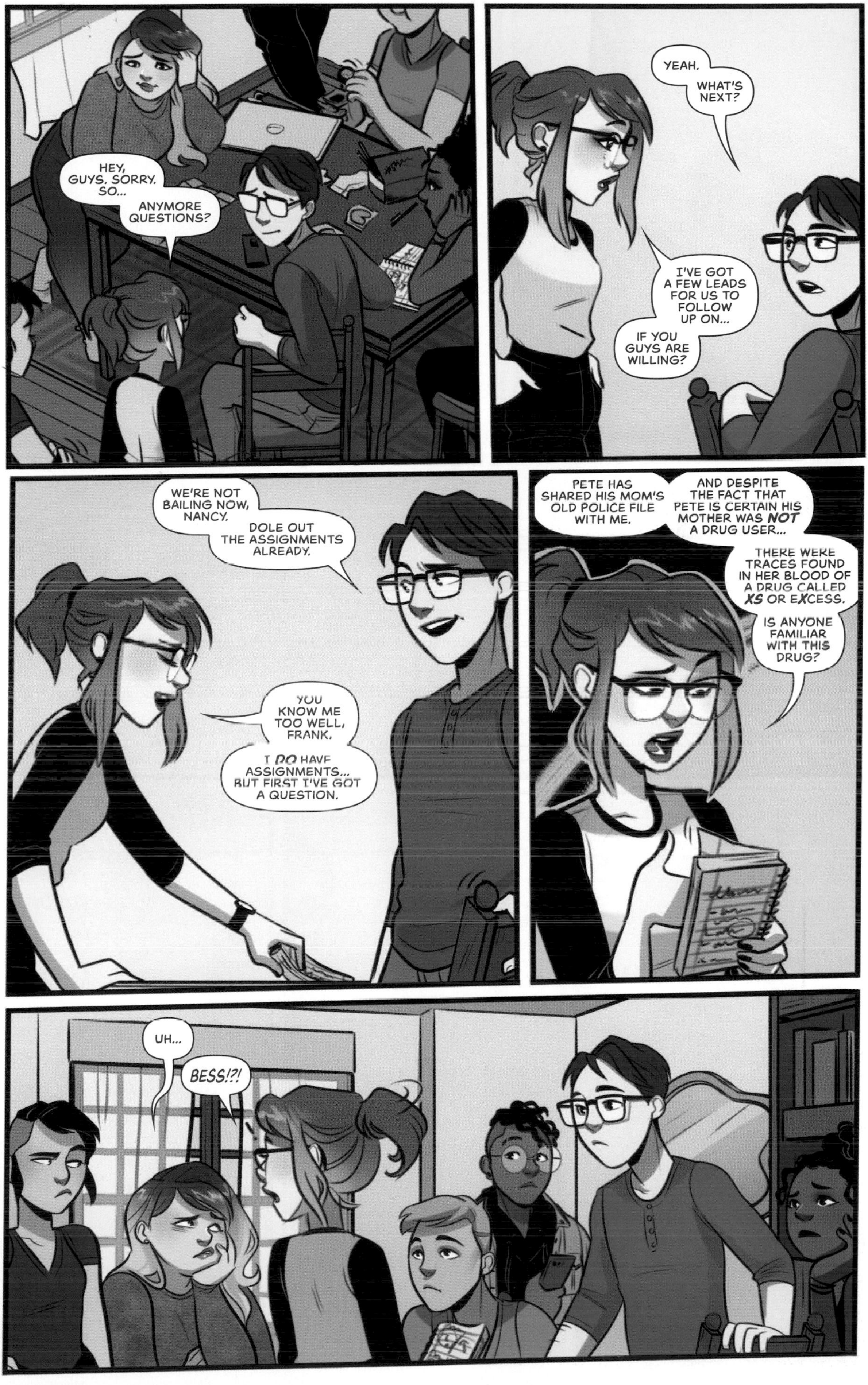
HEY, GUYS. SORRY. SO...
ANYMORE QUESTIONS?
YEAH.
WHAT'S NEXT?
I'VE GOT A FEW LEADS FOR US TO FOLLOW UP ON...
IF YOU GUYS ARE WILLING?
WE'RE NOT BAILING NOW, NANCY.
DOLE OUT THE ASSIGNMENTS ALREADY.
YOU KNOW ME TOO WELL, FRANK.
I DO HAVE ASSIGNMENTS... BUT FIRST I'VE GOT A QUESTION.
PETE HAS SHARED HIS MOM'S OLD POLICE FILE WITH ME.
AND DESPITE THE FACT THAT PETE IS CERTAIN HIS MOTHER WAS NOT A DRUG USER...
THERE WERE TRACES FOUND IN HER BLOOD OF A DRUG CALLED XS OR EXCESS.
IS ANYONE FAMILIAR WITH THIS DRUG?
UH...
BESS!?!

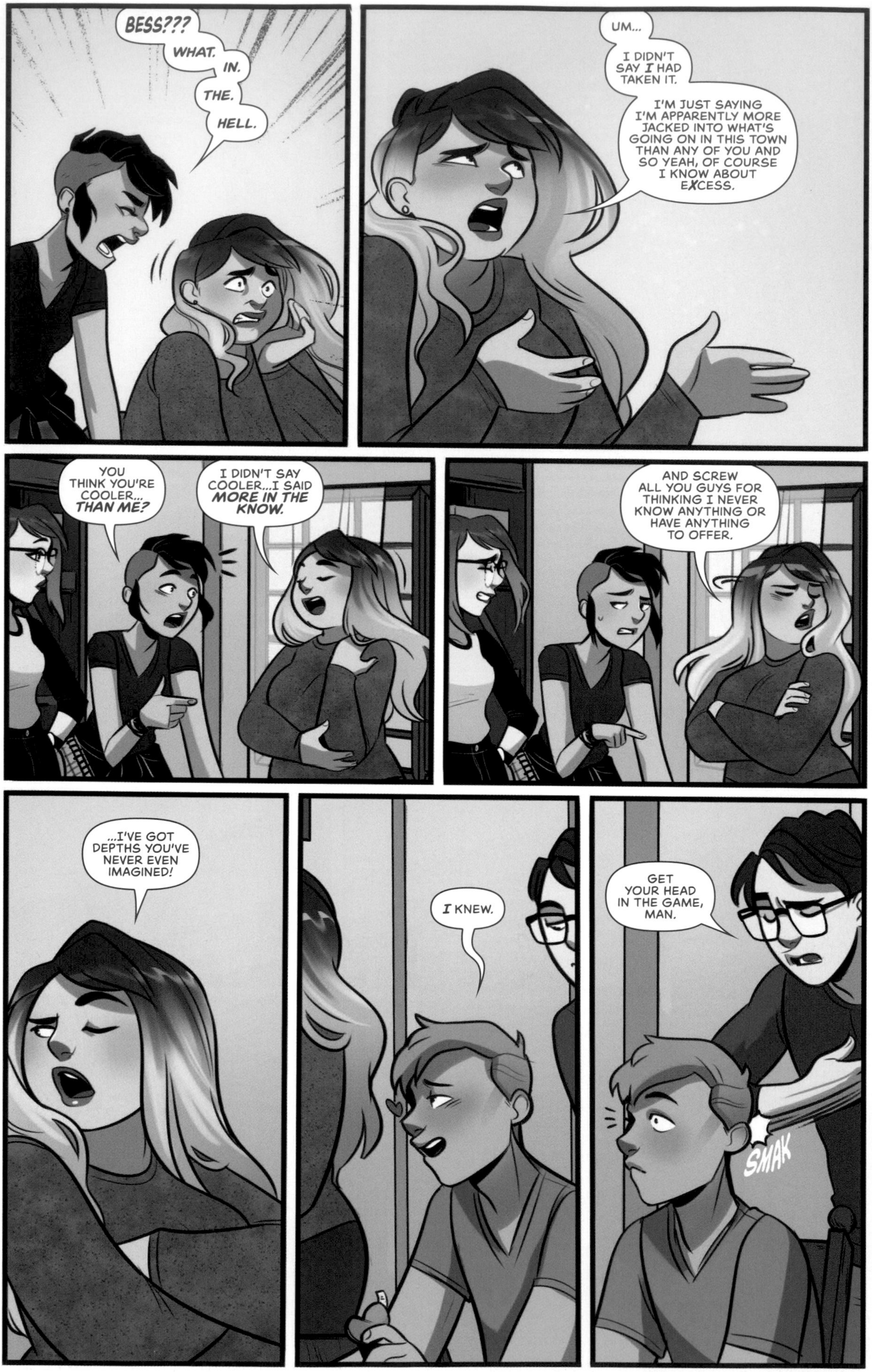

BESS??? WHAT. IN. THE. HELL.
UM...
I DIDN'T SAY I HAD TAKEN IT.
I'M JUST SAYING I'M APPARENTLY MORE JACKED INTO WHAT'S GOING ON IN THIS TOWN THAN ANY OF YOU AND SO YEAH, OF COURSE I KNOW ABOUT EXCESS.
YOU THINK YOU'RE COOLER... THAN ME?
I DIDN'T SAY COOLER...I SAID MORE IN THE KNOW.
AND SCREW ALL YOU GUYS FOR THINKING I NEVER KNOW ANYTHING OR HAVE ANYTHING TO OFFER.
...I'VE GOT DEPTHS YOU'VE NEVER EVEN IMAGINED!
I KNEW.
GET YOUR HEAD IN THE GAME, MAN.
SMAK

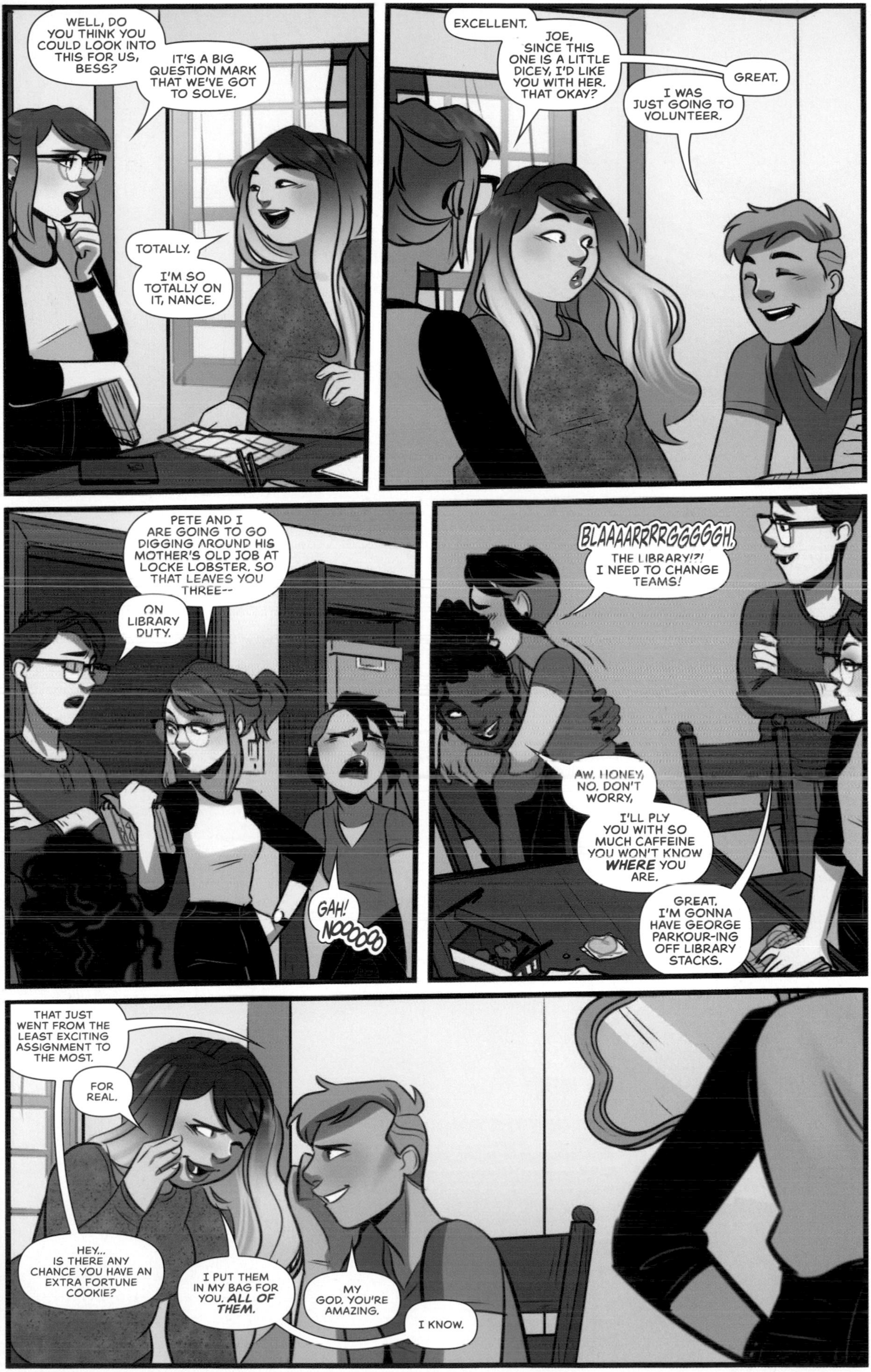
WELL, DO YOU THINK YOU COULD LOOK INTO THIS FOR US, BESS?
IT'S A BIG QUESTION MARK THAT WE'VE GOT TO SOLVE.
TOTALLY.
I'M SO TOTALLY ON IT, NANCE.
EXCELLENT.
JOE, SINCE THIS ONE IS A LITTLE DICEY, I'D LIKE YOU WITH HER. THAT OKAY?
GREAT.
I WAS JUST GOING TO VOLUNTEER.
PETE AND I ARE GOING TO GO DIGGING AROUND HIS MOTHER'S OLD JOB AT LOCKE LOBSTER. SO THAT LEAVES YOU THREE--
ON LIBRARY DUTY.
GAH! NOOOOOO
BLAAAARRRRGGGGGH.
THE LIBRARY!?! I NEED TO CHANGE TEAMS!
AW, HONEY, NO, DON'T WORRY,
I'LL PLY YOU WITH SO MUCH CAFFEINE YOU WON'T KNOW WHERE YOU ARE.
GREAT, I'M GONNA HAVE GEORGE PARKOUR-ING OFF LIBRARY STACKS.
THAT JUST WENT FROM THE LEAST EXCITING ASSIGNMENT TO THE MOST.
FOR REAL.
HEY... IS THERE ANY CHANCE YOU HAVE AN EXTRA FORTUNE COOKIE?
I PUT THEM IN MY BAG FOR YOU. ALL OF THEM.
MY GOD, YOU'RE AMAZING.
I KNOW.

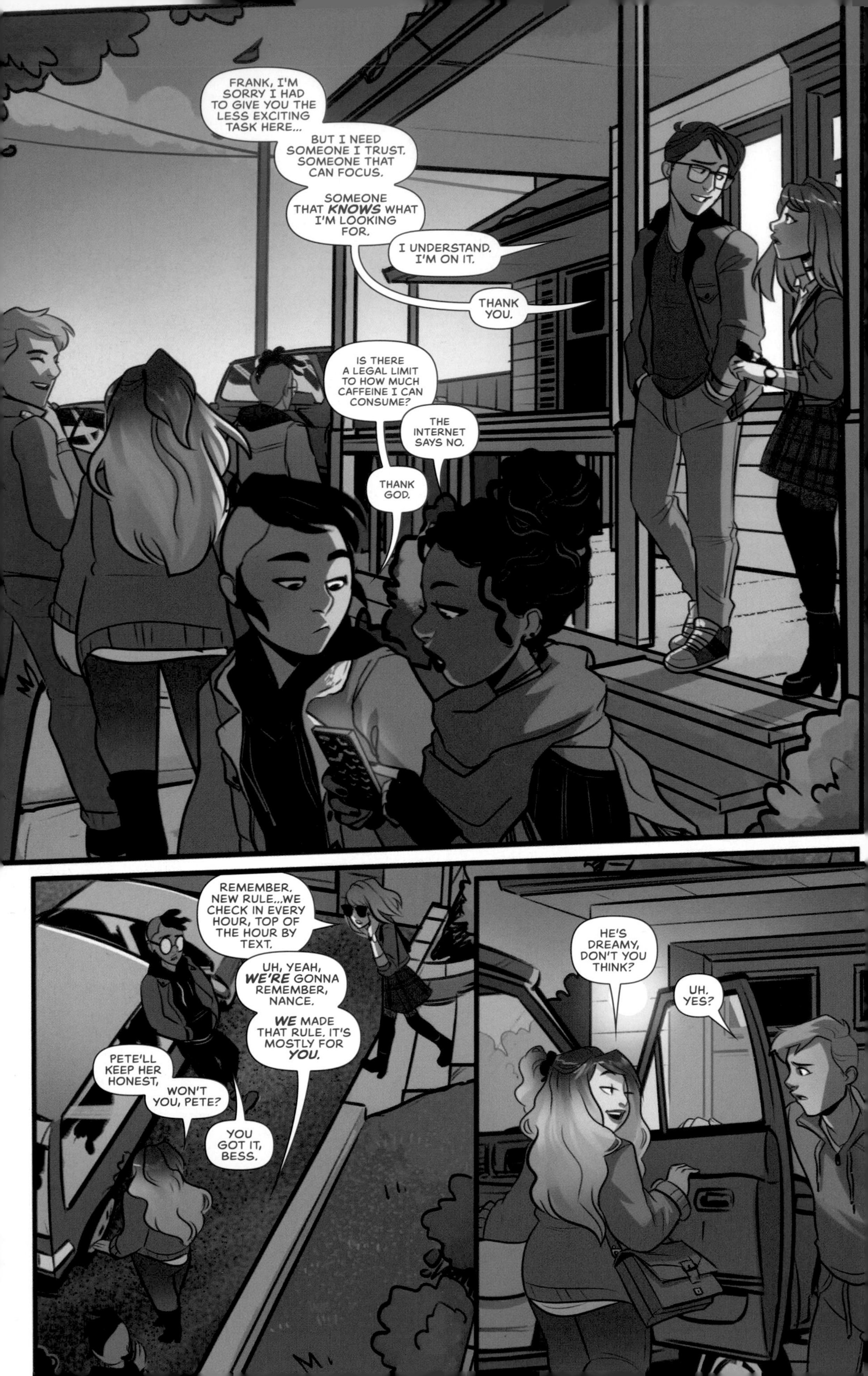
FRANK, I'M SORRY I HAD TO GIVE YOU THE LESS EXCITING TASK HERE...
BUT I NEED SOMEONE I TRUST. SOMEONE THAT CAN FOCUS.
SOMEONE THAT **KNOWS** WHAT I'M LOOKING FOR.
I UNDERSTAND. I'M ON IT.
THANK YOU.
IS THERE A LEGAL LIMIT TO HOW MUCH CAFFEINE I CAN CONSUME?
THE INTERNET SAYS NO.
THANK GOD.
REMEMBER, NEW RULE...WE CHECK IN EVERY HOUR, TOP OF THE HOUR BY TEXT.
UH, YEAH, ***WE'RE*** GONNA REMEMBER, NANCE.
WE MADE THAT RULE. IT'S MOSTLY FOR ***YOU.***
PETE'LL KEEP HER HONEST, WON'T YOU, PETE?
YOU GOT IT, BESS.
HE'S DREAMY, DON'T YOU THINK?
UH, YES?

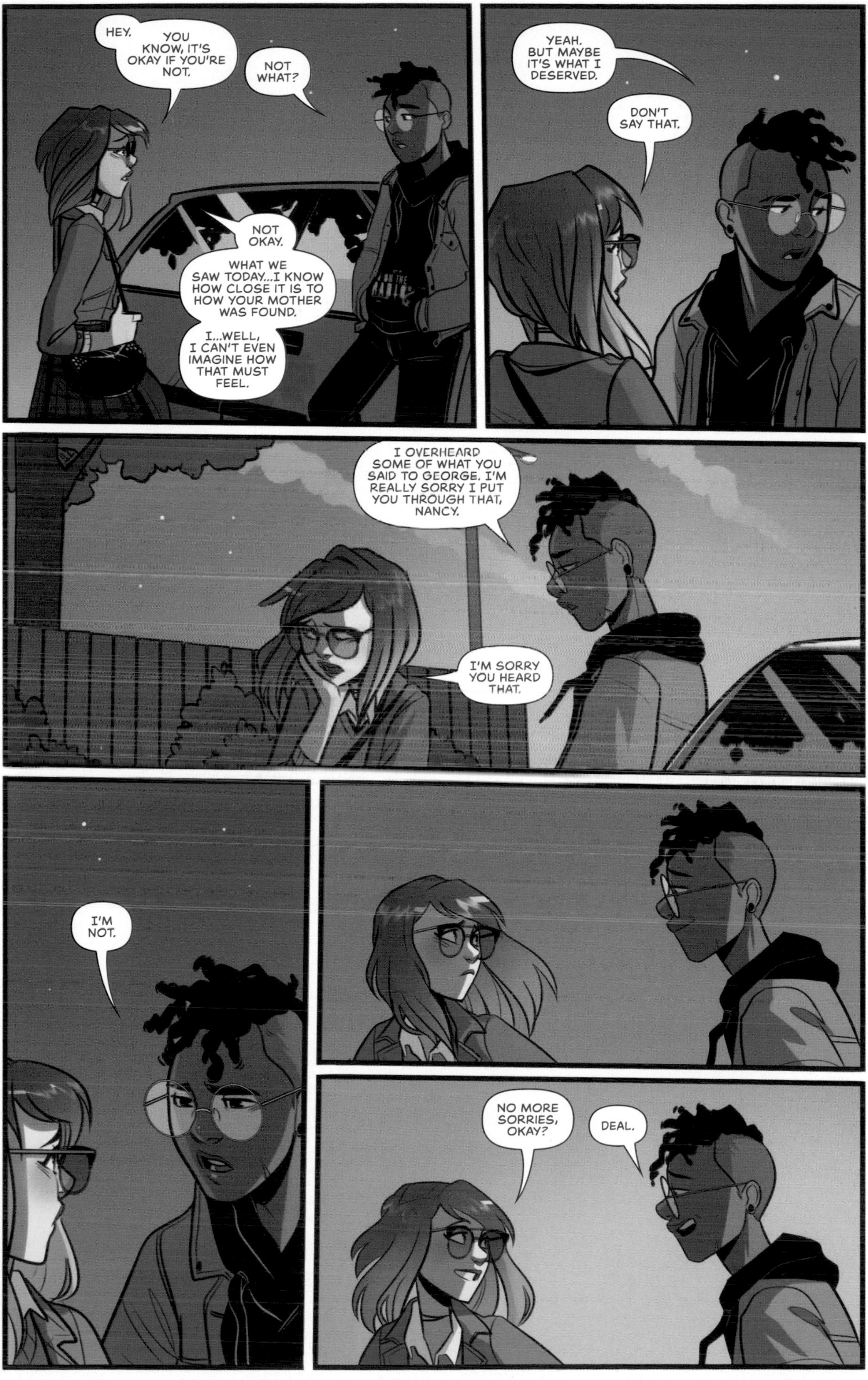
HEY.
YOU KNOW, IT'S OKAY IF YOU'RE NOT.
NOT WHAT?
NOT OKAY.
WHAT WE SAW TODAY...I KNOW HOW CLOSE IT IS TO HOW YOUR MOTHER WAS FOUND.
I...WELL, I CAN'T EVEN IMAGINE HOW THAT MUST FEEL.
YEAH. BUT MAYBE IT'S WHAT I DESERVED.
DON'T SAY THAT.
I OVERHEARD SOME OF WHAT YOU SAID TO GEORGE. I'M REALLY SORRY I PUT YOU THROUGH THAT, NANCY.
I'M SORRY YOU HEARD THAT.
I'M NOT.
NO MORE SORRIES, OKAY?
DEAL.

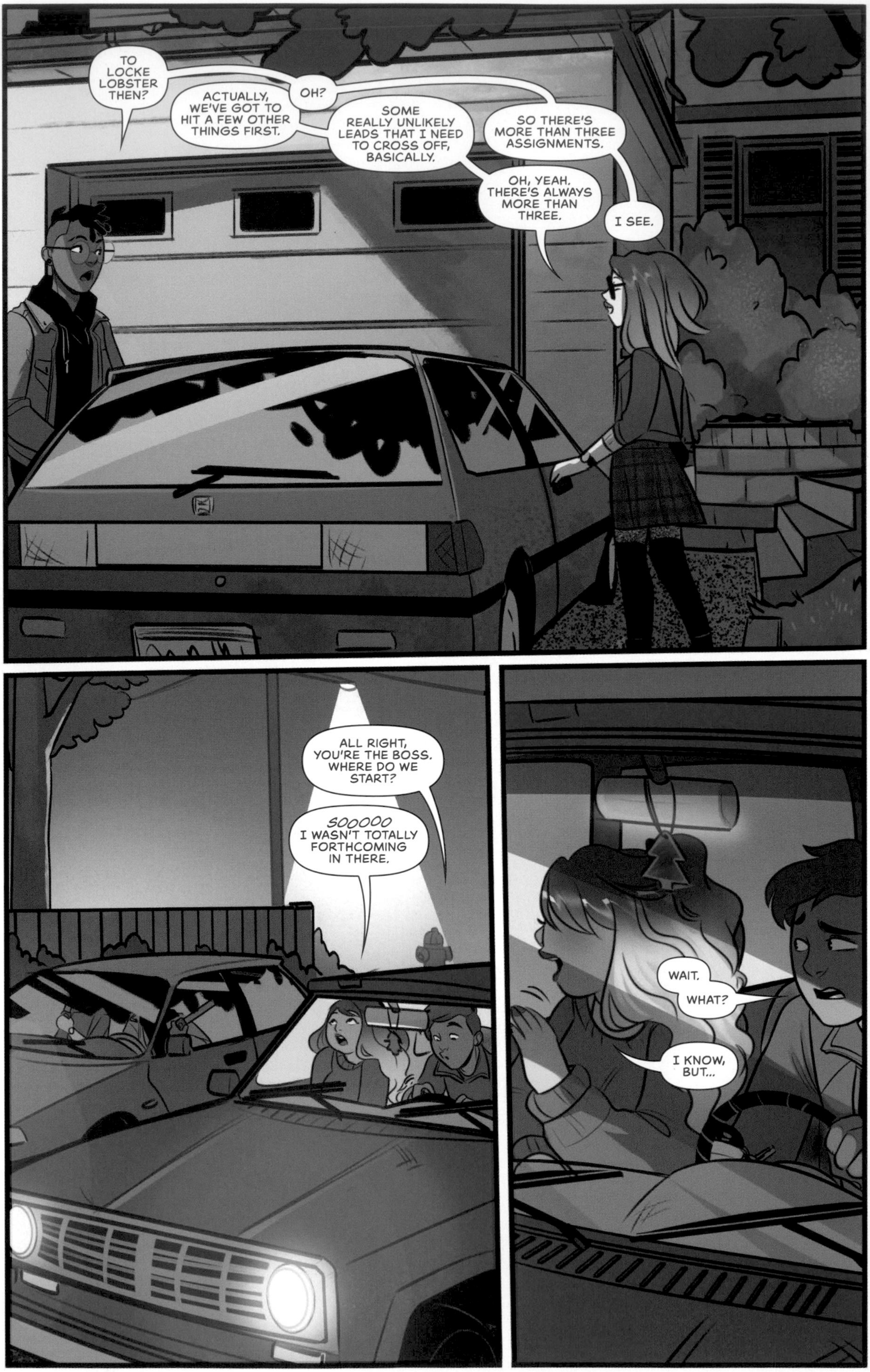
TO LOCKE LOBSTER THEN?
OH?
ACTUALLY, WE'VE GOT TO HIT A FEW OTHER THINGS FIRST.
SOME REALLY UNLIKELY LEADS THAT I NEED TO CROSS OFF, BASICALLY.
SO THERE'S MORE THAN THREE ASSIGNMENTS.
OH, YEAH. THERE'S ALWAYS MORE THAN THREE.
I SEE.
ALL RIGHT, YOU'RE THE BOSS. WHERE DO WE START?
SOOOOO I WASN'T TOTALLY FORTHCOMING IN THERE.
WAIT.
WHAT?
I KNOW, BUT...

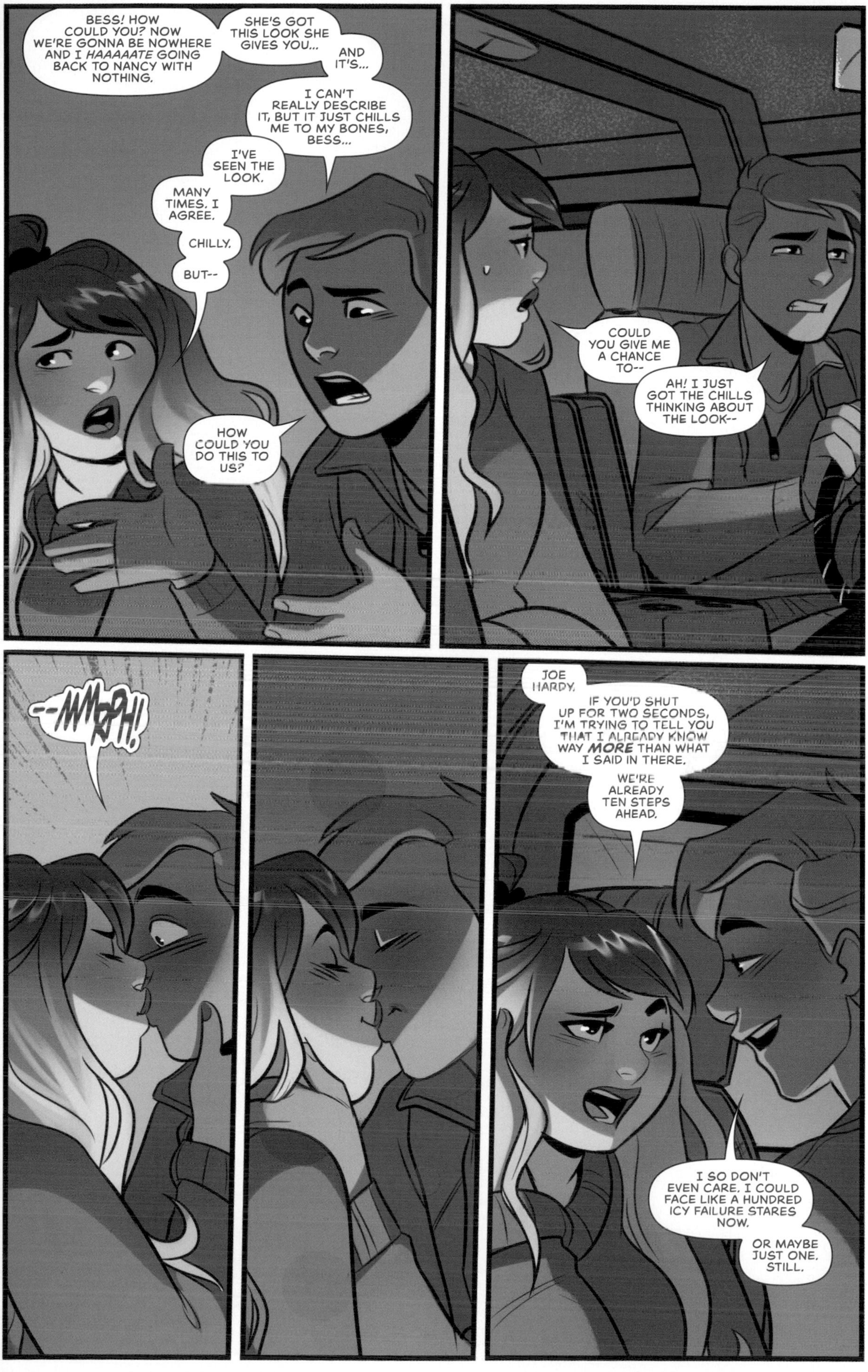
BESS! HOW COULD YOU? NOW WE'RE GONNA BE NOWHERE AND I *HAAAAATE* GOING BACK TO NANCY WITH NOTHING.
SHE'S GOT THIS LOOK SHE GIVES YOU...
AND IT'S...
I CAN'T REALLY DESCRIBE IT, BUT IT JUST CHILLS ME TO MY BONES, BESS...
I'VE SEEN THE LOOK.
MANY TIMES. I AGREE.
CHILLY.
BUT--
HOW COULD YOU DO THIS TO US?
COULD YOU GIVE ME A CHANCE TO--
AH! I JUST GOT THE CHILLS THINKING ABOUT THE LOOK--
--MMRPH!
JOE HARDY.
IF YOU'D SHUT UP FOR TWO SECONDS, I'M TRYING TO TELL YOU THAT I ALREADY KNOW WAY **MORE** THAN WHAT I SAID IN THERE.
WE'RE ALREADY TEN STEPS AHEAD.
I SO DON'T EVEN CARE. I COULD FACE LIKE A HUNDRED ICY FAILURE STARES NOW.
OR MAYBE JUST ONE. STILL.

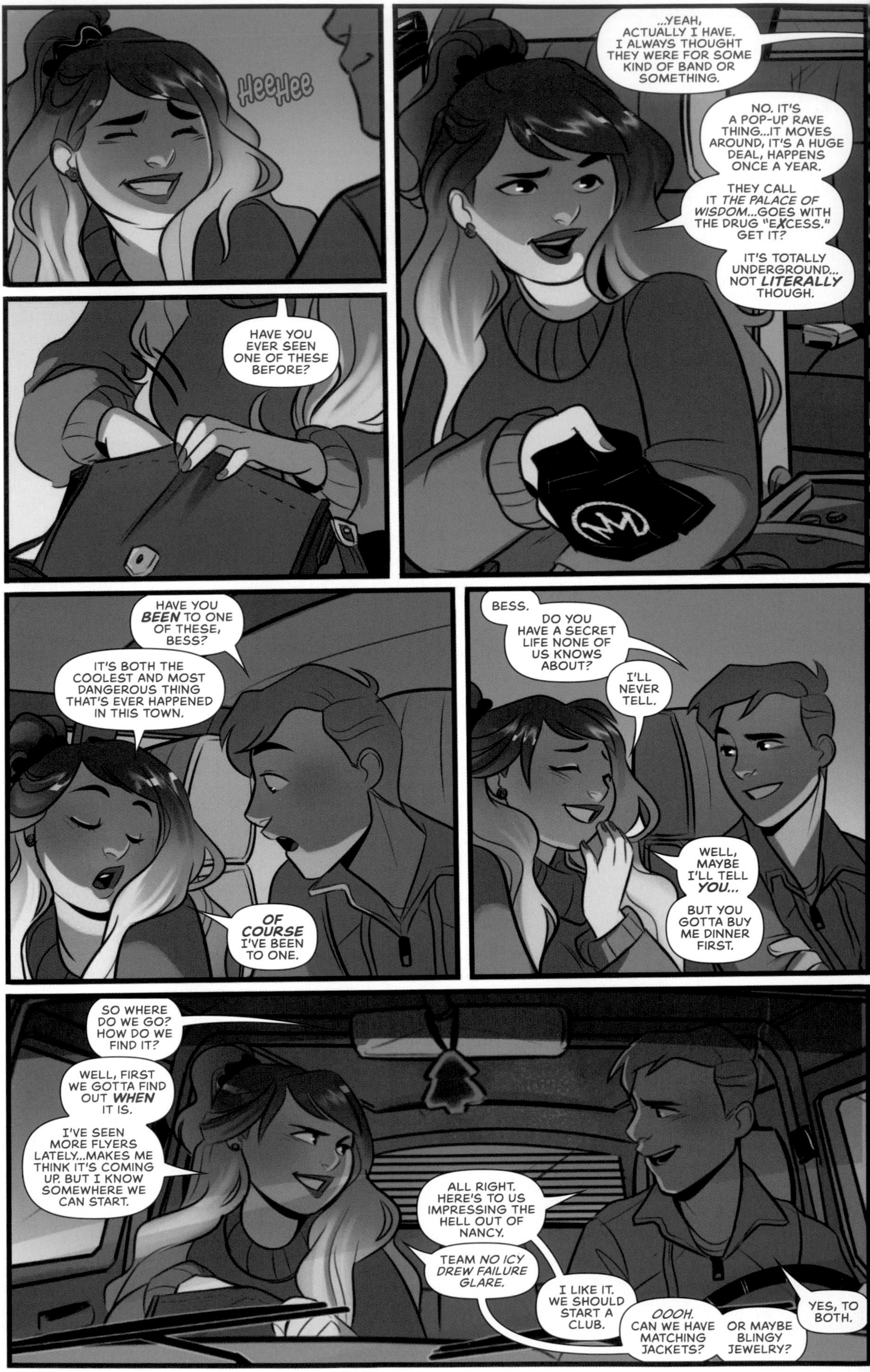
HEEHEE
HAVE YOU EVER SEEN ONE OF THESE BEFORE?
...YEAH, ACTUALLY I HAVE. I ALWAYS THOUGHT THEY WERE FOR SOME KIND OF BAND OR SOMETHING.
NO. IT'S A POP-UP RAVE THING...IT MOVES AROUND, IT'S A HUGE DEAL, HAPPENS ONCE A YEAR.
THEY CALL IT *THE PALACE OF WISDOM*...GOES WITH THE DRUG "EXCESS." GET IT?
IT'S TOTALLY UNDERGROUND... NOT ***LITERALLY*** THOUGH.
HAVE YOU ***BEEN*** TO ONE OF THESE, BESS?
IT'S BOTH THE COOLEST AND MOST DANGEROUS THING THAT'S EVER HAPPENED IN THIS TOWN.
OF COURSE I'VE BEEN TO ONE.
BESS.
DO YOU HAVE A SECRET LIFE NONE OF US KNOWS ABOUT?
I'LL NEVER TELL.
WELL, MAYBE I'LL TELL ***YOU...***
BUT YOU GOTTA BUY ME DINNER FIRST.
SO WHERE DO WE GO? HOW DO WE FIND IT?
WELL, FIRST WE GOTTA FIND OUT ***WHEN*** IT IS.
I'VE SEEN MORE FLYERS LATELY...MAKES ME THINK IT'S COMING UP. BUT I KNOW SOMEWHERE WE CAN START.
ALL RIGHT. HERE'S TO US IMPRESSING THE HELL OUT OF NANCY.
TEAM *NO ICY DREW FAILURE GLARE.*
I LIKE IT. WE SHOULD START A CLUB.
OOOH. CAN WE HAVE MATCHING JACKETS?
OR MAYBE BLINGY JEWELRY?
YES, TO BOTH.

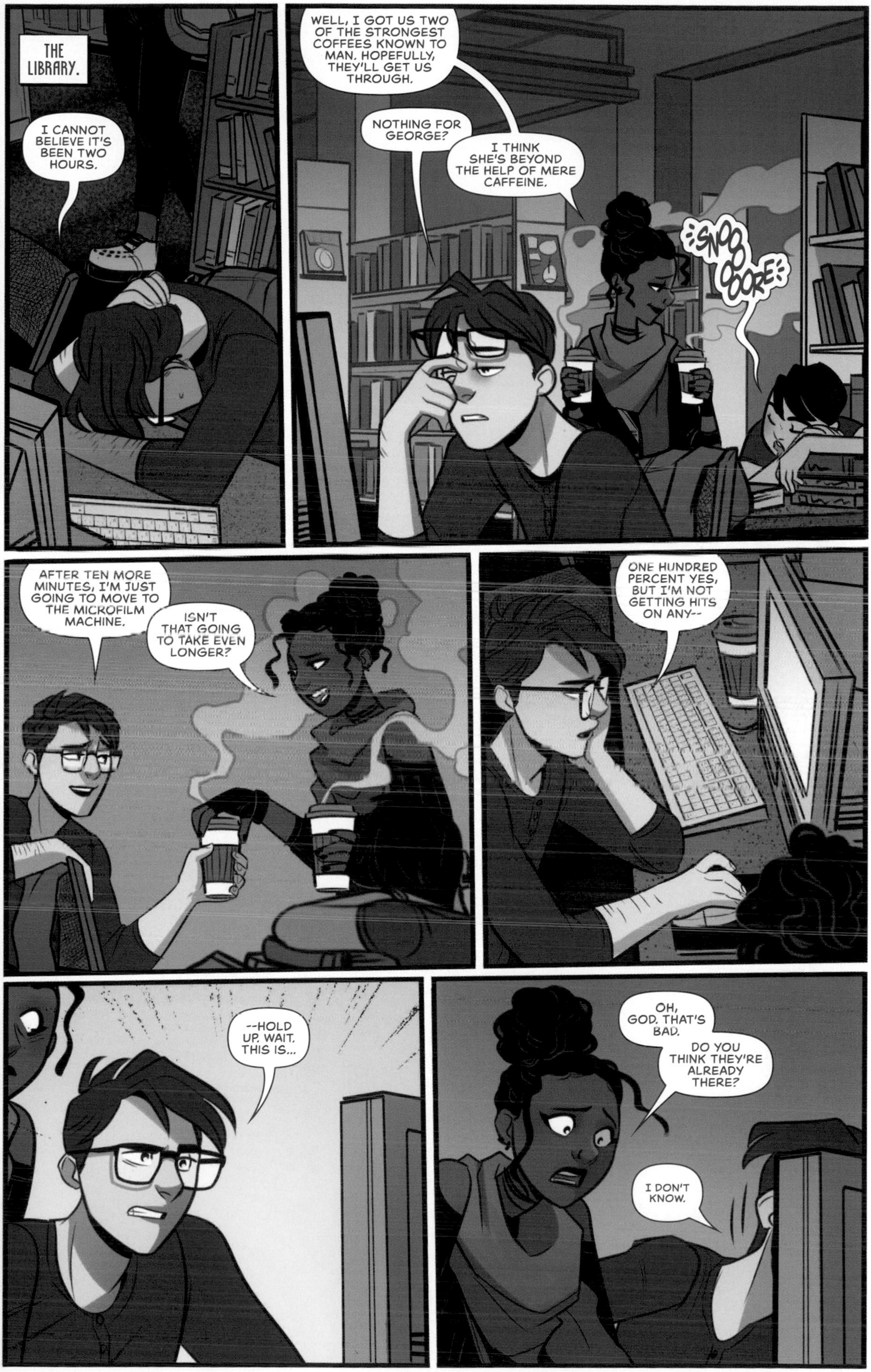
THE LIBRARY.
I CANNOT BELIEVE IT'S BEEN TWO HOURS.
WELL, I GOT US TWO OF THE STRONGEST COFFEES KNOWN TO MAN. HOPEFULLY, THEY'LL GET US THROUGH.
NOTHING FOR GEORGE?
I THINK SHE'S BEYOND THE HELP OF MERE CAFFEINE.
SNOOOOORE
AFTER TEN MORE MINUTES, I'M JUST GOING TO MOVE TO THE MICROFILM MACHINE.
ISN'T THAT GOING TO TAKE EVEN LONGER?
ONE HUNDRED PERCENT YES, BUT I'M NOT GETTING HITS ON ANY--
--HOLD UP. WAIT. THIS IS...
OH, GOD, THAT'S BAD.
DO YOU THINK THEY'RE ALREADY THERE?
I DON'T KNOW.

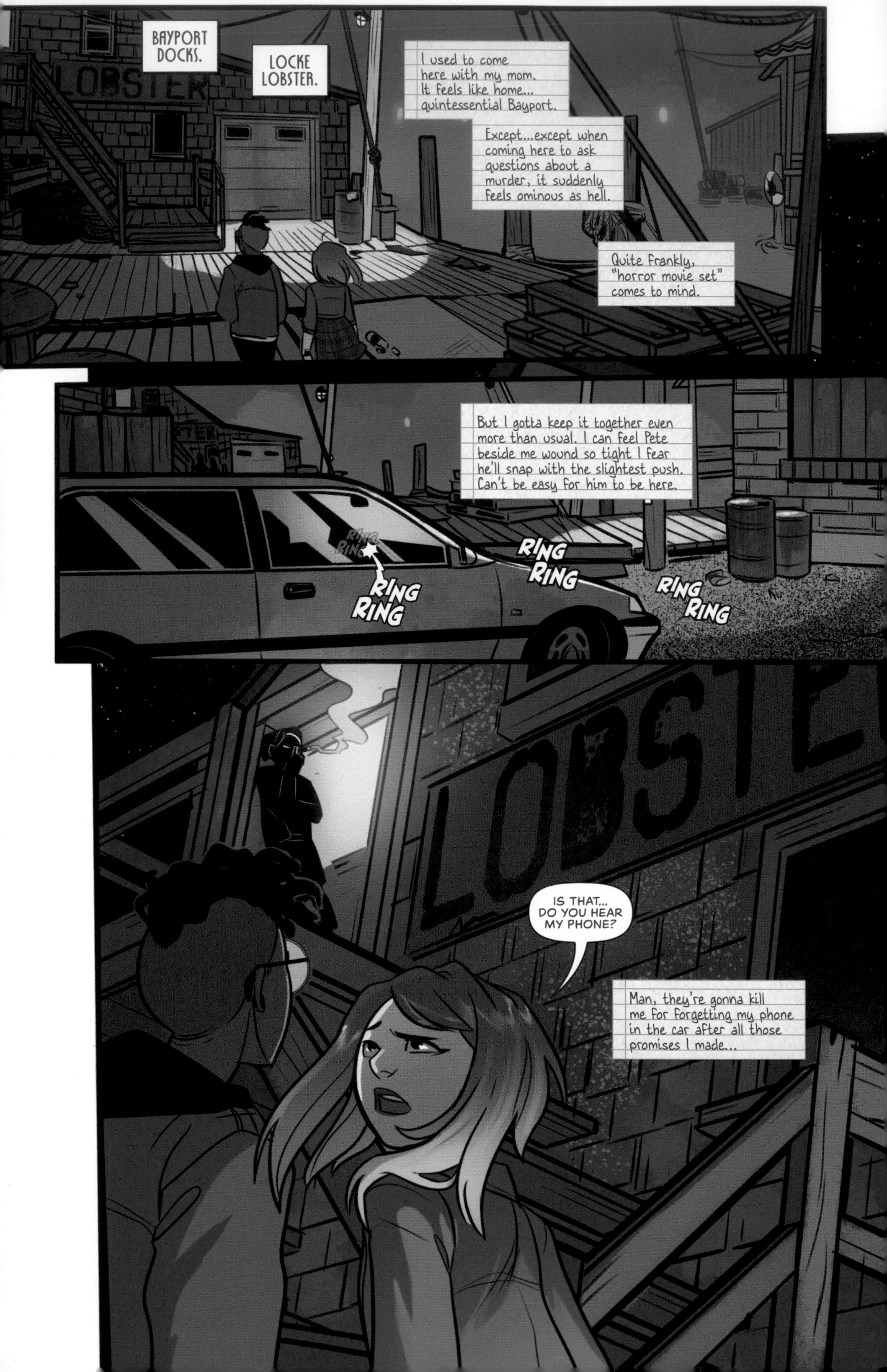
BAYPORT DOCKS.
LOCKE LOBSTER.
I used to come here with my mom. It feels like home... quintessential Bayport.
Except...except when coming here to ask questions about a murder, it suddenly feels ominous as hell.
Quite frankly, "horror movie set" comes to mind.
But I gotta keep it together even more than usual. I can feel Pete beside me wound so tight I fear he'll snap with the slightest push. Can't be easy for him to be here.
RING RING
RING RING
RING RING
RING RING
RING RING
IS THAT... DO YOU HEAR MY PHONE?
Man, they're gonna kill me for forgetting my phone in the car after all those promises I made...

CHAPTER FOUR

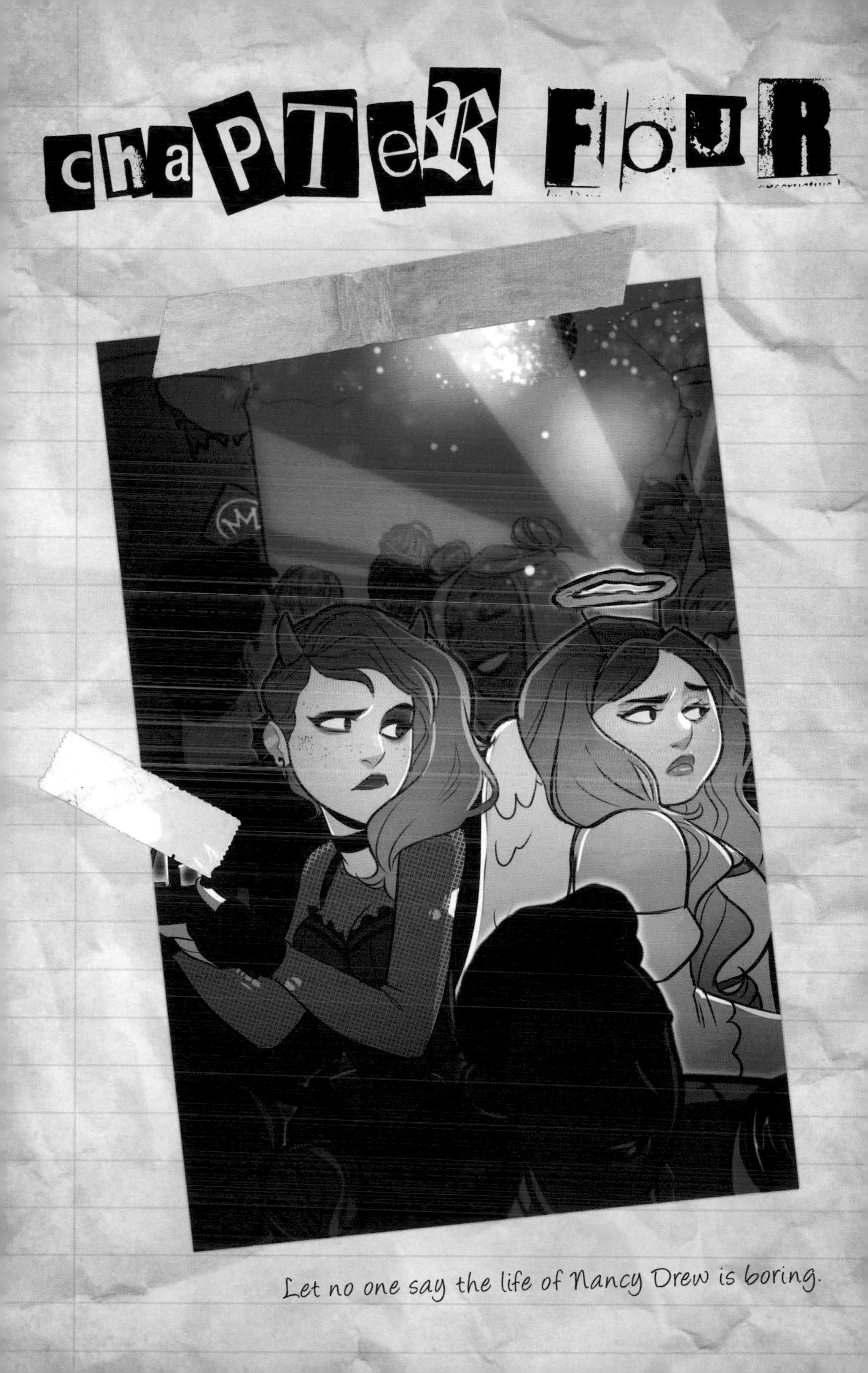

Let no one say the life of Nancy Drew is boring.

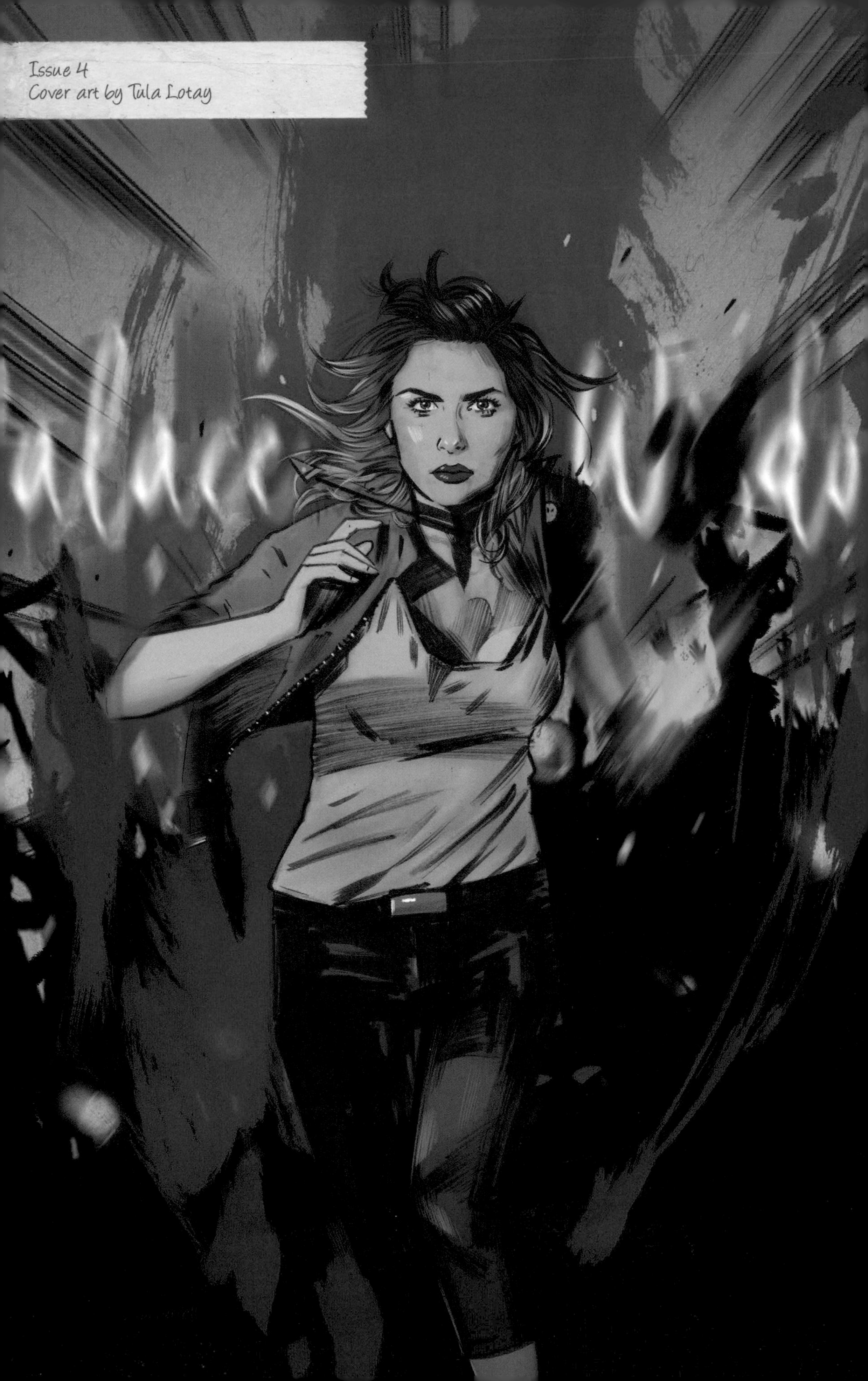

Issue 4
Cover art by Tula Lotay

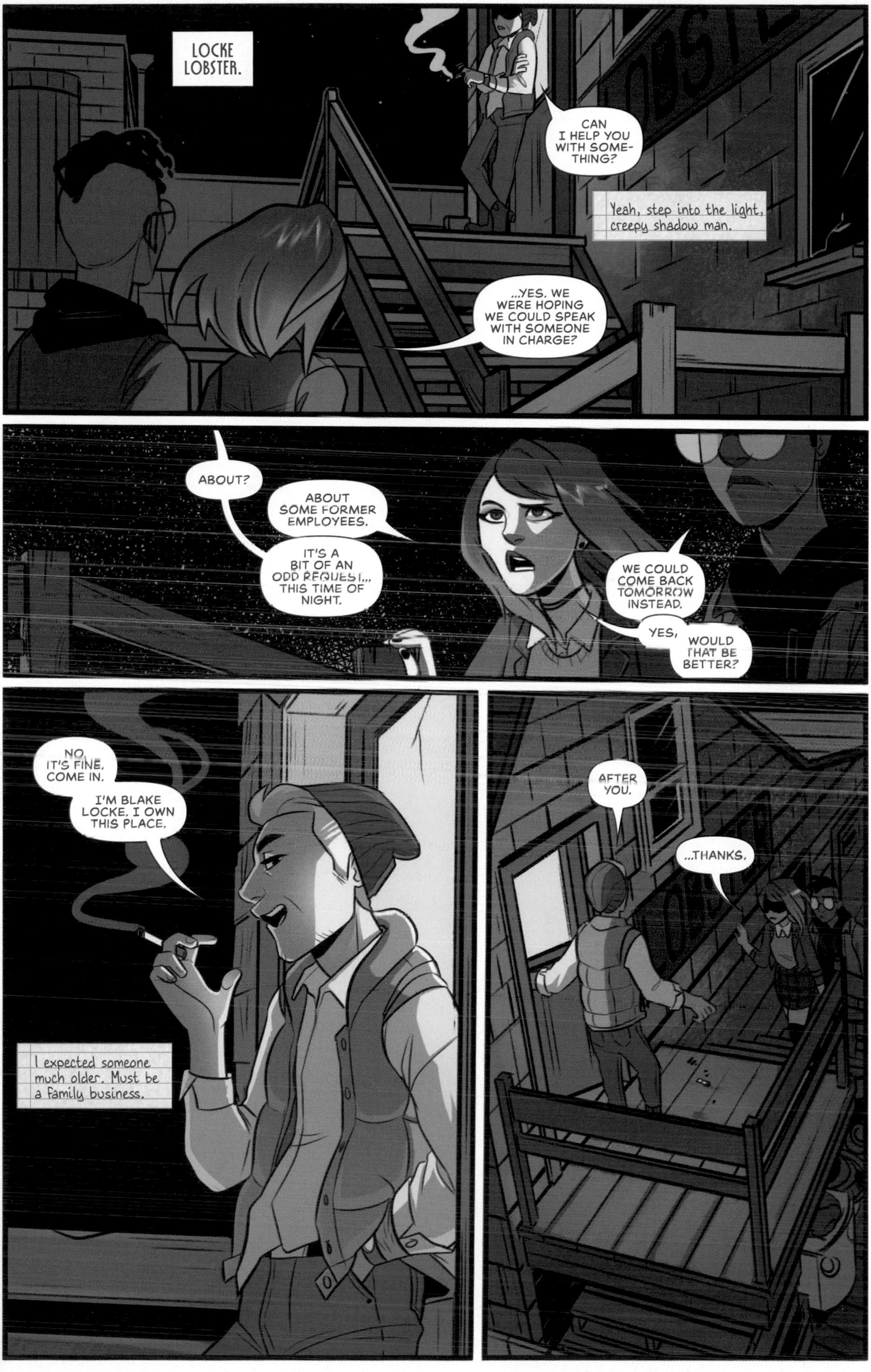
LOCKE LOBSTER.
CAN I HELP YOU WITH SOME-THING?
Yeah, step into the light, creepy shadow man.
...YES. WE WERE HOPING WE COULD SPEAK WITH SOMEONE IN CHARGE?
ABOUT?
ABOUT SOME FORMER EMPLOYEES.
IT'S A BIT OF AN ODD REQUEST... THIS TIME OF NIGHT.
WE COULD COME BACK TOMORROW INSTEAD.
YES, WOULD THAT BE BETTER?
NO, IT'S FINE. COME IN.
I'M BLAKE LOCKE. I OWN THIS PLACE.
I expected someone much older. Must be a family business.
AFTER YOU.
...THANKS.

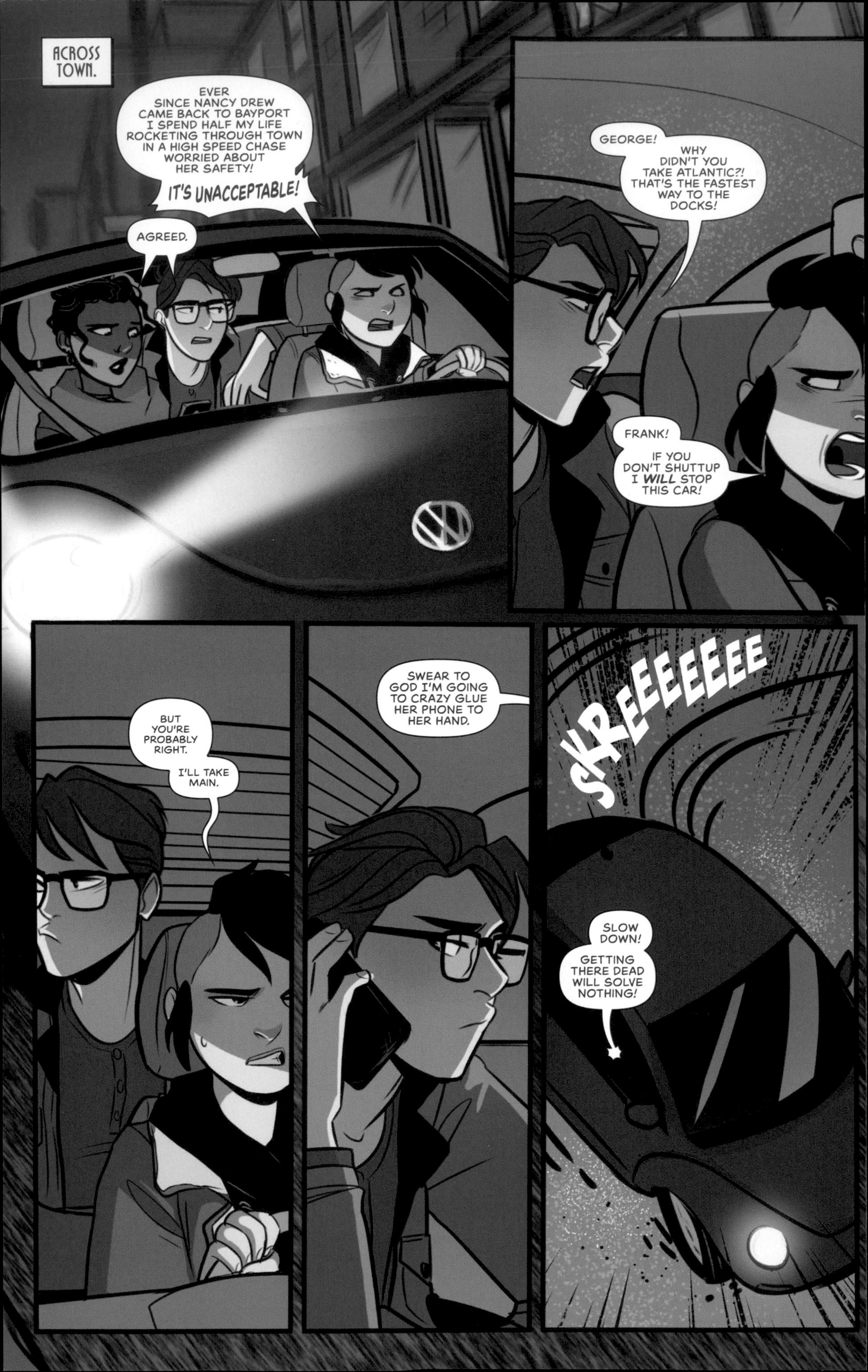
ACROSS TOWN.
EVER SINCE NANCY DREW CAME BACK TO BAYPORT I SPEND HALF MY LIFE ROCKETING THROUGH TOWN IN A HIGH SPEED CHASE WORRIED ABOUT HER SAFETY!
IT'S UNACCEPTABLE!
AGREED.
GEORGE!
WHY DIDN'T YOU TAKE ATLANTIC?! THAT'S THE FASTEST WAY TO THE DOCKS!
FRANK!
IF YOU DON'T SHUTTUP I WILL STOP THIS CAR!
BUT YOU'RE PROBABLY RIGHT.
I'LL TAKE MAIN.
SWEAR TO GOD I'M GOING TO CRAZY GLUE HER PHONE TO HER HAND.
SKREEEEEEE
SLOW DOWN!
GETTING THERE DEAD WILL SOLVE NOTHING!

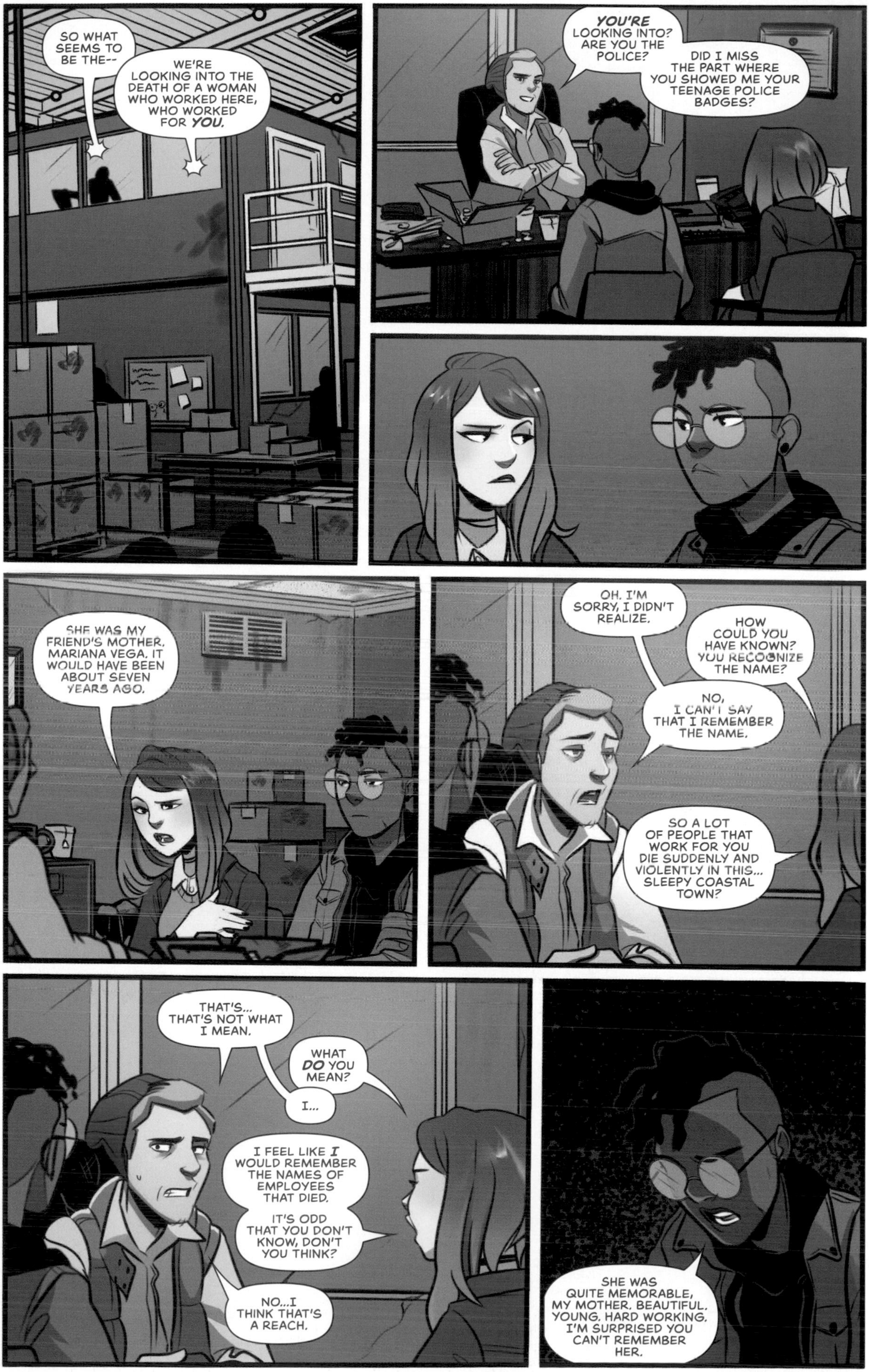
SO WHAT SEEMS TO BE THE--
WE'RE LOOKING INTO THE DEATH OF A WOMAN WHO WORKED HERE, WHO WORKED FOR *YOU.*
YOU'RE LOOKING INTO? ARE YOU THE POLICE?
DID I MISS THE PART WHERE YOU SHOWED ME YOUR TEENAGE POLICE BADGES?
SHE WAS MY FRIEND'S MOTHER, MARIANA VEGA. IT WOULD HAVE BEEN ABOUT SEVEN YEARS AGO.
OH. I'M SORRY, I DIDN'T REALIZE.
HOW COULD YOU HAVE KNOWN? YOU RECOGNIZE THE NAME?
NO, I CAN'T SAY THAT I REMEMBER THE NAME.
SO A LOT OF PEOPLE THAT WORK FOR YOU DIE SUDDENLY AND VIOLENTLY IN THIS... SLEEPY COASTAL TOWN?
THAT'S... THAT'S NOT WHAT I MEAN.
WHAT *DO* YOU MEAN?
I...
I FEEL LIKE *I* WOULD REMEMBER THE NAMES OF EMPLOYEES THAT DIED.
IT'S ODD THAT YOU DON'T KNOW, DON'T YOU THINK?
NO...I THINK THAT'S A REACH.
SHE WAS QUITE MEMORABLE, MY MOTHER. BEAUTIFUL. YOUNG. HARD WORKING. I'M SURPRISED YOU CAN'T REMEMBER HER.

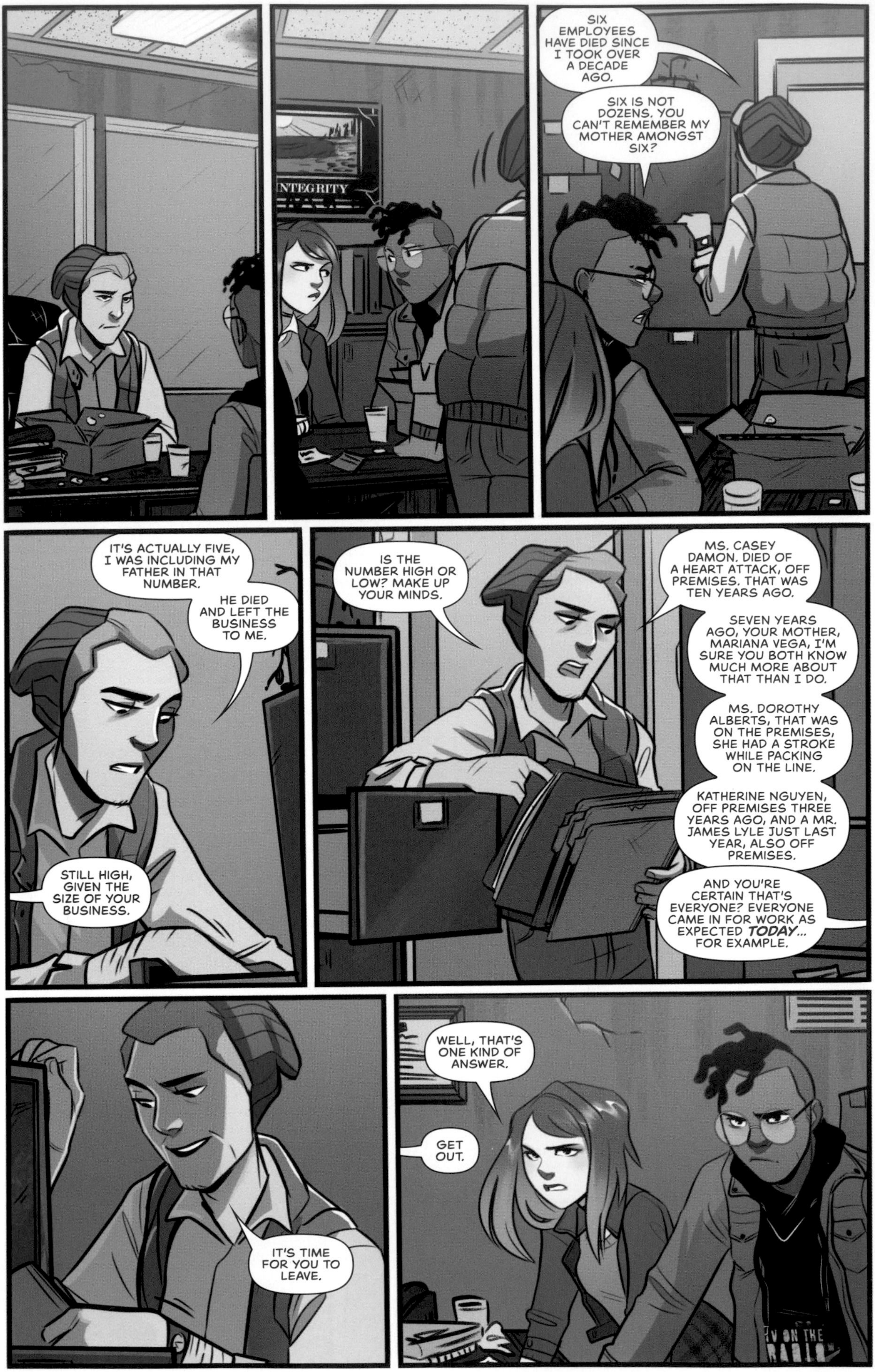
INTEGRITY
SIX EMPLOYEES HAVE DIED SINCE I TOOK OVER A DECADE AGO.
SIX IS NOT DOZENS. YOU CAN'T REMEMBER MY MOTHER AMONGST SIX?
IT'S ACTUALLY FIVE, I WAS INCLUDING MY FATHER IN THAT NUMBER.
HE DIED AND LEFT THE BUSINESS TO ME.
STILL HIGH, GIVEN THE SIZE OF YOUR BUSINESS.
IS THE NUMBER HIGH OR LOW? MAKE UP YOUR MINDS.
MS. CASEY DAMON. DIED OF A HEART ATTACK, OFF PREMISES. THAT WAS TEN YEARS AGO.
SEVEN YEARS AGO, YOUR MOTHER, MARIANA VEGA, I'M SURE YOU BOTH KNOW MUCH MORE ABOUT THAT THAN I DO.
MS. DOROTHY ALBERTS, THAT WAS ON THE PREMISES, SHE HAD A STROKE WHILE PACKING ON THE LINE.
KATHERINE NGUYEN, OFF PREMISES THREE YEARS AGO, AND A MR. JAMES LYLE JUST LAST YEAR, ALSO OFF PREMISES.
AND YOU'RE CERTAIN THAT'S EVERYONE? EVERYONE CAME IN FOR WORK AS EXPECTED ***TODAY***... FOR EXAMPLE.
IT'S TIME FOR YOU TO LEAVE.
WELL, THAT'S ONE KIND OF ANSWER.
GET OUT.

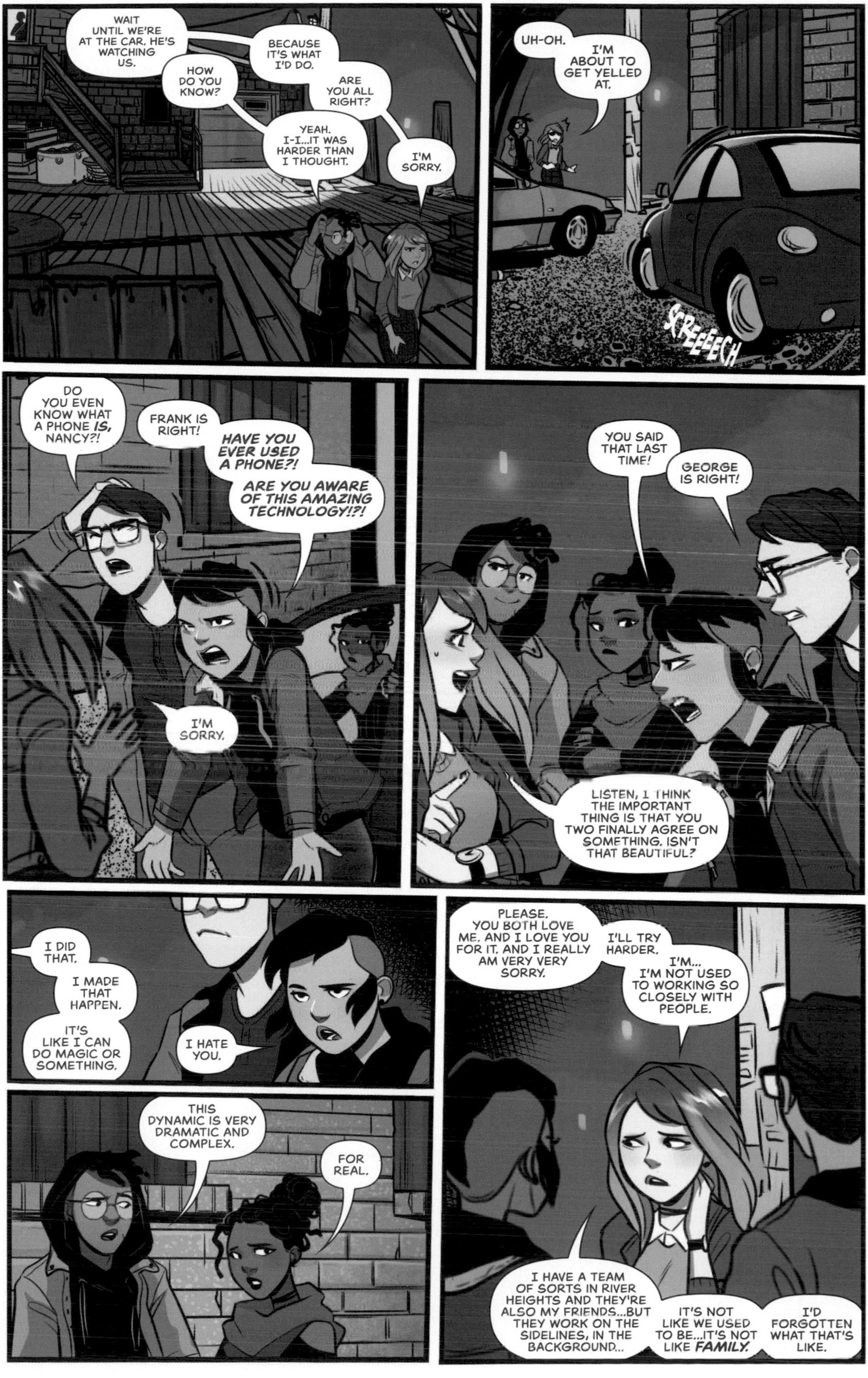
WAIT UNTIL WE'RE AT THE CAR. HE'S WATCHING US.
HOW DO YOU KNOW?
BECAUSE IT'S WHAT I'D DO.
ARE YOU ALL RIGHT?
YEAH. I-I...IT WAS HARDER THAN I THOUGHT.
I'M SORRY.
UH-OH.
I'M ABOUT TO GET YELLED AT.
SCREEEECH
DO YOU EVEN KNOW WHAT A PHONE *IS*, NANCY?!
FRANK IS RIGHT!
HAVE YOU EVER USED A PHONE?!
ARE YOU AWARE OF THIS AMAZING TECHNOLOGY!?!
I'M SORRY.
YOU SAID THAT LAST TIME!
GEORGE IS RIGHT!
LISTEN, I THINK THE IMPORTANT THING IS THAT YOU TWO FINALLY AGREE ON SOMETHING. ISN'T THAT BEAUTIFUL?
I DID THAT.
I MADE THAT HAPPEN.
IT'S LIKE I CAN DO MAGIC OR SOMETHING.
I HATE YOU.
THIS DYNAMIC IS VERY DRAMATIC AND COMPLEX.
FOR REAL.
PLEASE. YOU BOTH LOVE ME. AND I LOVE YOU FOR IT. AND I REALLY AM VERY VERY SORRY.
I'LL TRY HARDER.
I'M... I'M NOT USED TO WORKING SO CLOSELY WITH PEOPLE.
I HAVE A TEAM OF SORTS IN RIVER HEIGHTS AND THEY'RE ALSO MY FRIENDS...BUT THEY WORK ON THE SIDELINES, IN THE BACKGROUND...
IT'S NOT LIKE WE USED TO BE...IT'S NOT LIKE *FAMILY*.
I'D FORGOTTEN WHAT THAT'S LIKE.

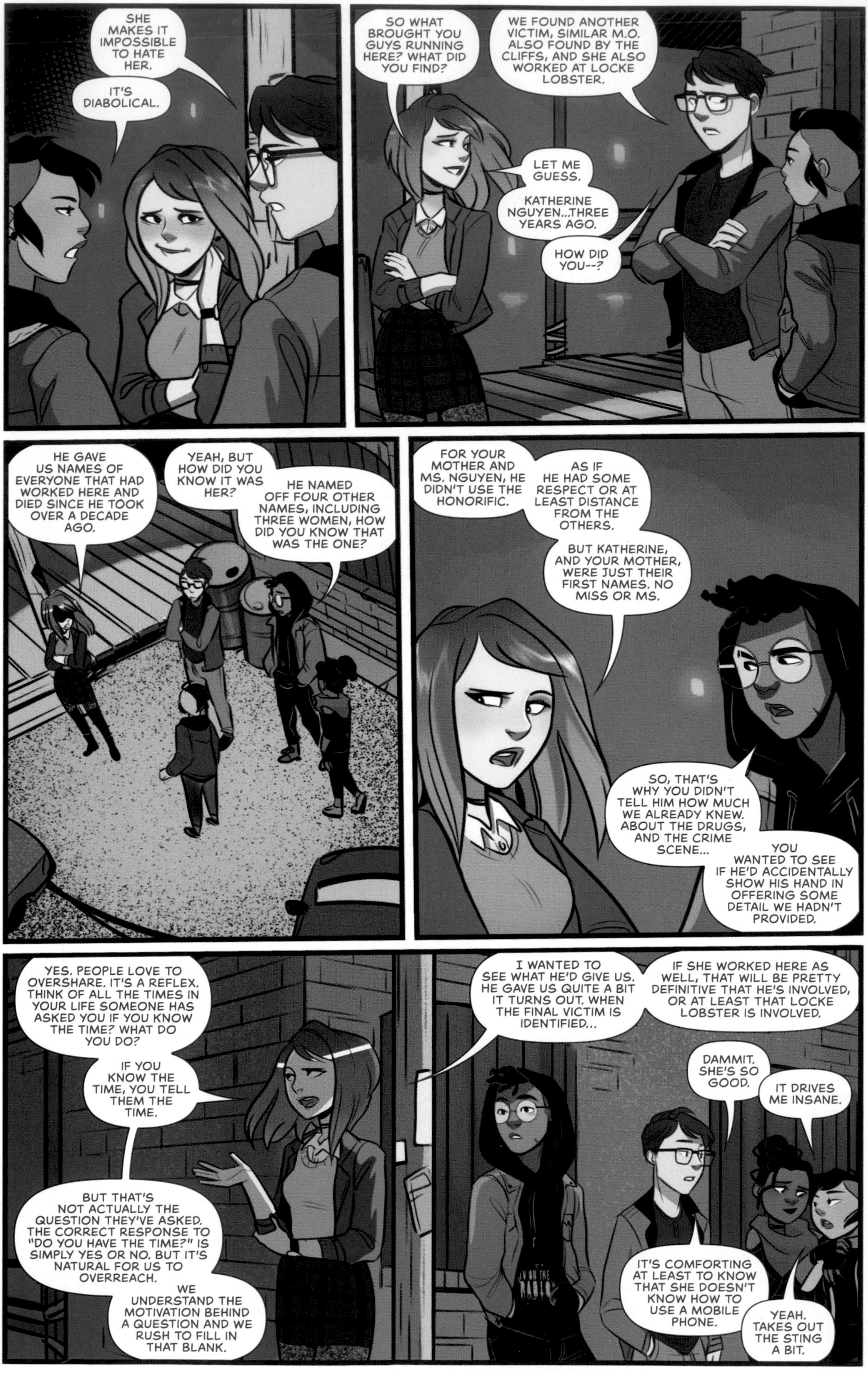
SHE MAKES IT IMPOSSIBLE TO HATE HER.
IT'S DIABOLICAL.
SO WHAT BROUGHT YOU GUYS RUNNING HERE? WHAT DID YOU FIND?
WE FOUND ANOTHER VICTIM, SIMILAR M.O. ALSO FOUND BY THE CLIFFS, AND SHE ALSO WORKED AT LOCKE LOBSTER.
LET ME GUESS.
KATHERINE NGUYEN...THREE YEARS AGO.
HOW DID YOU--?
HE GAVE US NAMES OF EVERYONE THAT HAD WORKED HERE AND DIED SINCE HE TOOK OVER A DECADE AGO.
YEAH, BUT HOW DID YOU KNOW IT WAS HER?
HE NAMED OFF FOUR OTHER NAMES, INCLUDING THREE WOMEN, HOW DID YOU KNOW THAT WAS THE ONE?
FOR YOUR MOTHER AND MS. NGUYEN, HE DIDN'T USE THE HONORIFIC.
AS IF HE HAD SOME RESPECT OR AT LEAST DISTANCE FROM THE OTHERS.
BUT KATHERINE, AND YOUR MOTHER, WERE JUST THEIR FIRST NAMES. NO MISS OR MS.
SO, THAT'S WHY YOU DIDN'T TELL HIM HOW MUCH WE ALREADY KNEW. ABOUT THE DRUGS, AND THE CRIME SCENE...
YOU WANTED TO SEE IF HE'D ACCIDENTALLY SHOW HIS HAND IN OFFERING SOME DETAIL WE HADN'T PROVIDED.
YES. PEOPLE LOVE TO OVERSHARE. IT'S A REFLEX. THINK OF ALL THE TIMES IN YOUR LIFE SOMEONE HAS ASKED YOU IF YOU KNOW THE TIME? WHAT DO YOU DO?
IF YOU KNOW THE TIME, YOU TELL THEM THE TIME.
BUT THAT'S NOT ACTUALLY THE QUESTION THEY'VE ASKED. THE CORRECT RESPONSE TO "DO YOU HAVE THE TIME?" IS SIMPLY YES OR NO. BUT IT'S NATURAL FOR US TO OVERREACH.
WE UNDERSTAND THE MOTIVATION BEHIND A QUESTION AND WE RUSH TO FILL IN THAT BLANK.
I WANTED TO SEE WHAT HE'D GIVE US. HE GAVE US QUITE A BIT IT TURNS OUT. WHEN THE FINAL VICTIM IS IDENTIFIED...
IF SHE WORKED HERE AS WELL, THAT WILL BE PRETTY DEFINITIVE THAT HE'S INVOLVED, OR AT LEAST THAT LOCKE LOBSTER IS INVOLVED.
DAMMIT. SHE'S SO GOOD.
IT DRIVES ME INSANE.
IT'S COMFORTING AT LEAST TO KNOW THAT SHE DOESN'T KNOW HOW TO USE A MOBILE PHONE.
YEAH. TAKES OUT THE STING A BIT.

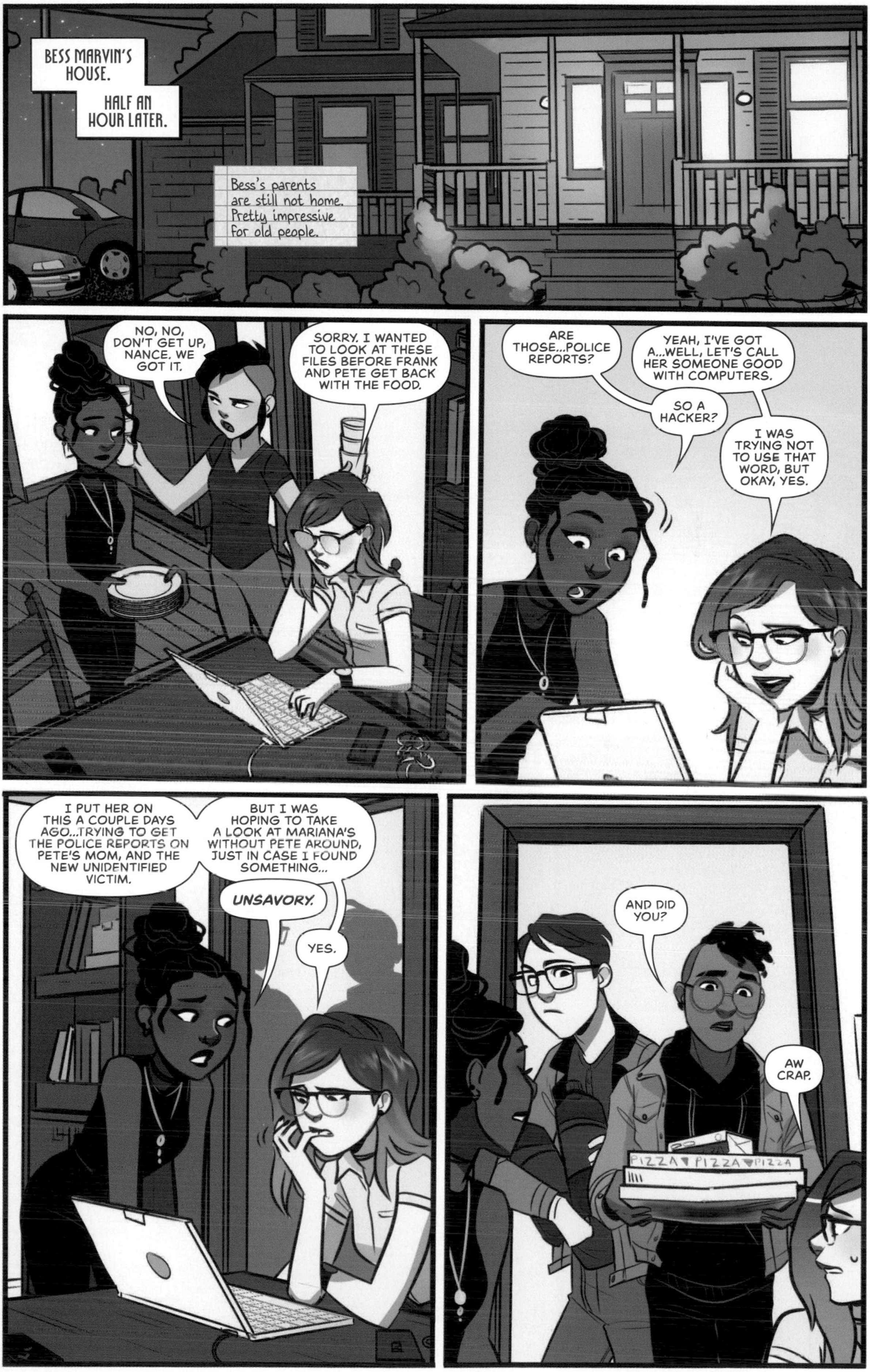
BESS MARVIN'S HOUSE.
HALF AN HOUR LATER.
Bess's parents are still not home. Pretty impressive for old people.
NO, NO, DON'T GET UP, NANCE. WE GOT IT.
SORRY. I WANTED TO LOOK AT THESE FILES BEFORE FRANK AND PETE GET BACK WITH THE FOOD.
ARE THOSE...POLICE REPORTS?
YEAH, I'VE GOT A...WELL, LET'S CALL HER SOMEONE GOOD WITH COMPUTERS.
SO A HACKER?
I WAS TRYING NOT TO USE THAT WORD, BUT OKAY, YES.
I PUT HER ON THIS A COUPLE DAYS AGO...TRYING TO GET THE POLICE REPORTS ON PETE'S MOM, AND THE NEW UNIDENTIFIED VICTIM.
BUT I WAS HOPING TO TAKE A LOOK AT MARIANA'S WITHOUT PETE AROUND, JUST IN CASE I FOUND SOMETHING...
UNSAVORY.
YES.
AND DID YOU?
AW CRAP.
PIZZA PIZZA PIZZA

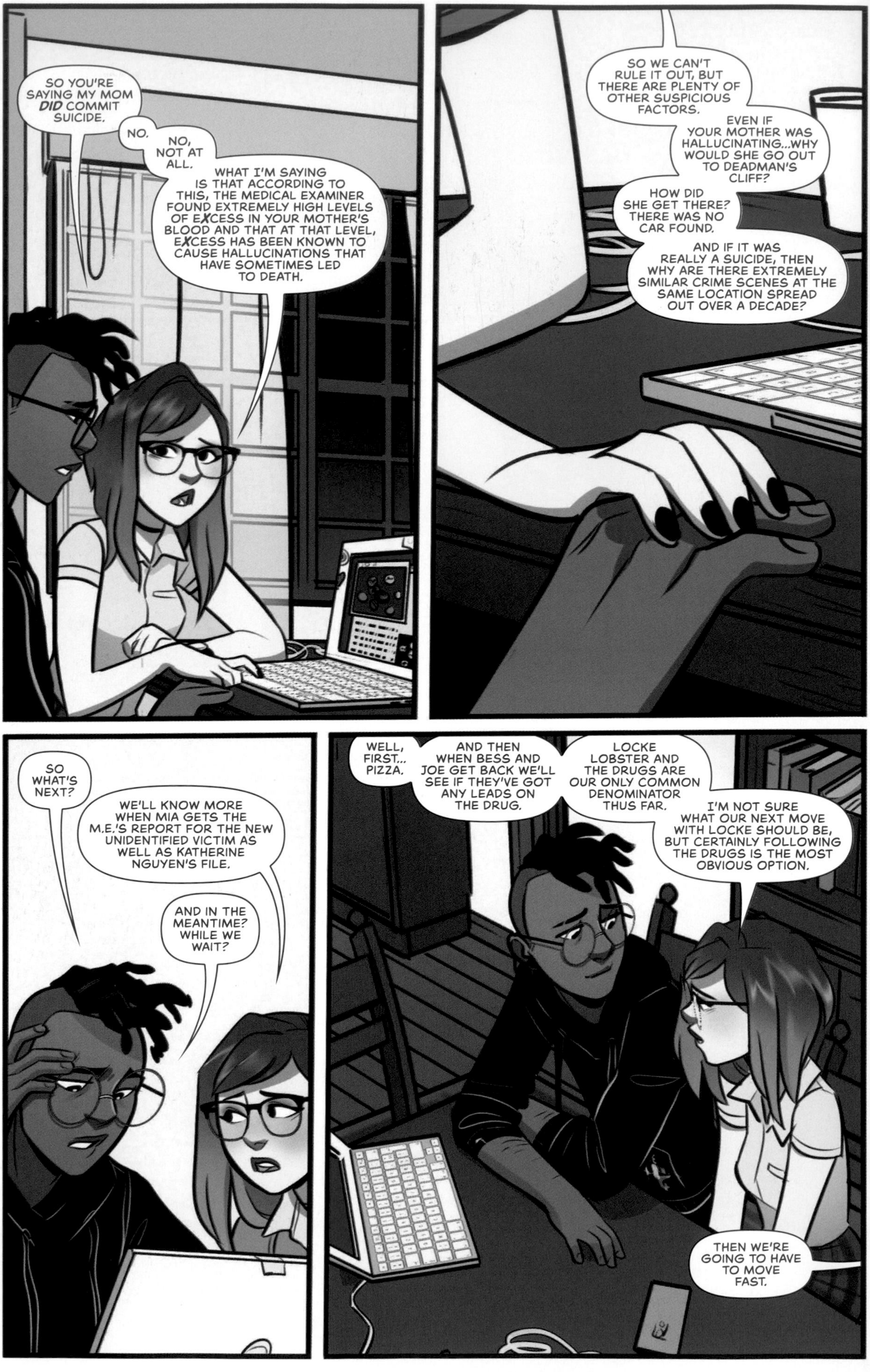
SO YOU'RE SAYING MY MOM *DID* COMMIT SUICIDE.
NO.
NO, NOT AT ALL.
WHAT I'M SAYING IS THAT ACCORDING TO THIS, THE MEDICAL EXAMINER FOUND EXTREMELY HIGH LEVELS OF EXCESS IN YOUR MOTHER'S BLOOD AND THAT AT THAT LEVEL, EXCESS HAS BEEN KNOWN TO CAUSE HALLUCINATIONS THAT HAVE SOMETIMES LED TO DEATH.
SO WE CAN'T RULE IT OUT, BUT THERE ARE PLENTY OF OTHER SUSPICIOUS FACTORS.
EVEN IF YOUR MOTHER WAS HALLUCINATING...WHY WOULD SHE GO OUT TO DEADMAN'S CLIFF?
HOW DID SHE GET THERE? THERE WAS NO CAR FOUND.
AND IF IT WAS REALLY A SUICIDE, THEN WHY ARE THERE EXTREMELY SIMILAR CRIME SCENES AT THE SAME LOCATION SPREAD OUT OVER A DECADE?
SO WHAT'S NEXT?
WE'LL KNOW MORE WHEN MIA GETS THE M.E.'S REPORT FOR THE NEW UNIDENTIFIED VICTIM AS WELL AS KATHERINE NGUYEN'S FILE.
AND IN THE MEANTIME? WHILE WE WAIT?
WELL, FIRST... PIZZA.
AND THEN WHEN BESS AND JOE GET BACK WE'LL SEE IF THEY'VE GOT ANY LEADS ON THE DRUG.
LOCKE LOBSTER AND THE DRUGS ARE OUR ONLY COMMON DENOMINATOR THUS FAR.
I'M NOT SURE WHAT OUR NEXT MOVE WITH LOCKE SHOULD BE, BUT CERTAINLY FOLLOWING THE DRUGS IS THE MOST OBVIOUS OPTION.
THEN WE'RE GOING TO HAVE TO MOVE FAST.

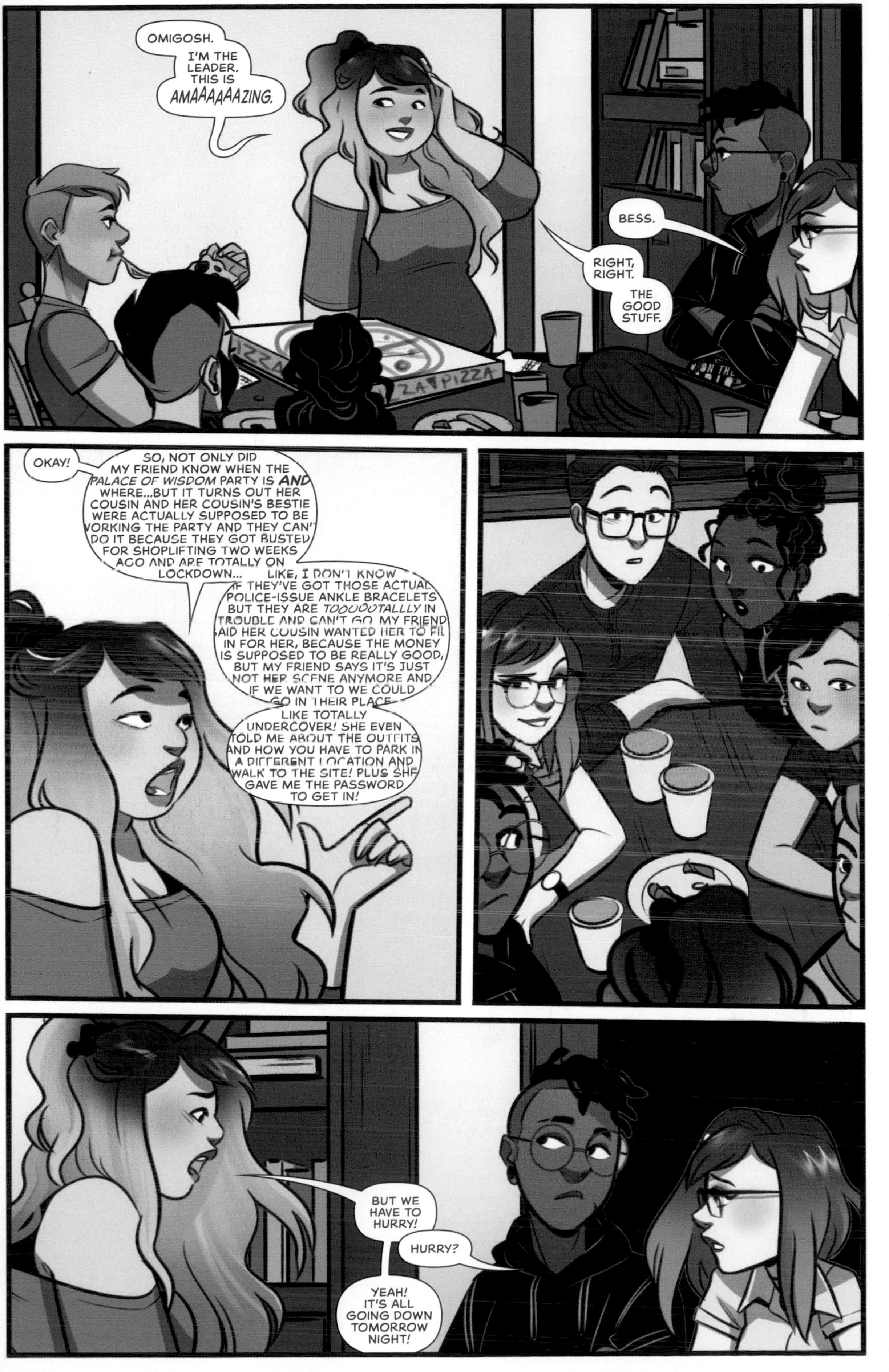

OMIGOSH. I'M THE LEADER. THIS IS AMAAAAAAAZING.
BESS.
RIGHT, RIGHT. THE GOOD STUFF.
PIZZA
OKAY!
SO, NOT ONLY DID MY FRIEND KNOW WHEN THE PALACE OF WISDOM PARTY IS AND WHERE...BUT IT TURNS OUT HER COUSIN AND HER COUSIN'S BESTIE WERE ACTUALLY SUPPOSED TO BE WORKING THE PARTY AND THEY CAN'T DO IT BECAUSE THEY GOT BUSTED FOR SHOPLIFTING TWO WEEKS AGO AND ARE TOTALLY ON LOCKDOWN...
LIKE, I DON'T KNOW IF THEY'VE GOT THOSE ACTUAL POLICE-ISSUE ANKLE BRACELETS BUT THEY ARE TOOOOOTALLLY IN TROUBLE AND CAN'T GO. MY FRIEND SAID HER COUSIN WANTED HER TO FILL IN FOR HER, BECAUSE THE MONEY IS SUPPOSED TO BE REALLY GOOD, BUT MY FRIEND SAYS IT'S JUST NOT HER SCENE ANYMORE AND IF WE WANT TO WE COULD GO IN THEIR PLACE--
LIKE TOTALLY UNDERCOVER! SHE EVEN TOLD ME ABOUT THE OUTFITS AND HOW YOU HAVE TO PARK IN A DIFFERENT LOCATION AND WALK TO THE SITE! PLUS SHE GAVE ME THE PASSWORD TO GET IN!
BUT WE HAVE TO HURRY!
HURRY?
YEAH! IT'S ALL GOING DOWN TOMORROW NIGHT!

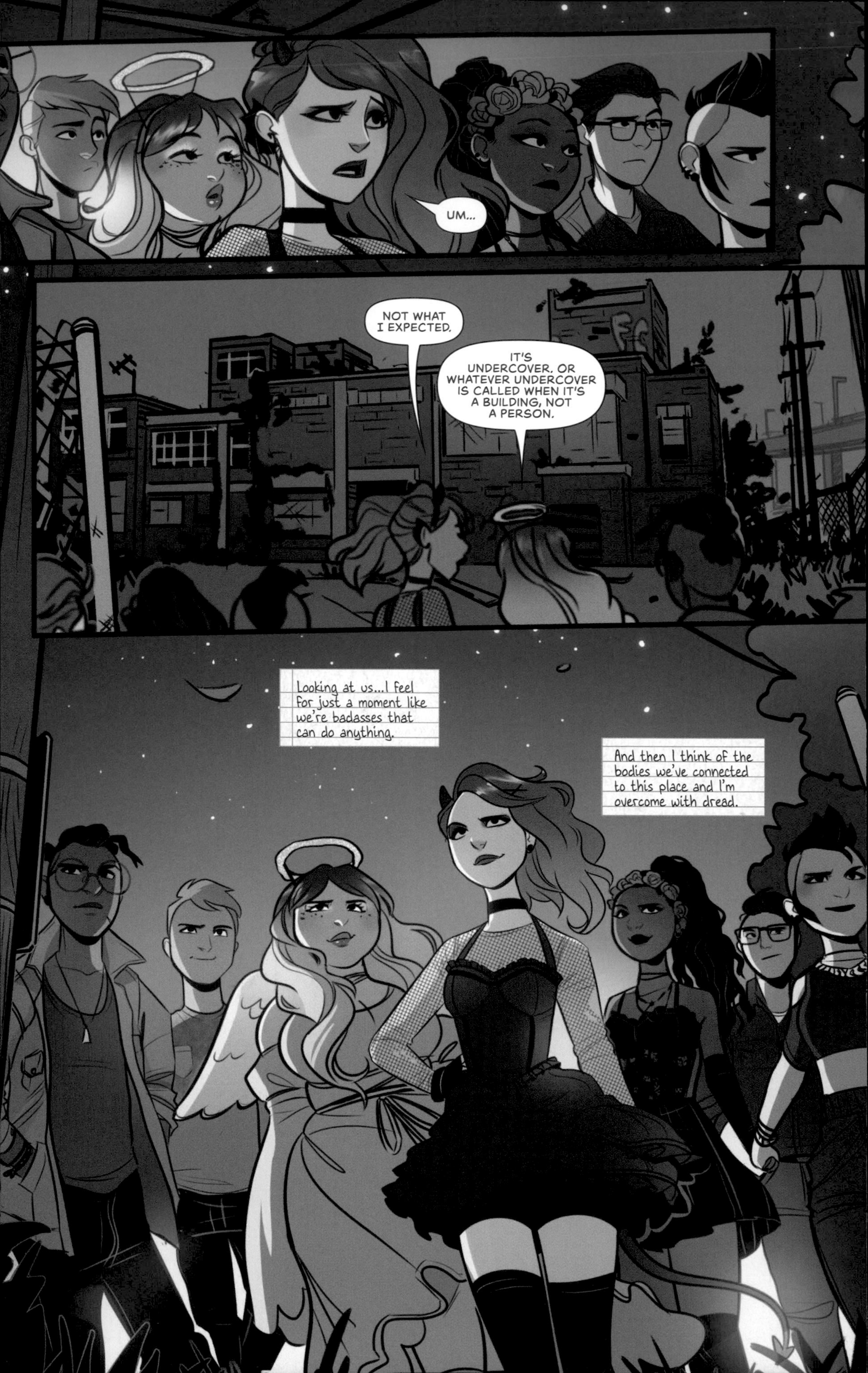
UM...
NOT WHAT I EXPECTED.
IT'S UNDERCOVER. OR WHATEVER UNDERCOVER IS CALLED WHEN IT'S A BUILDING, NOT A PERSON.
Looking at us...I feel for just a moment like we're badasses that can do anything.
And then I think of the bodies we've connected to this place and I'm overcome with dread.

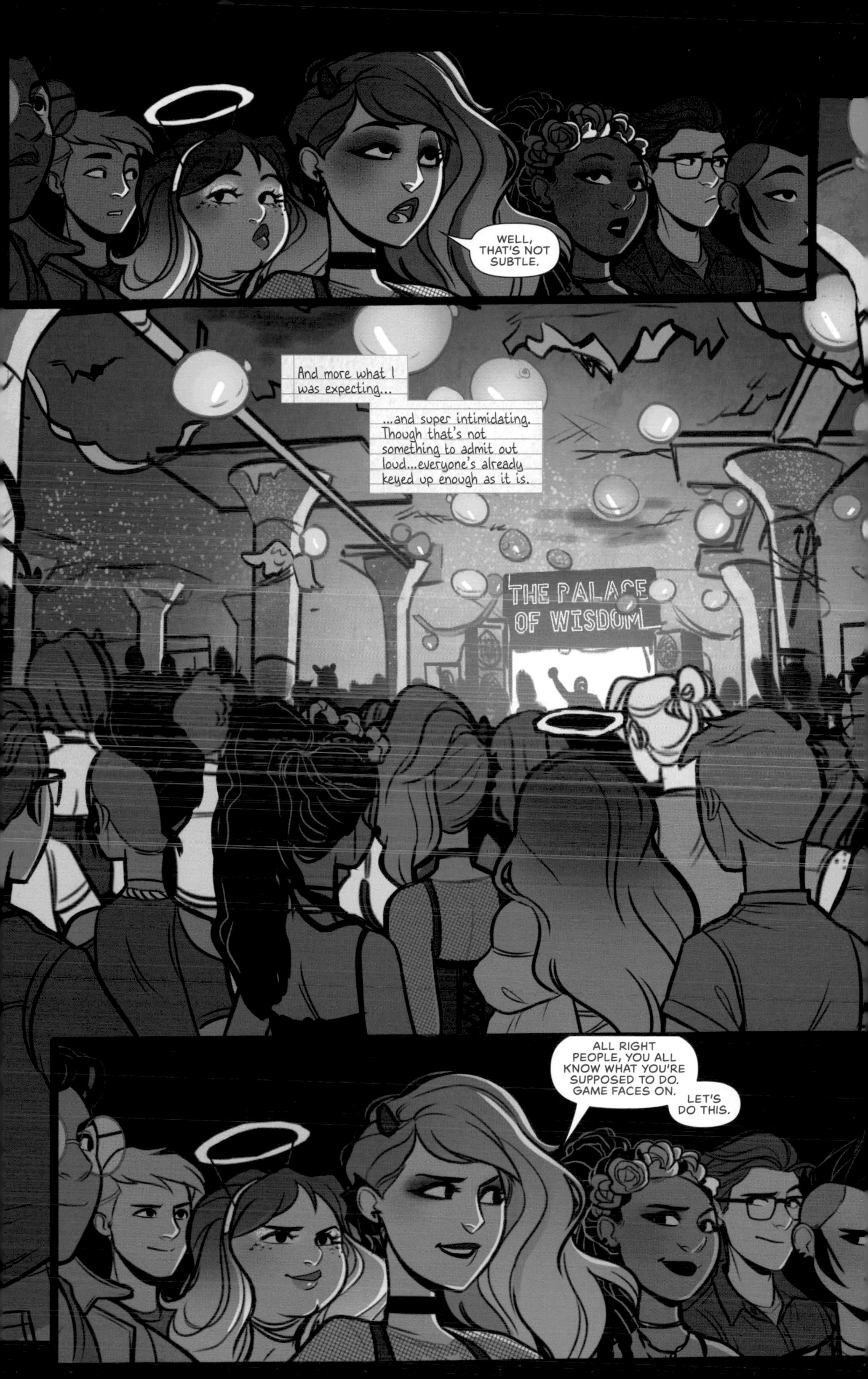
WELL, THAT'S NOT SUBTLE.
And more what I was expecting...
...and super intimidating. Though that's not something to admit out loud...everyone's already keyed up enough as it is.
THE PALACE OF WISDOM
ALL RIGHT PEOPLE, YOU ALL KNOW WHAT YOU'RE SUPPOSED TO DO. GAME FACES ON.
LET'S DO THIS.

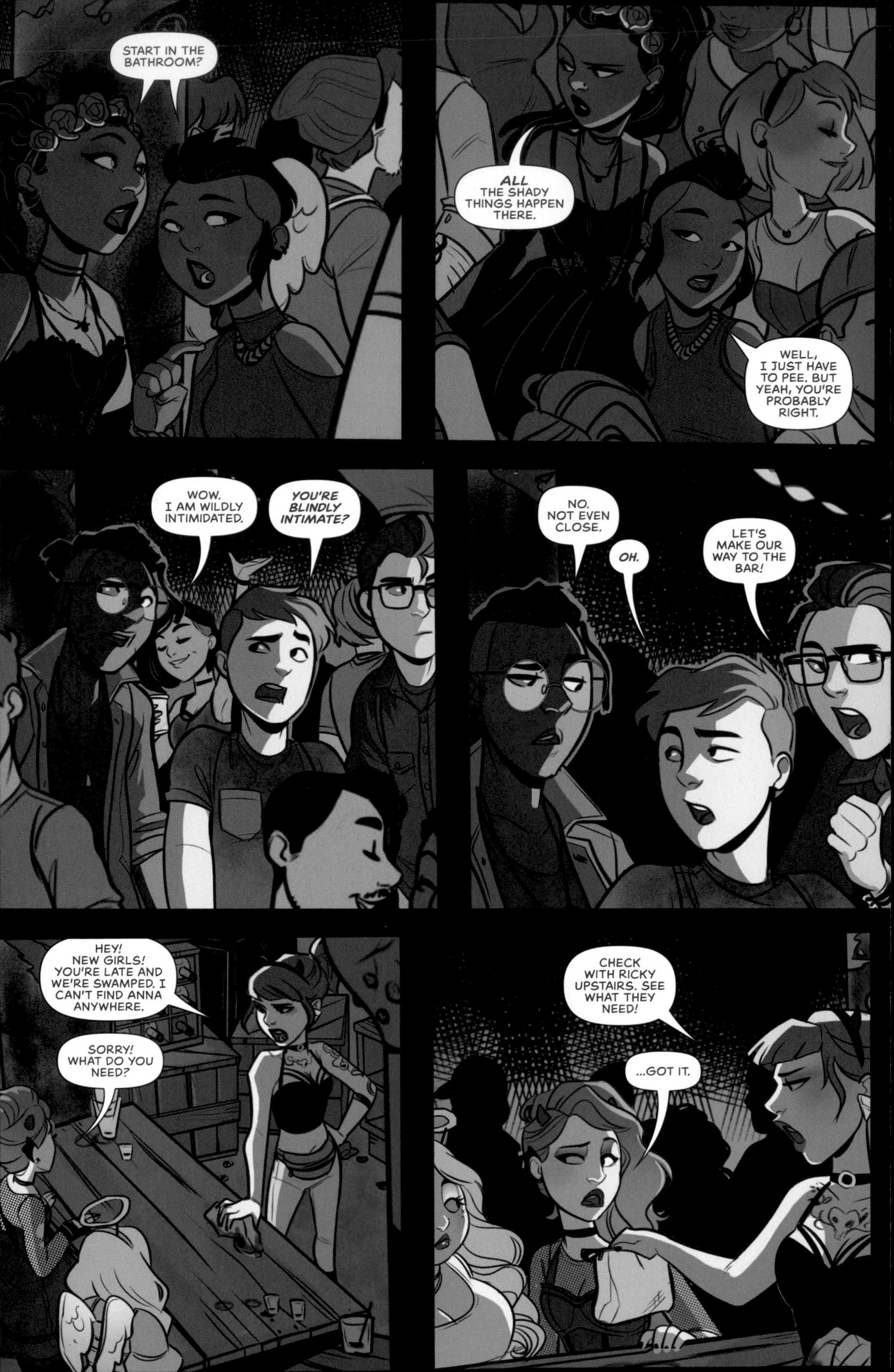
START IN THE BATHROOM?
ALL THE SHADY THINGS HAPPEN THERE.
WELL, I JUST HAVE TO PEE. BUT YEAH, YOU'RE PROBABLY RIGHT.
WOW. I AM WILDLY INTIMIDATED.
YOU'RE BLINDLY INTIMATE?
NO. NOT EVEN CLOSE.
OH.
LET'S MAKE OUR WAY TO THE BAR!
HEY! NEW GIRLS! YOU'RE LATE AND WE'RE SWAMPED. I CAN'T FIND ANNA ANYWHERE.
SORRY! WHAT DO YOU NEED?
CHECK WITH RICKY UPSTAIRS. SEE WHAT THEY NEED!
...GOT IT.

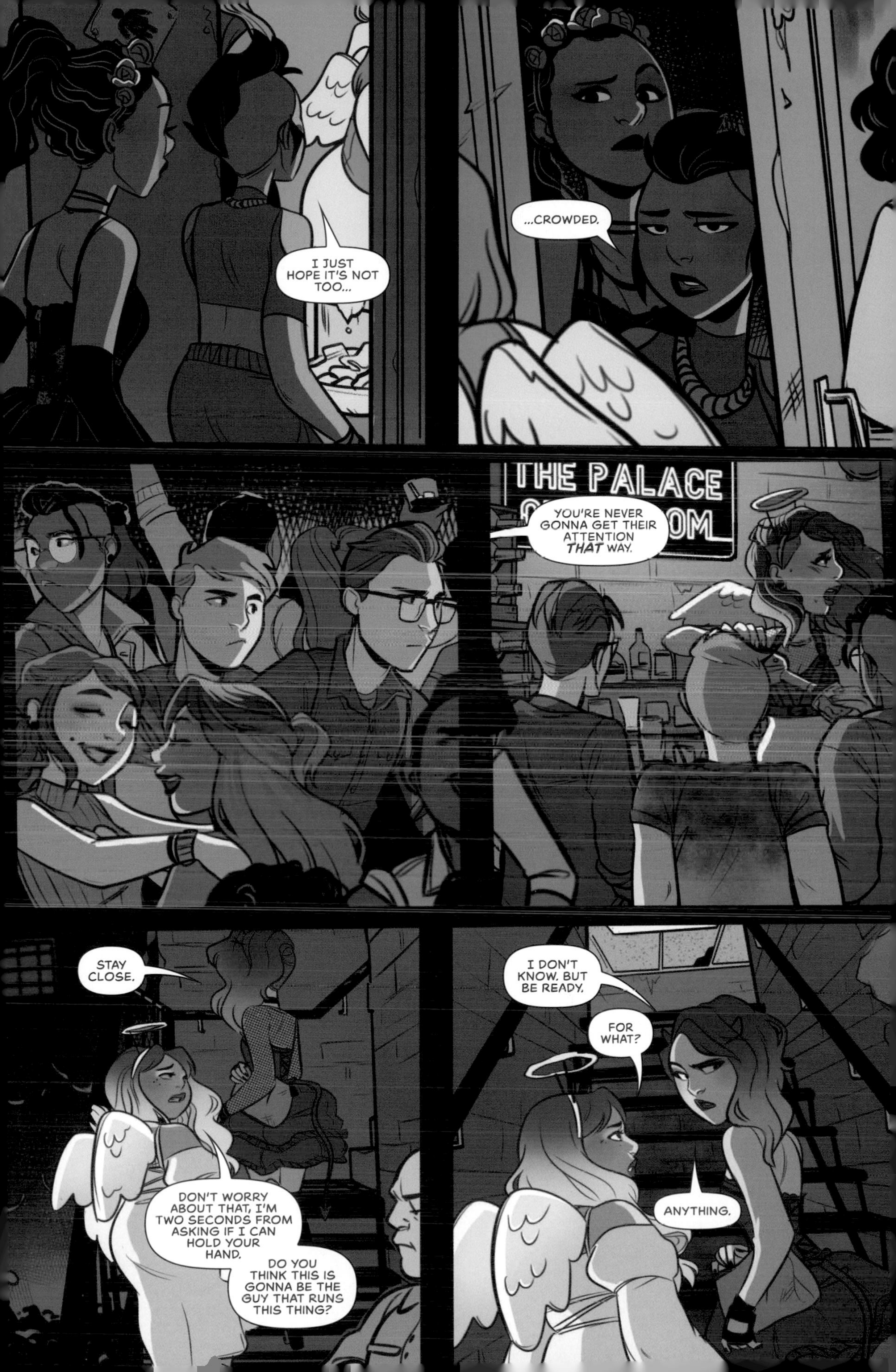
I JUST HOPE IT'S NOT TOO...
...CROWDED.
THE PALACE
OM
YOU'RE NEVER GONNA GET THEIR ATTENTION THAT WAY.
STAY CLOSE.
DON'T WORRY ABOUT THAT, I'M TWO SECONDS FROM ASKING IF I CAN HOLD YOUR HAND.
DO YOU THINK THIS IS GONNA BE THE GUY THAT RUNS THIS THING?
I DON'T KNOW. BUT BE READY.
FOR WHAT?
ANYTHING.

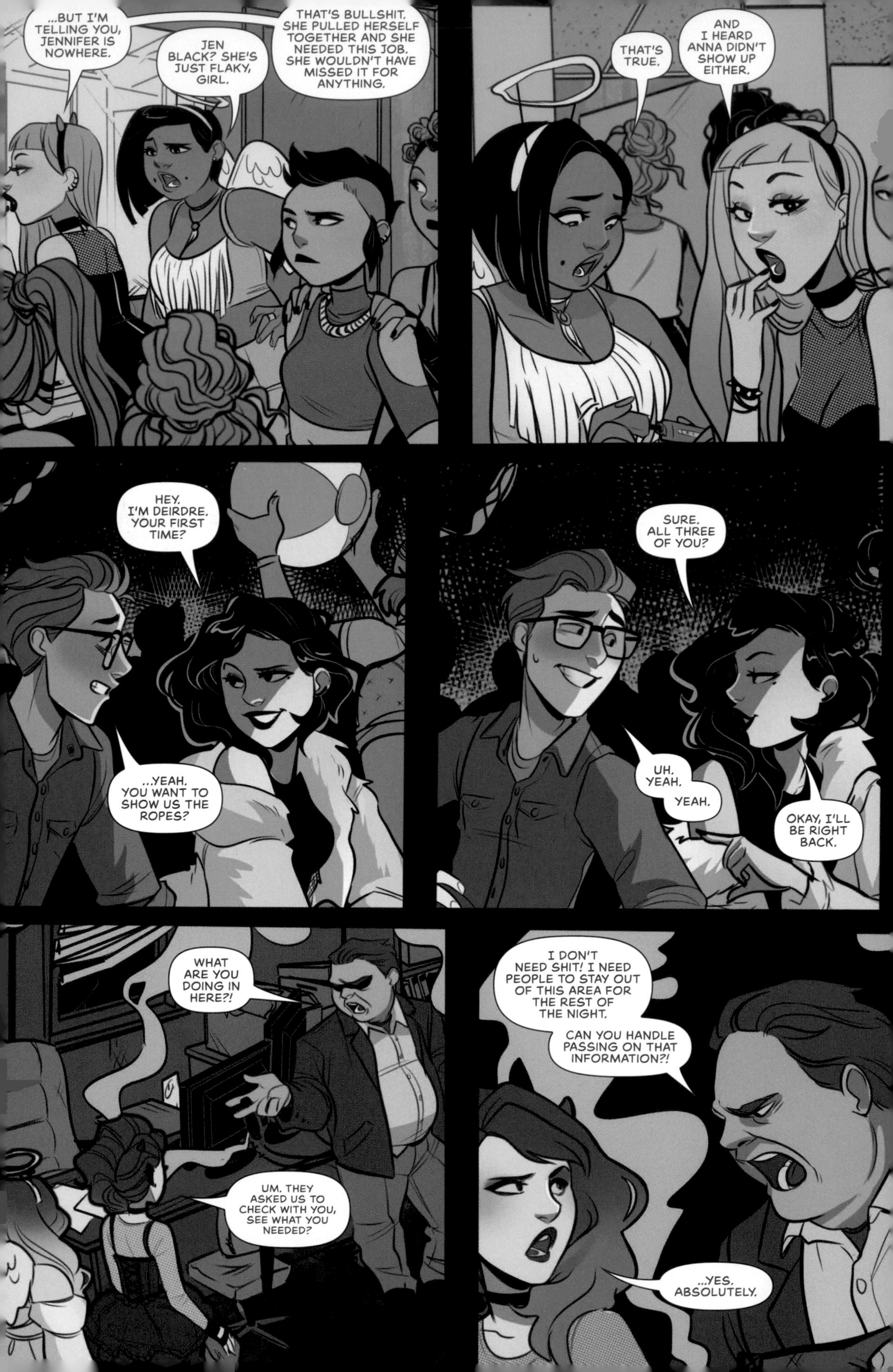
...BUT I'M TELLING YOU, JENNIFER IS NOWHERE.
JEN BLACK? SHE'S JUST FLAKY, GIRL.
THAT'S BULLSHIT. SHE PULLED HERSELF TOGETHER AND SHE NEEDED THIS JOB. SHE WOULDN'T HAVE MISSED IT FOR ANYTHING.
THAT'S TRUE.
AND I HEARD ANNA DIDN'T SHOW UP EITHER.
HEY, I'M DEIRDRE. YOUR FIRST TIME?
...YEAH. YOU WANT TO SHOW US THE ROPES?
SURE. ALL THREE OF YOU?
UH, YEAH.
YEAH.
OKAY, I'LL BE RIGHT BACK.
WHAT ARE YOU DOING IN HERE?!
UM, THEY ASKED US TO CHECK WITH YOU, SEE WHAT YOU NEEDED?
I DON'T NEED SHIT! I NEED PEOPLE TO STAY OUT OF THIS AREA FOR THE REST OF THE NIGHT.
CAN YOU HANDLE PASSING ON THAT INFORMATION?!
...YES. ABSOLUTELY.

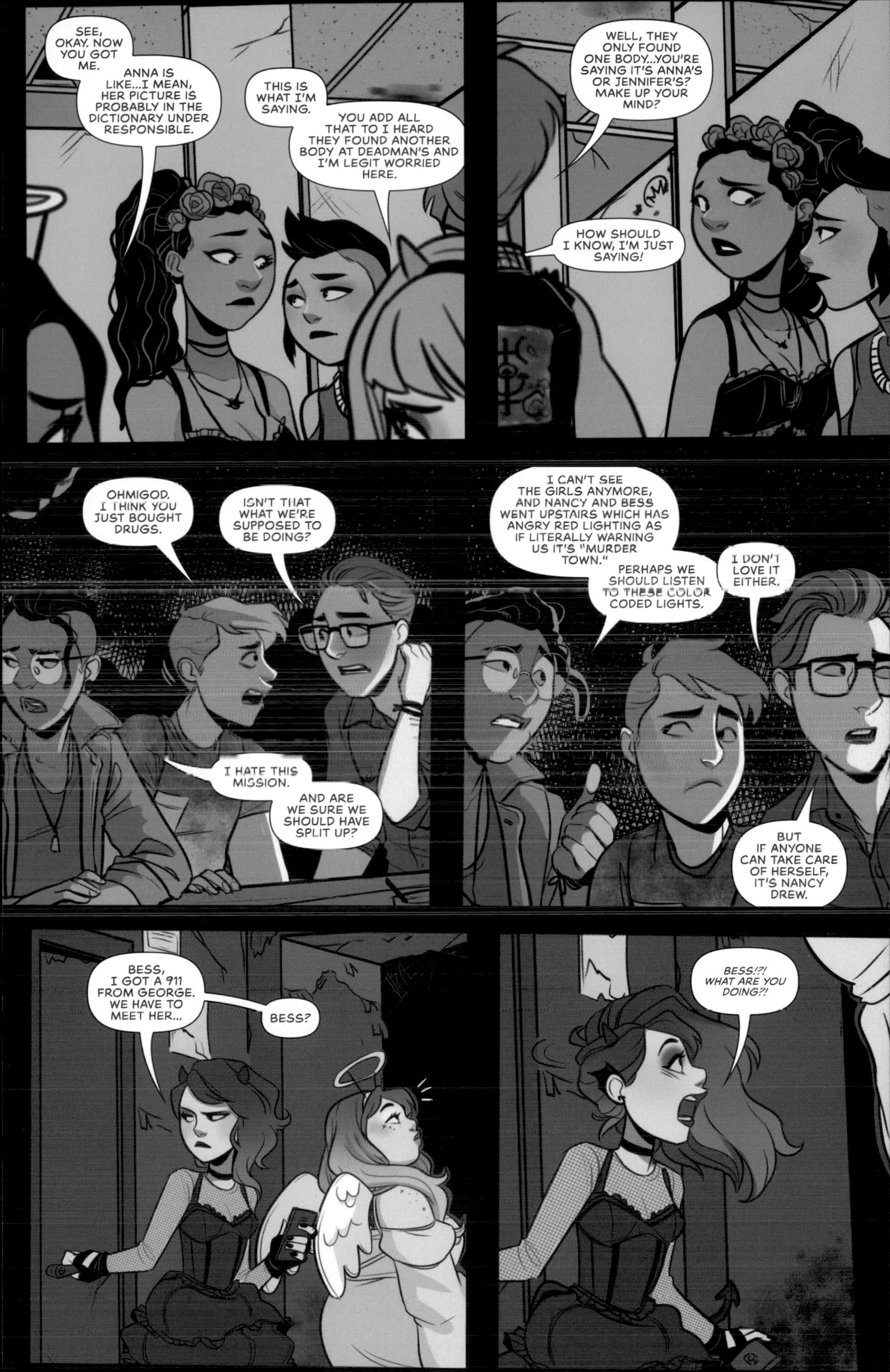
SEE, OKAY. NOW YOU GOT ME.
ANNA IS LIKE...I MEAN, HER PICTURE IS PROBABLY IN THE DICTIONARY UNDER RESPONSIBLE.
THIS IS WHAT I'M SAYING.
YOU ADD ALL THAT TO I HEARD THEY FOUND ANOTHER BODY AT DEADMAN'S AND I'M LEGIT WORRIED HERE.
WELL, THEY ONLY FOUND ONE BODY...YOU'RE SAYING IT'S ANNA'S OR JENNIFER'S? MAKE UP YOUR MIND?
HOW SHOULD I KNOW, I'M JUST SAYING!
OHMIGOD. I THINK YOU JUST BOUGHT DRUGS.
ISN'T THAT WHAT WE'RE SUPPOSED TO BE DOING?
I HATE THIS MISSION.
AND ARE WE SURE WE SHOULD HAVE SPLIT UP?
I CAN'T SEE THE GIRLS ANYMORE, AND NANCY AND BESS WENT UPSTAIRS WHICH HAS ANGRY RED LIGHTING AS IF LITERALLY WARNING US IT'S "MURDER TOWN."
PERHAPS WE SHOULD LISTEN TO THESE COLOR CODED LIGHTS.
I DON'T LOVE IT EITHER.
BUT IF ANYONE CAN TAKE CARE OF HERSELF, IT'S NANCY DREW.
BESS, I GOT A 911 FROM GEORGE. WE HAVE TO MEET HER...
BESS?
BESS!?! WHAT ARE YOU DOING?!

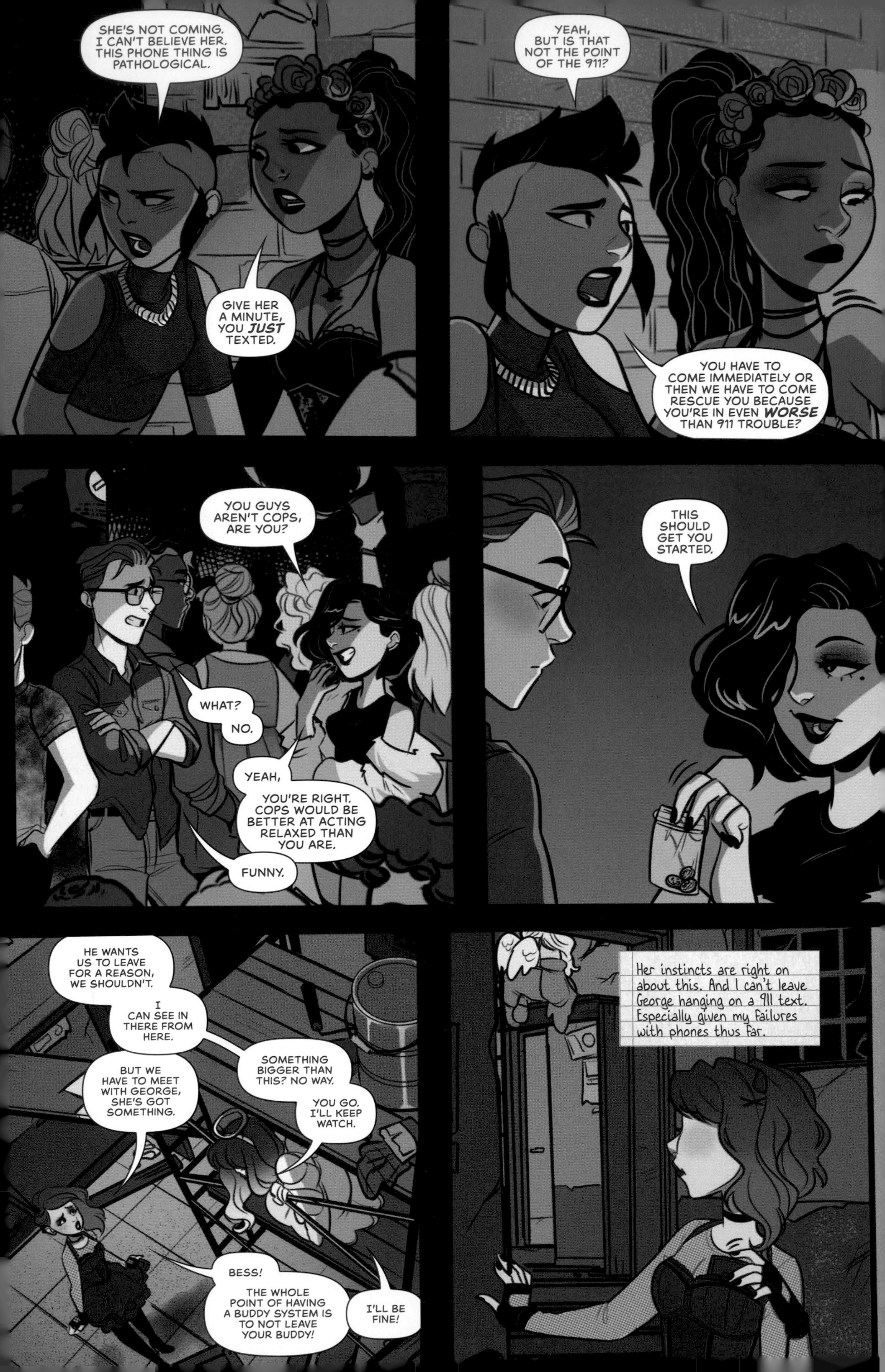

SHE'S NOT COMING. I CAN'T BELIEVE HER. THIS PHONE THING IS PATHOLOGICAL.
GIVE HER A MINUTE, YOU JUST TEXTED.
YEAH, BUT IS THAT NOT THE POINT OF THE 911?
YOU HAVE TO COME IMMEDIATELY OR THEN WE HAVE TO COME RESCUE YOU BECAUSE YOU'RE IN EVEN WORSE THAN 911 TROUBLE?
YOU GUYS AREN'T COPS, ARE YOU?
WHAT?
NO.
YEAH,
YOU'RE RIGHT. COPS WOULD BE BETTER AT ACTING RELAXED THAN YOU ARE.
FUNNY.
THIS SHOULD GET YOU STARTED.
HE WANTS US TO LEAVE FOR A REASON, WE SHOULDN'T.
I CAN SEE IN THERE FROM HERE.
BUT WE HAVE TO MEET WITH GEORGE, SHE'S GOT SOMETHING.
SOMETHING BIGGER THAN THIS? NO WAY.
YOU GO. I'LL KEEP WATCH.
BESS!
THE WHOLE POINT OF HAVING A BUDDY SYSTEM IS TO NOT LEAVE YOUR BUDDY!
I'LL BE FINE!
Her instincts are right on about this. And I can't leave George hanging on a 911 text. Especially given my failures with phones thus far.

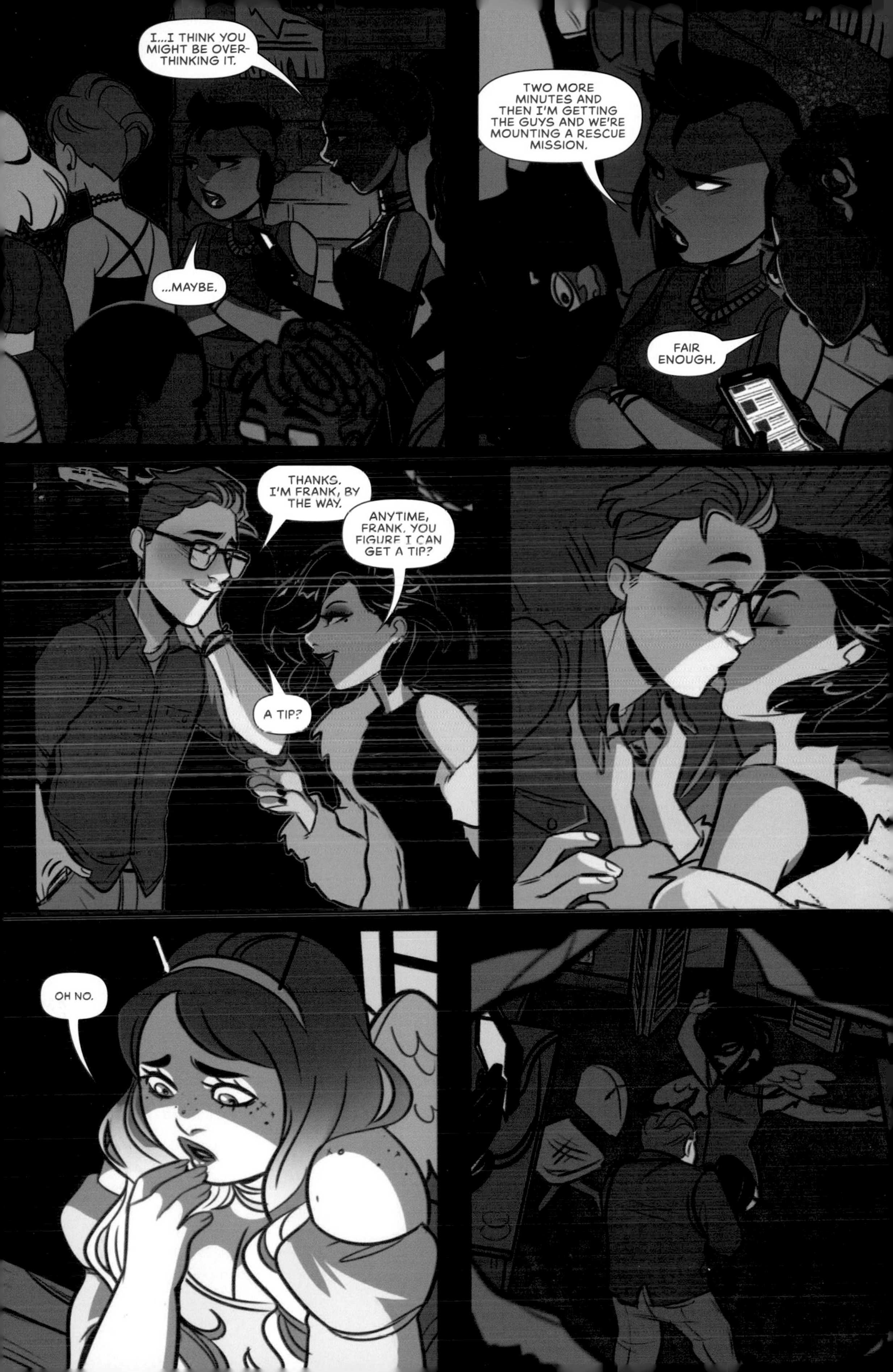
I...I THINK YOU MIGHT BE OVER-THINKING IT.
...MAYBE.
TWO MORE MINUTES AND THEN I'M GETTING THE GUYS AND WE'RE MOUNTING A RESCUE MISSION.
FAIR ENOUGH.
THANKS. I'M FRANK, BY THE WAY.
ANYTIME, FRANK. YOU FIGURE I CAN GET A TIP?
A TIP?
OH NO.

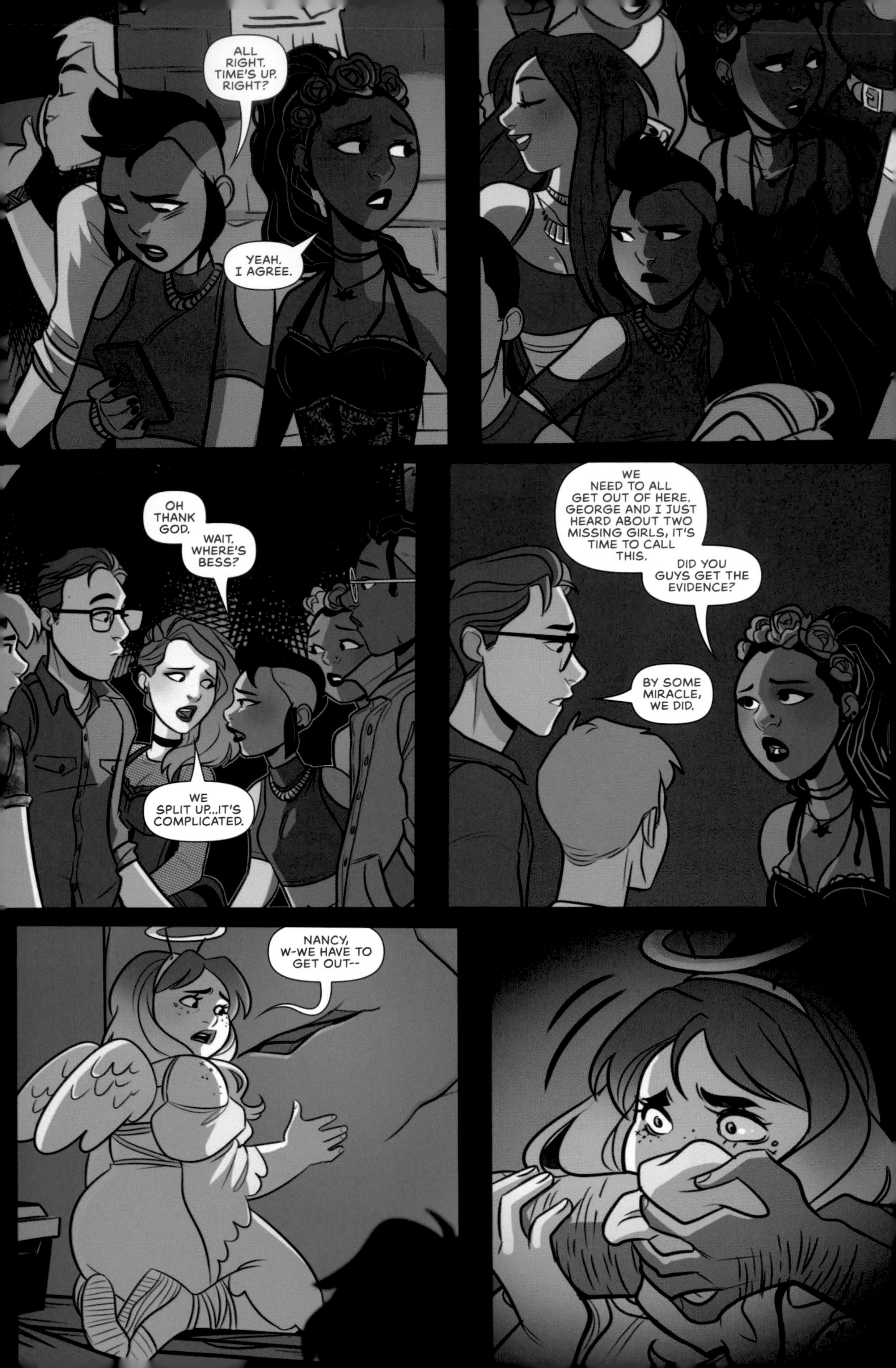
ALL RIGHT. TIME'S UP. RIGHT?
YEAH, I AGREE.
OH THANK GOD.
WAIT. WHERE'S BESS?
WE SPLIT UP...IT'S COMPLICATED.
WE NEED TO ALL GET OUT OF HERE. GEORGE AND I JUST HEARD ABOUT TWO MISSING GIRLS, IT'S TIME TO CALL THIS.
DID YOU GUYS GET THE EVIDENCE?
BY SOME MIRACLE, WE DID.
NANCY, W-WE HAVE TO GET OUT--

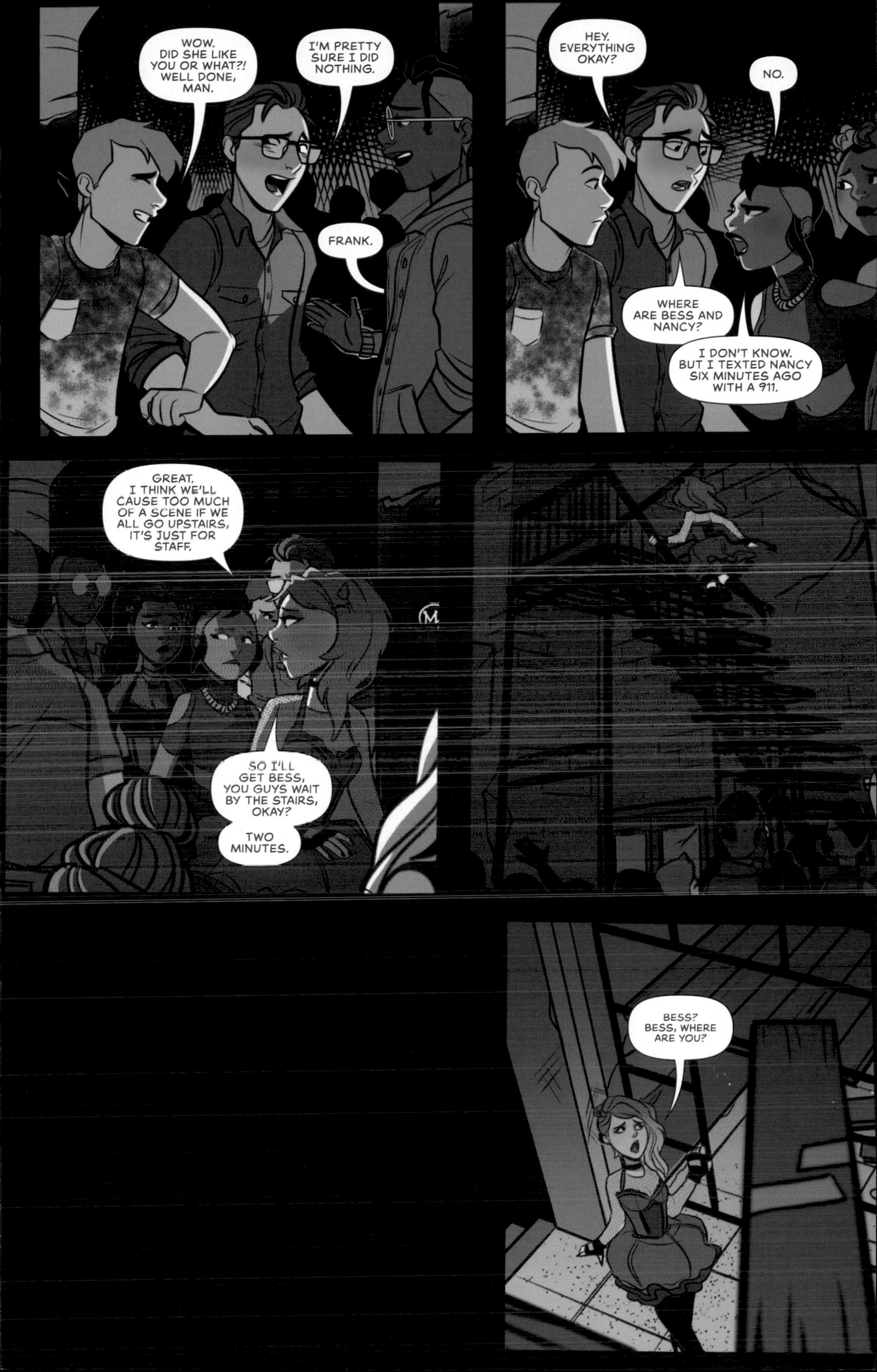
WOW. DID SHE LIKE YOU OR WHAT?! WELL DONE, MAN.
I'M PRETTY SURE I DID NOTHING.
FRANK.
HEY. EVERYTHING OKAY?
NO.
WHERE ARE BESS AND NANCY?
I DON'T KNOW. BUT I TEXTED NANCY SIX MINUTES AGO WITH A 911.
GREAT. I THINK WE'LL CAUSE TOO MUCH OF A SCENE IF WE ALL GO UPSTAIRS, IT'S JUST FOR STAFF.
SO I'LL GET BESS, YOU GUYS WAIT BY THE STAIRS, OKAY?
TWO MINUTES.
BESS? BESS, WHERE ARE YOU?

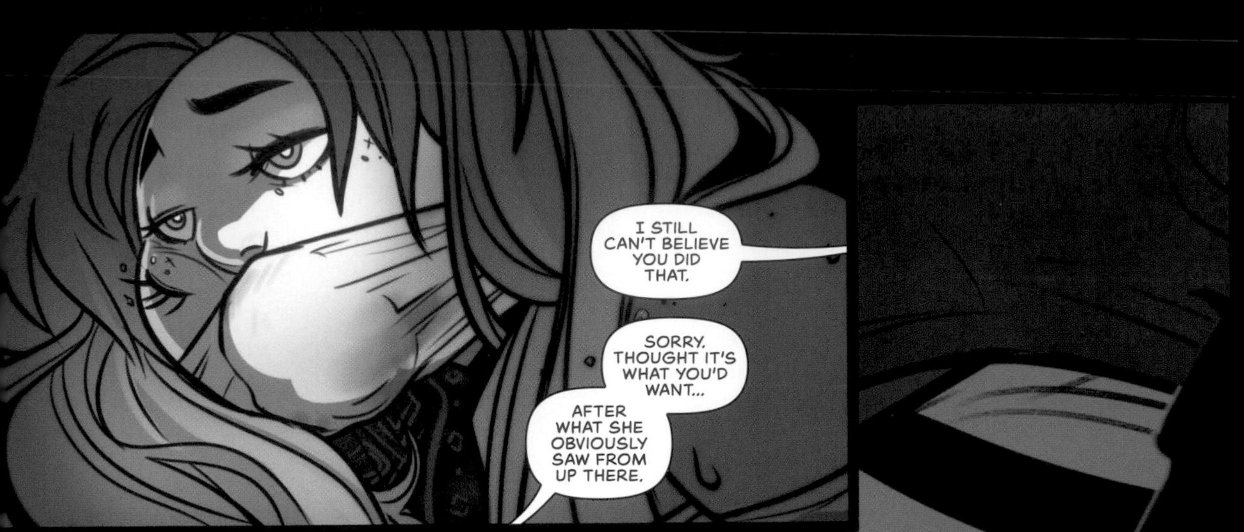
I STILL CAN'T BELIEVE YOU DID THAT.
SORRY. THOUGHT IT'S WHAT YOU'D WANT...
AFTER WHAT SHE OBVIOUSLY SAW FROM UP THERE.

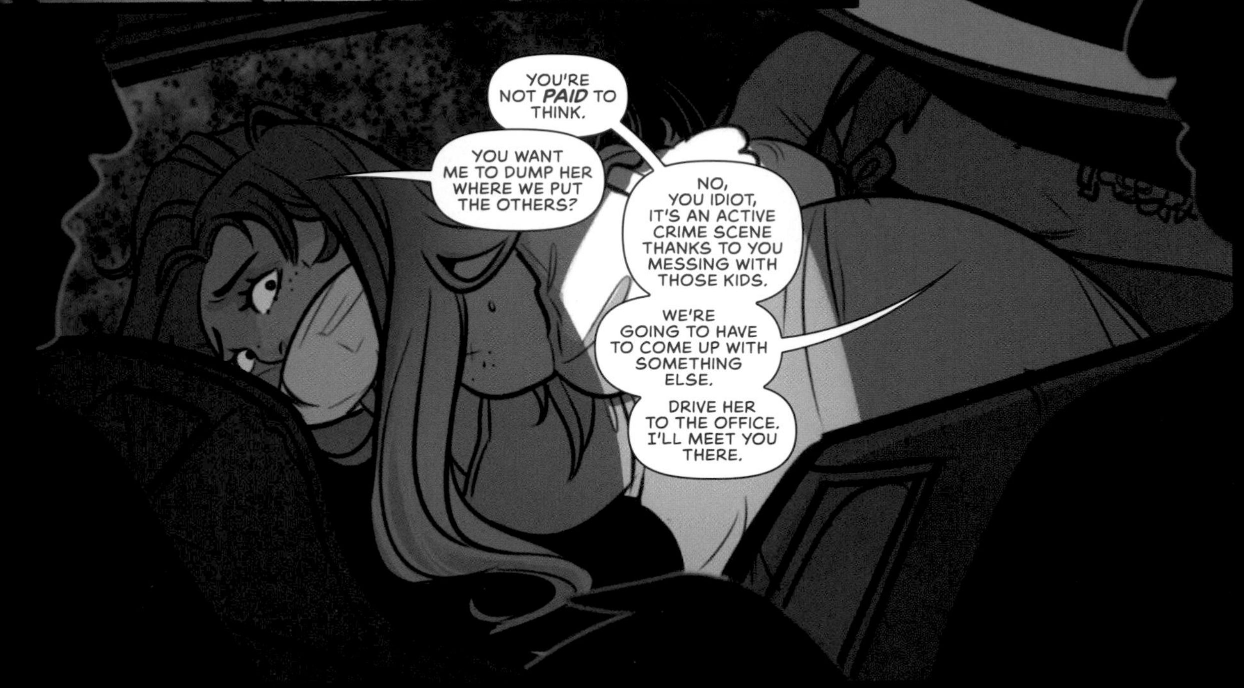
YOU'RE NOT PAID TO THINK.
YOU WANT ME TO DUMP HER WHERE WE PUT THE OTHERS?
NO, YOU IDIOT, IT'S AN ACTIVE CRIME SCENE THANKS TO YOU MESSING WITH THOSE KIDS.
WE'RE GOING TO HAVE TO COME UP WITH SOMETHING ELSE.
DRIVE HER TO THE OFFICE. I'LL MEET YOU THERE.

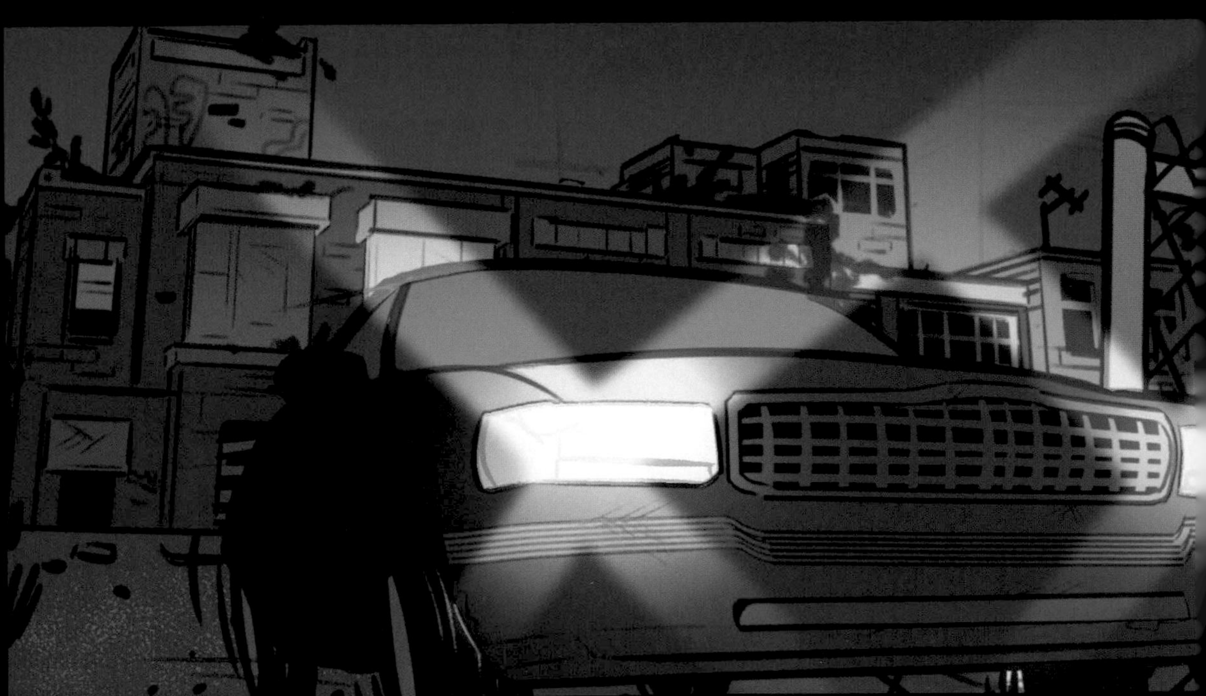

I always know what to do. But now it's like there's a big, blank spot in my brain and it's filling up with all the crap I usually repress...it's threatening to spill over.

chapTeR five

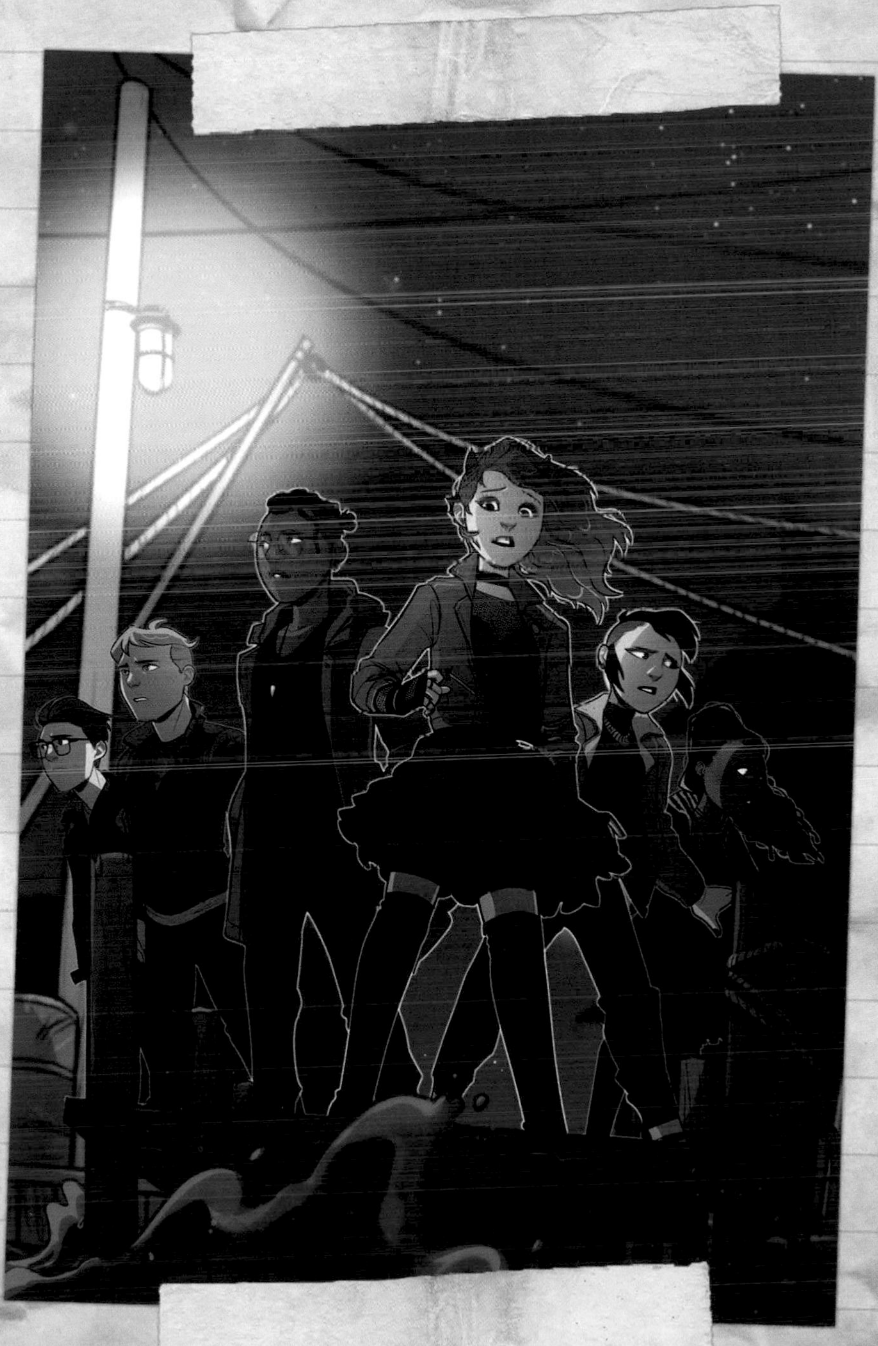

Issue 5
Cover art by Tula Lotay

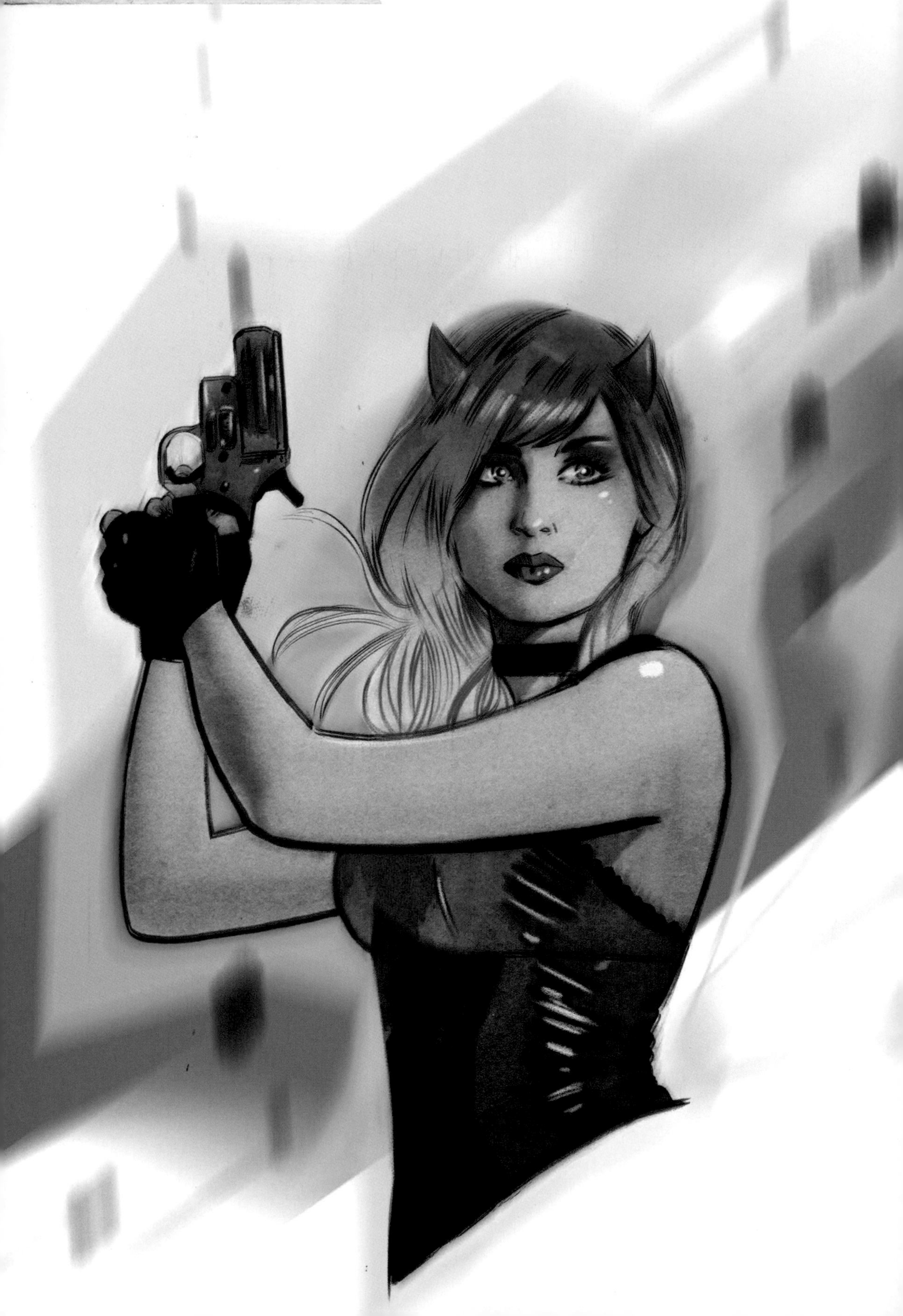

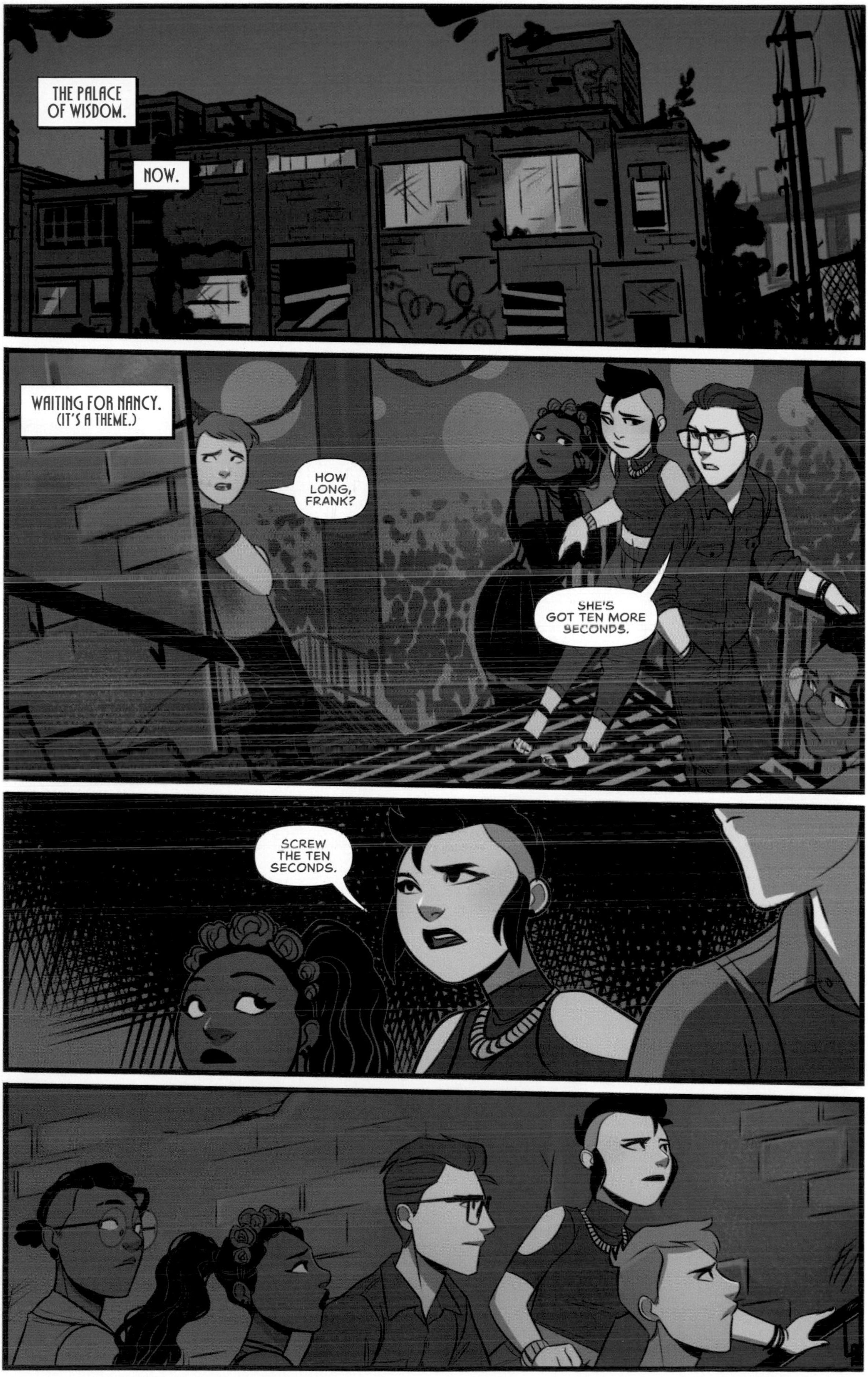
THE PALACE OF WISDOM.
NOW.
WAITING FOR NANCY. (IT'S A THEME.)
HOW LONG, FRANK?
SHE'S GOT TEN MORE SECONDS.
SCREW THE TEN SECONDS.

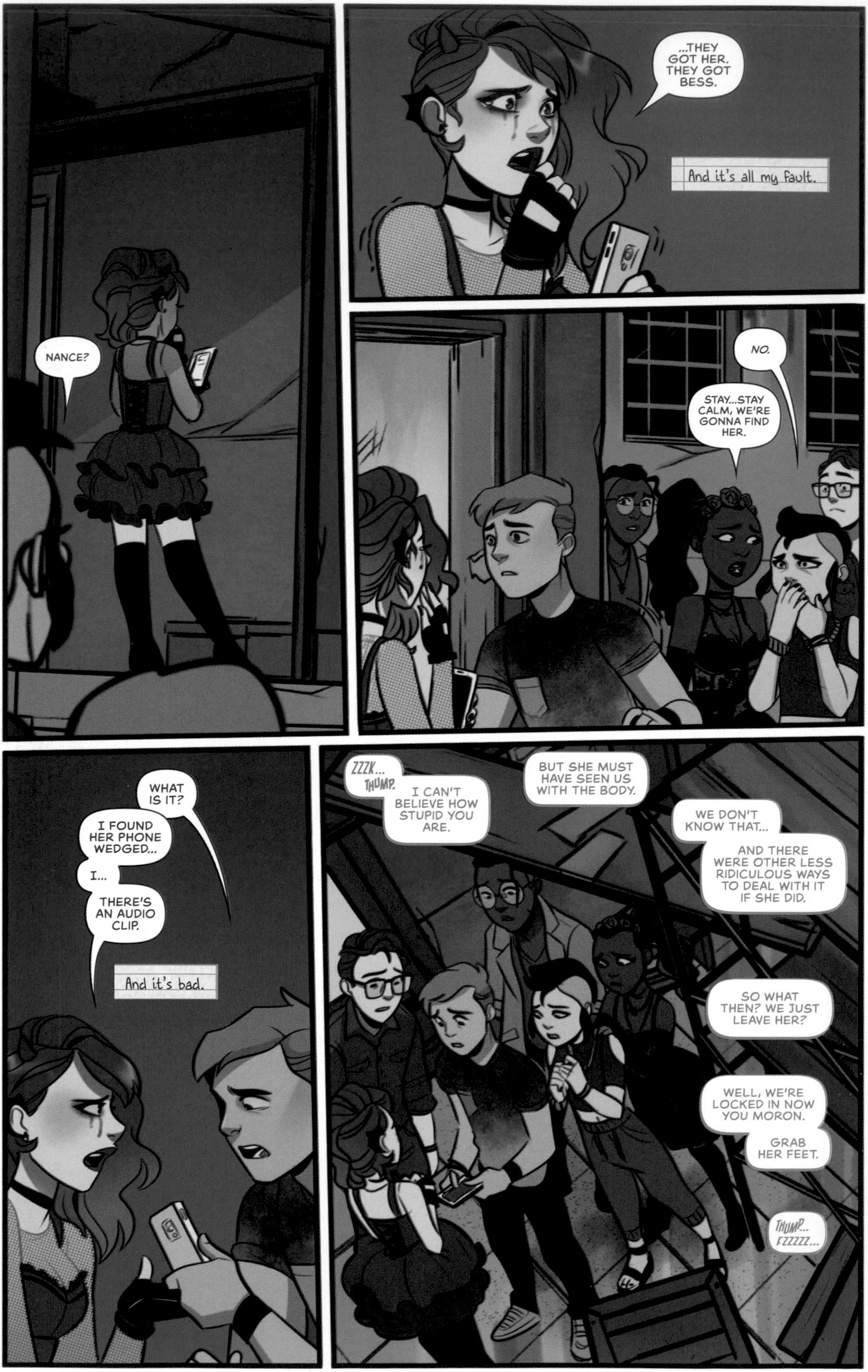
NANCE?
...THEY GOT HER. THEY GOT BESS.
And it's all my fault.
NO.
STAY...STAY CALM, WE'RE GONNA FIND HER.
WHAT IS IT?
I FOUND HER PHONE WEDGED...
I...
THERE'S AN AUDIO CLIP.
And it's bad.
ZZZK...
THUMP.
I CAN'T BELIEVE HOW STUPID YOU ARE.
BUT SHE MUST HAVE SEEN US WITH THE BODY.
WE DON'T KNOW THAT...
AND THERE WERE OTHER LESS RIDICULOUS WAYS TO DEAL WITH IT IF SHE DID.
SO WHAT THEN? WE JUST LEAVE HER?
WELL, WE'RE LOCKED IN NOW YOU MORON.
GRAB HER FEET.
THUMP...
FZZZZZ...

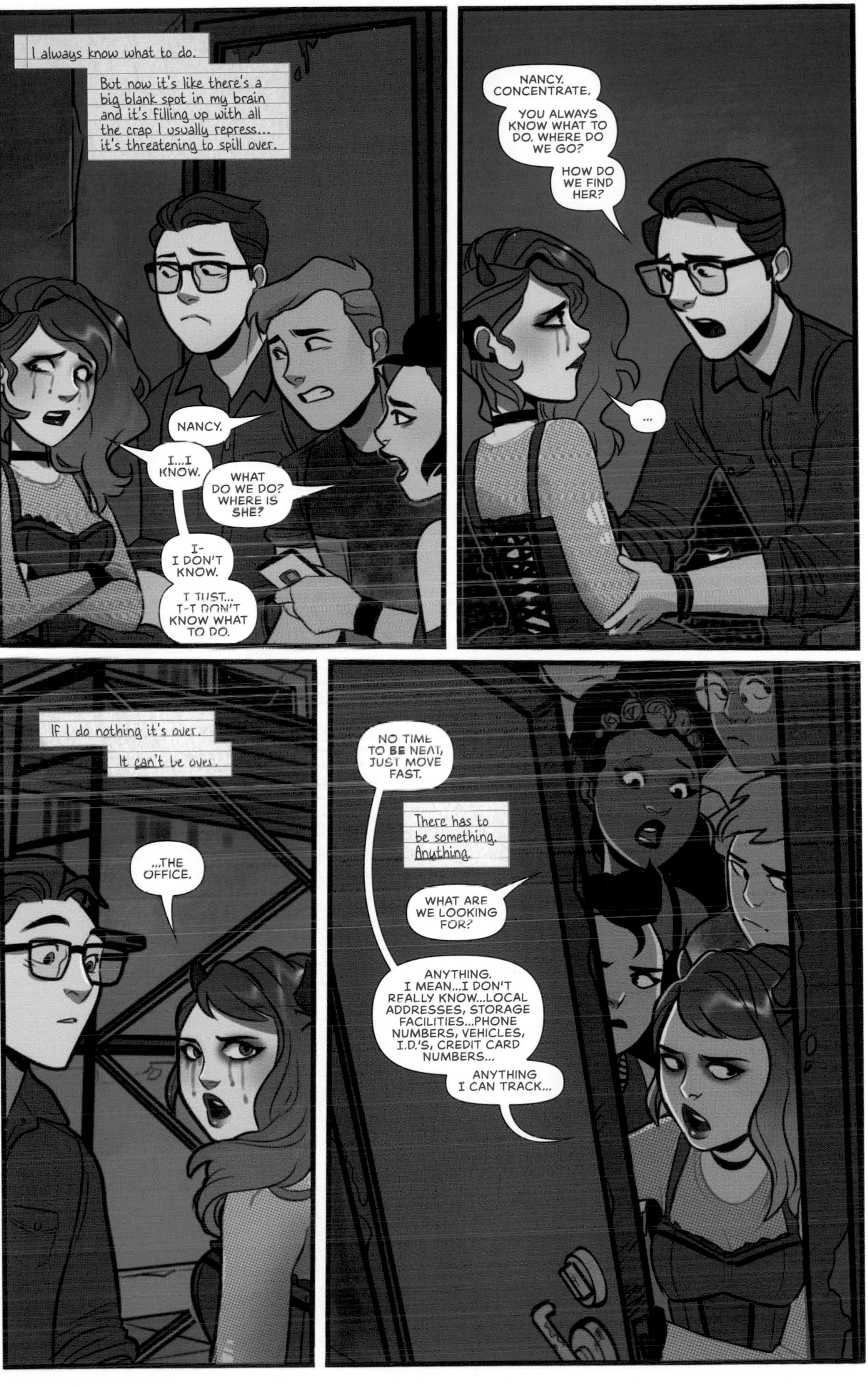
I always know what to do.
But now it's like there's a big blank spot in my brain and it's filling up with all the crap I usually repress... it's threatening to spill over.
NANCY.
I...I KNOW.
WHAT DO WE DO? WHERE IS SHE?
I- I DON'T KNOW.
I JUST... I-I DON'T KNOW WHAT TO DO.
NANCY. CONCENTRATE.
YOU ALWAYS KNOW WHAT TO DO. WHERE DO WE GO?
HOW DO WE FIND HER?
...
If I do nothing it's over.
It can't be over.
...THE OFFICE.
NO TIME TO BE NEAT, JUST MOVE FAST.
There has to be something. Anything.
WHAT ARE WE LOOKING FOR?
ANYTHING. I MEAN...I DON'T REALLY KNOW...LOCAL ADDRESSES, STORAGE FACILITIES...PHONE NUMBERS, VEHICLES, I.D.'S, CREDIT CARD NUMBERS...
ANYTHING I CAN TRACK...

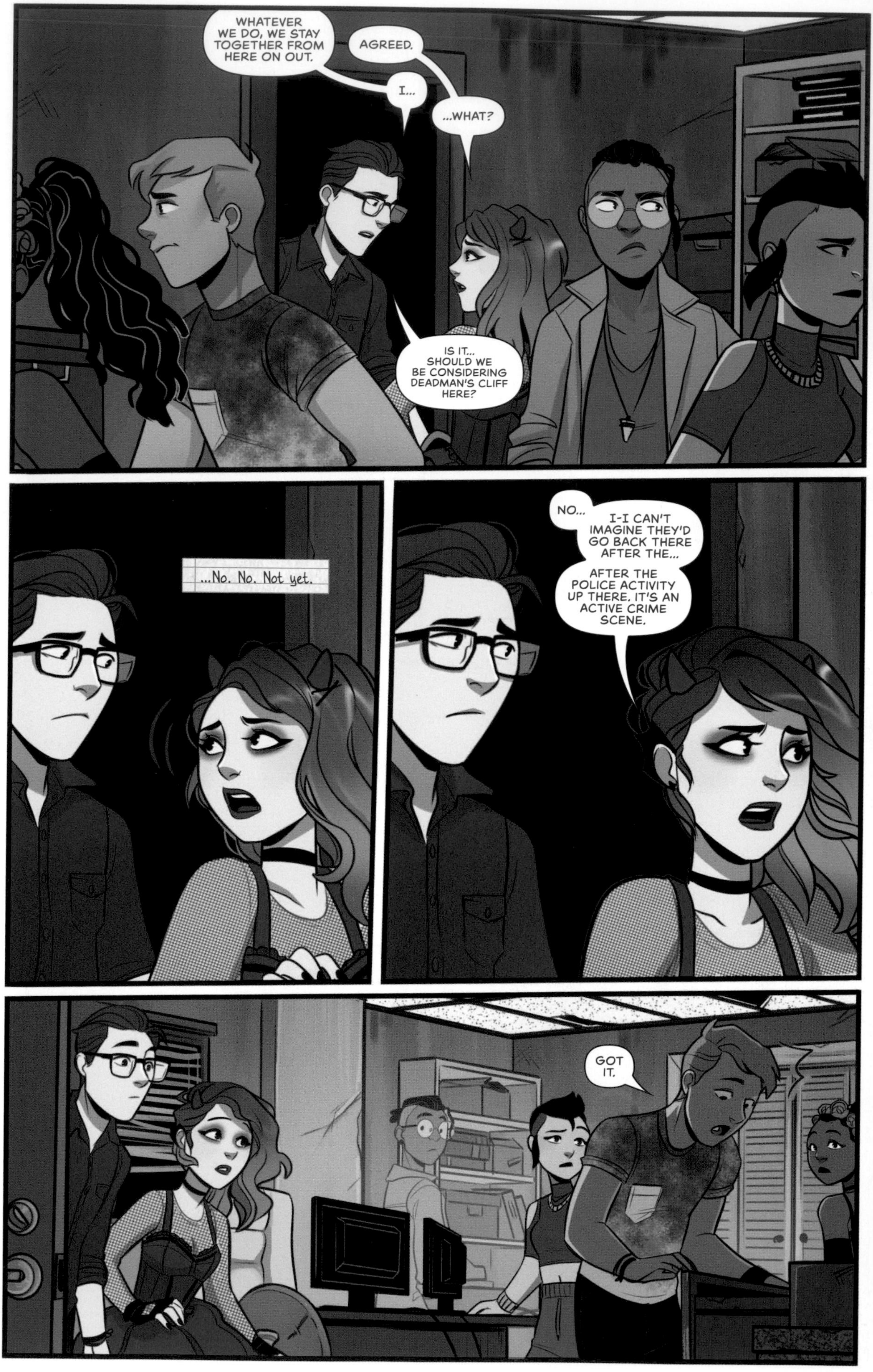
WHATEVER WE DO, WE STAY TOGETHER FROM HERE ON OUT.
AGREED.
I...
...WHAT?
IS IT... SHOULD WE BE CONSIDERING DEADMAN'S CLIFF HERE?
...No. No. Not yet.
NO...
I-I CAN'T IMAGINE THEY'D GO BACK THERE AFTER THE...
AFTER THE POLICE ACTIVITY UP THERE. IT'S AN ACTIVE CRIME SCENE.
GOT IT.

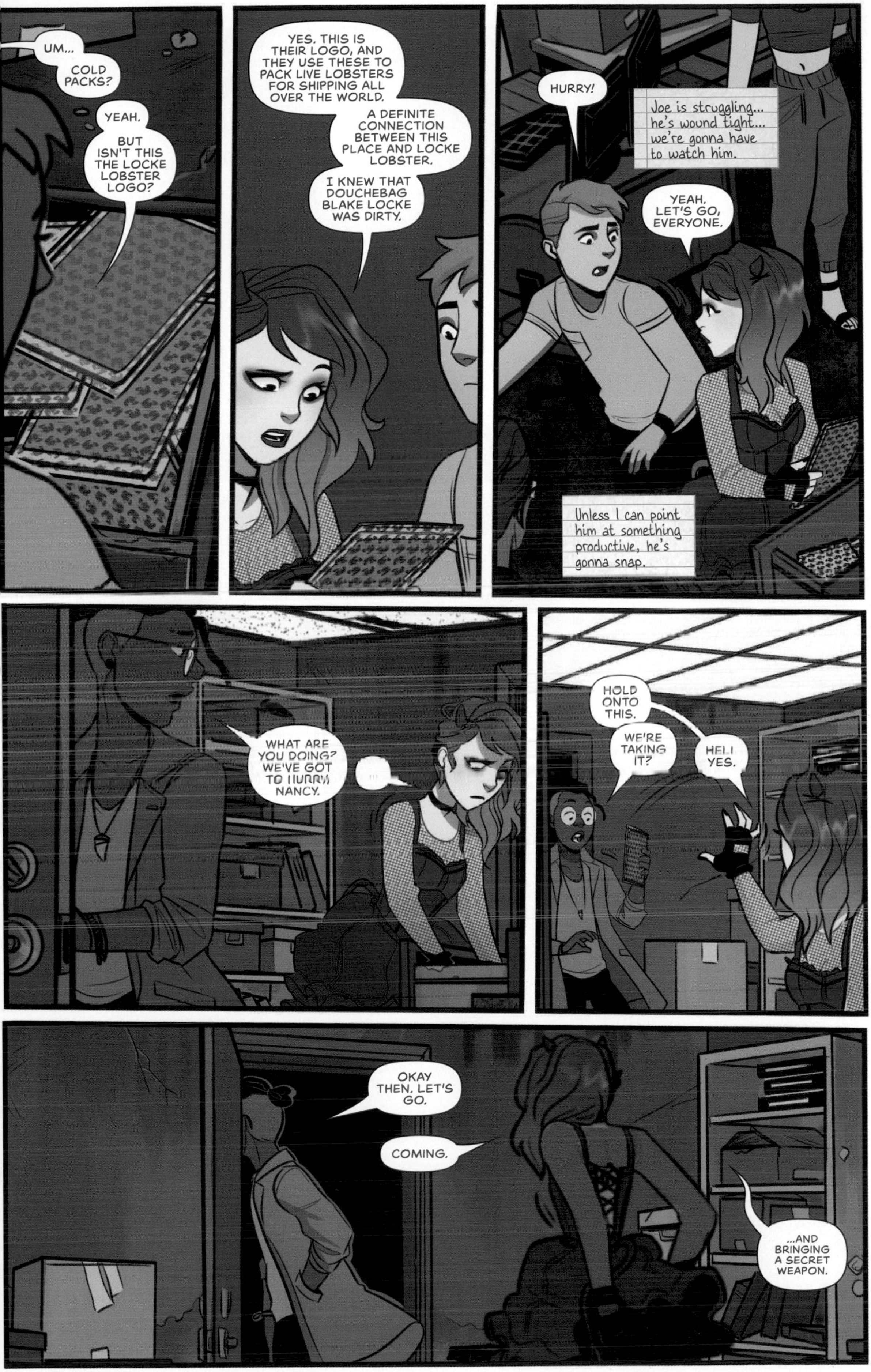
UM... COLD PACKS?
YEAH. BUT ISN'T THIS THE LOCKE LOBSTER LOGO?
YES. THIS IS THEIR LOGO, AND THEY USE THESE TO PACK LIVE LOBSTERS FOR SHIPPING ALL OVER THE WORLD.
A DEFINITE CONNECTION BETWEEN THIS PLACE AND LOCKE LOBSTER.
I KNEW THAT DOUCHEBAG BLAKE LOCKE WAS DIRTY.
HURRY!
Joe is struggling... he's wound tight... we're gonna have to watch him.
YEAH. LET'S GO, EVERYONE.
Unless I can point him at something productive, he's gonna snap.
WHAT ARE YOU DOING? WE'VE GOT TO HURRY, NANCY.
...
HOLD ONTO THIS.
WE'RE TAKING IT?
HELL YES.
OKAY THEN. LET'S GO.
COMING.
...AND BRINGING A SECRET WEAPON.

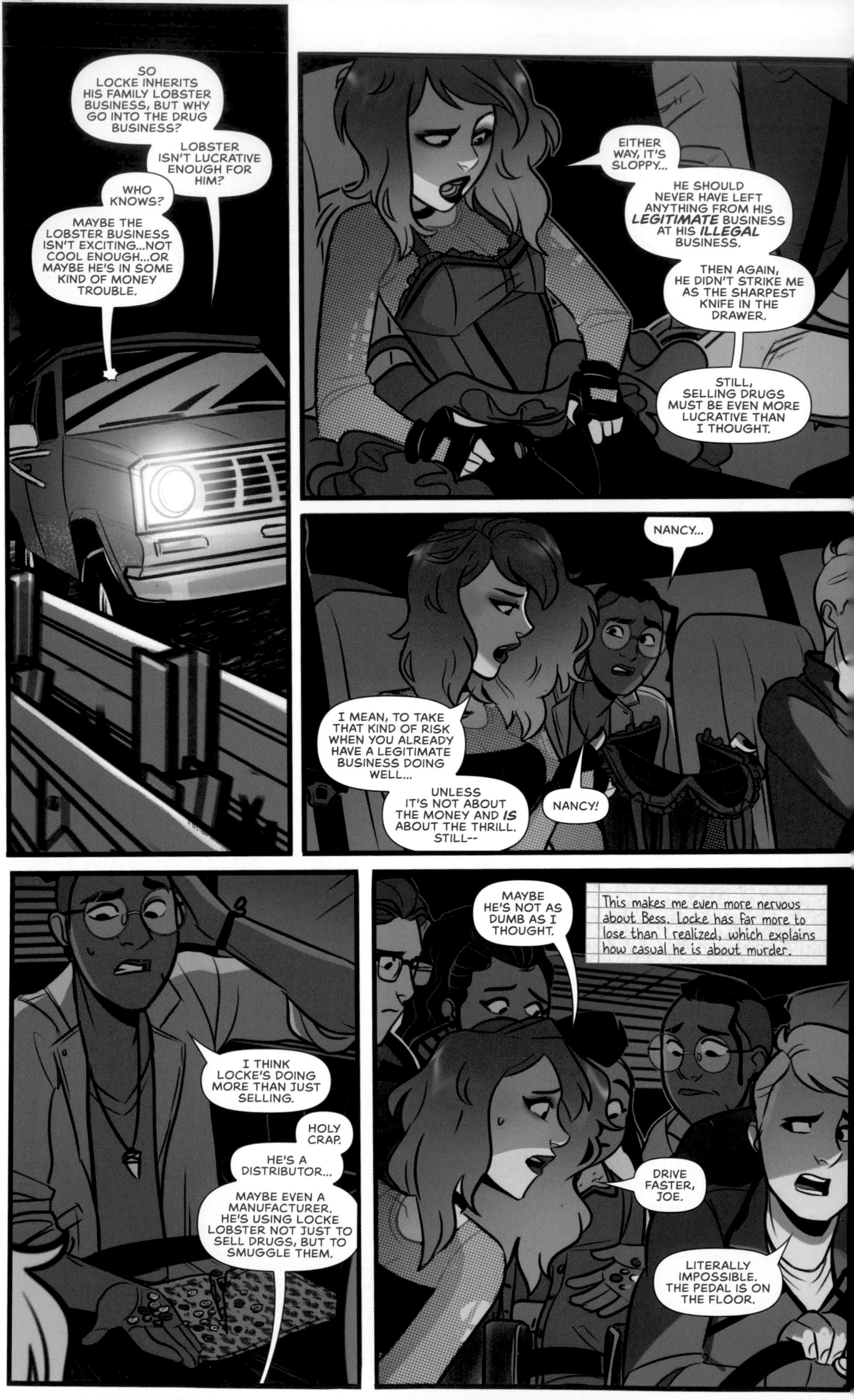
SO LOCKE INHERITS HIS FAMILY LOBSTER BUSINESS, BUT WHY GO INTO THE DRUG BUSINESS?
LOBSTER ISN'T LUCRATIVE ENOUGH FOR HIM?
WHO KNOWS?
MAYBE THE LOBSTER BUSINESS ISN'T EXCITING...NOT COOL ENOUGH...OR MAYBE HE'S IN SOME KIND OF MONEY TROUBLE.
EITHER WAY, IT'S SLOPPY...
HE SHOULD NEVER HAVE LEFT ANYTHING FROM HIS LEGITIMATE BUSINESS AT HIS ILLEGAL BUSINESS.
THEN AGAIN, HE DIDN'T STRIKE ME AS THE SHARPEST KNIFE IN THE DRAWER.
STILL, SELLING DRUGS MUST BE EVEN MORE LUCRATIVE THAN I THOUGHT.
NANCY...
I MEAN, TO TAKE THAT KIND OF RISK WHEN YOU ALREADY HAVE A LEGITIMATE BUSINESS DOING WELL...
UNLESS IT'S NOT ABOUT THE MONEY AND IS ABOUT THE THRILL. STILL--
NANCY!
I THINK LOCKE'S DOING MORE THAN JUST SELLING.
HOLY CRAP.
HE'S A DISTRIBUTOR...
MAYBE EVEN A MANUFACTURER. HE'S USING LOCKE LOBSTER NOT JUST TO SELL DRUGS, BUT TO SMUGGLE THEM.
MAYBE HE'S NOT AS DUMB AS I THOUGHT.
This makes me even more nervous about Bess. Locke has far more to lose than I realized, which explains how casual he is about murder.
DRIVE FASTER, JOE.
LITERALLY IMPOSSIBLE. THE PEDAL IS ON THE FLOOR.

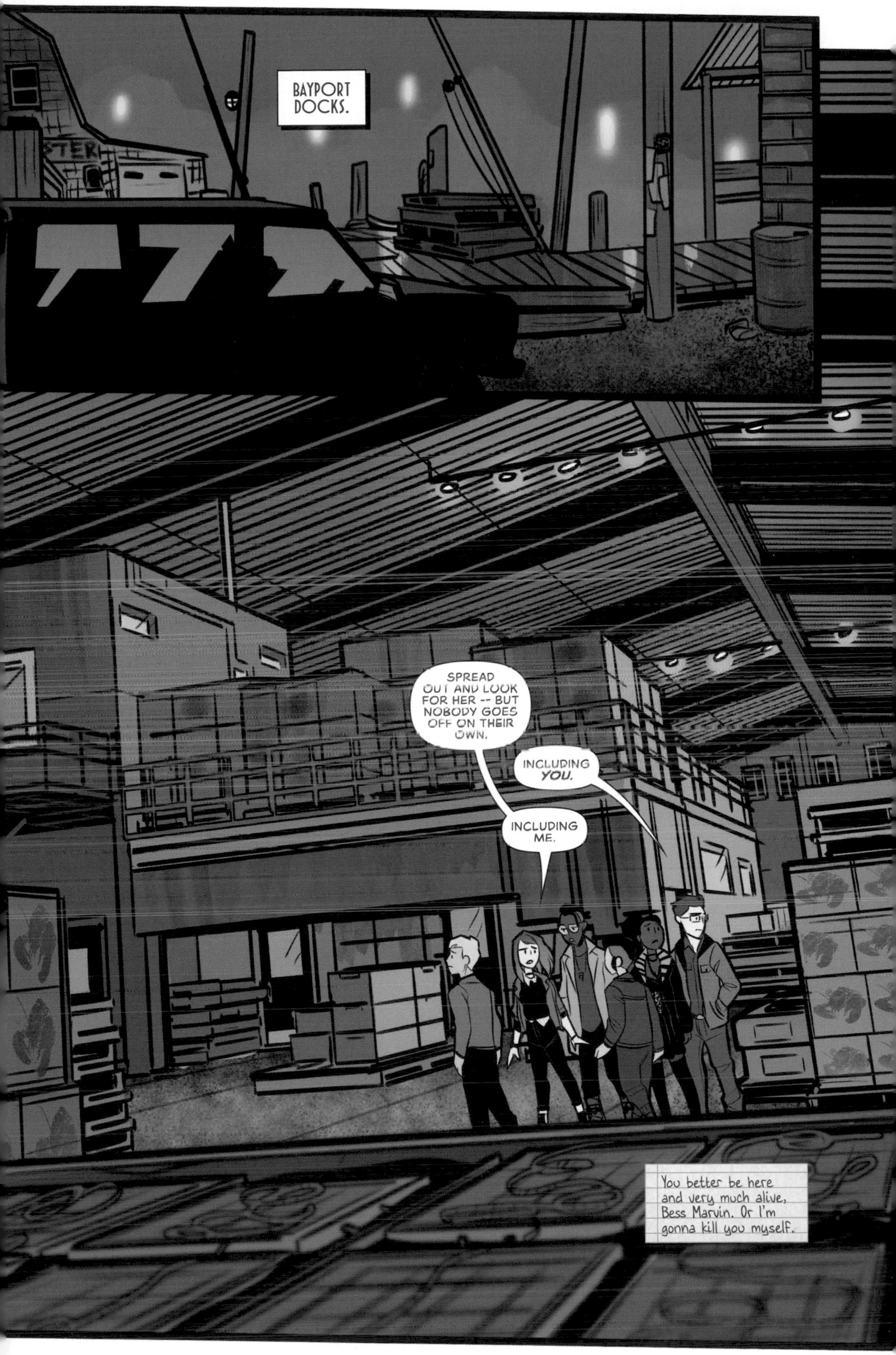
BAYPORT DOCKS.
SPREAD OUT AND LOOK FOR HER -- BUT NOBODY GOES OFF ON THEIR OWN.
INCLUDING YOU.
INCLUDING ME.
You better be here and very much alive, Bess Marvin. Or I'm gonna kill you myself.

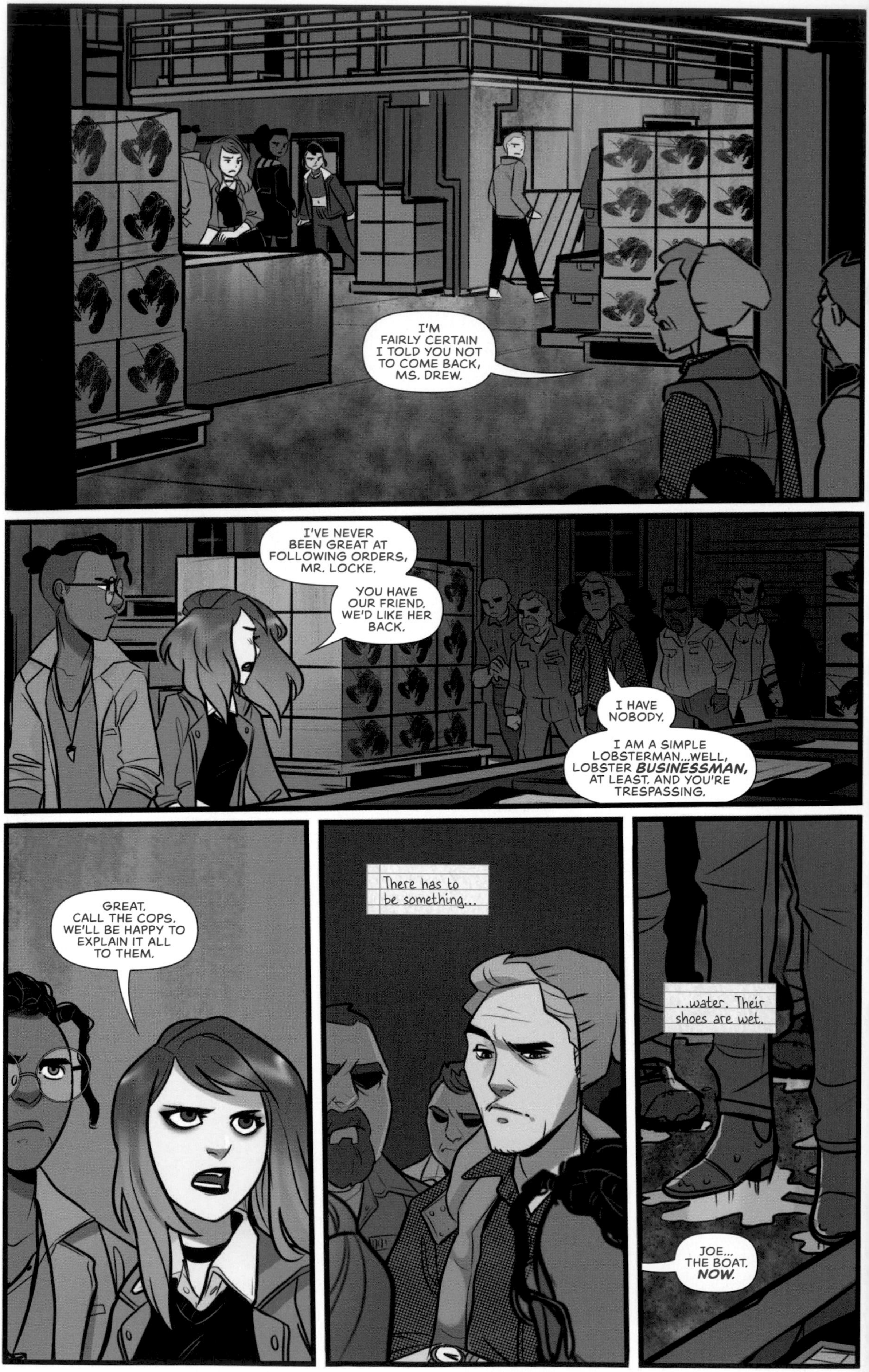

I'M FAIRLY CERTAIN I TOLD YOU NOT TO COME BACK, MS. DREW.
I'VE NEVER BEEN GREAT AT FOLLOWING ORDERS, MR. LOCKE.
YOU HAVE OUR FRIEND. WE'D LIKE HER BACK.
I HAVE NOBODY.
I AM A SIMPLE LOBSTERMAN...WELL, LOBSTER BUSINESSMAN, AT LEAST. AND YOU'RE TRESPASSING.
GREAT. CALL THE COPS. WE'LL BE HAPPY TO EXPLAIN IT ALL TO THEM.
There has to be something...
...water. Their shoes are wet.
JOE... THE BOAT. NOW.

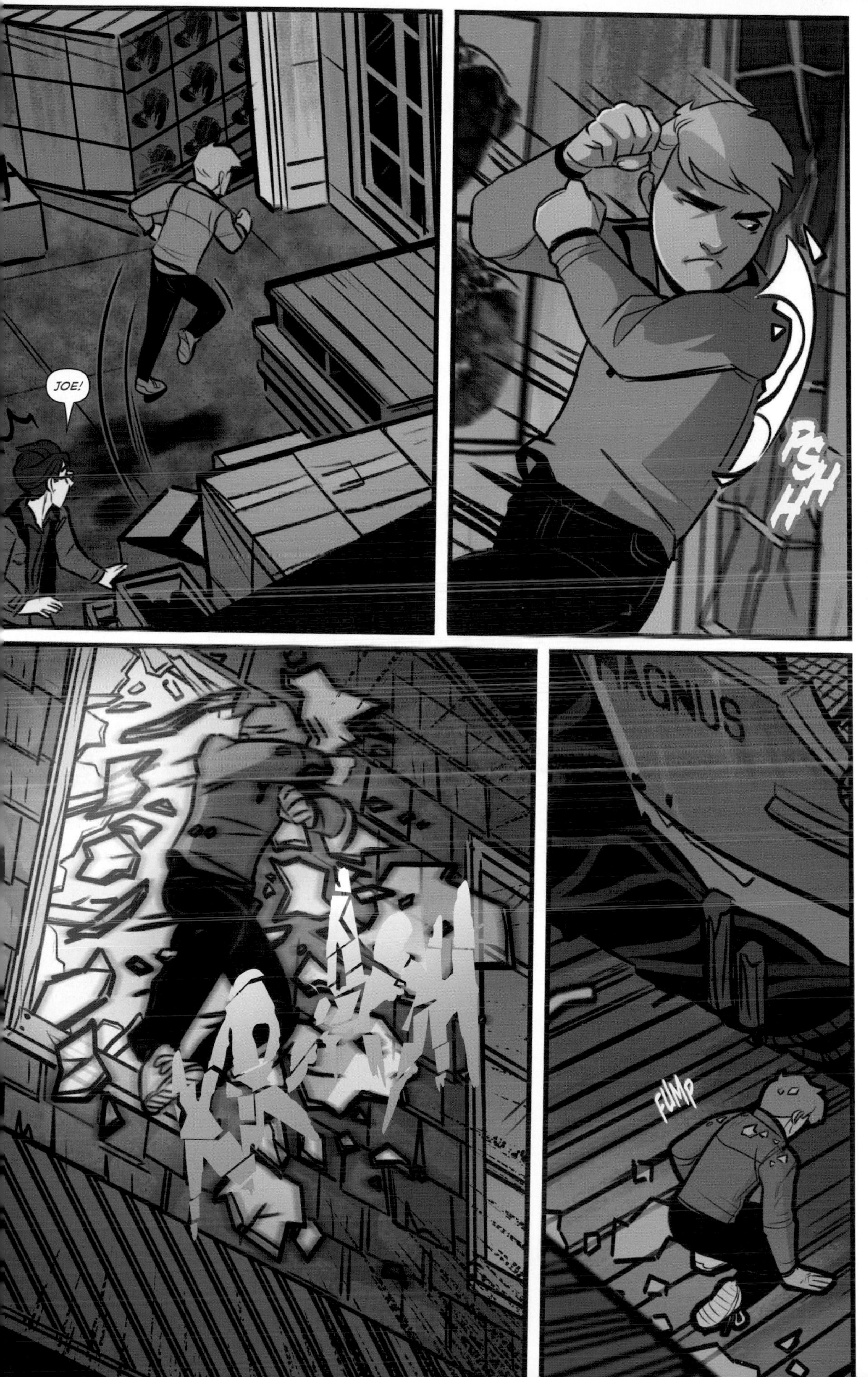
JOE!
PSHH
AGNUS
FUMP

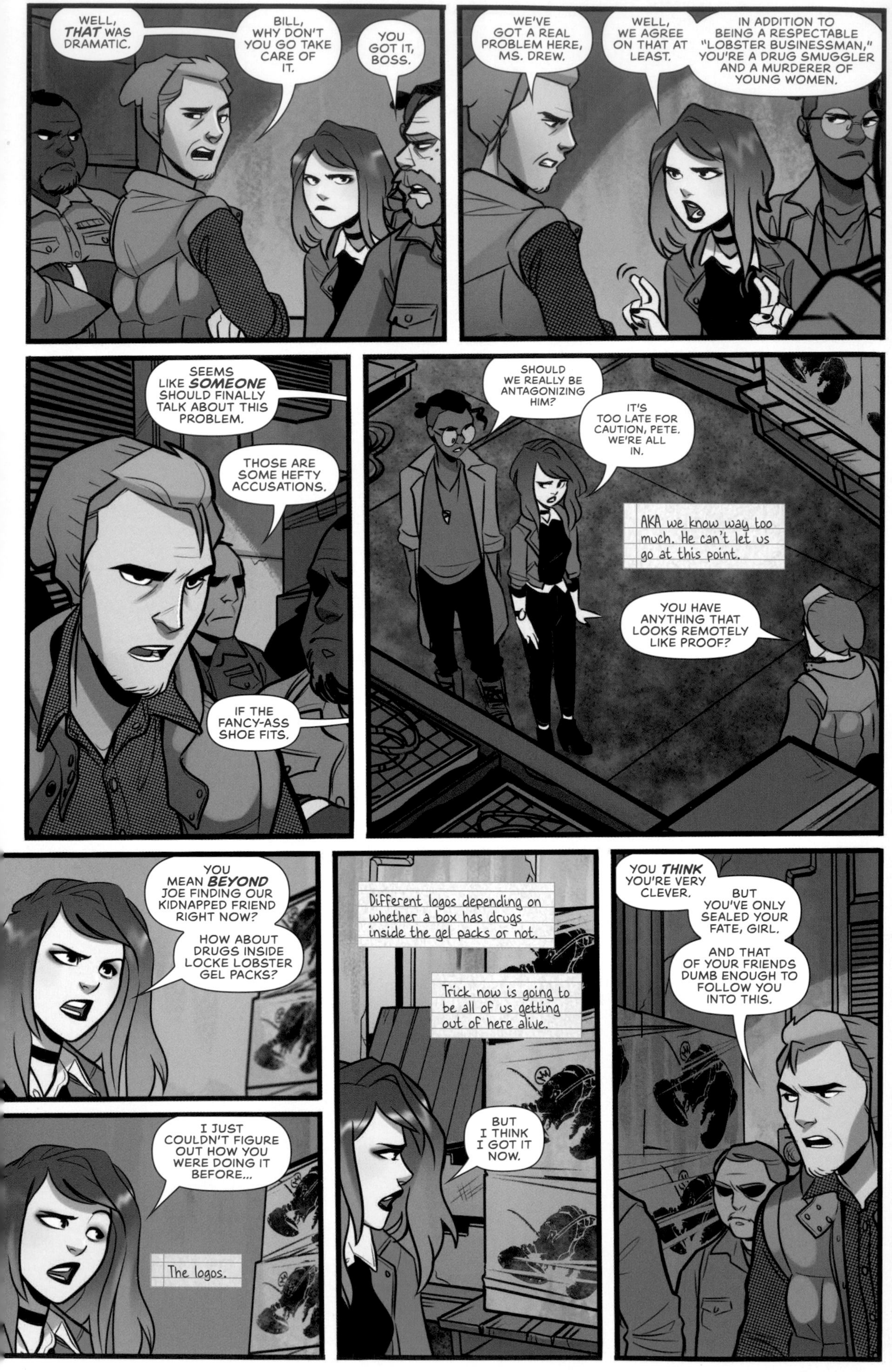

WELL, THAT WAS DRAMATIC.
BILL, WHY DON'T YOU GO TAKE CARE OF IT.
YOU GOT IT, BOSS.
WE'VE GOT A REAL PROBLEM HERE, MS. DREW.
WELL, WE AGREE ON THAT AT LEAST.
IN ADDITION TO BEING A RESPECTABLE "LOBSTER BUSINESSMAN," YOU'RE A DRUG SMUGGLER AND A MURDERER OF YOUNG WOMEN.
SEEMS LIKE SOMEONE SHOULD FINALLY TALK ABOUT THIS PROBLEM.
THOSE ARE SOME HEFTY ACCUSATIONS.
IF THE FANCY-ASS SHOE FITS.
SHOULD WE REALLY BE ANTAGONIZING HIM?
IT'S TOO LATE FOR CAUTION, PETE. WE'RE ALL IN.
AKA we know way too much. He can't let us go at this point.
YOU HAVE ANYTHING THAT LOOKS REMOTELY LIKE PROOF?
YOU MEAN BEYOND JOE FINDING OUR KIDNAPPED FRIEND RIGHT NOW?
HOW ABOUT DRUGS INSIDE LOCKE LOBSTER GEL PACKS?
I JUST COULDN'T FIGURE OUT HOW YOU WERE DOING IT BEFORE...
The logos.
Different logos depending on whether a box has drugs inside the gel packs or not.
Trick now is going to be all of us getting out of here alive.
BUT I THINK I GOT IT NOW.
YOU THINK YOU'RE VERY CLEVER.
BUT YOU'VE ONLY SEALED YOUR FATE, GIRL.
AND THAT OF YOUR FRIENDS DUMB ENOUGH TO FOLLOW YOU INTO THIS.

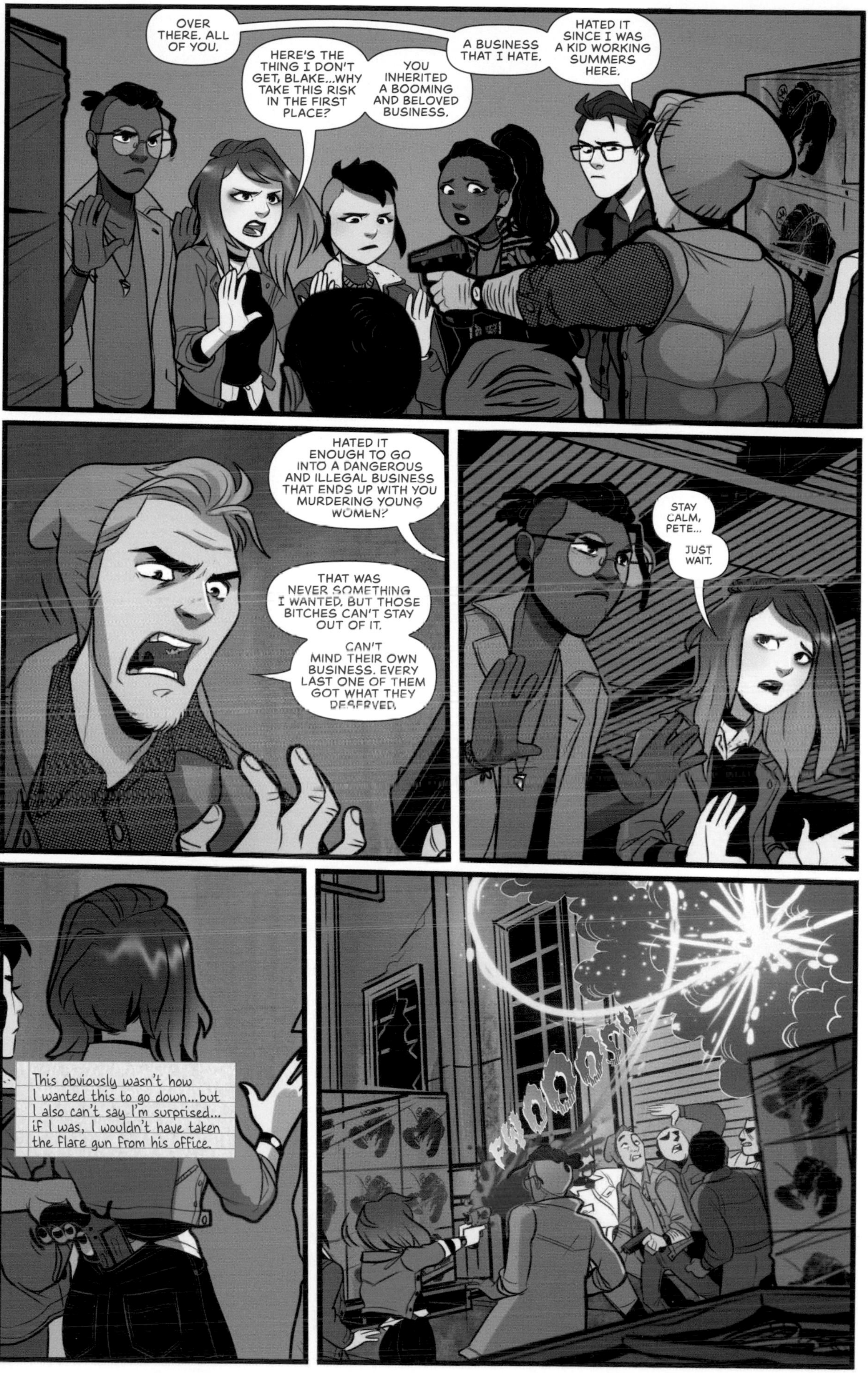
OVER THERE. ALL OF YOU.
HERE'S THE THING I DON'T GET, BLAKE...WHY TAKE THIS RISK IN THE FIRST PLACE?
YOU INHERITED A BOOMING AND BELOVED BUSINESS.
A BUSINESS THAT I HATE.
HATED IT SINCE I WAS A KID WORKING SUMMERS HERE.
HATED IT ENOUGH TO GO INTO A DANGEROUS AND ILLEGAL BUSINESS THAT ENDS UP WITH YOU MURDERING YOUNG WOMEN?
THAT WAS NEVER SOMETHING I WANTED. BUT THOSE BITCHES CAN'T STAY OUT OF IT.
CAN'T MIND THEIR OWN BUSINESS. EVERY LAST ONE OF THEM GOT WHAT THEY DESERVED.
STAY CALM, PETE...
JUST WAIT.
This obviously wasn't how I wanted this to go down...but I also can't say I'm surprised... if I was, I wouldn't have taken the flare gun from his office.
FWOOOOSH

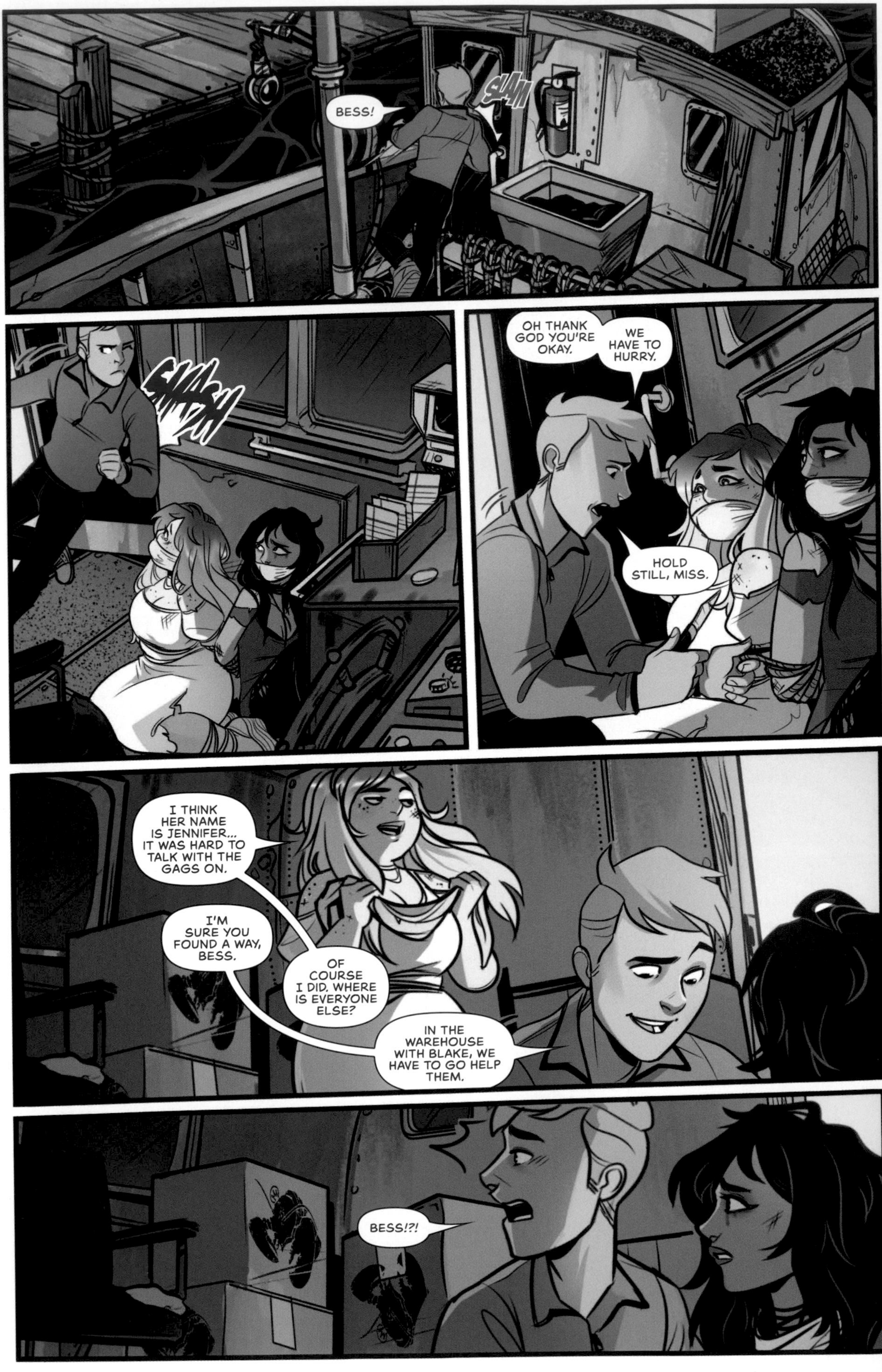
BESS!
SLAM
SMASH
OH THANK GOD YOU'RE OKAY.
WE HAVE TO HURRY.
HOLD STILL, MISS.
I THINK HER NAME IS JENNIFER... IT WAS HARD TO TALK WITH THE GAGS ON.
I'M SURE YOU FOUND A WAY, BESS.
OF COURSE I DID. WHERE IS EVERYONE ELSE?
IN THE WAREHOUSE WITH BLAKE, WE HAVE TO GO HELP THEM.
BESS!?!

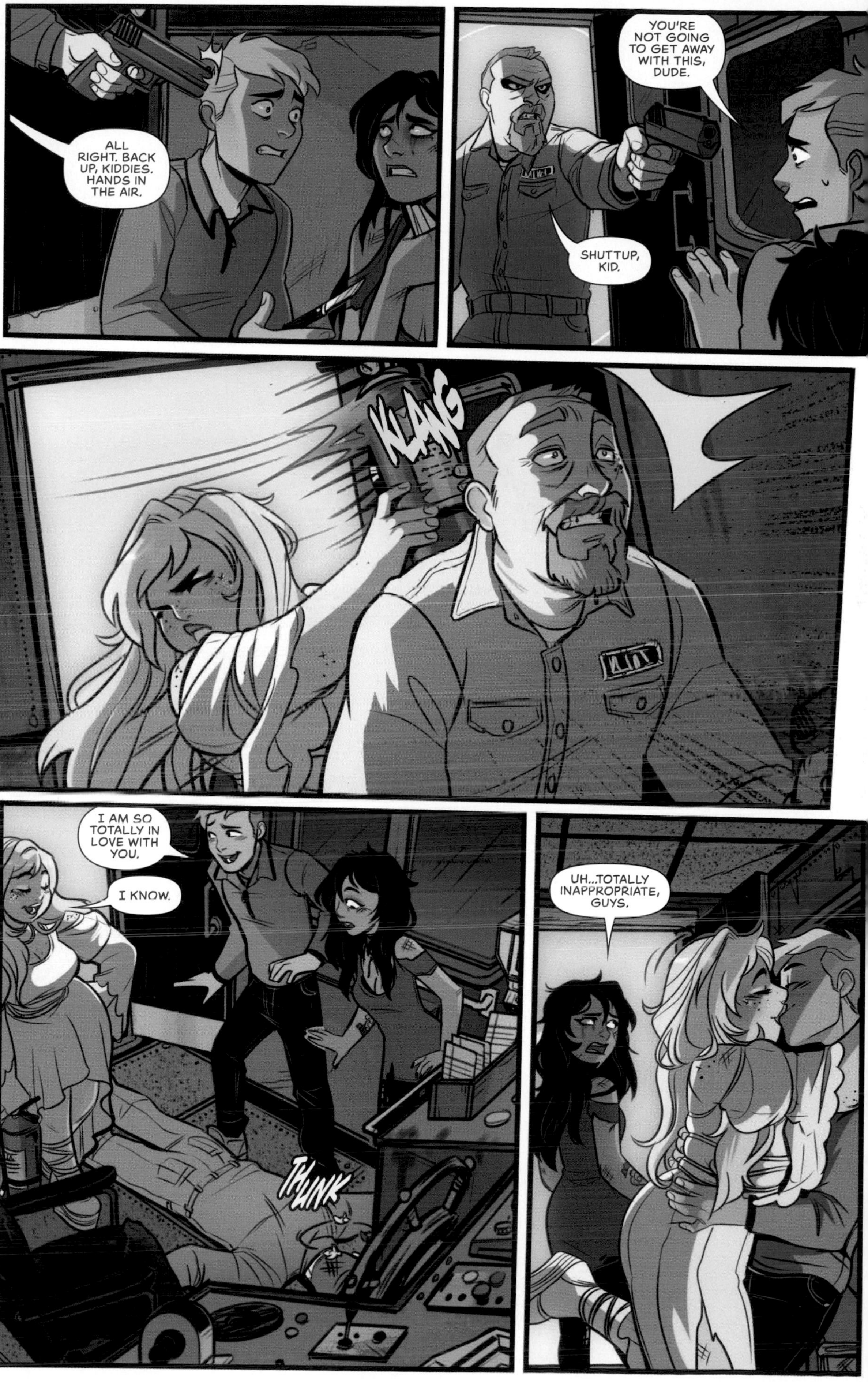
ALL RIGHT. BACK UP, KIDDIES. HANDS IN THE AIR.
YOU'RE NOT GOING TO GET AWAY WITH THIS, DUDE.
SHUTTUP, KID.
KLANG
I AM SO TOTALLY IN LOVE WITH YOU.
I KNOW.
THUNK
UH...TOTALLY INAPPROPRIATE, GUYS.

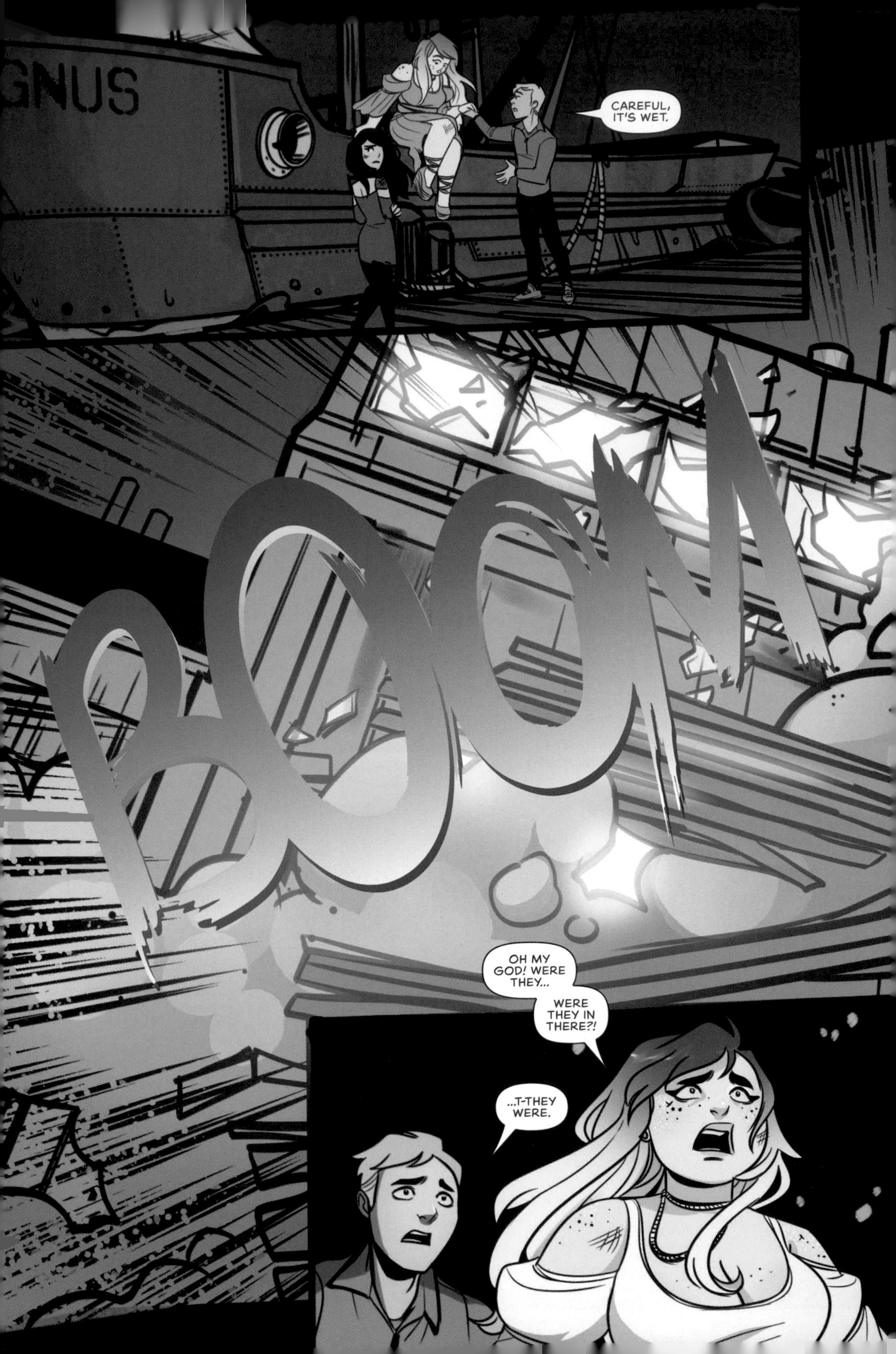
GNUS
CAREFUL, IT'S WET.
BOOM
OH MY GOD! WERE THEY...
WERE THEY IN THERE?!
...T-THEY WERE.

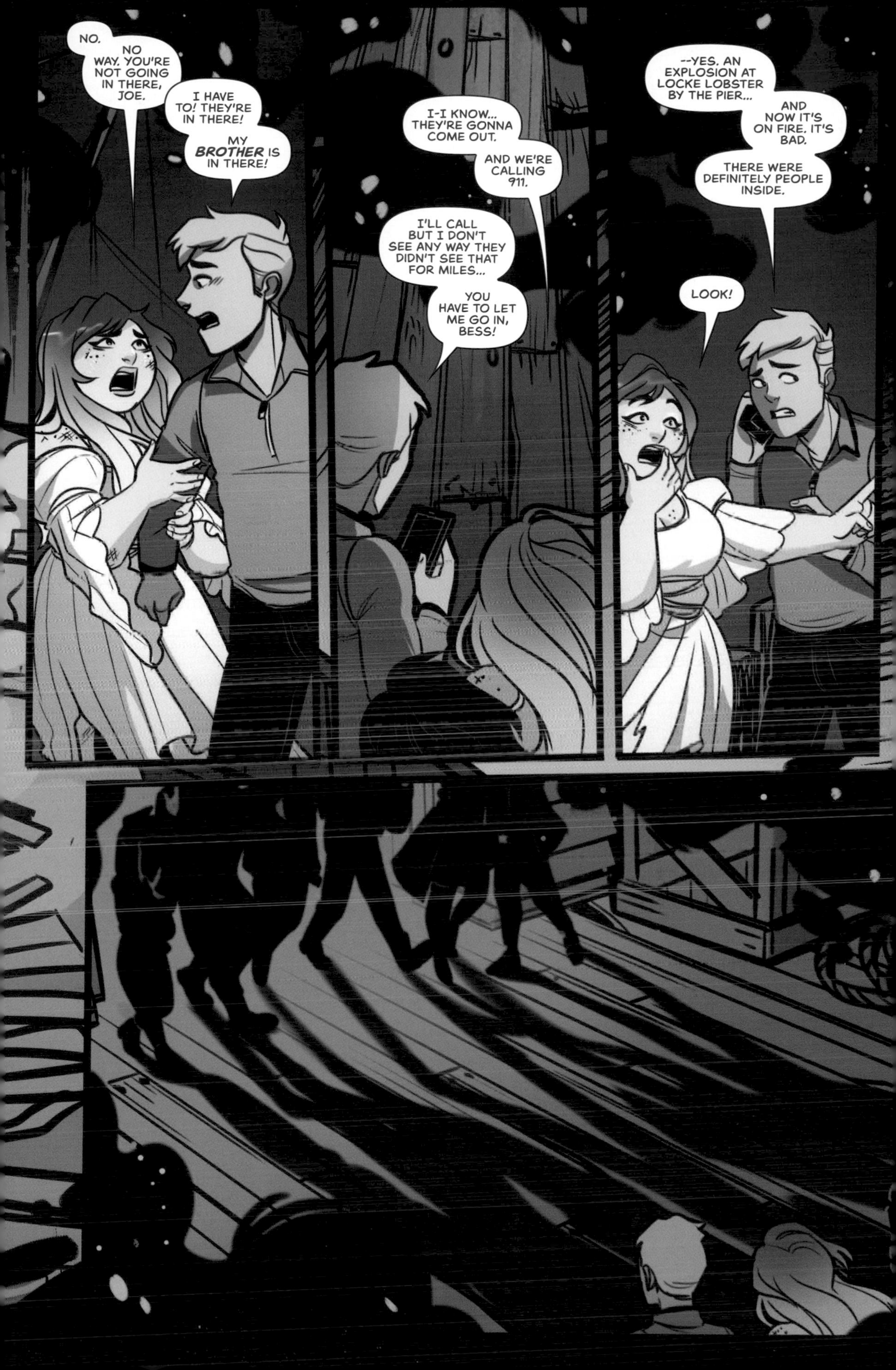
NO.
NO WAY. YOU'RE NOT GOING IN THERE, JOE.
I HAVE TO! THEY'RE IN THERE!
MY **BROTHER** IS IN THERE!
I-I KNOW... THEY'RE GONNA COME OUT.
AND WE'RE CALLING 911.
I'LL CALL BUT I DON'T SEE ANY WAY THEY DIDN'T SEE THAT FOR MILES...
YOU HAVE TO LET ME GO IN, BESS!
--YES. AN EXPLOSION AT LOCKE LOBSTER BY THE PIER...
AND NOW IT'S ON FIRE. IT'S BAD.
THERE WERE DEFINITELY PEOPLE INSIDE.
LOOK!

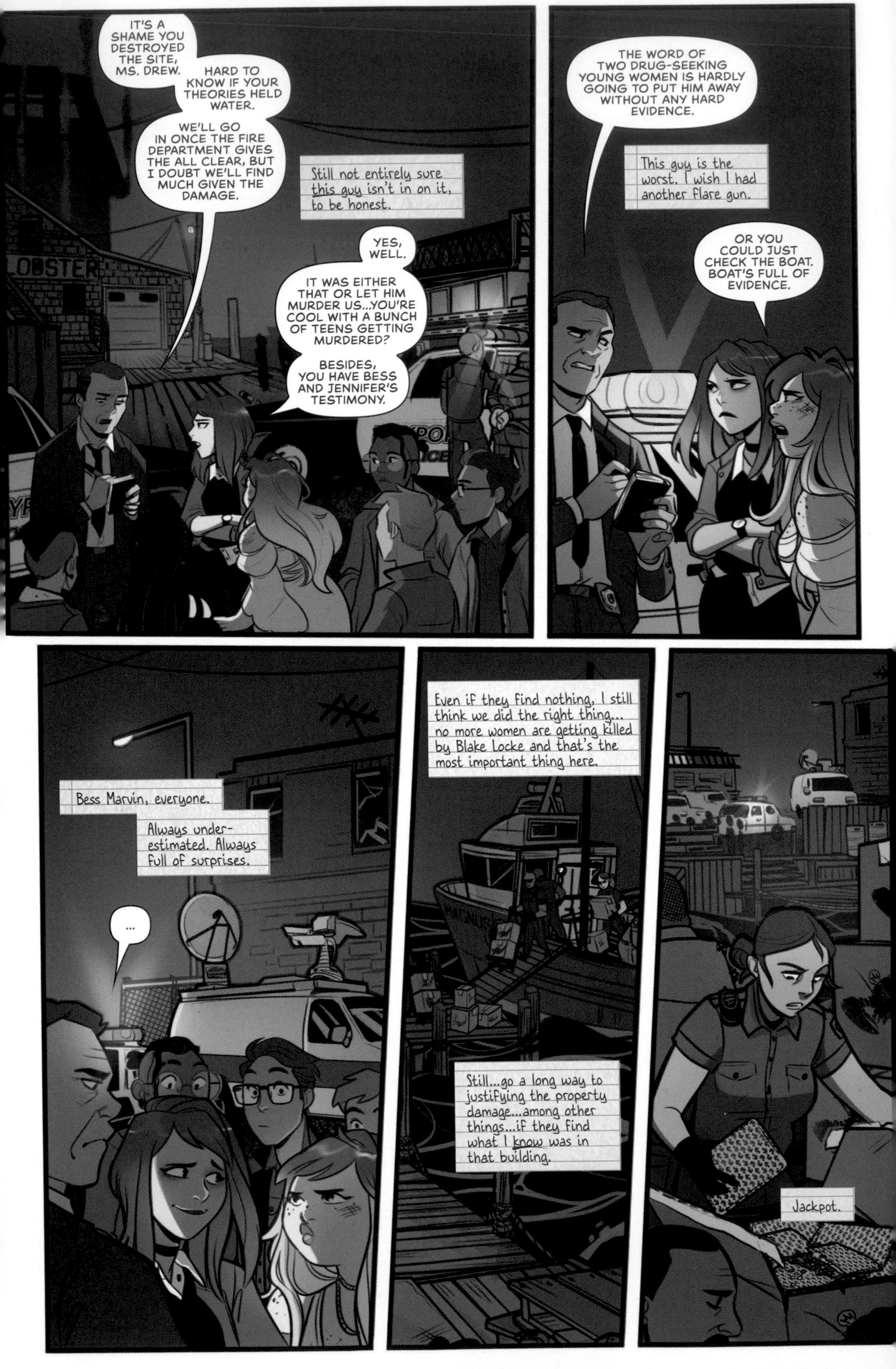
IT'S A SHAME YOU DESTROYED THE SITE, MS. DREW.
HARD TO KNOW IF YOUR THEORIES HELD WATER.
WE'LL GO IN ONCE THE FIRE DEPARTMENT GIVES THE ALL CLEAR, BUT I DOUBT WE'LL FIND MUCH GIVEN THE DAMAGE.
Still not entirely sure this guy isn't in on it, to be honest.
YES, WELL.
IT WAS EITHER THAT OR LET HIM MURDER US...YOU'RE COOL WITH A BUNCH OF TEENS GETTING MURDERED?
BESIDES, YOU HAVE BESS AND JENNIFER'S TESTIMONY.
LOBSTER
THE WORD OF TWO DRUG-SEEKING YOUNG WOMEN IS HARDLY GOING TO PUT HIM AWAY WITHOUT ANY HARD EVIDENCE.
This guy is the worst. I wish I had another flare gun.
OR YOU COULD JUST CHECK THE BOAT. BOAT'S FULL OF EVIDENCE.
Bess Marvin, everyone.
Always under-estimated. Always full of surprises.
...
Even if they find nothing, I still think we did the right thing... no more women are getting killed by Blake Locke and that's the most important thing here.
Still...go a long way to justifying the property damage...among other things...if they find what I know was in that building.
Jackpot.

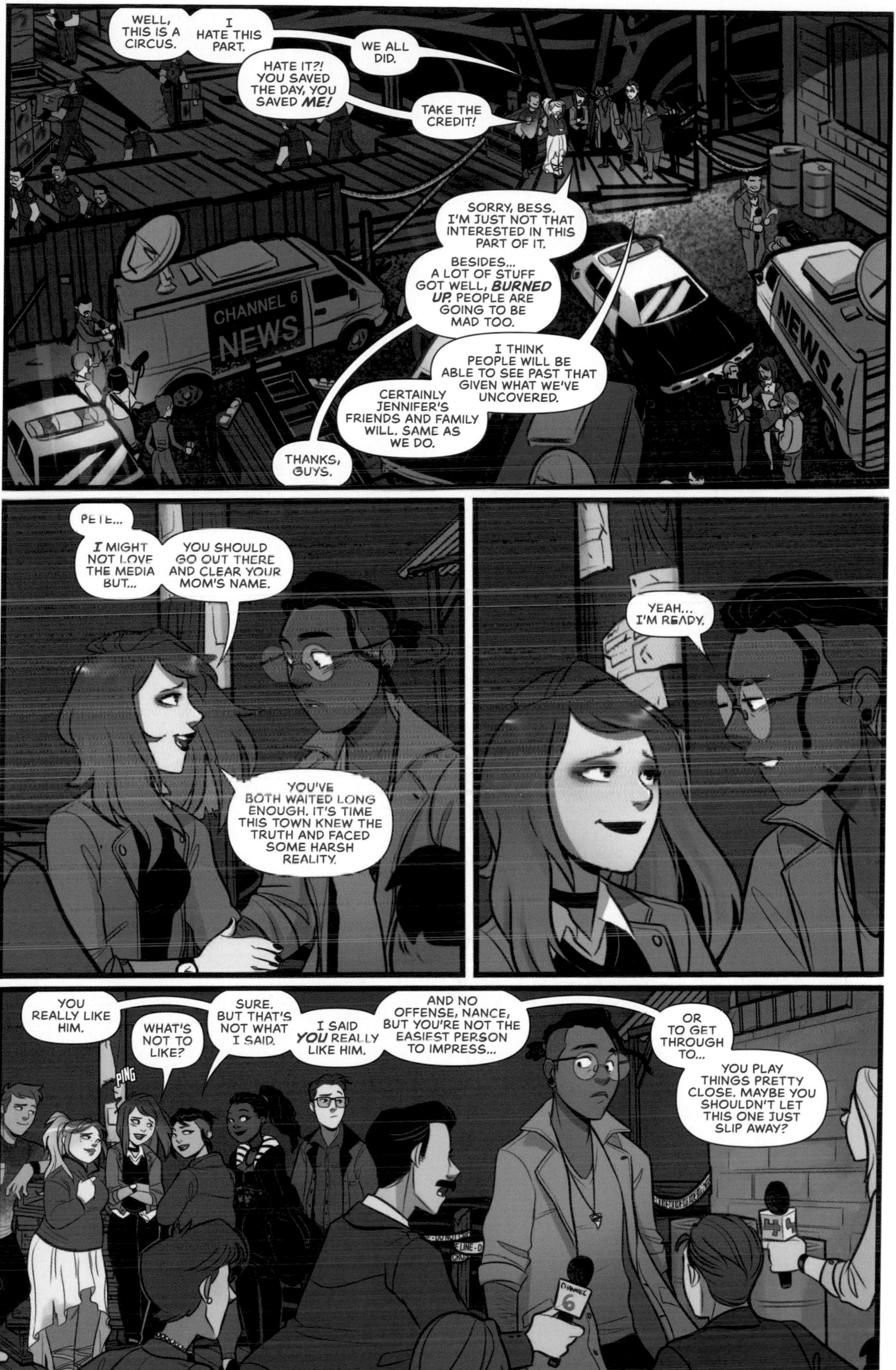
WELL, THIS IS A CIRCUS.
I HATE THIS PART.
WE ALL DID.
HATE IT?! YOU SAVED THE DAY, YOU SAVED ME!
TAKE THE CREDIT!
SORRY, BESS. I'M JUST NOT THAT INTERESTED IN THIS PART OF IT.
BESIDES... A LOT OF STUFF GOT WELL, BURNED UP. PEOPLE ARE GOING TO BE MAD TOO.
I THINK PEOPLE WILL BE ABLE TO SEE PAST THAT GIVEN WHAT WE'VE UNCOVERED.
CERTAINLY JENNIFER'S FRIENDS AND FAMILY WILL. SAME AS WE DO.
THANKS, GUYS.
CHANNEL 6 NEWS
NEWS 4
PETE...
I MIGHT NOT LOVE THE MEDIA BUT...
YOU SHOULD GO OUT THERE AND CLEAR YOUR MOM'S NAME.
YOU'VE BOTH WAITED LONG ENOUGH. IT'S TIME THIS TOWN KNEW THE TRUTH AND FACED SOME HARSH REALITY.
YEAH... I'M READY.
YOU REALLY LIKE HIM.
WHAT'S NOT TO LIKE?
SURE. BUT THAT'S NOT WHAT I SAID.
I SAID YOU REALLY LIKE HIM.
AND NO OFFENSE, NANCE, BUT YOU'RE NOT THE EASIEST PERSON TO IMPRESS...
OR TO GET THROUGH TO...
YOU PLAY THINGS PRETTY CLOSE. MAYBE YOU SHOULDN'T LET THIS ONE JUST SLIP AWAY?
PING

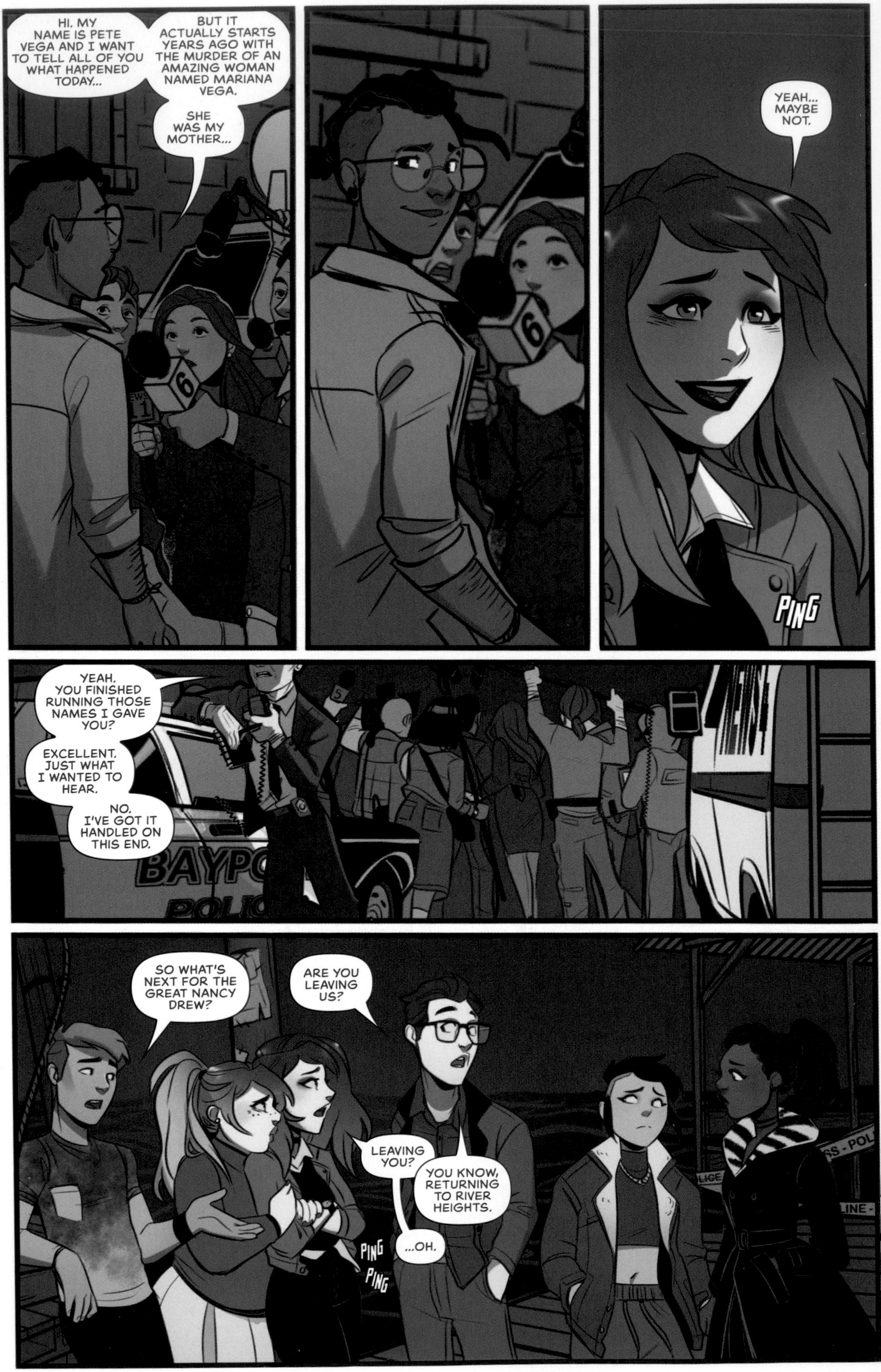

HI. MY NAME IS PETE VEGA AND I WANT TO TELL ALL OF YOU WHAT HAPPENED TODAY...
BUT IT ACTUALLY STARTS YEARS AGO WITH THE MURDER OF AN AMAZING WOMAN NAMED MARIANA VEGA.
SHE WAS MY MOTHER...
YEAH... MAYBE NOT.
PING
YEAH. YOU FINISHED RUNNING THOSE NAMES I GAVE YOU?
EXCELLENT. JUST WHAT I WANTED TO HEAR.
NO. I'VE GOT IT HANDLED ON THIS END.
BAYPO
POLIC
SO WHAT'S NEXT FOR THE GREAT NANCY DREW?
ARE YOU LEAVING US?
LEAVING YOU?
YOU KNOW, RETURNING TO RIVER HEIGHTS.
...OH.
PING
PING

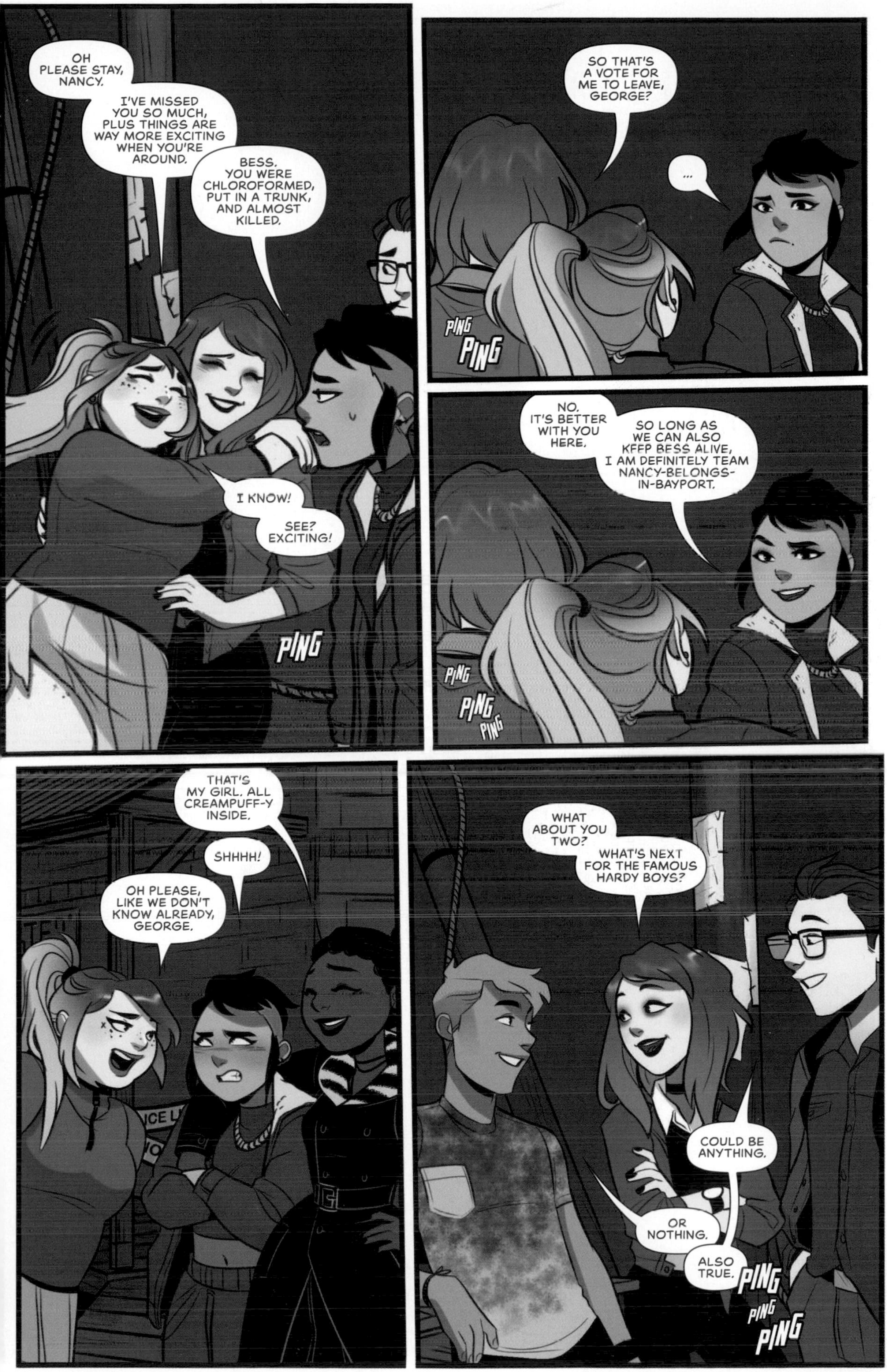
OH PLEASE STAY, NANCY.
I'VE MISSED YOU SO MUCH, PLUS THINGS ARE WAY MORE EXCITING WHEN YOU'RE AROUND.
BESS. YOU WERE CHLOROFORMED, PUT IN A TRUNK, AND ALMOST KILLED.
I KNOW!
SEE? EXCITING!
PING
SO THAT'S A VOTE FOR ME TO LEAVE, GEORGE?
...
PING
PING
NO. IT'S BETTER WITH YOU HERE.
SO LONG AS WE CAN ALSO KEEP BESS ALIVE, I AM DEFINITELY TEAM NANCY-BELONGS-IN-BAYPORT.
PING
PING
PING
THAT'S MY GIRL. ALL CREAMPUFF-Y INSIDE.
SHHHH!
OH PLEASE, LIKE WE DON'T KNOW ALREADY, GEORGE.
WHAT ABOUT YOU TWO?
WHAT'S NEXT FOR THE FAMOUS HARDY BOYS?
COULD BE ANYTHING.
OR NOTHING.
ALSO TRUE.
PING
PING
PING

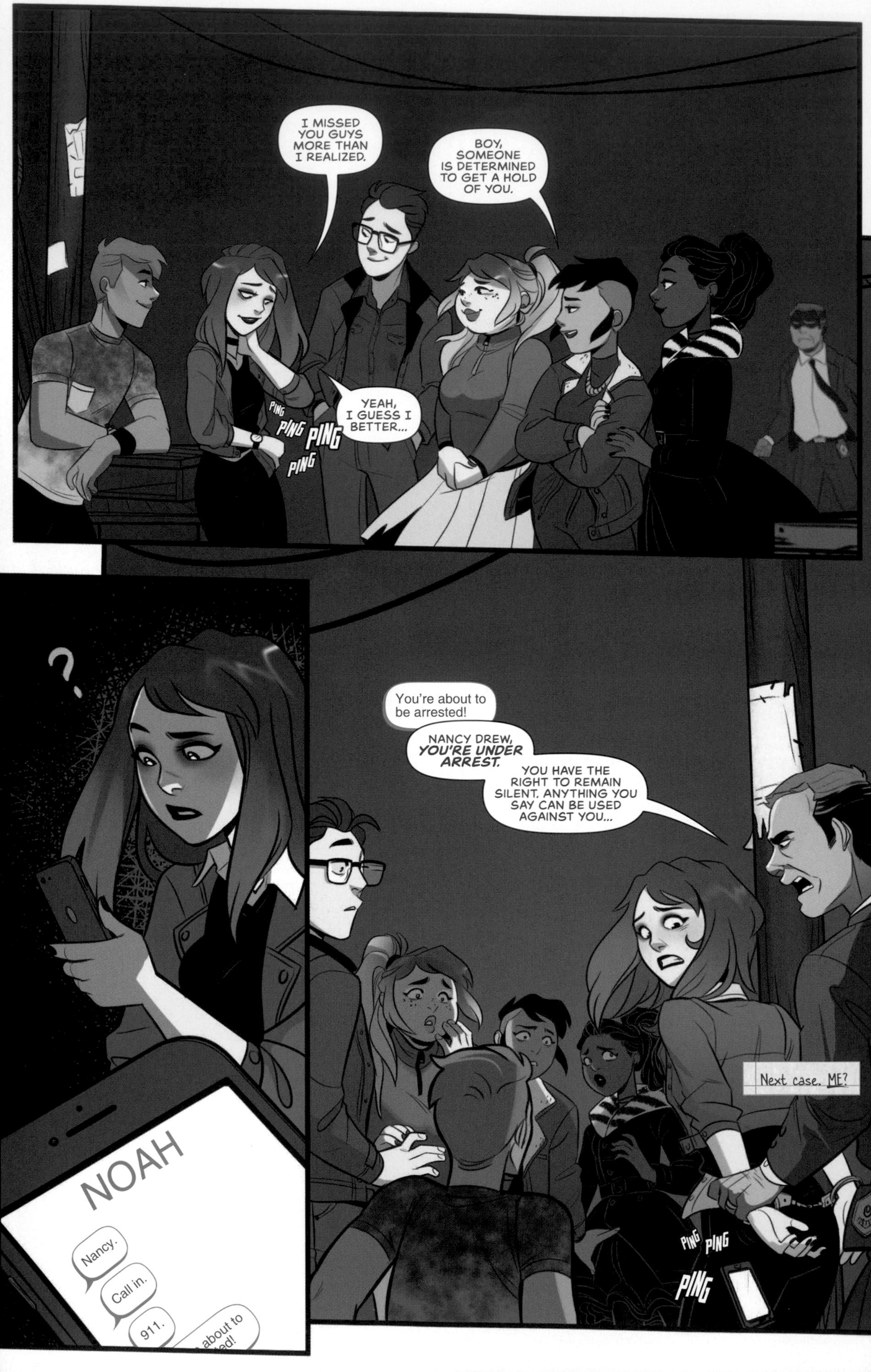

I MISSED YOU GUYS MORE THAN I REALIZED.
BOY, SOMEONE IS DETERMINED TO GET A HOLD OF YOU.
PING PING PING PING
YEAH, I GUESS I BETTER...
?
NOAH
Nancy.
Call in.
911.
You're about to be arrested!
NANCY DREW, *YOU'RE UNDER ARREST.*
YOU HAVE THE RIGHT TO REMAIN SILENT. ANYTHING YOU SAY CAN BE USED AGAINST YOU...
Next case. ME?
PING PING PING

Bonus materials

In my experience cops don't want to listen to a bunch of kids.

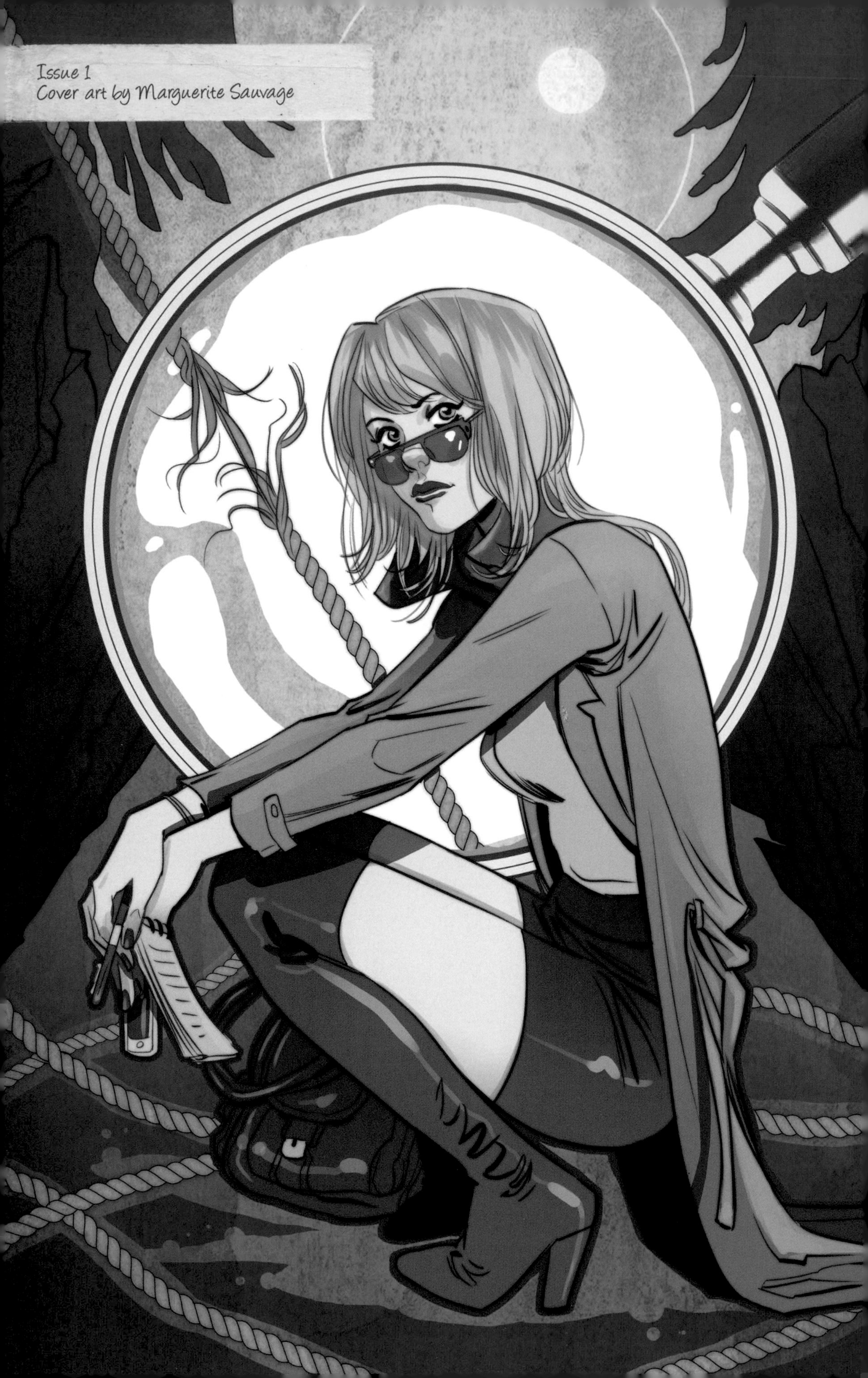

Issue 1
Cover art by Marguerite Sauvage

Issue 1
Cover art by Annie Wu

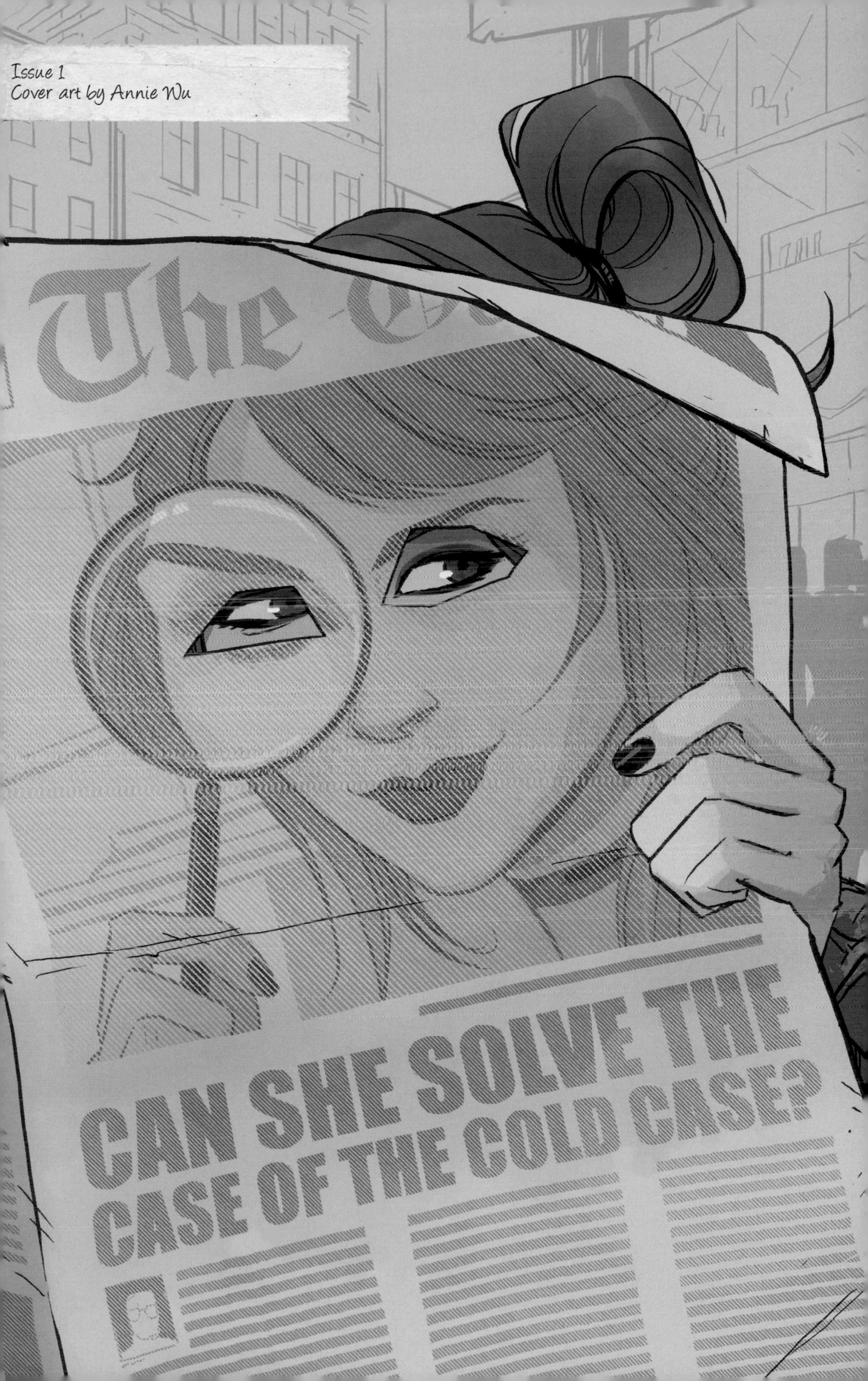
The
CAN SHE SOLVE THE CASE OF THE COLD CASE?

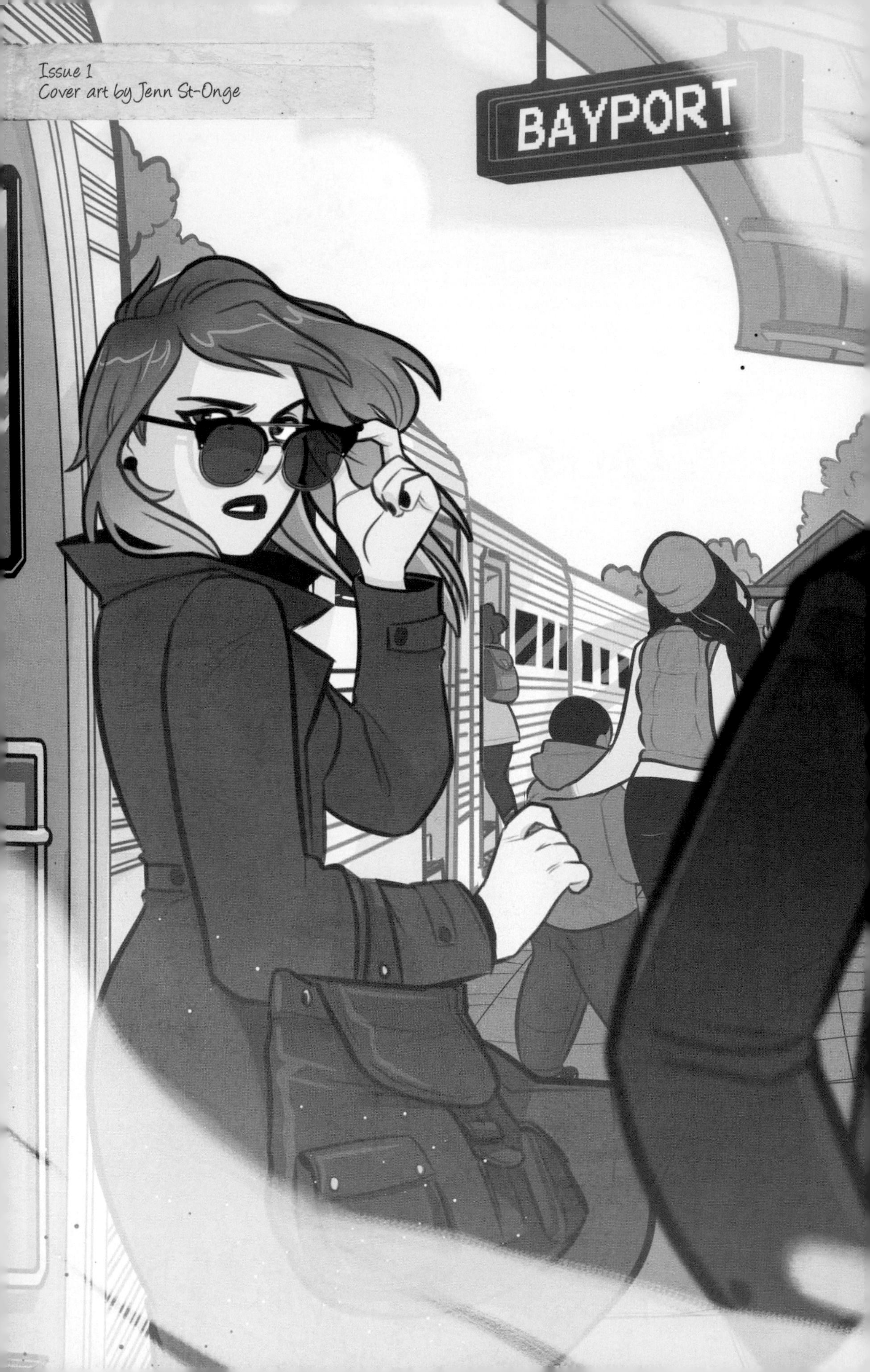
BAYPORT

Issue 1
Cover art by Jenn St-Onge

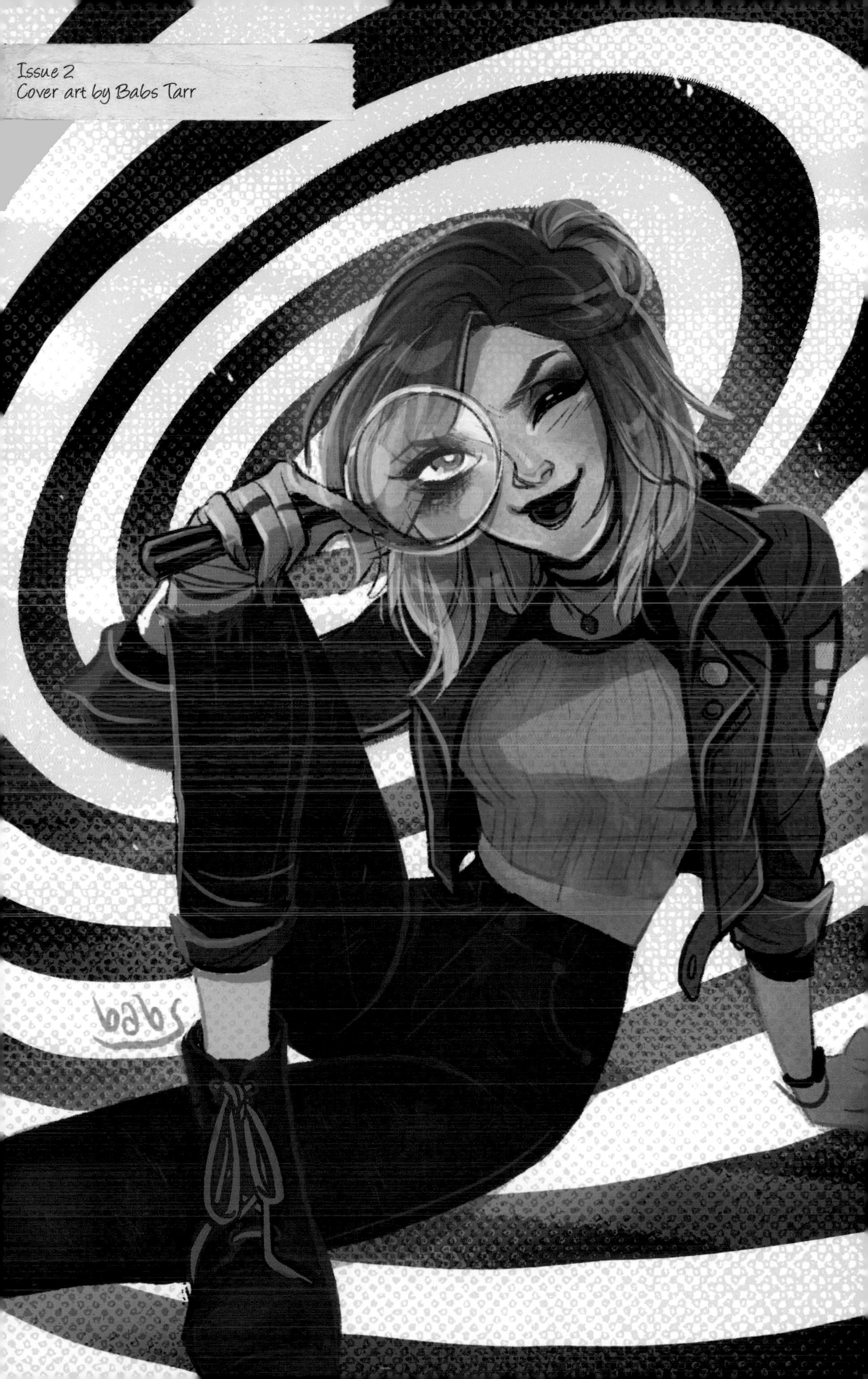

Issue 2
Cover art by Babs Tarr

Issue 2
Cover art by Jenn St-Onge

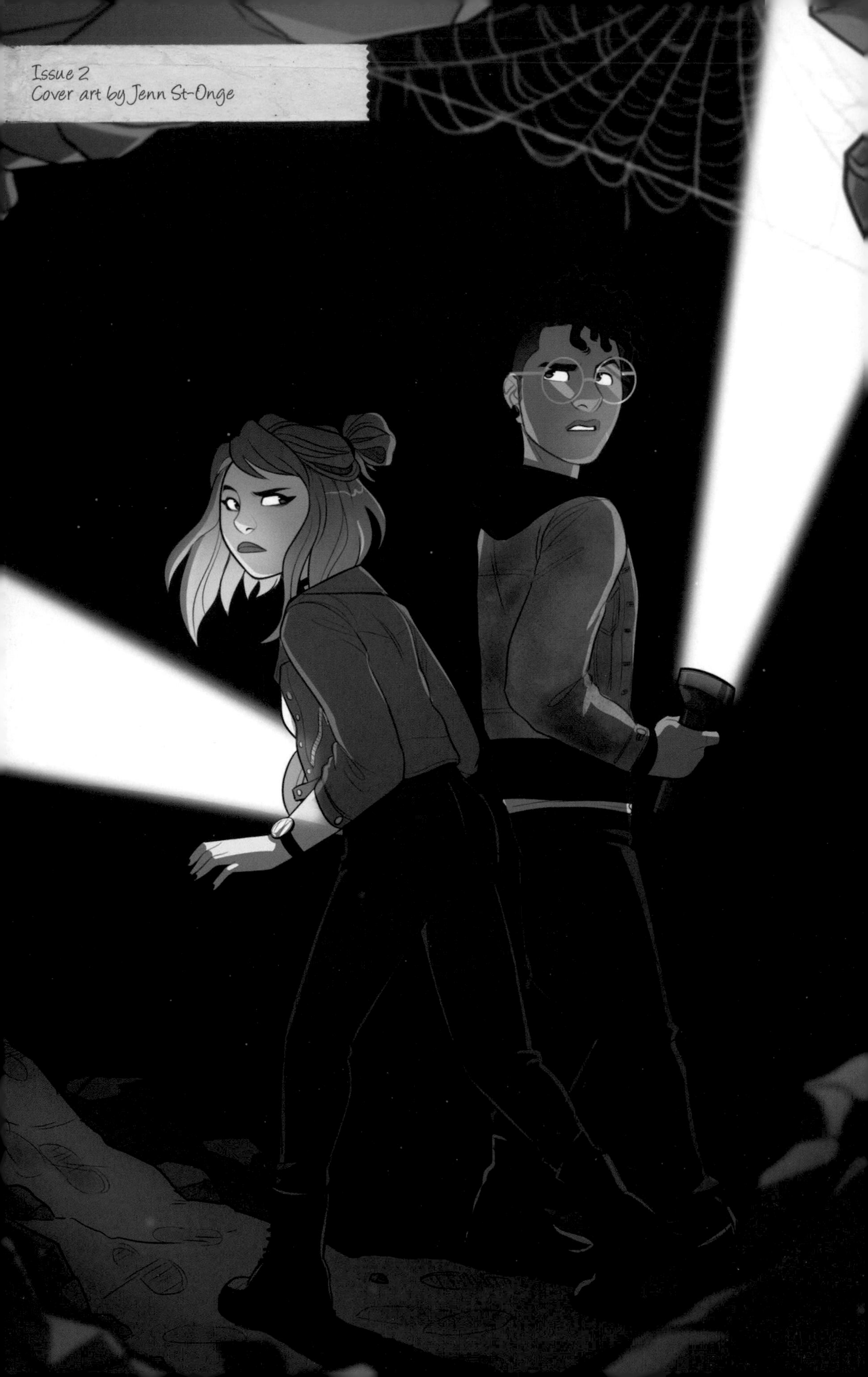

Issue 3
Cover art by Paulina Ganucheau

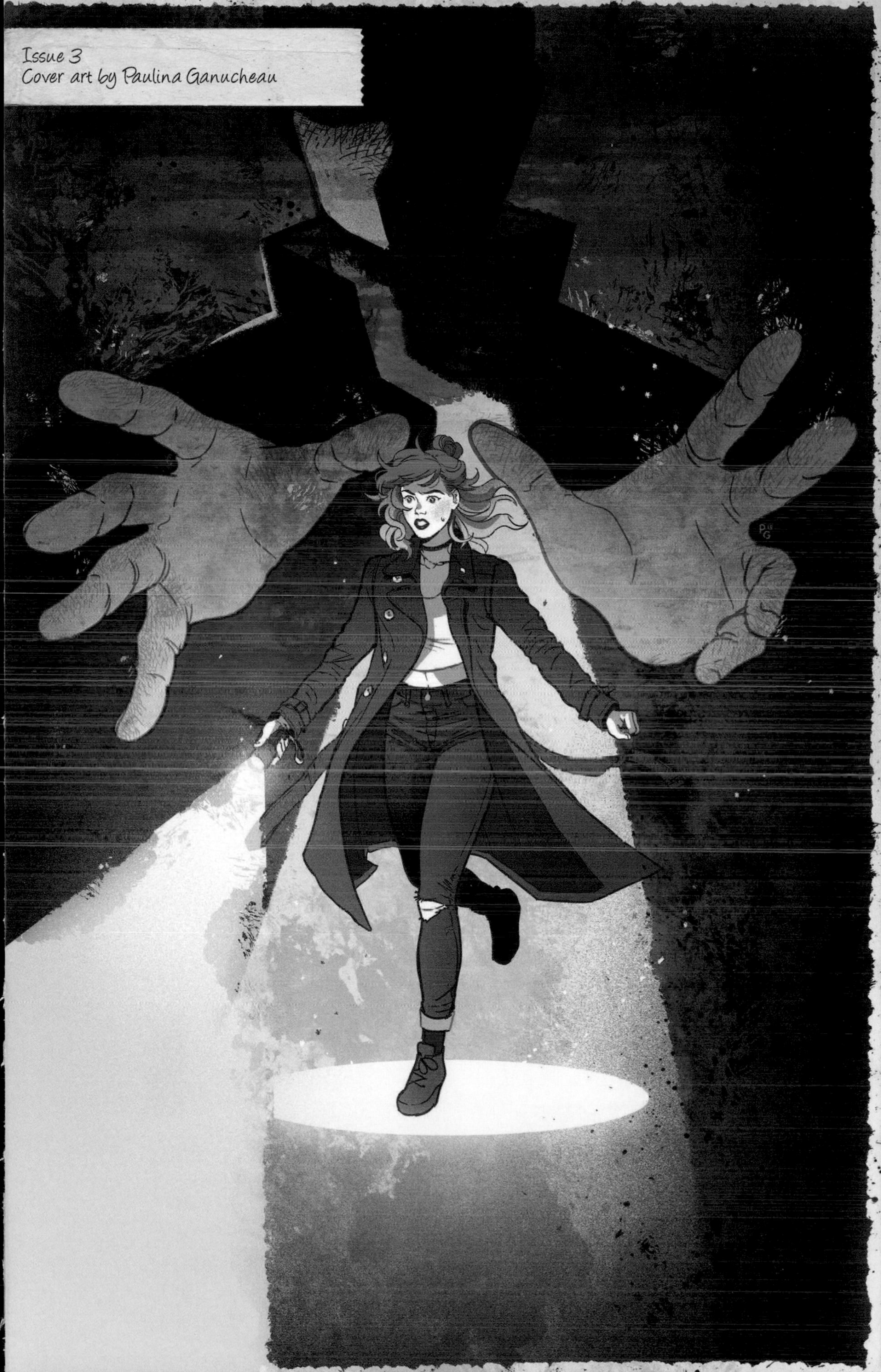

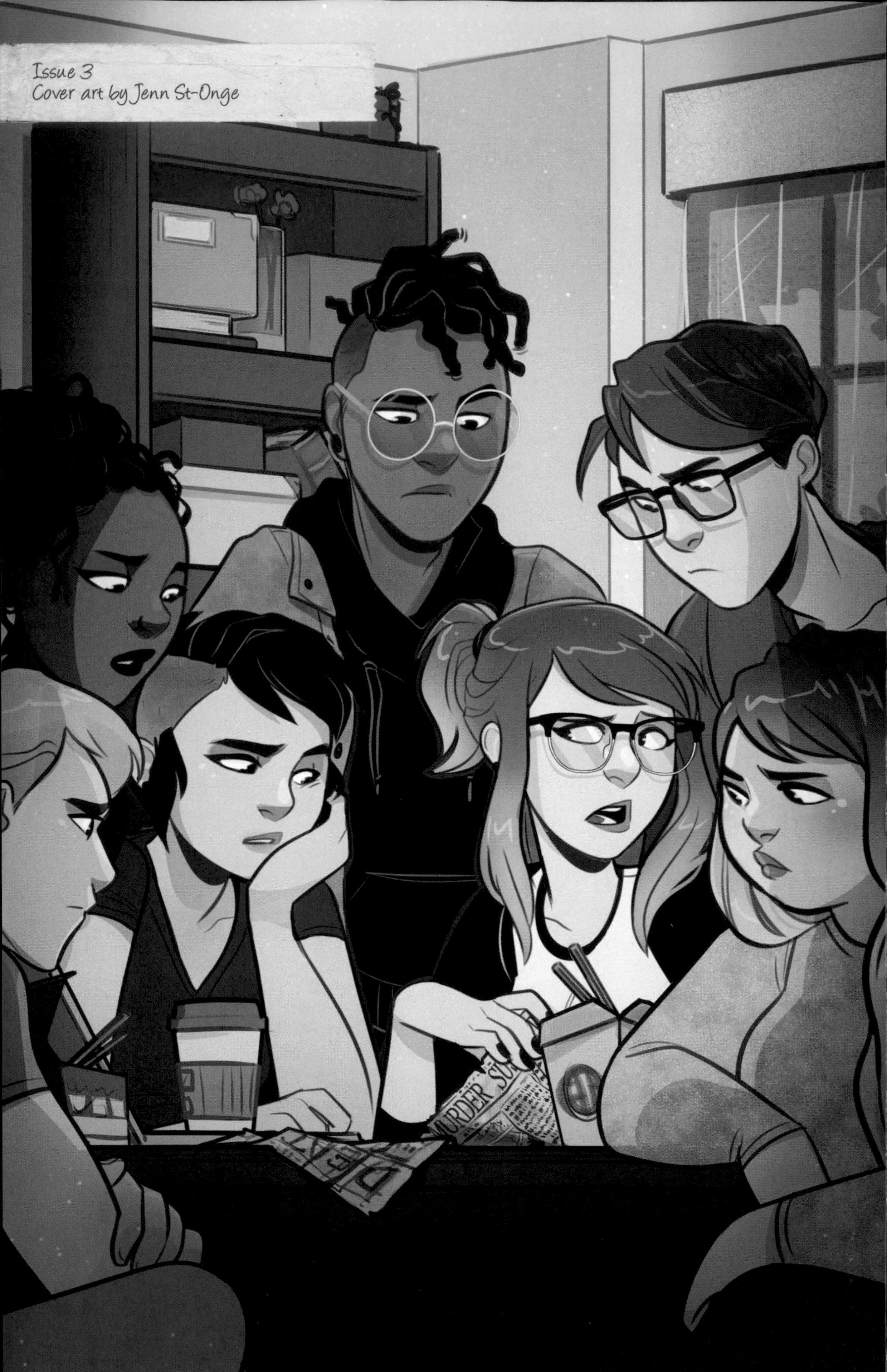

Issue 3
Cover art by Jenn St-Onge

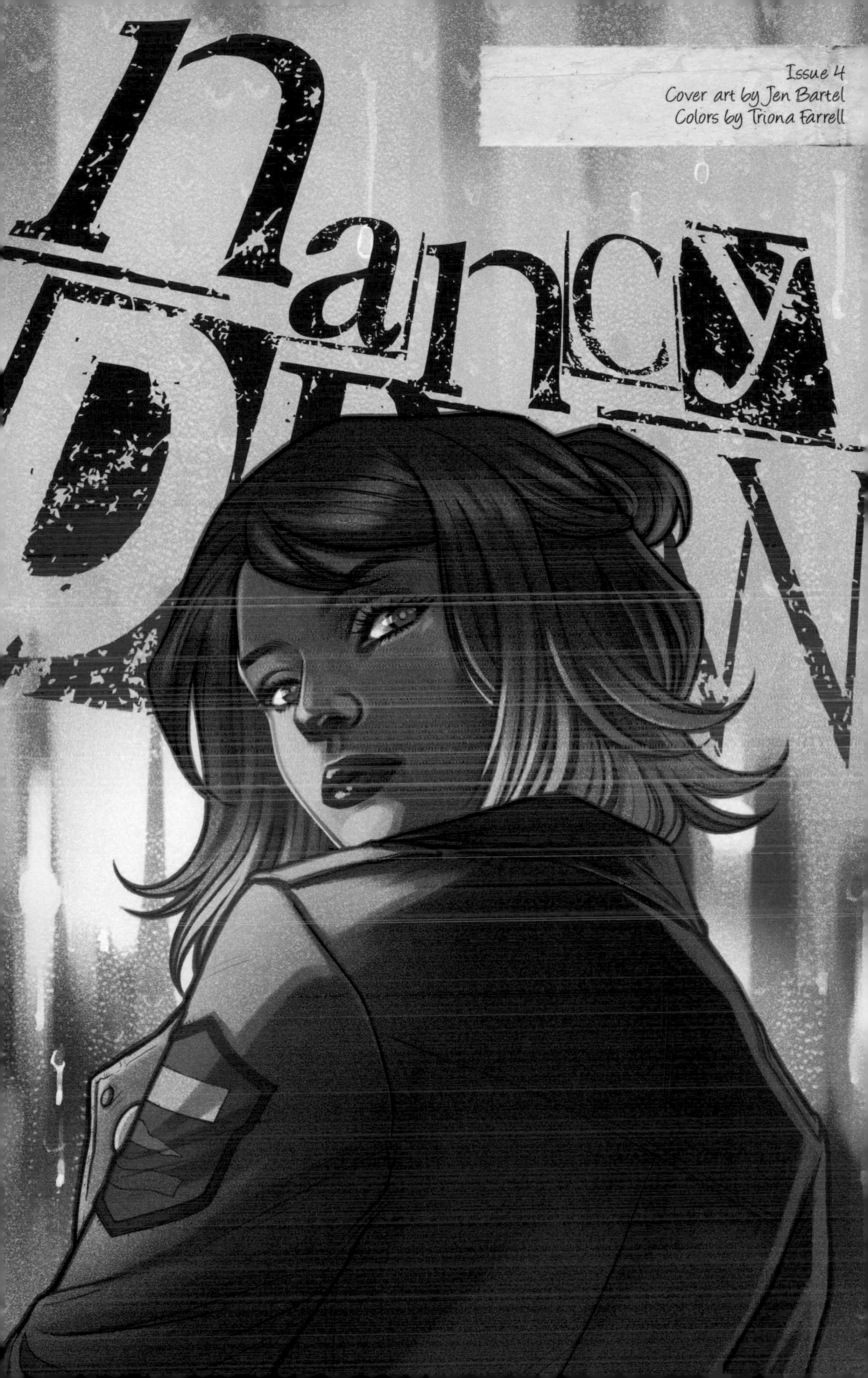
Nancy

Issue 4
Cover art by Jen Bartel
Colors by Triona Farrell

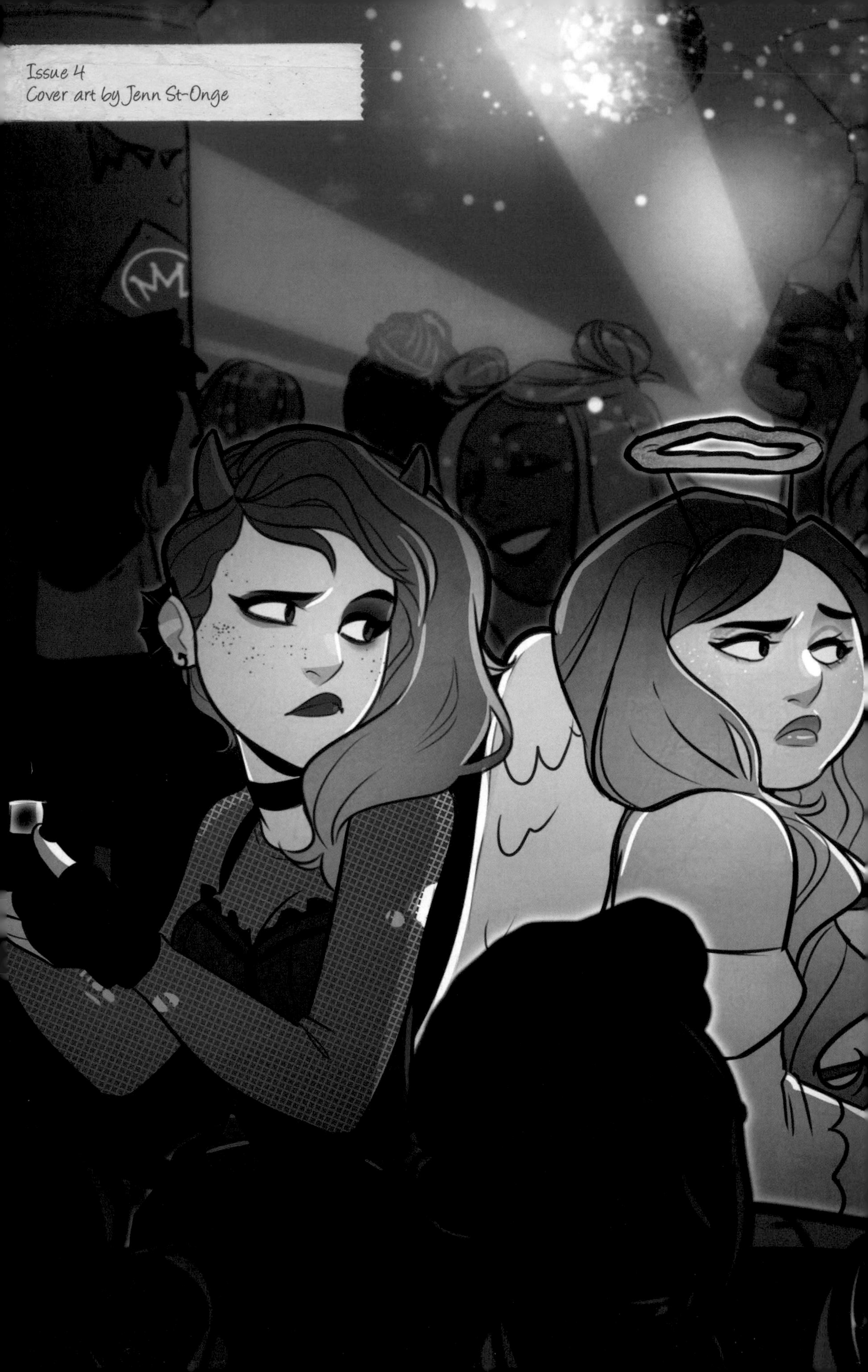

Issue 4
Cover art by Jenn St-Onge

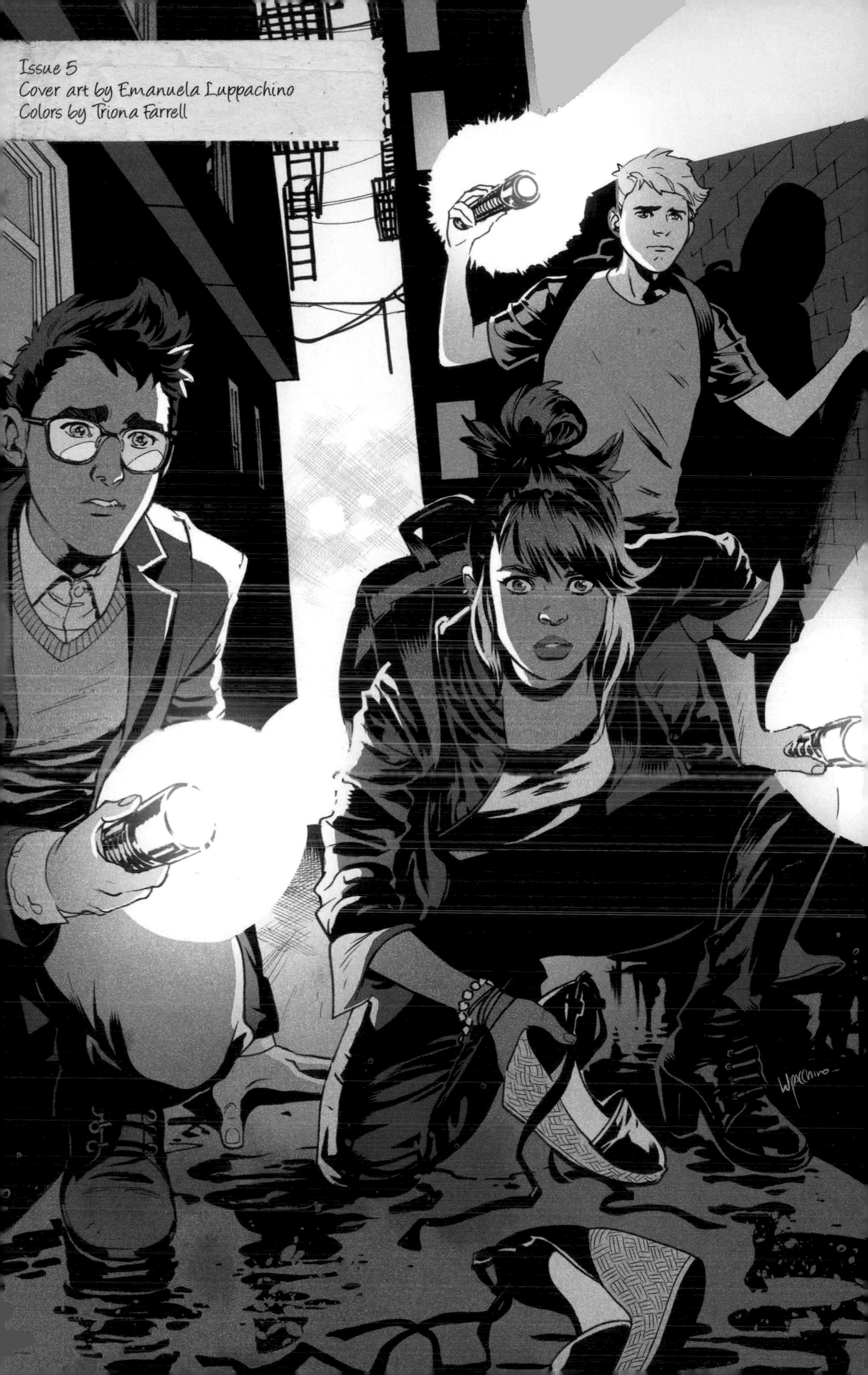

Issue 5
Cover art by Emanuela Luppachino
Colors by Triona Farrell

Issue 5
Cover art by Jenn St-Onge

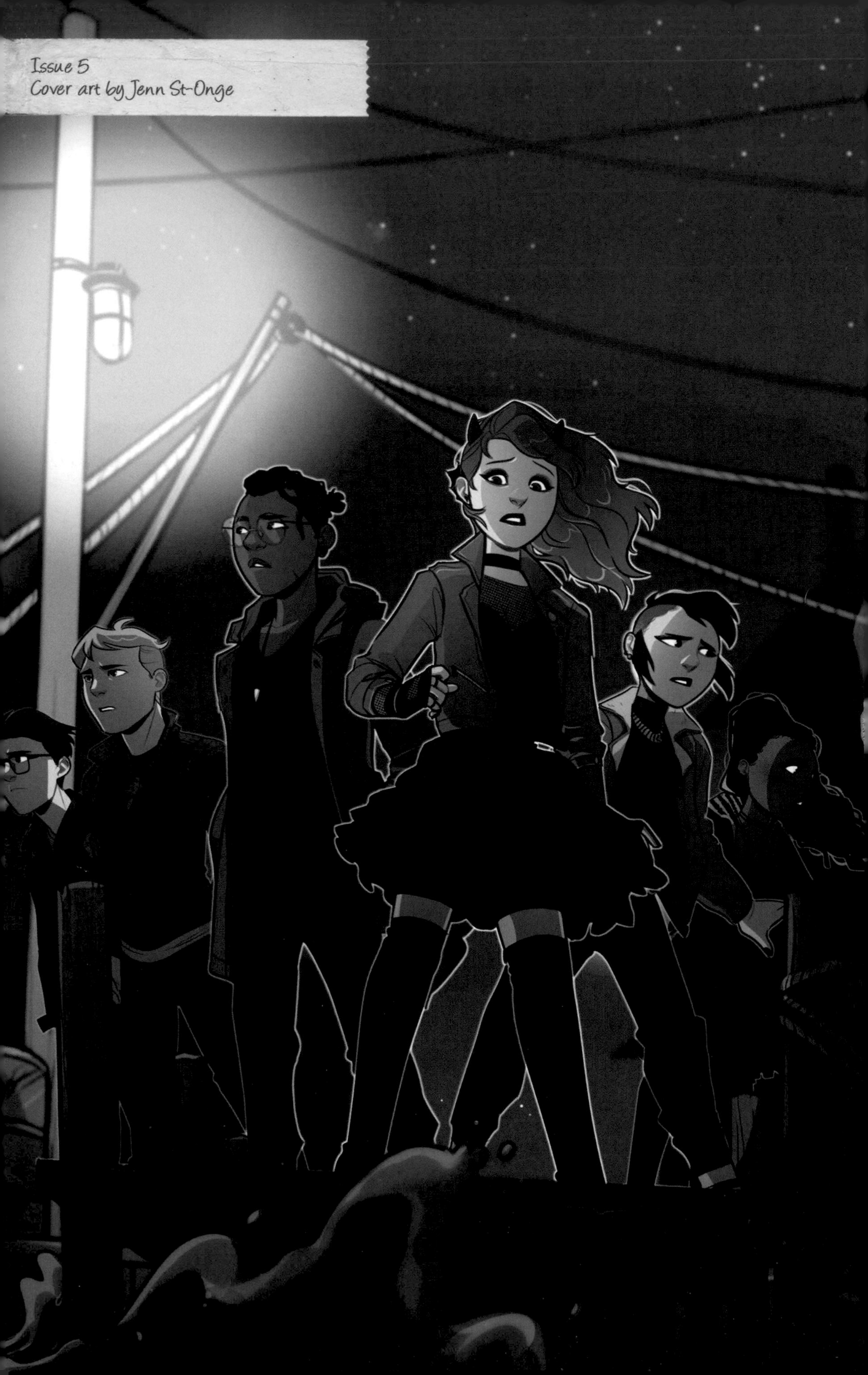

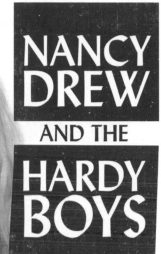

Nancy Drew

DReW

The Palace of Wisdom